"Your hair is silver in the moonlight, and you are as sweet as jasmine," he whispered.

She started. Had he heard what Odette said of her, the silver jasmine name?

He smiled down at her tenderly. "Odette pointed out the jasmine bushes near the house, have you seen them? I smelled their fragrance. I think she put some in your bath water, darling. And they call you silver jasmine—my lovely darling. It suits you—"

Then he bent to her again, and his lips burned a line from her throat to her thighs. The sheet was flung aside, they did not need the covering on the hot night.

She felt his lips go here, there, all about her. He kissed and caressed her ardently, and she felt herself melting under his gentle attack. . . .

"Darling—silver jasmine lovely—oh, you are so fragrant and beautiful—" he whispered against her mouth. He kissed the silver-blonde hair, light in the moonlight on the white pillow, kissed the dark eyes closed in passion.

She felt him come to her, slowly, deliberately, easy with her, yet an urgency driving him. She wanted to struggle, yet something inside was pushing her up to him instead. . . .

Also by Janet Louise Roberts

Golden Lotus

Published by
WARNER BOOKS

Silver Jasmine

Janet Louise Roberts

WARNER BOOKS

A Warner Communications Company

WARNER BOOKS EDITION

Copyright © 1980 by Janet Louise Roberts, Inc.
All rights reserved.

ISBN: 0-446-81998-0

Cover art by Elaine Duillo

Warner Books, Inc., 75 Rockefeller Plaza, New York, N.Y. 10019

W A Warner Communications Company

Printed in the United States of America

First Printing: April, 1980

10 9 8 7 6 5 4 3 2 1

Silver Jasmine

1

Tess Pritchard set down the quill pen carefully on the side of the battered ledger. The accounts of the past week were up-to-date, and her stepfather could search for some other complaint against her.

As the ink dried, she cupped her chin on her folded hands and gazed wistfully out the opened inn window to the sea. The Last Inn had been built near the end of the wharf of a small port on the coast of Cornwall. From here, she had seen many a gallant ship, sails fluttering and billowing in the winds, set sail for the Americas or the Caribbean.

How Tess longed for adventure! If only she had been a boy! Then she and her brother Vincent, now nineteen, could have signed on one of those sailing vessels, and left behind the life of drudgery, jumping to the snarl of orders, away from the petty meannesses of Hector Ryder.

However, Teresa Angela Pritchard was a girl of seventeen. Small, scrappy, too thin, she was still rounding out and becoming a woman. The small wistful face under the short blonde curls, the vivid blue eyes, were already drawing too much attention from sailors and others who frequented the inn.

Tess gazed absently at the pier, and the ship moored to it. The January day of 1816 was an unusually sunny blue one, and the sea glistened like shot silk. The tall-masted ship scarcely moved in its berth; only a faint wind stirred it. Sailors were painting the sides a gleaming white, others caulked the bottom as far down as the lapping gray green waters of the port. Out beyond lay the sparkling blue bay, and further yet—the open seas.

What a fine big ship she was. The *Marietta* was owned by an English company, and her captain, Amos Dillon, had been in and out of the Last Inn several times this week. She was outfitting for the Caribbean run, he had said proudly. He had a full complement of sailors, eight passengers, and a miscellaneous cargo of furniture, tools, farm machinery, silks and cottons, needles, thread, and suchlike for the island planters.

If only she and Vincent might shake off their bonds, slip away and be off. Tess was thinking it so fervently that she started wildly as the door to the small office burst open.

"Damme! Idling again! Dreaming away like your silly mother! Come to tend the bar, you brat, or you'll smart tonight!" Her stepfather bellowed at her across the room, glaring at Tess with black eyes gleaming.

I have just finished the accounts, Mr. Ryder," Tess said softly, closed the ledger and stood up. "I think you will find them all in order."

Her mother had cautioned her, "A soft answer turneth away wrath." But nothing seemed to turn away Ryder's fury.

"I should never ha' married your fool mother! Blinded by her beauty!" he growled. "Saddled wi' a pair of brats to raise!"

Tess opened her mouth to spit angry words. They more than earned their keep! But she saw her brother Vincent behind Ryder, and he was shaking his head in warning. She bit out the answer he always wanted: "We are both grateful to you, Mr. Ryder."

"Well, get to the bar and help out, then." As she passed him, sliding past his bulk, he reached out and smoothed his big wet hand down her back. She could scarce control the shudder, and skipped along the hallway to avoid any other touch of his hand.

She went behind the bar, smiling automatically at the two sailors lounging there. "What's for you, gents?"

She poured the foaming ale, slid the glasses deftly before them, managed to avoid big red fingers that sought to clasp hers, and moved back to whisper to her brother.

"What has him so riled?"

"Tweedy."

Tess felt a shudder down her spine again, a cold shiver like someone walking over her grave. She hated the hot-eyed Marquess of Tweed who had taken to haunting the inn lately. He was gentry, and Hector Ryder fawned over him, even when he lost money to the marquess. They played for high stakes at times, and Tess secretly worried that her stepfather was going into debt to the man.

And Elias Shippen, Marquess of Tweed, stared at Tess whenever she was about. He touched her, grabbed at her in corners, fondled her unless she could slide out of his reach. She hated him, and feared him. He had money and power, and he was spoiled by women, Ryder said with a laugh.

Vincent helped at the bar until the afternoon rush

was over, then was sent back to the stables to help with the horses and muck out the slime. Ryder enjoyed sending him on that task; he hated the thin hard-working high-toned boy who was his stepson. He worked him as hard as he dared; not to kill the lad, for he was smart. He did not kill the hands under him, but he stopped short of it—just short.

Tess stayed at the bar, sliding foaming glasses of ale or beer automatically to the heavy fists of loud-talking sailors, to an occasional tradesman, to the man who ran the town stable.

Her stepfather sat in a corner, watching all that went on with a sharp eye, even as he drank his pint. His face was red, sullen. Yes, something was bothering him, thought Tess, even as she rushed to the kitchen to prepare a thick sandwich for one sailor, and dashed back with it.

She was at one end of the bar, leaning on it, with one foot up to ease the ache in her foot, when a different man came in. She noticed him at once; so did Ryder.

The man was tall, with bright red hair and the most vivid blue eyes Tess had ever seen. He walked with a sailor's rolling gait, he wore the blues of an officer, but over his shoulder was a red plaid tartan fastened with a silver brooch. Her eyes widened as he came forward to the bar.

As he moved, she thought, "I bet he's going on one of them ships!" and her heart ached. If only she were free to go, to stride out eagerly in such polished boots, to hold up a head and not worry about being pinched on her tender bottom. Oh, to be a man, and such a man as this—

Everyone in the bar turned to stare at him. Two sailors moved aside automatically to let him have space at the bar. Tess went up to him.

"Yes, sir?"

The vivid blue eyes appraised her, the short blond

curls almost covered by the white mob cap, the blue-and-white print woolen dress, the white apron dirty now by the work of the day. She wiped her red wet hands, and repeated, "Yes, sir? Drink, sir?"

"Later, miss. I'd like to bespeak a room, if you have such."

Tess glanced toward her stepfather. He liked to do the honors with nobs such as this. Ryder got up with an effort, and strode forward.

"Room is it? We got a good front room, two shillings a night. How long you staying?"

"Until the *Marietta* sails," said the stranger, and his voice had a soft different sound to it, an accent that blurred rough speech.

"That'll be three nights, in advance. The *Marietta* sails on Thursday," said Ryder importantly. He liked to give the impression that he knew everything that went on in this port.

The man nodded briefly. Tess felt that he knew that information and much else. "I'd like to see the room, if ye will."

She was not mistaken, he had a strong Scottish accent, and with that plaid—

"Your name?" asked Ryder. "And where you come from?"

"Morgan Hamilton. From His Majesty's navy, lately discharged."

He looked down at Ryder, and then picked up his leather bags as though they weighed nothing.

"The girl will take you up," said Ryder. "You'll come down for a drink on the house?"

The man nodded. "And thanks." He followed Tess up the stairs she indicated. She kept well ahead of him, for men usually tried to nip at her legs or bottom. But this man stayed just behind her, but not touching.

She opened the door to the front room. It was a nice one, with the same view of the sea as the small parlor where she did the accounts. The bed had been made fresh that morning, she had done it herself. She showed it to him silently.

He looked about, pulled back the down quilt to examine the sheets critically, then nodded. "I'll take it," he said. "Three nights. I'll see the landlord. What is his name?"

"Hector Ryder," she said, trying not to show the distaste she felt for her stepfather. "He owns the Last Inn."

"Umm. Would it be possible for ye to fix a small luncheon for me? And a pot of tea?"

She did show surprise then. Most men asked for a large bottle of ale or rum. "Tea, sir?"

"Aye. I have a great thirst," he said solemnly. Then he smiled, slowly, and it was like the sun coming out on the sea. So warming, and lightening, and glowing. She caught herself staring at him, and looked down hastily.

"Yes, sir. Right away, sir."

She dashed down the stairs to the kitchen. Ryder followed her out. "Did he take it?"

"Yes, sir. And wants food. I thought the roast beef, and bread and cheese." She was reaching down the cups and plates as she spoke.

Ryder rubbed his hands. "Charge him a shilling for that also," he said gleefully. "I'll collect in advance tonight."

He must be short of the blunt, thought Tess, as her stepfather went back to the bar. Collecting in advance, for three nights! The man was a gent, and he didn't usually make them pay ahead. Had Ryder been gambling again? Probably, and with Lord Tweed. She gave a grimace at the teakettle as she filled it with fresh water. She set the battered tin tray carefully with a fresh white napkin, and tin knife and fork and spoon. She searched until she found a cup without cracks, and plate to match, folded another napkin neatly beside the plate, sliced a big piece of roast beef into neat thin slices, layered them. She added a huge basket of bread, a hunk of good farmer cheese.

Then she hesitated. A shilling! It was too much for this. Hastily she reached into the pantry, brought out a round orange from the last shipment a sailor had left them. She washed it, set it on the tray. Then she chopped some onion, some greens and herbs, and added a bit of oil and vinegar in the bowl. There! That was more like a gent's meal!

She took it up the backstairs, moving softly, hoping her stepfather would not catch her. The tray was heavy, but she was used to that.

She tapped at the door, Mr. Hamilton opened it, smiled, and was about to take the tray from her.

"I'll set it on the table, sir," she said hastily, primly. She felt him staring at her as she walked to the table under the opened window. So he liked the sea air and the view also.

She set the tray out neatly, with the pot of tea and the cup to one side. She bobbed a curtsey, as her mother had taught her. "I hope you enjoy your food, sir," she said, and left the room.

She heard him say, "Thank you, miss," behind her.

She skimmed down the front stairs to the bar, to find a waiting line of sailors. One cheered her when she came. "There's our Tess! Hey, Tess! Going out with me tonight?"

She answered their banter with coolness, endured the many stares, avoided the fingers, slid glasses along the wet bar, until her arms ached with weariness and her back seemed permanently bent to the tub of ale.

If her mother Angela could only see her, how she

would weep! Maybe the angels did weep in heaven, as her mother had said. When Tess and Vincent had lost their father—Henry Pritchard had died five years ago, gallantly, in the wars in the peninsula under Wellington—they had felt lost. But they had their mother and each other. They would manage.

Angela had worried. She had never been strong. When Hector Ryder came courting, an important innkeeper, a man of substance, so they said, Angela had not asked many questions. She had married him. Her frailty had enraged him. He had thought to marry a beauty, who would attract more men to the inn, a woman he could be proud of. Instead, his heavy-handed lovemaking had increased her illness; she had died within two years.

Ryder had been left with young Tess, then fourteen, and her brother Vincent, then sixteen. He had already put them to work in the bar, without her mother's knowledge and consent. Angela had lain in the back room, so white and thin, so uncaring of the world, and smiled feebly when Tess kissed her in the morning. "My poor darlings," murmured Angela, as she lay dying.

What she would think now! Tess avoided two sailors deftly, as she carried four ale mugs in her small hands over to the corner table. She left the mugs, gathered up the coins, and returned to the bar. Ryder held out his big hand. She set the coins in them silently.

Ryder never let her and Vincent keep any of the money. They never handled it, except to hand it to him. He was afraid of their having money, said Vincent scornfully to Tess. He knew they would leave him in a flash.

But you got nowhere without money.

Sailors left coins for Tess, giving her big smiles. She would nod and thank them, knowing full well Ryder would demand them. Vincent had tried to keep some money, coins tossed to him by men from horseback after they mounted, or by coachman, pleased by his attention to their horses. But Ryder had taken to turning out Vincent's jacket pockets and even his pants pockets, and taking them all. It was simpler and less humiliating to hand them over at once.

Mr. Hamilton came down the stairs, and paused by the bar.

"Yes, sir?" said Tess automatically.

The blue eyes studied her. "Thank you for the excellent lunch. I set the tray in the kitchen," he said.

"Thank you, sir," she said, and as soon as she could, she scurried to the kitchen to get rid of the betraying orange peel and wash the dishes. He had eaten every scrap of food, he must have been hungry.

When Tess returned to the bar, Mr. Hamilton was sitting at a table with Hector Ryder, a mug of ale before him. He was doing all the listening, Ryder all the talking.

Between customers, Tess tried to hear what they were saying. She was strangely interested in this quiet-voiced red-haired sailor.

Ryder asked questions. "Where might you be sailing?" he asked in his jovial voice, and gave a hearty laugh. "To the Caribees? Eh?"

"That's right, Mr. Ryder," and Mr. Hamilton took another drink of the foamy ale, and wiped his mouth with his handkerchief.

"What island, eh?"

"Do you know the Caribbean islands, sir?"

The polite way he talked! And the way he answered one question with another question! It pleased Tess, that he was so smart. Not many could outsmart her stepfather, who was shrewd and cunning, for all his hearty innkeeper manner.

They finished their ale. Mr. Ryder urged, "Stay and

have another one, on the house! There'll be gaming later, you'll be interested, shorely?"

"Not tonight, sir; perhaps tomorrow. I have been traveling several days a-horseback, and am weary. May I bespeak a breakfast from the young maid at the bar?"

"Oh, aye. Tess!" bawled Ryder. Tess came over to them, wiping her wet hands on the wet apron.

"Yes, sir."

"Breakfast for Mr. Hamilton in the morning. What hour would you wish it?"

Tess glanced toward the tall red-haired man who had stood as she came to the table.

"At about eight o'clock, if that be convenient," said Mr. Hamilton. "What have ye to offer?"

Tess hesitated suspiciously. Did he have a double meaning in his words? No, maybe not. "Sir, there's ham, and eggs, and sometimes fresh bread. And tea if you please."

"That sounds fine. Good night to you all, then," and he bowed courteously in the general direction of Mr. Ryder and Tess, and went up the stairs to his room.

Tess went back to the bar. Vincent came in presently, weary from long hours of hard work, and so dirty. She slipped to the kitchen with him, gave him slices of roast beef and bread and cheese, recklessly, and some hot tea. If Mr. Ryder saw her, he'd have them both whipped! But Vincent did look so exhausted, he made her heart fail her. What if something happened to her brother? She would have nobody in the world who cared a tinker's curse what happened to her.

He washed his hands and sat down to the feast she had prepared. "Looks good, sis, if I wasn't so awful tired." He picked up the bread, nibbled at it. "Dear God, I wish we could get away from this hellhole!"

She glanced swiftly at the kitchen door, afraid of who

might be listening. The cook went home at seven, but sometimes hostlers hung about, or sailors, or Ryder himself.

"Watch your tongue, Vincent! We'll get away one day," she whispered, her hand on his shoulder comfortingly.

"In a wooden box," he muttered gloomily.

Someone yelled, "Tess! Tess!" from the bar, and she sped back. She was busy pouring more beer, when something made her look up. The door had opened, and a gust of cold sea air had swept in, and something else. A man in a black riding cloak.

The Marquess of Tweed! His gray eyes were staring right at her, and he was pulling his gloves from his hands, slowly, still staring her up and down as she set mugs on a fresh-washed table.

Ryder rolled up to him. "Ah, good evening, my lord! Your table is right here, ready for you!" And he showed him over to the fine corner table, cleared of all but a fresh pack of cards.

It was past ten o'clock. How late would he stay? By the flush of his face, he was already drunken. Tess sometimes had to work until midnight or one o'clock, when there was drinking and gaming, and she was so bone-weary.

She scrubbed at the bar. Ryder beckoned her. "Fine wine for my lord," he said sharply. "And be quick about it."

"Yes, sir."

She got out the special bottles of red wine and brandy, and brought the first glasses silently, and set the bottle of burgundy on the table with them. The gaming had started, the cards were set out. The Marquess looked up at her, and grinned.

"Well, Tess, you haven't said good evening to me," he said.

"Good evening, sir, my lord," she said impassively, and returned to the bar.

She saw her stepfather passing money across the table to Lord Tweed. It seemed much money was going between them than ever before. Twinges of uneasiness flashed over her, especially when Tweed kept glancing toward her and grinning. What was on his mind?

He was a wealthy, spoiled young man of about thirty-four or thirty-five. Some said he had been disinherited in his youth, but his charm had won back his elderly father, and the man had made him his heir. When his father died, and Elias Shippen came into the title and estates, he had gone wild. Gaming, women, London pranks, dogfighting, horse racing, all the amusements of the London bucks were at his command. He ran through money like a waterfall over rocks, some said.

Yet he always seemed to have more, gold to spill on the table, coins to flip at Tess. He had a sort of pokerish face, without expression at times when he was playing. A red scar slashed across his right cheek clear to his eye. From a duel, they whispered. He had once been handsome, but dissipation and the scar had blurred the fine lines of his face, and the evil in his eyes was something to shudder at. Tess had seen him whip one of his footmen until the man lay bloody and unconscious on the ground, for some fault with the horses. She had never forgotten or forgiven that.

One of their glasses was knocked to the floor and smashed as Tweed moved his arm irritably. Tess hastened over, to sweep up the glass and bring a fresh one to them.

She caught the gist of their words. "New man . . . Hamilton . . . pockets full, I'll warrant," whispered Ryder excitedly. "He ain't against gaming, he will join us tomorrow. Come over early—"

"What has he got? How much money? Any horses?"

"He sold his horse when he got here. I saw his wad of notes, and he jingles gold in his pocket. He'll be here three days—"

Tess finished sweeping up, and moved away silently on her soft black leather slippers, with their flat soles. So they were gaming with the red-haired man! She wondered if she should warn him.

No, he was no downy bird to be plucked by them, she thought. If he was smart, he would not let himself be drawn into any game with those two! And if he wasn't smart— Well, she had enough troubles of her own.

It came midnight, and she was yawning. Most of the sailors had left. Ryder was losing steadily to Tweed, and by his dark frown he wasn't happy in the playing. Tess ventured over to them. Vincent had signaled from the hallway that he was ready to escort her up the steep stairs to the attic rooms they had. She never went up alone; someone might lie in wait for her.

She brought a full bottle of golden brandy over to them, and stood silently while the one play was finished. Ryder cursed. Tweed grinned as he swept up the coins on the table, and looked up at Tess.

"Want to play, sweetheart?" he jeered. His eyes wandered over her, the gaze making her feel dirty. She did not look again at him, but kept her look at her stepfather.

"Mr. Ryder, might I retire now? It is midnight, and I would be getting up early tomorrow," she said steadily.

He frowned, blinked at the tall grandfather clock that ticked steadily in the corner. "Midnight? Hell, no, it's only ten o'clock."

"I beg pardon, Mr. Ryder, it is midnight, and most of the sailors have left, sir."

He cursed her, and she tried to close her eyes to it.

"Oh, let her go to bed, and get her sleep! I vow I'd

like to see the pretty maid sleeping! Shall I take you upstairs, sweetheart?" And Tweed's hand came out and clapped hold of her arm. She tried to pull away.

Ryder watched alertly, his black eyes narrowed.

"Let me go, if you will, my lord," said Tess, trying to keep her temper. She pulled and tugged, but strong as she was, he was much stronger. He yanked her to him, and tried to pull her down on his lap.

"A kiss before you go to your innocent bed, my sweet!" he told her thickly, and the big red lips came close to her cheek. She shuddered in revulsion at the closeness of his hot body.

Vincent raced into the room. "You let my sister go!" he raged. "Let her go! She's not your plaything! Tess, come here!"

She would have gladly come. But it had to be by trick. Her arm swept out as Tweed laughed and tried to pull her closer. She managed to knock his glass of red wine over him, and it spilled down over his white shirt and silver silk waistcoat as he sat in shirtsleeves.

He cried out curses, and let her go. She jumped up, and backed into Vincent. He grabbed her, and started for the door.

"One minute, my little spitfire!" yelled Tweed. His face had turned red as the wine spilled over his white ruffled shirt. "Come here! I'll take that kiss—"

Vincent tried to take a swing at him. But he was smaller, more frail, and Tweed saw the blow coming. He swung smartly at Vincent and knocked him flat on the floor of the barroom. Tess cried out, and knelt down in the sawdust beside her brother.

"Vincent—oh, Vincent—" He shook his head groggily, tried to get up. She helped with her arm about him, glaring at Tweed with stormy eyes.

"You are a bastard!" she cried. "Hitting a boy like that—you should be ashamed—"

Tweed glared down at them both. "You need to be taught manners, my girl!" he said grimly. "And the time ain't so far away when it'll be my pleasant task to do just that!"

Ryder had gotten up also. His bull-like head swayed from side to side, as he tried to puzzle out what was happening. "My lord, sit you down, and I'll have Tess wash out your shirt," he begged, trying to get Tweed to his chair. "By God, I'll whip her for this! Little bitch! Tess, you take the lord's shirt and git it washed—"

Just then the doors opened, and some drunken sailors swayed in, singing. Tess had never been so glad to see the blue-clad men, who lunged inside the warm room, and called out for drinks. They swept around the Marquess and Ryder, and for a few moments Tess and Vincent were separated from them.

"Up—fast—come on, Vincent—" She half pulled, half pushed her brother to the door and out, up the narrow stairs to the next floor. Breathless, she paused to listen for any signs of being followed.

The sailors were calling for ale, for beer, for service, pounding on the bar. She heard her stepfather call out jovially, "With you right now, boys, right now!"

They had escaped—for tonight. She and Vincent scurried up the next flight of stairs, and the next, to the attic rooms. Inside, and locked in, with Tess in the far room and Vincent in the near one, Tess felt close to tears. It had been a very narrow escape tonight.

But what about tomorrow? And what had Lord Tweed meant—about teaching her manners soon? Her mind fumbled wearily at the puzzle as she stripped to her petticoats and washed in the cold water in the basin.

She fell into the narrow bed, with relief. Blessed

sleep. Maybe tomorrow would be better. But it never was better. It got worse and worse.

She said her prayers, and was asleep before they were over, worn out, her thin body shivering under the thin blanket, but too weary to mind even that in the cold attic room. She had some hours to sleep, then she must rise and start again, another long wearisome worrying day.

2

Morgan Hamilton wakened early as he usually did. He lay in the lumpy inn bed, his arms behind his head, and thought. The limp white curtains at the open window had not begun to billow with the dawn wind. He gazed unseeingly at the darkness outside.

It had been a noisy night, but he was accustomed to it. Still, in his weariness, he had not slept until the inn had grown silent. He had heard curses, glasses breaking, singing, raging, laughter. He had heard a man go out into the night, raging in a quiet deadly voice at the innkeeper. He had heard Mr. Ryder calling after him, "But ye'll be back tomorrow night! Dinna be angry, I'll make the maid apologize!"

Hamilton had lain awake a while longer, frowning slightly. The girl at the bar had been so small and thin, so sturdy and determined to be polite and quick. But he had seen the weariness in her face and the droop of her thin shoulders. He had seen the quick fear flash in her blue eyes when the big husky innkeeper staggered near. Was she so desperate that she had to work here? An inn on the waterfront of a tough port like this one was no place for a nice girl.

But then he didn't know much about girls and women. He knew men; he had fought with them, lived with them, held them as they died, quickly or slowly, painfully, of wounds, of disease, of coughing illnesses, in the chill and mud of the peninsula. He knew men all right; he knew their faces, he watched their eyes, he knew the fears that ran them through before the sword had its turn.

His family was gone. Broken up by the Clearances in Scotland, his clan had scattered to the ends of the world. Some had gone to America, some to Canada, some to Australia. Some went to the cotton mills in Glasgow, and the woolen weaving mills, and the ship foundries, and all that. He himself at twelve had found himself orphaned. His father dead, his mother dying of a broken heart, his only sister gone to the house of a madam on the wharf of Glasgow. She had not lived long; he was thankful for that.

He had gone to the cotton mills, working at the bobbins, then at the loom itself, weaving, drawing out the threads, until his fingers bled, until he hardened and grew older.

Then one day on the wharf as he ate his evening cheese and bread, sitting on a pier, a press gang had swept along. They caught up the sixteen-year-old lanky lad, and when he protested, they caught him such a blow on the head that he did not wake up until the ship was out at sea. He had been in the Navy since then. Twelve years.

A knock came at the door. Hamilton got up and shoved away the chair he had tipped under the knob. He never let himself sleep without some such protection. There were too many about who would kill a man for his bit of blunt, a rifle, anything.

He opened the door, and a tall thin lad came in, carrying a hot pitcher. "Your hot water, sir," mumbled the boy.

"Thank you, lad. Your name?" Morgan asked pleasantly. He had a resemblance to the maid at the bar, blond hair, blue eyes, a sort of delicate patrician look that louts in an inn did not usually have.

"Vincent, sir." He set down the pitcher carefully beside the basin, tipped the slops out the window, and wiped out the basin again. "The maid will bring your breakfast in half an hour, sir."

"Thank you. Are you son to the innkeeper?" Morgan asked, on impulse.

A look of outrage and distaste came in the boy's face. "Stepson, sir. He's our—stepfather, Mr. Ryder is."

Ah, that was it. Free labor, thought Morgan, and nodded as the boy left. He splashed the hot water lustily over himself, dried himself with the thin but clean towel, and dressed. He was about to pull on his boots when another knock came at the door. He opened it, his stockinged feet silent on the wooden floorboards.

Tess stood there with the heavy tray in her hands. He let her in, she set the tray on the table near the window. He noted the large pot of hot steaming tea, the clean plate and cup. She was neat and quick. He liked the movements of her slim body, without a wasted motion to her. Her face was clean and fresh, she had washed that morning. Her apron was fresh also, and white, over the green-and-blue striped woolen gown. Her mobcap was fresh and stood up stiffly about her curls.

But there was a shadow about her, dark circles under her eyes, and bruises on her wrists where the sleeves were rolled up to the elbow. He thought the bruises had not been there last evening, or he would have noted them.

"Good morning, miss," he said pleasantly. "What is your name?"

"Tess, sir. Anything else?" She stood away from him, suspiciously, ready for flight.

"No, thank you. I believe it was your brother who brought the hot water."

"Yes, sir." She was poised near the open door, ready to dash out.

"I believe your—stepfather—said there would be gaming tonight. Does he game with the sailors?"

A look came into the wide blue eyes. A hesitation.

"Tess!" A heavy voice bawled up the stairs. "Tess? Where are you? Come down this minute!"

She said quickly, "He games with—Lord Tweed. Marquess of Tweed, sir. They game—much." She paused, as though she would say more; then she fled.

Hamilton closed the door. A Marquess, eh? Gentlemen usually prided themselves on being honorable at cards, however else they acted in private or public life. Hum. It might be an interesting evening. Tess had been about to warn him about something, he thought keenly, as he sat down to his breakfast.

Slices of roast ham, slices of fresh cheese, thick slices of fresh warm bread. He ate hungrily, with appreciation. And the tea was just right. The maid was a jewel! He thought of the orange yesterday, and wondered. Not many oranges about in January. Must have come on a ship from the Caribbean.

As he ate, and drank the hot tea, he gazed from the window at the lightening sky. Dawn brought wisps of rosy clouds, a darkly purple sky that changed slowly to a pale blue. The ship at anchor showed first black against the sky, then the dawn light brought out the colors and shapes

26

of her. A pretty ship, the *Marietta,* and he looked forward to sailing in her.

He would go over and introduce himself to the captain today, he thought. It might make the trip go more quickly, to make friends with the man, if he was so inclined. He could count on a month at sea, more if the winter storms came up in their path.

Now there was a stirring on the dock, some sailors came off the ship yawning and stretching. He saw a uniformed man on deck, pointing instruments at the sky, taking note of their variance.

He finished his breakfast, leaned back and drank the last of the tea in the pot, enjoying it to the last drop. Yes, the girl could fix good tea, and she was light and graceful—

Hummm, he said to himself, smiling a little. He had no place in his life for a woman! He had avoided them like the plague! A sailor had no time for lasting ties.

He had stayed in the Navy because it was a bit better life than in the factory. He had worked his way up, from crude sailor managing the ropes, to crack rifleman, cannon worker, on up to a deck officer. He had ended up as First Mate, and been offered a captaincy—when the wars had ended. Then all of them had been turned off, except the wealthy who could buy their positions. England had no need of so many sailors in peacetime.

Soldiers and sailors, so valuable just two years ago, now roamed the English and Scottish countryside, looking for work. They had defeated Napoleon in the peninsula, Wellington had praised their work; some had medals to show for it, the ones who had lived. Then had come Waterloo—and the end of it all. Now Europe was safe, England was safe from invasion. "Thanks very much, we don't want you anymore," muttered Morgan bitterly.

He shrugged off the thoughts. He had done his best

for England, now she shoved him down into the gutter. Well, he would not stay there. He would leave her.

He got up, put on his boots, and went out. The bar was silent. He left his tray in the kitchen, heard the soft voice of the maid out in the stable yard, talking to her brother.

About the only minutes of the day when they could have peace, he thought, with some pity. Let them alone.

He went out through the bar, which was neat and clean, the floor fresh-washed, the bar shining with cleanliness. The bar glasses stood ready for the next invasion.

He left the large barroom, and went outside. It had been dark when he had come in. He met the fresh crisp January air with a feeling of welcome. The air off the sea, so clean, so salty, smelling of fish and seaweed and tea being brewed somewhere.

He strode off briskly toward the *Marietta*. He kept glancing at the ship, evaluating her. An older ship, but well kept: neat lines, sturdy, the sails folded well. One could judge a ship and her officers by just looking at her, he thought, after all those twelve years of service. A sloppy sail meant a sloppy crew and officers.

The officer leaned over the rail, gazing down at him. Morgan lifted his hand. "Ahoy, the *Marietta*. May I come aboard?"

"Aye, and welcome."

Morgan Hamilton took the wood steps lightly, and came up on deck. The officer came toward him. He wore a captain's uniform.

"You'll be Captain Dillon?" said Hamilton. "May I introduce myself? Morgan Hamilton, late of His Majesty's Navy."

The hands clasped. The captain had a huge red ham of a fist, and was big built to match. His sea blue eyes met Hamilton's frankly, and went over him just as openly.

28

"Aye, Amos Dillon, at your service. Come and have a pint."

They went to the captain's quarters. They were small, but neat, with everything in its place.

"So—of the Navy, eh? How late discharged?" Amos Dillon had done the honors. They sat with pints of ale in their hands, and appraised each other. "How long service? Have I met you somewhere?"

"We might ha' met at Lisbon, or thereabouts. But not to speak our names," said Morgan. He settled himself comfortably in the armchair. The boat swayed gently at anchor. This was his life. "It was in the Navy for twelve years, until the end at Waterloo. Then pitched out to make my way, as so many of us were. I had been first mate on the *Cormorant*."

"Aye, were you then? I saw her sometimes in Lisbon harbor. And how did ye go in? From Scotland, are ye?"

He was genial, not prying. Morgan wanted to make friends with this man, he would need a favor later.

"Aye, I was pressed off the Glasgow docks when I was a lad of sixteen. From the factories there, cotton mills. I liked the new life, and I stayed."

"Is that a fact? Well, well. Many a lad has come to the sea in that manner. And you're one of our passengers. You'll be going to the Caribbees?"

"Yes. I'd like to tell you about that."

"Do so. I'm listening."

Navy men liked a good story. It was one of their few amusements at sea. Morgan took off his warm plaid, laid it back on the chair, and began.

"My family are all gone, the Clearances, you ken. Well, when I come out of the Navy, I went up to Scotland, to see if anybody was aboot of the old clan. Could find nobody but some old folks in the glen where we had lived these many generations. But one old fella, he said someone had come looking for me. Now, he was going to warn me to stay hid, but I didn't have anything to hide about, you ken?"

"Oh, aye, being busy with His Majesty's wars," grinned Captain Dillon, his sea blue eyes sparkling. "So what happened?"

"The old gent said, it was a solicitor fella from Glasgow who went looking about for me, or anybody of the Hamilton ilk. The direct line being about gone, it left me. So I went to Glasgow and inquired about. Found the solicitor's office, and he welcomed me with open arms, so to speak. He had been all about Scotland a-searching and a-searching for some heir of one Thomas Hamilton."

"Oh, aye? A fortune, you have?"

Morgan grimaced. "I don't know what I have. It seems that this one Thomas Hamilton was of my great-uncle's line. He went off to America, and had some luck with a plantation in the Carolinas. He was a hard worker, said the solicitor, and he had some slaves and a family. He built up a big estate; then came the American Revolt from us. Thomas Hamilton, he was a Loyalist, and thought the war would go that way. He was wrong, and the locals went after him with a tarbrush and rope, so they said. He sold out, when he could, and went to the Caribbees."

"Aye, aye, so did many a man from the Americas!" exclaimed Amos Dillon, lighting up a long pipe after first offering some Virginia tobacco to Morgan, who refused. "So he went to the islands, then?"

"Aye. With his wife and other relatives. It seems he prospered there with his slaves, on a sugarcane plantation. There was much market for the sugar and for the rum that he made."

Dillon chuckled. "So you'll be making rum, eh? That's fine for a good Navy man like yourself!"

"That jumps ahead of my story," complained Morgan

dryly, which drew another hearty chuckle from Dillon. "The solicitor asked me for my identification. Well, I had that, the family Bible, and some words from clan in Glasgow who remembered me. So he turned over to me the papers. It seemed that Thomas Hamilton knew my name, and made a will. His wife and three children had died of a fever, of which there are many in the islands. He struggled on, and died just last year, with his plantation remaining to him. Called the Last Hope."

"Last Hope, is it?" mused Dillon, crinkling his red face. "Now, do I remember that name?"

"On an island called Elysia," added Morgan, watching him alertly. The brow cleared.

"Oh, aye, I know Elysia. Tis south of the Bahama Islands. Fine place, a small island, but pleasant. Banana trees, and coconut, and miles of sugarcane. I stop at their port at times. Leave supplies of furniture usually. A mirror, this trip! And some glass chandeliers!" Dillon chuckled. "Would ye believe it, chandeliers, for a plantation house?"

Morgan drew a deep breath. "This is very good," he said, trying to control his excitement. "I want to be left off as near Elysia and my plantation as possible. And you know it! This is splendid!"

"Well, well, well, so you're heir to some great plantation. Fine, fine!" Captain Dillon drew on his pipe thoughtfully. "Course, it's a pile of work, managing slaves and all, with that hot sun, and the insects a-pestering, and some disease. You have a wife?" he shot at Morgan unexpectedly.

"I? A wife? Nay, then. I've no time to marrying."

"You should have," said the Captain, shaking his head. "It's lonely for a white man, and there be few white women on the islands Best to take a wife before you depart. A man with property wants a wife, and sons to follow him. Eh, that's your business, and none of my own! Care to see about the *Marietta*, eh?"

Morgan followed him, and they spent the next hours roaming the ship. Morgan was pleased to find it neat and well kept, as he had thought on first seeing her. The cannon did surprise him though, a dozen in all, six on a side.

"Pirates," said the captain, laconically. "There be many of the devils roaming the islands still. This'll scare them off, and my men will do the rest, should they sneak up in their small boats to board us."

Morgan had luncheon with him at a restaurant in town, and finally returned to the Last Inn well satisfied. He liked the captain and trusted his seamanship. The man kept a keen eye on everything on board, and his officers respected him and moved smartly. The words he had spoken lingered though. Take a wife! It is lonely there for a white man.

He went up to his room, and was disturbed a bit to find his luggage moved about a bit, some papers disturbed and crumpled in place in his one case. He frowned down at it, with resignation. Useless to complain. The landlord himself had probably been checking on him. Fortunately, Morgan kept his little store of money on his own person, and slept lightly.

Tess brought him a supper tray, with more tea, and he thanked her, watching her as she left the room on her light quick feet. A nice girl, young yet; too bad if she went bad here on the waterfront. With all the sailors about, it would be inevitable.

About nine o'clock, he went down to the bar, having put some coins in his pockets, and reserved the rest in a cloth pocket sewn inside his jacket. He would play for a time, and test his skill. If things went against him, he would shrug and go to bed.

Ryder greeted him eagerly, with a mug of ale soon

to hand. Morgan sipped it cautiously. He didn't want to get drunk, it would not help his play. If he played well, his stake for the islands would increase. And he did not know yet what kind of condition the plantation would be in. It might be a wild gamble that did not pay off, and he would have to turn to some other work.

He did not know plantation work either. He must learn it quickly, and make it pay, if the place was in somewhat decent shape.

He played a few hands of cards with Ryder, enough to find the man cunning and shrewd, but likely to stick to a few good methods of winning. He let the man win a hand or two, which made the landlord bold, then Morgan moved in and took the next two.

At ten o'clock, the inn doors opened, and a gust of January wind blasted in. Morgan glanced up from his place in the corner, his back to the two walls. He had taken the seat before Ryder could protest. Morgan liked to see what went on before him, and have a good wall to his back, an old sailorly trick.

He saw now a tall man with ash blond hair, splintery gray eyes, garbed in black, black cloak, black shiny boots, black suit and white frilled shirt. He heard the husky whiskey-voice of the man, and recognized it as the one under his window last night.

He rose for introductions. Ryder said, "My lord, this be one Morgan Hamilton, arrived last night. Mr. Hamilton, my lord, Marquess of Tweed." By the heavy respect in Ryder's voice, Morgan figured the man was a frequent and valued guest.

They bowed briefly to each other. Tweed looked Morgan over curiously, arrogantly, then seated himself. Morgan glanced at the hands, long, supple. A gambler, he thought, for all he was a gentleman. He noted the pistol at his belt, the sword, and also the reddened face and the eyes. Drunk already.

Morgan noted the prompt appearance of a bottle of burgundy, glasses of the finest. Tess brought them. He glanced up at her, found her face blank of expression, but the blue eyes worried as she half-looked in his direction.

"Miss Tess," he said quietly. "When you have the time, would you bring me a roast beef sandwich?"

"Yes, sir." She went off to the kitchen at once, and returned with a platter of beef, bread, cheese, and a pot of hot tea. He smiled with appreciation. If he wanted to stay sober, she would help him!

"Tea!" Mr. Ryder raved. "Whatever are you thinking about, Tess?"

"The gentleman likes his tea," she said quietly, her hands in the apron.

"Right you are, Miss Tess," Hamilton said heartily. "Thank you. That's all."

She skipped away quickly. Morgan poured out some tea and drank, to his companions' disapproving looks, and he noted a quick secret glance between them.

They spoke of the stakes which were not very high, but high enough for a seafaring man. The Marquess tossed some gold coins on the table, carelessly, and Ryder's eyes gleamed.

The men began to play. Although the other two were drinking heavily, Morgan managed to avoid the wine altogether. He played carefully until he learned the style of the Marquess, then began to work out his own strategy.

Morgan watched carefully for a time, to make sure there was no cheating in the dealing. He couldn't detect it, and after all, gentlemen prided themselves on their gaming, so maybe there would be none of that.

He moved out a small stack of shillings, lost them, bet again on the next hand more carefully. Tweed had gathered in the coins casually, most contemptuously, but his icy gray eyes shone. He liked to win, even small amounts.

They went on, playing as the sailors came and went. Tess was kept busy at the bar. Morgan noted between hands how she scurried about, racing from kitchen to bar, to tables and back to bar, great mugs in her small hands, moving carefully to keep from spilling any. When a table was cleared, she took her tray and removed the glasses, mopped the table, and had it ready for the next. Ryder paid scarcely any attention to the men, Tess was doing it all, and she looked tired, Morgan thought.

Vincent came in from the stables. Brother and sister whispered for a moment, then disappeared into the kitchen. Tess returned first, presently Vincent returned, and they worked together at the bar, kept busy with the constant demands of the sailors. They knew her, and bawled out her name and Vincent's. Yet she managed to parry them, serve them quickly, and avoid their hands.

Ryder shoved forward the last of his stack. He had a red face now and he breathed heavily over his hand. From the look of his own hand, Morgan thought Ryder must have a good one; his own was very poor.

He threw in his cards, so did the Marquess, and Ryder grinned in triumph and gloated, "There, I knew I had it! Had the cards for it this time! Lady Luck is in my corner tonight, I feel it!"

Tess brought a bottle of golden brandy to them, at her stepfather's signal. She opened it, poured out three glasses. Morgan left his untouched, pretending to examine his new hand.

He had a little more money than when he had started, but not much. Dared he risk more? He could risk all on the table, then quit, claiming to be wiped out. That would doubtless be best. On the other hand, he might win.

The hand was good, he studied it, face expressionless. Lord Tweed frowned over his, then smoothed out his face. His face was bloated from excesses, probably alcohol and rich food. They played, Morgan raked in the winnings, and was quietly pleased that he had some of Lord Tweed's gold coins with the pot.

Should he stop? Not yet. He took another hand, studied it. Ryder was squirming with excitement, probably had a good hand. They played, Ryder was drinking too much brandy, and fumbled with the cards. He played badly, lost, and was cleaned out of the coins before him.

"Get more," Lord Tweed said without looking up.

"I—I ain't got more—not tonight," whined Ryder. He bit his thick lips. "Maybe I could put up some on paper credit," and he looked hopefully at the Marquess.

"Put up what?" snapped Lord Tweed, arranging his cards with meticulous care. "Not the Inn, I don't want it."

"What about a note, I'd take care of it soon. Except I'll win, I'm sure of it," said Ryder, whining his appeal. They both ignored Morgan. He thought this scene had probably been played between them a dozen times in the past.

"You got something I want," said the Marquess, laying down his cards, face down. His gray eyes took on a hot gleam.

"What's that?" asked Ryder.

"Tess."

For a long minute, Morgan thought he had not heard right. Ryder glanced over toward the girl at the bar. She had heard, her young pale face had turned white as her apron, and she held a glass in nerveless young hands, staring at them aghast.

"Tess? I couldn't write a note on her," protested Ryder. "She's me own daughter!"

"Stepdaughter, and don't pretend to give a damn

36

about her," the Marquess laughed coarsely. "You always say you'll be glad to be rid of her. I want her."

Morgan had stiffened. He was going to protest, when he saw his hand. His heart thumped. Aces! He kept quiet. He wasn't sure what he was going to do, but the appeal in the great blue eyes had reached him.

He let the men argue it out. Finally Ryder wrote on a piece of paper, which he ordered Tess to bring to him. Her hand was shaking as she handed the quill pen to him, and held the ink bottle.

"What shall I write?" Ryder asked, scowling.

"Just write her name. 'Tess'—whatever," said Lord Tweed, and reached out and sharply nipped Tess's bottom. She flinched, her blue eyes staring as her stepfather wrote down her name.

Morgan saw the words and deadly rage filled him as the man wrote.

"Mr. Ryder," she protested. "Don't—oh, I beg you— don't do this! I cannot let you!"

"You can't let me! You little bitch! When have you not been trouble to me!" snarled Ryder, and scrawled out, "To whoever wins her. Hector Ryder."

A sailor gave out a yell, and others laughed at the bar, drowning out her protest.

"Please, please, don't do this. I can't—he must not—" Tess was trying to protest, her face white, as her stepfather threw the note into the pile of coins in the center of the square table.

"Hey Tess! Another beer here!" a sailor yelled.

"Go back to the bar," her stepfather said harshly.

Morgan watched her stumble back to the bar. Her brother was not in sight. Alone, her small figure moving back and forth, filling glasses automatically, putting the coins in a box at the end of the bar, she still kept glancing apprehensively toward the three men at the corner table.

Morgan pretended to study his hand, then closed the cards. "None," he said quietly.

The other two men paid no attention, they thought the contest was between them. Ryder's black eyes blazed as Lord Tweed shoved some more gold coins out to the table.

They bid, Morgan quietly, Lord Tweed with a contemptuous curl to his big heavy lips, Ryder in a squeak of excitement. The bidding went higher, but Ryder had already put in the amount written on the paper, "Tess Pritchard."

Ryder flung down his hand. Lord Tweed grinned, and showed his, reaching out hungrily for the paper on top of the coins.

Morgan stopped him. Laid down his cards. "Three aces, and a pair," he said quietly. "My pot, I believe, gentlemen!"

He took the paper, and scooped it into his pocket, then deliberately took the gold coins. Lord Tweed glared at him in hot fury, and half rose from the table. Morgan watched his right hand sharply.

"You can't have it! That paper is mine—" the Marquess panted.

"No, I won it fair and square. You can see my hand," said Morgan casually. He pushed back his chair and stood up, "My thanks for an interesting evening."

Lord Tweed staggered from the drink, and put his hands heavily on the table; he began to curse Ryder. "You damn fool, he took the paper! Why didn't you stop him?"

Ryder's head swung from one to the other of them, like a great bewildered bull. "He can't have that—give it back, Mr. Hamilton! That wasn't fer the likes of you. Give it up, I say!"

"I won it fair and square," Morgan Hamilton said,

his hand to his belted hip. He pushed back his jacket, they all saw the dirk in it. "I'll take Tess with me on the ship when I sail in a couple of days. I'm sure she will enjoy the sea voyage!"

Tweed fell back into his seat, and raised one weak hand to his befuddled head. Morgan strode over to where Tess stood at the bar, her hands on it, gazing in horror and disbelief at him.

"Miss Tess," he said gently. "You heard? You belong to me now. I'll talk to you tomorrow."

She did not answer, only staring at him as though he were a monster risen from the depths of the ocean. He bowed and said, "You best go to bed. We have much to do tomorrow. Is your brother about?"

She gestured toward the doorway. Vincent stood there, paralyzed, his face dismayed and incredulous. Take her upstairs," said Morgan.

The boy gulped, took his sister's arm, and led her to the stairs. Morgan waited a minute, to make sure the Marquess would not follow them, then bowed ironically to the two men frozen at the table in the corner. With a slight smile, he went up the stairs to his own bedroom.

3

Tess slept little that night. The door was open between their rooms as she and Vincent whispered, desperately trying to plan.

"Maybe I could talk to the red-haired man," she whispered. "He seemed gentleman enough."

"Gentleman!" Vincent said bitterly. "They're all the same—after a woman like a dog after a bitch! I wouldn't trust him an ell. No, we got to get you away from here."

"But where?"

They talked about that in low tones. They were alone in the attic rooms, but sometimes one of the hostlers slept in a third-floor room, or Ryder came creeping up to check on one of his "guests."

"You best go north in the morning, Tess," Vincent said, quietly. "I'll follow you when the hue dies down. I'll steal a horse for you—"

"Come with me," she urged.

"We'd be easy spotted. Besides, I might turn them off the path."

Tess was silent. If she disappeared, they would take it out on Vincent, whip him, beat him. She was still so dazed and incredulous, she could not believe what had happened. That her stepfather had gamed her away at cards! It was horrible! She was no longer safe here, even if they had laughed and taken back what they said. Even if Ryder had won, she would never feel safe again.

And the red-haired man! She had thought he was a nice gentleman! All the time he had been calmly looking her over! Now he planned to carry her off with him on a ship, and make a shame of her! What would he do with her when he tired of her? She shuddered. He would put her off on some strange island, and sail away, and there she would be, far from England, her brother—

"Vincent?" she whispered.

He stirred, he had been half asleep. "Yes, Tess?" he asked gently, knowing of her fears.

"If he does—if that man does get on a ship—come along, will you? Sign on, or creep aboard somehow, I'll help you! I cannot be alone, I cannot!"

He came more fully awake, his voice more lively. "That I will, Tess! It might be a good idea, at that! We'll get away from him one day—and start over again somewhere else! Away from Ryder and his hateful inn!"

She sighed. In the meantime, she would have to endure whatever the man Hamilton chose to do to her. But her brother would not be involved, he would be safe. Grimly, she knew she must just endure.

She wakened restlessly about four, and rose to wash in the ice-cold water. She put on her warmest dark navy blue gown, stuffed some clothes in a small cloth bag, then woke Vincent. He got up, alert at once, for all the lack of sleep.

"Ready?" he whispered. He had lain down in his clothes, and all he had to do was put on a coat.

They crept down the backstairs, conscious of the creaking of the steps. Cautiously they opened the back door from the kitchen to the stable yard. All was silent, the hostlers were asleep in the hay of the barn.

Tess went silently behind Vincent as he opened the stable door. He crept in, took the first horse, which was that Mr. Hamilton had sold to the stable keeper when he arrived.

It was a fine big horse, and she eyed him with a qualm; she could ride, but it was so huge—

Vincent was saddling it, with cold fingers, and Tess was standing silently near the door, when she felt someone coming in. She looked nervously over her shoulder. How could they explain to the stable keeper or a hostler? They had no money to pay bribes . . .

Morgan Hamilton stood there! Booted, in his dark blue clothes, with the red plaid over his shoulder! He was gazing right at them in the darkness of the stable yard, with the horses in the stable stirring and puffing at all the people coming.

Vincent had not seen him. He led the horse forward. "There you are, Tess," he whispered. "Now get on and ride, I'll come for you when I can. Get a job in an inn further north and east—" He stopped abruptly, as Morgan loomed before him. He gave a little squawk of terror and surprise.

"Put the horse back," said Morgan, evenly, in his deep soft voice. "I'll take the girl inside. She goes nowhere, but with me!"

He grabbed Tess by the arm and hustled her back to the kitchen. In the stable yard she began to fight. She scratched and clawed, driven by fury, desperation, fear. She scratched with her fingernails as he tried to control her arms. She kicked out at him with slippered feet, but but made no impression on his boots.

"Come on now, kitten," he was laughing, and that made her more furious. "Give over now. It won't do a bit of good!"

"I'll see you in hell before I go anywhere with you!" she cried, and swung a thin arm and fist at him.

He caught it easily with his big hand, and held her more firmly. Finally he just picked her up and tucked her under his arm and carried her into the kitchen. As she kicked, squirmed, and cursed him in words she had heard in the bar but rarely used, he simply held her, carefully, not hurting her, but keeping her from hurting him.

When she paused for breath, gasping, still held firmly under his big arm, he said, "When you're finished, I'd like some breakfast."

She gaped at him. He swung her down to her feet, and held her by the shoulders, watching alertly for any swing of her fist. She had no strength left for fighting. She could have wept, but she was too proud. She blinked once, twice, and tossed back her loose blond hair. She had not paused to tie it up, and it ran free under the navy bonnet.

"Through? Good. We have much to do today. The ship sails tomorrow morning with the tide," he said.

Vincent came in the back door, hesitantly. Morgan gave him a look over his shoulder. Tess thought he can hear anyone coming, he knows what goes on all around him, and it made her more afraid. He could be smooth-tongued, but he was tough and hard, this stranger. How had he known they would try to escape this morning?

"Go and wash," said Morgan. "We'll be going into town in about two hours, when it is dawn."

Vincent stared at him, then at his sister, then slowly went back up the stairs.

"I'd like some breakfast," said Morgan to Tess.

Tess drew in her breath. "I'll see you in——"

"The tune is worn, sweetheart!" He grinned. "Breakfast, and some of your fine tea." He let her go, and sat down at the kitchen table, drawing up a chair with a leisurely hook of his booted foot. "You can take off your bonnet and coat, you won't need it for a time."

Tess's hands were shaking as she drew off the bonnet, and laid her coat jacket on a chairback. Morgan was watching her every minute, for all his leisurely lying back in the chair. She went to the pantry, came back with ham and cheese, looked absently for the bread that had been rising.

She put the bread in the oven, and began to slice the ham. Then she took out the tea canister, and remembered she had not put on the teakettle. He said not a word. He just watched.

Tess felt like a mouse in a corner, being watched by a great lazy cat which could spring at any moment. Her arms ached from his grasp. She would be bruised all over tomorrow, she thought. *Tomorrow.* She would be aboard ship, and in his grasp—and the night before her made her sick at the thought of it—

She took down a cup and a plate.

"Three," Morgan said. "We'll all eat before we go out."

"I have to clean up the bar and wash the glasses," she said feebly.

"Not anymore. You don't belong to Ryder. You belong to me," he said simply, and grinned at her. "I think you'll like it better, Tess. I won't beat you, so long as you behave. And you'll like the island——"

"What island?" Was he daft?

His blue eyes narrowed, as though he faced the sun,

or was being cautious. "The island in the Caribbean where we are going to live," he told her. "I'll tell you of it tomorrow, on the ship, or maybe later. We'll have a month on the ship."

A month! Alone with him, in some tiny stinking cabin, where he could do as he pleased with her—maybe turn her over to rough sailors when he was done with her. A month . . .

She felt sick at her stomach. She had not slept much, and now fear made her limp.

Her hands shook as she reached for the teakettle. "I'll do that," he said, and got up with a single lazy movement. She was so startled, she backed up and stood almost at the stove, but he reached out and yanked her away from the fire.

"Careful, you'll be burned," he said. He took the teakettle and filled the pottery jug with water. "Now sit down."

She sank into the chair he held. Her mouth was dry, she felt she could not eat a bite. Vincent came down the stairs, in boots and coat, ready for anything.

Morgan nodded to him. "Where's the nearest preacher?" he asked, as the two men sat down opposite each other.

"Preacher?" asked Vincent blankly.

Tess muttered, "On Front Street, next the church with the white steeple."

"Good. We'll go there."

"What for?" asked Vincent.

"I'll marry Tess this morning," said Morgan, and cut the ham with his sharp dirk. He was eating and chewing, all unconcerned, as the two stared at him.

"Marry?" whispered Tess. "I won't—marry you—"

"Yes, you will. The captain won't like it, to have a woman on board who isn't married," explained Morgan.

"We never allowed a single woman on board a ship, unless she was young and with her parents or a chaperon."

They gazed at him with the fascination of two wide-eyed children. "Is the bread burning?" he asked casually.

Tess jumped up, wrapped her hand in a cloth, and took out the first loaf. Still in a state of shock, she cut it, brought the sliced bread to the table, and set it down. Morgan reached out for it.

"You'll make a good wife, cooking like you do, Tess," he said kindly. "Can you sew?"

She gulped.

Vincent said quickly, "She makes all her dresses and my shirts. She's neat and good with a needle. And she cleans up fine, and works hard."

Morgan smiled at her brother. Tess could have hit them both! It was bad enough to be won at cards, but to hear herself described like—like a woman being bought at auction!

"Eat, Tess," said her new lord and master. He turned to Vincent and they talked.

Tess ate mechanically. She drank tea thirstily, she felt dried out. The two men talked more easily. She realized Vincent was telling him their life story, but she felt too numb to stop him. He was telling about their father dying in the peninsula, and their mother, so frail and pretty. "She married Mr. Ryder, thinking to give us a good life. She said we would be taken care of," said Vincent bitterly. "And look what happened! We was working before Tess was thirteen, and in the bar! Mother never knew, we kept it from her. And she died three years ago."

"Tough, but not unusual," said Morgan, so easily that she could have hit him. She gave him a blue-eyed glare across the table, and his vivid blue eyes returned the look with interest. His eyes looked like the sea on a calm day, she thought. Deceptive, though. Behind that calm was deadly energy and purpose. "I was pressed off the docks of Glasgow, after working in a cotton mill. My folks long gone, and my sister also," and a shadow crossed his bronzed face. His hand ruffled his red hair absently. He had tossed back the heavy red tartan plaid.

"You're from Scotland, I take it?" asked Vincent. "And you've been in the Navy for many years?"

Tess only half-listened, hating it that her brother was going over so easy to the enemy. It was all right for men, but she was a woman! She was the one who would have to endure his wet kisses, his pinches on her bottom . . .

They talked so long that when dawn came it startled Tess. Morgan stood up easily. "All right, we'll be off."

"Oh! I haven't cleaned up the bar!" Vincent went pale.

"When does Ryder get up?"

"About noon."

"Plenty of time. Come along." He swept them both with him. They went off, out the front door, past the messy bar with its dirty floor, glasses sitting where they were left last night and the whole place smelling like stale ale.

Tess was glad to get out in the fresh hair, keen and sharp though the wind was. Morgan had her arm in his big hand, she could not have run off if she wanted. He saw her shivering, and set his plaid about her and himself, drawing her to his side so she was out of the wind. Vincent had plunged his hands in his coat pockets, and was head-bent against the sharp breeze off the sea.

At the preacher's house, the man wanted to protest. "The banns have not been called," he said.

"We're sailing tomorrow," said Morgan patiently, and slipped a gold coin in his hand. Tess saw him, and glared. A man could buy anything!

They were married then, with Vincent giving her away. Morgan kept his hand on her arm, as though thinking she might dart off. She would have, too, she told herself fiercely, saying the words in a choked whisper.

"I Teresa Angela Pritchard, do take you. . . ."

He slipped a heavy signet ring on her left hand; it was too big, and she had to close her hand to keep it on.

After the ceremony, they went outside, and paused on the plank sidewalk. "You best go back to the inn," said Morgan, to Vincent. "We have some shopping to do. We'll see you before we depart."

Tess wound her arms about her brother's neck. She put her lips near his ear. "Tonight, after work—the ship—" she whispered desperately.

He nodded, and kissed her cheek. "Be happy, Tess," he said quietly and went off down the street, hunched against the rising January wind.

Tess was biting her lips. Morgan said, "Don't cry, maybe one day he can visit us."

She did not answer. He would be furious when he found Vincent on the ship, but hopefully that would be when they were far off at sea!

He took her arm again, and marched her down the street. She had to skip to keep up with his long strides. He found a goods shop, and turned in with her. The woman was just opening for the day.

Morgan looked over the goods, keeping his left hand on Tess, as though fearing she would slip away. She would too! if she but had the chance, she kept thinking. He bought some lengths of cotton cloth, for shirts for himself, she thought contemptuously.

He would think of his own comfort! He explained, chattily, to the woman, "We're going to the tropics, and will need lighter clothing."

"You'll have been in the Caribbees before," said the woman, beaming at them both. It was a good day for her, with all these sales, and so early in the day.

"Aye, that I have," said Morgan. "My ship stopped in the islands three times during the wars. There be palm trees with coconuts there for the plucking, and trees with huge bunches of bananas just growing there. Nobody would go hungry, just lying under a tree."

"Fancy that!" the woman said, eyes large.

Tess sniffed. Telling her tales like that! Morgan grinned down at her, and squeezed her arm. "You'll see, sweetheart," he said to her.

"Just married?" the woman asked brightly.

"Aye, that we are. Do you carry rings?"

"Not I, but the shop halfway down the street, marked Regent's, they have a sight of fine rings."

He thanked her, told her he would send a sailor for the packages, and they went off. He paused in another shop, to buy some bonnet frames. "You'll need bonnets in the tropics," he said to Tess. "Thin material over the face, to keep out the burning hot sun."

Those also were left for a sailor to fetch. Then they went to the jewelry shop. There Morgan mulled over the rings, carefully, and finally chose a small gold one for her finger. He took back his signet, slid it on his own hand, and put the gold ring solemnly on her left hand.

She thought they would go right back to the inn after that. Instead, he stopped at a restaurant in town, and they had a fine cooked meal. Tess felt odd, sitting there and being waited on. She hardly knew how to act, not jumping up to fetch and carry.

Morgan watched her like a hawk. He never took his gaze from her long, just to speak to the waitress, or choose something from a tray. He ate with enjoyment the fresh fish, the potatoes cooked in butter, the green salad and the rich trifle. Her nerves were in such a state that she could scarcely touch a thing.

He was going through with taking her with him. She

was married to him, married tight, according to the beaming preacher.

And tonight—she gulped against the gall rising in her throat. Tonight would be—unspeakable horror!

They went back to the inn. Morgan stopped a sailor he seemed to know, and paid him to collect his purchases and take them to the *Marietta*.

"Now to pack our things," he said, slipping his big hand back into Tess's arm. "You're cold!" he said, as she shivered.

It was fear, but she was too proud to admit it. "A chill wind today," she said, in a steady voice.

He paused at a shop window showing cloaks. "We'll get a cloak for ye," he said. "The ship will be chilly also, this January, weather." They went in, and he bought her a fine dark blue cloak with a hood on it. She put it on, and felt immediately warmed. He was buying her, she thought. Buying her regard.

He had won her at cards, and he was trying to buy her with cloaks and bonnets. But he would never succeed in buying her regard, she thought bitterly, hating him. He was taking her away from England, all she had known. He cared nothing that he was removing her from her only relative, her beloved brother!

They returned to the inn, to find Vincent washing out the floor of the inn, scrubbing down on his knees. Ryder was coming down the stairs as they walked in.

He stared at them, his face red and flushed. His breakfast must have been a bottle of brandy, thought Tess. It often was.

"There you are," he snarled. "I come looking for you! Why ain't the bar ready to open?"

"Are you speaking to my wife?" asked Morgan Hamilton, still holding on to her. "She no longer works for you."

Ryder gaped in shock. "Wife, is it?" he said. "Wife, is it? You're mad, you are!"

"Ask the preacher," said Morgan. "We'll be packing and leaving. I won't require my room tonight. We'll sleep aboard ship, and be off in the morning. Tess, say good-bye to your—stepfather. This is the last you will see of him."

Much as she hated her situation, Tess did enjoy the sight of Ryder's stunned red face, his helpless flailing hands. "You don't mean this!" he wailed. "A joke is enough! I'll laugh at it with you. But you ain't leaving, not you, Tess!"

Tess managed to say, "I'm leaving, Mr. Ryder. I—I will thank you for the years of taking care of us both—"

Ryder turned his irate gaze on Vincent, standing with the cloths in his hands. "I'll beat you until you weep blood, boy!" he snarled. "Letting your sister slip from me like this! I suppose you was at the wedding, eh?"

"I would take good care of Vincent, and not damage him," said Morgan Hamilton in a soft smooth voice. "Now that you have lost Tess—and a good worker she was— you will need Vincent in good condition, won't you?"

Ryder was glaring at them all, unable to take it all in, when the inn doors banged open. Lord Tweed strode in, in his black cloak, his face pale now, glaring from one to the other.

"There she is. Tess, you'll come with me," he ordered, and tried to catch hold of her. "Your stepfather owes me much, I have been counting the papers I have of his—"

"That has nothing to do with my wife," said Hamilton. Now he dropped her arm, and shoved her a little to one side, toward Vincent. "We were married this morning. Now, you were saying, my lord?"

Lord Tweed was sober for once. He caught his breath sharply. "Married?" he whispered. "You couldn't have. There wasn't time—"

"Oh, aye, just time," drawled Morgan easily, his hand on the handle of the dirk in his belt. "You'll see her ring." He took his left hand, and raised Tess's left hand to his lips, not taking his eyes from the furious face of Lord Tweed.

"You cannot have her!" Lord Tweed said sharply. "I have planned for a year. I must have her—I want her—"

"But she is my wife," Morgan smiled. Somehow Tess thought he was the more deadly of the two, though Tweed's words make her shake inside. "Now, if you will excuse us, we must pack our goods."

Somehow he had moved Tess to the stairs, while the Marquess gazed after them in cold deadly fury, and Ryder stammered to him, "I am sorry, my lord, my lord, I am most sorry, I did try—the lass would ha' been yours in time—I swore it—"

Morgan shoved Tess up the stairs, to her rooms on the top floor. He stood over her as she packed hastily, shoving things into her two small trunks which her mother had left to her. There were her few clothes, her dresses, and a black Sunday bonnet. She packed some dresses that had been her mother's: a blue silk, a white muslin, a green shot silk, a bonnet of blue of an old style. She lovingly wrapped pictures, one of her father, one of her mother and one of her family, when she and Vincent were children. She added a small box, with her mother's last rings in it. That was about all.

He stopped her when she would have lifted one of the trunks, to carry it down the stairs. "No, I'll arrange that." He stepped to the window, and yelled down to the stable yard to a hostler, who put his hand to his forehead and nodded. "You'll come up and carry down two trunks and a valise!" Morgan yelled, with a voice that would have carried from one ship to another at sea, Tess thought tartly.

His back turned to her, Tess thought it was her

chance. She slipped out the door, and raced down the first flight of stairs. He was right after her, and caught up with her in the hall landing. He put his hand on her wrist, and held it easily, his fingers meeting around her thin wrist.

"No, no, sweetheart, we are eager to be off, but not *so* eager," he smiled narrowly down into her wide eyes. He took her with him down the next flight, and then to his room at the front. He shut the door, and nodded to a chair. "Be seated, if you will, dear wife, while I pack."

She sank into the chair, glaring at his back, and stuck out her tongue at him. He caught the look in the mirror as he gathered up his brushes and shaving tackle.

"Now, wife, is that any way to treat your so very new husband?" he laughed. "I must teach you proper respect!"

To her, the words were menacing. She sat, still and pale, while he packed up his shirts and undergarments, averting her gaze from his intimates. He had stared enough as she packed her nightdress, her petticoats. She flinched. Tonight! It was not the garments she needed to worry about: it was her own intimate person that no man had known.

He finished, then looked about to make sure he had left nothing. They went downstairs, his fingers again about her wrist, as though lovingly. Tweed and Ryder were drinking in a corner, their heads together. As Tess went past them, Tweed looked up, and stared her over, from head to foot. She shrank against Morgan. He put his arm about her deliberately, and led her out. Vincent was not in sight, but pans rattled in the kitchen. He must be working hard, poor dear Vincent. A sob caught in her throat.

If Vincent did not make the ship tonight . . .

But he must, he must. She could not be alone with this monster, who looked so pleasant, and talked so soft, and could be so hard. When they left the inn that had been her home—held her prison—for so many years, Tess did not look back.

They walked down to the ship, and the keen wind blew more fiercely. An officer was leaning over the deck rail, smoking a pipe, staring as they approached. Morgan waved at him.

The newly married pair walked up the slippery planks to the ship. Tess's slippers kept sliding and Morgan finally picked her up, swung her into his arms, and carried her up the rest of the way. He set her down lightly on the fresh-washed deck.

He grinned at the captain. "Well, Captain Dillon, I took your advice. May I introduce Captain Dillon to you, my dear Mrs. Hamilton?"

The red-faced captain took the pipe from his mouth and stared. He peered under the broad brim of Tess's bonnet. "Tess? Tess from the Last Inn?"

"Yes, Captain Dillon," she said, in a muffled voice.

"Well, bless me! Best wishes to you both! You'll not want to be sharing a cabin with a gent this trip." The captain began to grin all over.

"Aye, no," Morgan Hamilton said, and kept his arm about Tess, as he drew her toward the inside part of the vessel. "I'll show you to your cabin, my dear. Our purchases and your trunks should have arrived, and you can unpack before the vessel moves. Do you get seasick?"

"I don't know." She turned pale at the thought. "I haven't been on a ship at all."

"Well, we shall soon see," he said cheerfully, and flung open the door to a small neat cabin paneled in shiny wood. "There we are, our first home, my dear!"

He moved her in, with a gentle shove at her back, as she stood motionless in the doorway. He shut the door after them. He looked down at her, as she gazed about the cabin. The packages had arrived, they lay on one of the neat bunks. She shivered. She was unable to tear her look from that bunk.

"I might be a terrible sailor," she said fiercely, lifting her head and glaring at him. "I might be an awful wife! I will hate you forever for taking me away from England —why did you marry me?"

He moved to touch her shoulder, she shrank from him. He dropped his hand, and spoke quietly. "Well, you're a smart strong girl," he said. "You'll do as well as the next girl, for a wife. And in the Islands, I'll need a wife. There aren't many white women there."

She wanted to cry, but she blinked back tears, and lifted her chin. She had to endure it, until he wearied of her. May it be soon, she thought angrily.

"Why don't you unpack now," he urged. "I'll go up on deck, and have a talk with the captain. I may go ashore also for a couple more errands."

She was silent, thinking frantically of how to escape while he was gone. He tipped her chin back further, to gaze down into her eyes. She flinched from the strong fingers, though they did not pinch her chin.

"And don't try to run away. The sailors will only laugh, and I'll have the trouble of carrying you back again."

He went out and shut the door quietly after himself. Slowly she untied her bonnet, and took off the thick cloak, and sank down into an armchair beside the bunk. Her lips trembled. If only she could cry! But she would not, for he would laugh at her.

4

Tess unpacked, set her things and his in the cunning little built-in cupboards and wardrobe, then sat in the chair near the window, watching from there the movements of the deckhands. She could just see the shore, and make out the tall narrow building that was the Last Inn.

She could not believe all that had happened to her. Had it been only a couple days ago that she had sat at her desk, and dreamed of the sea? She shivered. One should be very careful of a dream, she decided, it just might come true!

Her blue eyes widened as she realized that she had been wishing she could get away on this very ship! And here she was. But her dream did not include being tied and shackled to a tall red-haired stranger, nor did it include going off to some strange tropical island . . .

The door opening startled her. Morgan came in

informally, shedding his plaid. His cheeks were red from the wind. "Errands all done," he said with satisfaction, and dropped some parcels on the floor near the wardrobe. "Come up on deck, and get some fresh air. You look pale."

She thought of defying him, but the look in his eye told her he did not stand for disobedience. She stood up. He took her dark new cloak from the wardrobe and put it about her, and pulled the hood over her curls. "Like guinea gold," he said, as he absently touched one of the curls.

Morgan took her arm, and piloted her through the narrow corridors, up the stairs, and out on deck. He steered her through a maze of sailors, coming aboard with trunks, valises, strongboxes, iron stuff, all manner of goods. They went over to stand near the railing overlooking the dock, and watched the endless business procession.

It was strange to Tess to stand in idleness, and with a man's arm about her possessively, watching while others worked. She would work soon enough, in the island house, she thought. He would probably have her cooking and slaving for him. How long would she last?

Maybe if Vincent got aboard, they could both escape into the strange port and hide out. They were both strong and sturdy, they could work in any inn. Just so Vincent got aboard! She leaned on the railing, strained her eyes this way and that, but did not see her brother.

An older woman, gray-haired, came up the steps to the deck, clinging to her husband.

"Planters," Morgan said in Tess's ear, his lips touching her earlobe. She stiffened in shock. "And those men in the carriage, just coming—see? Planters also. You can tell by their garb and their faces."

They were dressed in navy blue, their faces were ruddy and tanned, they did not walk with a rolling walk, but hard and firm with their booted feet. Still, she wondered how Morgan knew.

Dusk came, and they went down to the large cabin which served as dining room for the paying passengers. The captain's chair was empty, he was busy on deck, and the sailor serving them made his formal excuses.

Another chair was vacant, but the other eight were occupied. Morgan Hamilton introduced himself and Tess, the others bowed and smiled. The older woman and Tess were the only women.

"I shall be seasick if it be rough," said the older woman, weakly. "I always am. I cannot wait to get to our islands!"

"Now, dear, don't think so," said her husband firmly. "It is in your mind."

"Not when the ship rolls back and forth, and the soup spills, and the dishes go flying," his wife said, shaking her gray head.

Tess's apprehension showed on her face. Morgan laughed, and took her hand. "Don't let them frighten you, my dear," he said. "You may not be sick at all. I'm sure you'll be a good little sailor."

The men looked their envy, as he held her hand. All were bronzed, hearty, outdoormen. They began to speak of their plantations, and Morgan listened with keen interest as they described the sugarcane, the making of molasses and rum, how to manage the huge slave population. It was a different world they were going to, Tess thought.

They walked on deck for a short time following dinner. However, it was not safe, for the deck was slippery with the seas that sloshed the docks, and the sailors still streamed back and forth carrying goods.

Morgan said, "We'll go below, my dear." Something

in his tone told of excitement. Tess swallowed in fear. Her throat felt dry and raw.

In the cabin, he began to strip off his coat, then his shirt and trousers. She turned her back on him, and removed her bonnet and the shawl she had put about herself on the deck. Her hands hesitated at the fastening of her dress, her fingers were cold. She felt rebellious and sick.

Morgan blew out one of the lamps, leaving only one alight swinging from the ceiling. "Shall I help you, my dear?" he asked quietly. She thought he mocked her. She flung around, her blue eyes dark with rebellion.

"No. I'll not go to bed, I'll sit up the night! I need no sleep—"

"Who said anything about sleep?" he smiled, his red hair ruffled. He came to her, and began to unfasten the buttons of her gown. She tried to slap his fingers away. He frowned down at her.

"Tess, if you are gentle and quiet, it shall go well. If you fight me, you will only hurt yourself," he said ominously.

While he spoke he managed to unfasten three more buttons.

"No, no, no!" she cried, and pushed him away, and kicked at him with her slippered feet. He had yanked off his boots.

He scowled. "Quit that, or I'll give ye a spanking ye won't forget!"

"It would be like you—brutal . . . horrible!" she panted, backed against the bunk by his advance. "You let me alone, let me alone!"

"You're my wife," he said firmly. "You'll have a much better life with me than with old Ryder and that Inn. And don't forget his Lordship! He'd ha' given you a brutal time, and don't mistake it!"

She shuddered. He pounced, and while she was thinking of the Marquess, Morgan had her dress unbuttoned all the way down. He pulled it up, and over her head, revealing her in the white petticoats and pantalets with the lining showing under her skirts.

She cried out, and crossed her arms protectively across her slight breasts. He was so much taller, stronger, rougher—she eyed him with wide-eyed fear. He gentled, and stroked back her tumbled blond curls.

"Don't worry, Tess, I'll take good care of ye!" he said. "Just you be a good gentle girl, and naught will happen that is bad. I'll see to it—"

"Let me alone, let me alone!" she moaned. Then her fighting spirit came to the fore as his big hands reached for her petticoats. She began to fight him again, kicking and scratching, his fists and her fingers with their sharp nails reaching for his face. He swore, and caught her under his long arm.

"Quit that, or I'll make ye smart!"

She kicked at him again, and he gave her one sharp spank on her bottom. She cried out in outrage. While she struggled, and kicked at him in futile attempts to get from his grip, he had her pants off, and lying on the cabin floor. Then he plunked her down on the blanket of the bunk, and as she tumbled back, off balance, he yanked up her petticoats and off her head.

She was practically naked then. She could have cried with humiliation as he stared down at her. He had left only her little chemise, and it scarce covered her.

He stood back, and pulled off his undergarments. She closed her eyes tight against the shame of his nakedness before her. It was a mistake. While she cringed against the side of the cabin, cowering on the bunk, he pulled back the blanket and slid her neatly inside the covers. Then he followed her in, and he was so big, it was a close fit in that narrow bunk.

She tried to fight him again. Kicked at him, with bare feet, flailed with her thin arms, bit at him with her sharp teeth when he tried to kiss her mouth. He had his troubles just holding her close to his naked body.

"Aw, Tess, now give over," he said in an accented soft tone. "Come along now, give over the fightin'. I'll not hurt ye if ye'll be still for me."

She did not believe him. She fought him in silence, until his strong arms had subdued her, and she was wet and panting for breath. He had rolled over, and half lay on her, his strong, muscular legs holding her down. He was so much bigger, that she feared him, and thought he would kill her.

His hands moved over her. She tried to hit him with her fist. He simply caught both fists in one hand, shifted his grip to her wrists, and held them above her head. Her blue eyes glared at him in the dim light of the overhead lamp. He gazed down into her frightened face, his own eyes blazing with desire.

She felt his hard body against her softness and thinness. He would smother her to death, she thought, as he bent down and kissed her cheeks, and put his big red head down in the hollow between her chin and shoulders. She felt his wide lips kissing there, here, and down to her uncovered breasts.

She shuddered. His lips were not dry nor wet. They felt—strange. Nobody had touched her there, ever, though men had tried. His lips went over her, and his free hand stroked over her body. He pulled off the chemise, and she was naked in the rough covers.

Tears of humiliation streaked her cheeks; she was not crying, she told herself fiercely, she was just so mad!

His big hand went lower, over her thighs. Then she

felt his fingers moving between the thighs, to her private parts. She stiffened in shock, as his fingers moved on her.

He was talking to her softly, soothingly. She felt hypnotized by the soft words, some in English, some in a language she did not know. "There, now, little Tess, lie still for me. Ye are so little and so full of softness—give to me, eh? Give to me . . ." She felt him moving to cover her completely.

Would he kill her yet?

Pain came, sharp and terrifying. She tried to scream out, her body stiffening in shock. He covered her mouth with his, his lips opened against hers, and his tongue came into her mouth. She writhed, moaned, but it was done.

She could not move while he held her like that. He moved, slowly, then more swiftly, and it hurt fiercely in her virgin body. He was so big, so strong—

She thought she fainted. She felt wetness, was it blood? Had he done it then, killed her?

He drew out, and lay breathing very quickly. His head was against her soft shoulder, and he kissed her on the arm. She tried to shrink from him, but there was no room, she was crammed against the side of the cabin wall, caught in the blankets.

Then he was talking, quietly, softly, into her ear, his big hand stroking soothingly over her trembling limbs. "There, it is done, little Tess. The first time is the hardest for ye, I promise it. The next time will be easier, and lovelier for ye. As ye are so pretty and so bonny, ye'll be a good wife, and I'll be a true husband to ye . . ."

He went on and on, and somehow his words and the turmoil of her mind made her weary. She closed her wild blue eyes, and he held her closer, and she slept.

She wakened once in the night. The light had been blown out, and she could see only the dim shadow of the night as the lamp swung over their heads. The porthole was open, the fresh night wind blew in. It was the last night in England . . . the first night of her marriage . . .

She lay with a man's arm tightly about her, holding her even in his sleep, and his body so close there was not room for a sheet of paper between them. She shifted uncomfortably, and he moved with her, turning over on his back. But she still was caught close in his arm.

She slept again, so tired with the fighting and the hating and strangeness, that she could not stay awake.

When she did finally waken, there was a dim dawn light in the room. She opened her eyes, knew she was alone in the bunk. Then her eyes widened in pure shock. *He* was standing at the fitted dresser, naked as the day he was born, sloshing water over himself! And humming to himself, pleased as a dog with a new bone!

She shut her eyes tight after that one long look at the tall body, the hard-muscled back and thighs. Fortunately he had his back to her!

She heard the movements, as he tossed the basin water out the porthole into the sea. Then the sounds as he dressed, and pulled on his boots.

She hoped he would go out. There was one more chance to escape. She would dress, throw on a few clothes, and flee the ship! She must get away, find Vincent . . . unless he had come aboard in the night—

There was the rustle of movement behind her. Morgan sat down on the bunk, leaned over her turned body, and kissed her neck.

"Tess? The ship is moving now, out from the port. Dress and come up on board. I'll be there, and we'll have our last look at England!"

She froze, unable to speak. Their last look at England! There was something exultant in his voice she did not understand. Was he glad to be leaving England forever?

He got up when she did not move. "There's hot

water in the pitcher. Come along now, no need to lock the door. I'll be near the entrance, a-waiting for ye." He went out of their tiny cabin and softly shut the door.

She was tempted to defy him and lie in. But naked like this she felt very vulnerable. She rolled over, peered warily about. Yes, he had left the cabin.

She got up, and washed in the hot water tipped into the basin. He had set out a large dry towel for her. She supposed she must be grateful, she thought sourly. He was being considerate! Here she was a new bride, and she felt it—the pain in her thighs, and her whole body bruised from head to toe.

He would probably say it was her fault for fighting him.

She did not pause long to examine her bruises. She finished washing, and dried herself. She felt the sway of the cabin floor in some surprise. They must be going out to sea! She felt now the waves she had watched so wistfully year after year, from the inn windows.

As she dressed hastily in a fresh white chemise, white petticoats, and her blue and white woolen dress, she thought, with a shake of her head, "And I was a-longing for this all that while! If only I was going to sea with my freedom, not as a wed woman! How happy I would be! If only—if only I did not have to bed with him, this would not be half bad!"

She felt a rising excitement, suddenly. No Mr. Ryder, she realized, no bar glasses to wash, no floors to scrub— at least for a time! And no sailors to evade, no Lord Tweed coming in and trying to pinch her when she turned away from the table.

Tess started timidly out the door, her cloak about her, hugging her new excitement to herself. If *he* was not about—if the ship had not yet left the pier—she might escape! She could slip out and be gone . . . She went up the narrow stairs, her small black slippers silent on the steps. On the deck, she stared up with surprise at the billowing white sails over her head.

She looked over toward the pier. It was becoming smaller and smaller, as the ship moved away from the shore!

An arm slipped about her waist. "See the shore, sweetheart? We're going out to sea on the tide!" Morgan said quietly in her ear. Tess stiffened at once, but if Morgan felt it, he gave no sign of displeasure.

She looked toward the Last Inn, saw it grow smaller and narrow in the distance. The tiny figures on the wharf were growing indistinct. They moved over to the railing where other passengers stood. In silence, they watched the shores of England slip away from them.

"A new life, sweetheart," Morgan said softly. "A new beginning! We will have a grand life! The tropics are warm, with fruit and flowers growing in abundance, and the cane is higher than my head. We'll work hard, true, but not like here! Not in the cold bitter winds and the rain that freezes the bones. Not waiting on others, and bowing respectfully to our betters! Out there, we'll be in charge!"

The shore faded from view, as they stood there. Then, when she could no longer distinguish the Last Inn, they went down to breakfast. Tea was poured and ham and fried eggs were served while the couple chatted with the other passengers.

One chair at the long deal table was still empty. "My roommate," one of the planters said, who had introduced himself as Mr. Grantly. "A spoiled brat of a younger son of an Earl. Ran through a fortune in two years, and is being sent to the Islands to manage a plantation. I wish him luck!"

"Aye, he'll come whining back in a year," prophesied another planter, with a grin. "His kind don't stick. No guts

—beg your pardon, ladies!—no backbone," he amended hastily.

"Aye, it takes backbone to stick with it," Captain Dillon said thoughtfully. "There be the heat and the dampness at times, and no cool wind for a month. Then the storms come raging, pulling up trees like they was so much tinder. Folks hide their heads, and seek shelter in a ditch when them storms come, I'll tell ye! But cane grows so fast you can see it coming up! And vegetables and fruits— why they come up while you sit and rock! A rich land, and a paradise for them as can manage to live there, and get along with other folks."

Tess listened with wide eyes at their stories, and thought they were exaggerated for her benefit, as so many of the sailors' stories were. But Morgan was nodding his agreement, and drinking it all in. He believed them, she thought.

After breakfast, she tried to evade him, but he followed her about, slipping his hand in her arm, or taking her fingers in his big grip. He talked to her with seeming casualness, but was always asking questions.

"It'll be a fine life on the islands. I'll probably be riding about the place day after day. Ha' ye ever directed the work of slaves, Tess?"

"Slaves? No," she said, shocked. "Will we—must we have slaves?"

"I'm told there are more than forty slaves on the island my uncle left to me," he said and told her a little about his uncle and the plantation. "Can ye do sums and read?"

"Yes," she nodded. "I kept the accounts of Mr. Ryder. He was fair lazy, and was after me night and day to keep the accounts up. I kept them more than three years."

"That's good. I'm no good on sums, but we could manage together. And the reading, Tess?"

"I can read," she said warily. "But we won't have books, will we?"

He looked mighty pleased with himself this morning, she thought, as he grinned down at her. The sea was no more a vivid blue than his eyes, against his dark tanned face.

"Sure we will. What do ye think I went ashore for at the last? I thought to myself, sure there will be long winter nights for us to be reading, sitting on the porch and rocking and talking. And I bought a case of books, in the little bookstore on the wharf. Got them ashore and put in storage for us. I ordered the gazettes sent out to us by ship regular. The news will be a month late, but better than never. I talked to Captain Dillon, and he says our plantation might be away from the town a piece, so we best provide our own amusements. Might be other planters about, though. We'll be visiting with our neighbors."

"And me with no fancy dresses," she returned tartly, surprised at him. He was planning for a lifetime, sounded like to her!

"Oh, aye, ye will have plain dresses and fancy ones. I bought some blue shot silk for ye, and taffeta. There are the cottons too. Ye can sew, can't ye? Ye might while away the voyage with sewing, and making bonnets," he suggested.

"It was one way to slip away from him. She thanked him primly for his foresight, and went down to the cabin, to take out a favorite dress and measure it against a length of cotton. He had bought long lengths, he must have thought her a big girl!

He came down to the cabin after her. He was always about, sharp-eyed and watchful, she thought snappishly. He watched with interest as she laid out the dress and measured it on the cotton.

"You could use the dining table while it is cleared, if

ye want more space," he suggested. He gathered up the fabric for her, and went with her to the cabin steward who let them use the table between the meals.

She managed to cut out the first dress, for all his interfering and suggesting. "You'll want it loose fitting," he said.

She thought he meant because of a child to come. Thought pretty far ahead, he did! Then he added, "The tropics are hot and wet. You'll want a dress more loose than in England; I noticed the women there wear their dresses fair tight."

Mrs. Grantly, the woman with gray hair at their table, confirmed his words at luncheon, as she and Tess talked more confidentially. "Aye, it is fair hot there, and you should make gowns that fit more loosely. The native women sometimes just wrap cloth about their bodies." She nodded her disapproval. "Fair loose women, *they* are," she added, "but one can tell you're not the kind. You'll want nice dresses for town, also, in silk and satin. However, the stores there often have goods from England. And bonnets, the latest out from home."

In the afternoon, Tess went out on deck, with the first lengths ready for sewing. Morgan had bought her a pretty sewing box, all fitted with three pairs of scissors, needles and threads of many colors, and a neat gold thimble. She thanked him again, with more feeling.

"I never did see such a pretty box for sewing," she said, admiring the golden woven basket and rose lining, as well as its contents.

"I am glad you are pleased," he said, grinning down at her. "You'll be all right, if I leave you to your sewing?" He had found her an armchair to set on deck, with her basket at her feet.

"I'm fine," she said primly. As soon as he left, she laid down the sewing, and started looking over the sailors.

She was anxious to know about Vincent. She had not caught one glimpse of him! Had he made it aboard, or was he working and scrubbing and slaving for Ryder?

She sewed all the afternoon, glancing up at times whenever anyone came past. But not a look did she have of Vincent, until the evening sky began to purple and the sun cast golden and orange flames across the sea and horizon.

A tall thin sailor had been working his way along the railing, businesslike in his scrubbing of the rail and the deck. As he came closer, Tess glanced up hopefully, to meet a bright blue eye and a wink under a sailor cap. She stared, then she finally knew it was Vincent.

His cheeks were rosy from the wind, his eyes sparkled with joy. He had come!

"Oh, Vincent!" Tess whispered. He gave her another wink, then bent to his task once more. She leaned back in the chair, and looked down blindly at her sewing.

He had made it! Now that she knew her brother was safe on board this ship her happiness was complete. No matter what the future held, they were together, and they would remain together, no matter what her new husband said.

Morgan came along the deck, sliding easily with his low-heeled shoes. He had changed from boots to deck shoes, and seemed to have changed even his gait. She watched as he would pause at a railing, gazing out at the sea, then turn to her with the sea in his eyes, and a content look about him. Clearly her husband loved the sea, she thought.

"Time to come in for dinner." He paused at her side. "Why, you've sewn a good deal today," he commented admiringly, picking up the basket for her.

She managed a smile. She could have sewn more if she hadn't stopped to peer anxiously at every sailor!

"It's going on a pace, Mr. Hamilton," she said demurely.

He helped her up, with a possessive hand in her arm. "You'll call me Morgan, not Mr. Hamilton. I'm not a man for formality between husband and wife," he said in a low smooth voice in her ear, and managed to kiss that earlobe once more. She was annoyed that it sent a tingle down her spine.

They went to dinner, and Tess enjoyed the company. The Captain talked of the smooth sailing before them, his full cargo, agreeable passengers, with the only smart fellow sick in his bunk from too much drinking. He answered the questions of the planters about the news of the islands.

Tess listened in eager silence. This was a new life she would have and she knew Vincent would be sharing it also. She was determined that Morgan would not turn him away. For once, the fates were being kind—except in giving her this husband! She would make the most of the joy she felt.

The Captain looked into her eager blue eyes, and smiled. "Now, Tess—Mrs. Hamilton, I should say—ye'll have a grand, a glorious, time on the island, I know it. Hard-working little lady that you are, you'll make a home there, and keep your husband a happy man. I envy him! I'll warrant you'll have a fine house, and several dozen acres of land, and in a few years, a houseful of children—"

Tess blushed wildly at the kindly laughter that went up around the table. Morgan got some envious looks as the captain went on.

"And I'll come and see you in my old age, and tell you how you come out on my ship, young and hopeful and just married, and made a good life in the islands. Gentlemen, let us drink to the new young couple sailing with us. A good voyage, and a fine new life for them!" He raised his filled glass, and they all drank solemnly to Tess and Morgan.

Morgan stood up, and answered for them. "I'm thanking ye for your good wishes and toast to us. For years, it seems, both my wife and I had a rough voyage of it through our days. She with her mother dying and having to work so hard. Me with my family gone, and a rough life at seas in the wars against France. But the war is over, and we have met and married, and may our days be peaceful ones. And ye'll all be welcome to come and stay wi' us in our new home!"

They raised their glasses and drank and cheered at that. Tess was silent, thoughtful. There was poetry and passion in his soft accented voice, and for the first time she felt moved by that voice. Although he was hard, and had been tough with her, a tiny little feeling of emotion crept into her heart. Would it stay lodged there to nuture and grow or would it be squelched when it pleased him?

5

That night, Morgan slept in the other bunk. Tess lay uneasily awake afraid he might slip over to her when she got drowsy and off her guard. However, he was soon sleeping soundly, she knew by the even breathing.

She did not sleep even then for a time. Arms under her head, she watched the lazy swinging of the darkened lamp over her, and the shadows as they went past the porthole, as the moon rose and drifted in and out of the clouds. The washing of the waves against the sides of the ship made a cradle of her bunk, and she rocked back and forth, back and forth . . .

A new life. A chance to start again in a new land! Hope had come from her deep despair. How her life had changed since that tall red-haired sailor had marched into the inn! All in a matter of days, in a twinkling of an eye, it seemed, she was upside-down and whirled around, and now out to sea on a ship—bound for the Caribbees!

Her heart thumped, she put one hand on her breast to still its excitement. Would it be a good life? Dared she hope that life would be good with this man? Other men liked him, she could see that. She had watched men come and go in the inn, and she knew instinctively that some were good and some bad. But some put up an appearance, and only when in a fight did they show the stuff of which they were made.

She finally slept, swayed back and forth by the movement of the sailing vessel.

She wakened to the soft feel of a kiss on her lips, an unfamiliar form beside her on the bed. Widened eyes surveyed her husband as he grinned down at her.

"Good morning, Tess! You sleep soundly, just like a baby," and he wound his fingers teasingly in her golden curls. "Want to get up, or shall I bring you some tea first?"

"I never had tea in bed before," she said drowsily.

"The sea is getting a wee bit rough." He said seriously. "Mrs. Grantly got sick in the night, I heard the voices outside. I'll bring ye a cup of hot tea and some biscuits. That helps if you have them first, and lie still a wee while."

He got up and went out. She lay wondering. He was waiting on her! Her—Tess, from the inn, who had flown about to do the bidding of everybody else! What did he want of her? He sure was being nice to her! He must want something, she decided.

He brought the tray to her, and sat beside her, drinking his own tea in a big mug. She sat up against the pillow, eyeing him warily as she sipped at her hot sweetened tea, and ate the biscuits. They were hard and cold, but welcome to her stomach.

"I hope we're not in for a rough voyage," he was saying thoughtfully. "I want you to enjoy it. You're a thin piece, and you've had a hard time of it. This is a holiday for ye, I'm hoping. Do ye like it, Tess?"

She said slowly, "I used to dream about going to sea. I used to sit by the window of the inn after I did the accounts, and look at the blue waves and the ships, and wish I was a-going to sea. But I wished I was a man, maybe a sailor."

He smiled, gently, at her small thoughtful face, and put a finger on her cheek, and drew it down to her chin. "I'm glad you're a woman," he said softly.

She stiffened, and drew back. He picked up another biscuit, and his strong teeth made short work of it.

"Well, I'll wash and dress," he said, more practically. "Ye could stay abed a time, but not for long. Ye'll be better for walking about."

She closed her eyes tight as he stripped off his nightshirt, and washed at the basin. That was not to say she didn't take a peep or two at him as he hummed and dried himself. He did have a fine form, she thought; broad shoulders, narrow waist, back with smooth muscles rippling, a couple of narrow scars along the shoulder, slim hips, and long muscled legs like a racehorse.

She caught his gaze in the mirror, and he grinned at her. Crossly, she shut her eyes again, and turned her face to the wall.

He left the room to her, and she got up and washed and dressed, staggering a little at the unfamiliar feel of the rolling deck beneath her feet. She had to concentrate. "I will not get sick, I will stay well," she muttered fiercely. The hot tea had helped. Morgan walked the deck with her. The dawn came up slowly, piercingly beautiful, with slashes of red flame across the horizon. Morgan frowned at it. "Storm's coming," he muttered.

"How do you know that?" Tess asked with interest. He launched into an explanation involving clouds and the way the sun looked, that she didn't understand. But it seemed to make him happy to talk about the sea. His eyes shone, his face was open and happier even than it had been when she had first met him.

They went down to breakfast. Only five persons were there. Captain Dillon said, "All seasick. Glad to see you up and about, Mrs. Tess!"

"Thank you. How is Mrs. Grantly?" she asked, with sympathy.

"Poorly. And now her husband down," he said gloomily. "I had hoped we would not be plagued with this until further out to sea."

"Maybe I could go down and see her this morning," Tess offered. "I could take her some tea?" she asked Morgan, appealing to him naturally.

"Aye, that's a good thought. I'll take ye down there," he said. "But stay not for too long a time in the cabin, you'll be sick yourself. Tis better to remain in the fresh air on deck."

She and Morgan took a tray of tea and biscuits to Mrs. Grantly, who was moaning in one bunk, and her husband in the other. Morgan took charge deftly, and got some tea down Mr. Grantly, while Tess, feeling sorry for the woman, washed her face and tied her hair back and smoothed the sheets.

"You're an angel, you are," muttered Mrs. Grantly, sinking back into the bunk.

"We'll come back this afternoon," Tess promised.

"Best thing to do is go up on deck, even if you're sick," Morgan said firmly.

Mrs. Grantly groaned and closed her eyes. Morgan took Tess's arm and guided her back up on deck. "Now ye'll sit down and be quiet a time, or ye'll get sick in turn," he told her. "We'll walk later."

She was glad enough to sit still, her eyes shut, until she felt less queasy.

A storm did come up, as Morgan had predicted. Tess went back to her cabin, tried to sew, and ended up lying down on the bunk, while the ship creaked and swayed and rolled slowly back and forth with sickening precision. She wondered how Vincent was faring as a sailor through the storm.

Morgan kept coming to her, and getting her up again, walking the deck, the next couple days. In spite of rain and wind, and the ship swaying about, he would hold her by the waist, and shelter her inside his plaid, and walk her about until even Tess got the feel of the ship. She felt gloriously alive and sparkling, with her cheeks rosy and her blue eyes shining, as they paced the wet deck in the rain and wind.

"Aye, ye'll make a fine sailor," Morgan approved in her ear, kissing her earlobe.

Mrs. Grantly did not get up for several days. Tess went down morning and afternoon with hot tea and biscuits, and some oranges the steward had provided. She insisted that the woman should eat, that was what Morgan had advised. Finally the woman was able to get up and out on deck, holding to her husband's arm.

The *Marietta* rode out the storm, and they sailed into calmer water, further south toward the equator. It was warmer now, and Tess did not need her cloak on deck.

The sailors whistled and hummed as they worked about the ship, moving with sure bare tanned feet on the wet decks, or climbing up the ropes to sight for long distances, or pulling and hauling at the ropes to change the direction of the sails.

Tess saw Vincent several times, and exchanged happy looks with him. When they got to their island, she would tell the kindly captain, and he must surely allow Vincent to come with them.

She was sewing on deck one afternoon, when Morgan

approached her, holding a sailor by the collar. He looked completely furious. Tess glanced up, saw them, and dropped her sewing.

"Is this your brother, Vincent?" asked Morgan ominously.

Tess nodded, gulped. "He—he decided to come along with us," she said.

"Oh, he did, did he? And does the captain know he is your brother, coming for a jaunt?"

Morgan looked so angry that Tess quailed for a moment. Then she stood up, and put her hands on her hips defiantly. "I told Vincent to come!" she blazed. "I wanted him with me! I won't be separated from my only brother! He doesn't have anybody else in the world, and neither do I!"

They were attracting an audience. Several planters looked curiously at them, Mrs. Grantly peered at them over her spectacles.

"You dared to arrange this, behind by back!" Morgan roared.

Tess kept her head up, and her blue eyes blazed. "Yes, and I'd do it again! He is my brother, we have never been separated!"

"It was my idea," Vincent said anxiously. He glanced from one to the other. "I—I told Tess—I wanted to sail—"

"No, he didn't," Tess volunteered. "I told him to come! I told him to come aboard after work that night, and get away from Mr. Ryder! That man is a beast, and he would only beat Vincent to death one day, and I never knowing—"

She hated it that her voice broke in the middle.

Morgan scowled. "We'll go to the cabin and discuss it," he said, looking about. "Without an audience, and your voice so high," he added, glaring at Tess.

She stalked before them down the stairs, and into the

cabin. Her heart was thumping wildly. She had never seen Morgan in such a temper. In fact, he was usually so calm, no matter what happened, that she was worried.

But no matter what he did or said, he could not throw Vincent overboard! Nor would the captain turn back to let one sailor ashore!

She stood in the cabin, chin up, hands clasped tightly together. Vincent was shoved into the cabin, followed by Morgan who slammed the door after them.

"Now, the story," said Morgan. "Whose idea was it to come with us?"

"Mine," Vincent said promptly.

"No, it was mine," Tess said.

Morgan slammed his fist on the dresser, making the brushes and combs and pin boxes jump. "Now, damn it, tell me the truth!" he roared. "Do ye think me so soft, I'll take on all your relatives?"

"I don't care what you think! He's my only relative, and we won't be parted!" She was shouting also, her hands on her hips, sounding like a fishwife. She screamed at Morgan, "I didn't know you at all, at all! How did I know what you would do with me, eh? You might ha' discarded me when you was done with me! How did I know? I told Vincent to slip aboard and come with us, because then when you was done with me, we would make a life in the islands together!"

Somehow Morgan had calmed down a bit. He was staring down into her furious face. "You thought I would *discard* you?" he asked, more quietly.

"Sure, and you might!" she cried defiantly. "Then Vincent and I can hire on an inn, maybe in the islands, and make our own way. I told him to come, and we can manage together, you'll see!"

To her surprise, Morgan sank into a chair, as though his legs were weak. He put his hand over his face, rubbed it slowly, and then his fingers went through his red hair. He was looking from Tess to Vincent, standing awkwardly in his blue sailor suit, his bare feet rubbing together.

"Why didn't ye ask me if ye might come?" he asked Vincent, more in his own soft voice.

Vincent looked surprised. "I didn't think you would let me come along, not having the money for my passage," he said.

"He works hard," said Tess anxiously. "He is not a lazy one. He has always worked hard."

"What can you do, besides scrubbing and washing dishes?" Morgan asked a little wearily.

"He's fine with horses!" snapped Tess. "And there be plenty who would hire him on, and me too! There ain't anything he don't know about horses, Vincent can fix them up when they're limping and sore. He knows his way about them, all right! And he can turn his hand to fixing anything."

"I do like horses," said Vincent quietly. "And I will work hard, you'll see. If you don't want me at the plantation, I'll hire on in town until Tess is—I mean—"

"Tess is not leaving me," Morgan snapped, furious again. "Make up your mind to that! She is my wife, and I'm not letting her go."

Tess stared at him, her mouth open. He scowled at her. "Well—how did I know?" she asked defensively. "You didn't say. Besides, you might not have meant it. A man tires quick of a woman, I hear!" and she nodded wisely, her babyish curls bobbing.

Morgan was staring at her. He did not laugh, but he did not look angry anymore. The anger had been wiped right out of him by something.

"Well, Vincent, you'll go with us. I'll have a word with Captain Dillon, and make sure he'll let you off at the island with us," Morgan said unexpectedly. "Did you sign on for the whole voyage, back again to England?"

"Aye, but some say they jump ship at the islands, and the captain expects it," Vincent said. "He hires on more at the islands, who want passage back home to England."

"You cannot be hopping back and forth," Morgan said sternly. "Man, you must make up your mind what you want in this life, and go after it. That's the only way. If you dither and fritter, you can't have anything worth having."

"Yes, sir," Vincent said respectfully, and stood up straighter.

Morgan had snapped at him like a commanding officer, thought Tess resentfully. But maybe since he had let Vincent off easy, and said Vincent could come to the plantation . . .

"Vincent is a right good worker," she said hopefully.

"All right, all right!" Morgan sighed. "You go back to work, and report to Captain Dillon about this. I'll tell him myself ye signed on without my knowledge, but I'll be responsible for ye, Vincent. We'll straighten out the matter. Go on then," and he nodded his dismissal.

Vincent backed to the door, and went out, closing the door softly after him, just as he had done with Mr. Ryder. Tess glared at Morgan.

"He is not a slave," she said, in fiery tones.

Morgan scowled at her. "Nor are ye," he said, unexpectedly. "Ye're a wife, my woman, and don't ye forget it! Now I'll be about my job of persuading Captain Dillon not to be furious about this matter!" He went out.

Tess sat down, her legs and whole body feeling weak. They had won! She did wonder if Morgan might change his mind about letting them both stay. However, she and Vincent were good hard workers. If Morgan didn't want them on the plantation, then they could get work in town.

With that thought in mind, she sought out Mrs.

Grantly. With a little guile, the good woman was led to talk about life on a plantation.

"You'll need to learn how to manage the slaves," she said. "That might be the most difficult piece of it. Just remember, some are new from Africa, and cunning rascals. Beware of them. Do you know how to shoot?"

"Shoot?" echoed Tess, her eyes round. "No, ma'am!"

"Best have your husband teach you, at least a pistol," advised the woman, busily sewing on a seam for one of Tess's new dresses. She was bent on paying Tess back for being so good to her when she and her husband had been ill. "And it won't hurt to learn a rifle, how to load it at least. Never let the field hands in the house. Only the docile house servants. And lock up every night, have heavy bars on all the doors, and keep the first floor windows locked."

"Are you scaring my wife?" Morgan asked in cool tones. He had returned soundlessly on the deck, and now he sat down on the deck floor at Tess's feet, easily. "I won't have her terrified, now, ma'am."

"Don't hurt to know what to expect," Mrs. Grantly said. "I think you should teach your wife to shoot, and that right soon. The captain would let you practice with sighting over the deck rail at the birds, when we get close enough to the islands to have them flying about. She should learn how to clean and load a rifle. I know, and heavens above, I ain't that bright about it. But if a slave insurrection comes about, you'll be prepared."

Morgan listened to her, and so did Tess. During the next days and weeks, there was much talk about the islands. The lazy smart-aleck son of an earl had finally gotten up from his bunk, and lay on a deck chair much of the time. He flitted his handkerchief disdainfully under his nose, and seemed about as helpless as a newborn babe. However, he was unexpectedly knowledgeable about surgarcane, molasses and rum, and soon Morgan and Tess had laid aside their prejudice about him, and listened to him discourse in his languid tones about the making of a really fine rum.

The Captain had been furious at first about Vincent, then more resigned. He allowed Vincent to join them of evenings, after the lads work was done, to hear their conversation. "You'll need to know more than sailoring, to work on a plantation," said Captain Dillon dryly.

Vincent was silent most of the time, but drank in all they said. Tess listened eagerly also, bewildered at first by the terms they used and the advice about living on the tropical lands.

"Always wash the fruit," Mrs. Grantly advised. "And the vegetables. Test the water to make sure it is pure. If the birds drink freely from it, it will be all right. Protect your water supply."

"How can water be on an island. Are there rivers?" asked Tess.

"Some have rivers, but not the smaller islands. You will find that the smaller islands have a layer of limestone, and the seawater comes up through the layers," Mr. Grantly said, on his favorite subject, the islands. "On top of the seawater, is a layer of fresh water. No salt in it, or hardly any. I reckon the rainwater comes down, and lays on top of the heavier seawater. Anyway, that's your fresh water supply. Elysia? Yes, that's one of the smaller islands. About fifty miles wide and thirty miles deep at its broadest. The town is at one end, I have heard, and the plantations at the windward side. Towns are usually set to leeward, on the Caribbean side," he further explained. "With the harsh Atlantic winds on the windward, the towns are usually established first on the leeward side, which is more gentle and not so likely to be blown about by the winds."

"Tell them about the coral reefs, and not to go swimming recklessly," said Mrs. Grantly, pulling her needle deftly through the muslin fabric of Tess's dress. With her aid, Tess had completed four dresses; two of white muslin, one of blue, and one of pink. She was now working on a muslin bonnet to match the blue dress, making sure the brim was deep against the sun.

"Aye, yes," said the captain shaking his head. "Look out for the coral reefs. They can rip the bottom of a ship to pieces afore you know you're on it! And what they do to a person—tell them, Grantly, about the fellow who swam ashore—"

Grantly grimaced. "There was a slave off one of the slavers," he said. "Got out of the chains, God knows how, and tried to swim ashore. The coral tore his legs to bits, but he made it, and my slaves were sheltering him, and trying to fix him up. He was terrified of me and of any white person, but I managed to get a doctor out to see him. We saved him between us, but it was months before he could walk. One of my most devoted slaves now—a fierce fellow, but gentle as a lamb to me and the missus."

"I wouldn't trust him an inch," said the earl's son languidly. "They will all turn on you. Never let him in the house, or be alone in the field or wood with him."

"That's true enough of most of them, rough men they are, and women also, fit only for field work," said Grantly, nodding his head. "But this one saved my life twice, once when a snake bit me: he drew out the poison with his mouth! Yes, saved my life then. And another time, a tree would have fallen on me, but he yelled out, and dragged me free. Yes, I would trust him. When they become devoted to you, they would give their lives for you, with no thought of betrayal."

"I wouldn't trust one of them," the man said again, stubbornly.

Tess took in all they said, in a puzzled way. They were talking of human beings, but they spoke of them as possessions. Slavery was not something she had thought much about. She had heard of it, and sometimes a slaver came into harbor—you could smell the stink of it for miles, even as they careened the vessel and cleaned it good with salt water. But slavery—capturing and using a human being for his labor—that was an odd and frightening idea.

The Honorable Billy just shook his head, and turned the conversation to rum-making. There his eyes would light up, and he spoke as one expert in drinking the rum as well as making it. The planters had learned he knew of what he spoke, and gave him their attention, as he told of how to boil the molasses at once after cutting the cane, how to test it, how to distill it, and so on.

He asked Morgan how many acres he had, and how he had learned of the land. Morgan told the full story, of his uncle who had been a Loyalist in the American Revolution, of how he had fled from the Carolinas with his slaves and family.

"And how many slaves do you have?" the Honorable Billy asked.

"About forty, it is said, on the papers."

"Humm, not a huge plantation, but a decent size," mused the earl's son languidly, waving his white hand. "You probably have a couple hundred acres—set out in sugarcane as you said? Yes, well, from that you should get enough to make sugar for export. Or if you take my advice, you will turn to making rum. Only be sure, let it age, at least a year, and for preference, from one to three years. The longer it ages, up to at least six years, the better the quality of the rum. Age it in oak barrels. You can get them from the United States, I have heard. I plan to obtain some for myself as soon as possible, and make a fortune in the rum business. There is a thirst that cannot be quenched for that stuff! Nothing like it in the tropics also. You prepare it with a base of fruit, stir it with a stick of pineapple or cinnamon, add a goodly dash of aged rum, and—" He kissed his fingertips eloquently, shaking his head. "Drinks for the gods! Nectar!"

The days grew warmer, they had left winter behind them. Now they sometimes sighted land at a distance, islands with palm trees waving feathery fronds. Tess hung on the railing, unable to sew for hours at a time, staring at the incredible blue of the seas, the way the waters turned to a turquoise near the creamy sands of the beaches. They would sail slowly past one, and how she longed to be on that land! If only their own island could be so beautiful!

Morgan would stay on deck with her, and talk eagerly about the months to come. "It is time to cut the sugarcane, so the Honorable Billy says. From February to June, it is cut, and turned into molasses, and then to sugar or rum, if we so wish. I hope there are planters within a couple hours ride; I shall need much advice! Would that some of our friends were going to Elysia!"

The Captain had agreed to turn aside from his main port on Elysia, to let them ashore at a small town closer to their plantation. He knew a man who had horses and carriages to let or sell. They could make the plantation in one day that way, and save themselves from a night or more in town. He knew they had little money to spare, and would need all they had.

The reefs were dangerous near the smaller port, few ships went there. But the Captain was skilled and confident. He would see them close enough, and the longboat would take them and their goods over the reefs and the churning waves onto the land.

It was now mid-February, and hot. Tess felt Morgan's shoulder close to hers, and blushed as she remembered the nights they had spent in the same bunk, sheets off against the stifling heat of their cabin. Morgan had made love to her again and again. She was almost accustomed to it— but still wary of him.

She had a feeling he would tire of her quickly, though he seemed so ardent now. It would burn low and die, she thought. She rather wished she could see the larger town on Elysia and survey the work possibilities for herself and Vincent, should Morgan tire of her, and want to get rid of them both as burdens.

Also, Mrs. Grantly had told her confidentially of the incredible sultry beauty of some of the black slave women. He might turn to one or more of them, Mrs. Grantly had warned her. The earl's son was notorious for his affairs, and others more discreet kept their mistresses about the house or in a separate cabin near the slave quarters.

Yet Tess recalled a recent night with Morgan, when he had not tired of her until close to morning, when a dawn wind had risen and cooled their heated bodies. He had caressed her body with his warm hands, had kissed her from her curly head to her small feet, saying words that she grew hot to remember.

Well, they would soon be on the island, and she would see how it was—and how Morgan was. She had a sense of fatalism, that life would dump on her unsuspecting head what it chose to dump, like a rainstorm coming up out of the skies and the sea, wetting her thoroughly. She would have little choice in the matter.

If Morgan kept on wanting her, and was kind, she would remain and work hard. If not, she could escape, and work where she and Vincent could find jobs. That was all she could plan ahead.

6

Morgan and Tess stood on the small dock at the town of St. John's, and stared about them. Vincent was helping carry ashore one of the huge boxes from the longboat. They had said farewell to Mr. and Mrs. Grantly, and all the others.

Morgan smiled a little at the wide-eyed wonder of his little wife. How small, yet sturdy and pretty she was, standing there in her new blue muslin dress with her blue bonnet shading her eyes. What a sweet little thing she was, all fiery sometimes, and yet at night, like honey melting in his arms.

He had found himself a splendid wife, he thought. The luck he had now! After all the years of turmoil and change, of wars and death, of grief in the Highlands, of blood in battle. Now this—

This paradise, this Elysia! He stared about in wonder, as Tess did, caught up in the enchantment. The Captain had guided his boat among the reefs at high tide in the early morning hours, and taken the *Marietta* in as far as he dared. They had anchored, and gone ashore in the longboats, the Captain with them, to introduce them to some acquaintances of his.

They stood on a creamy sand beach, beyond them turquoise waters, and out further the purple of the Caribbean Sea. Further along on the shore, palm trees waved lazily in the dawn winds. The town was small, just a dozen or so buildings.

Black men came along, wearing only shabby white trousers, their bronzed chests bare and magnificent. Tess shrank against Morgan. He figured she had probably never seen men like this before.

A white man came from one low-front whitewashed building.

The captain hailed him, they shook hands. He was introduced to the couple as Jonah Falconer. He owned a general store, the livery stable, everything in town, it seemed.

"Aye, I'll rent you two horses and two carriages," Jonah said. He waved away payment. "Keep it. If you like them, you can buy them after the cane harvest. Everybody pays after harvest," he said, and grinned in a friendly manner. "Got enough rifles? Need anything? Send for it, or come yourself. It'll be good to see some more white faces about—especially as pretty as your missus," he added, gazing at Tess in admiration.

Morgan felt uneasy about not paying him anything. He insisted on giving him a couple guineas on account, which the man accepted and stuck in his pocket.

Captain Dillon confided in Morgan's ear, "It's the way of doing business here. He'll keep an account ledger for you at the store, and you can charge anything. Pay after the cane harvest. You arrange to send the cane sugar or the molasses, or rum if you have it, on one of the ships; the captain pays you on consignment. Then you pay him and any other bills you have. That's the way of it."

It seemed a very casual way of doing business, but the Captain always knew what he was talking about. The carriages were loaded, the owner of the store gave them directions to their plantation.

"Hamilton's Last Hope, is it? Well, well, so you're the new owners. Judson won't be half-mad," Jonah said, with a fat chuckle. His belly shook under the loose white shirt. "Judson? He's your next neighbor, and figured to take over when Hamilton died. I told him, fine property like that, someone will claim it, but he thought not! Just be firm with him, and keep your rifle close to your fist. He ain't bad—got a pretty wife too."

They said their farewells and thanks to Captain Dillon, who shook their hands firmly. "I'll be back this way, come summer, on my way back to England. Take any messages for you, and orders for goods," he said, with a trader's gleam in his eyes. "You'll have some sugar by then, maybe I'll have room for it. But don't wait for me! Any ship comes along with an honest captain, you send your cargo along. That's the way of it."

He was still giving them advice, shouting as the longboat returned him to the *Marietta.* "And keep your rifles close, and a weather eye out for any of them storms! Especially along toward July and August. Remember to go down cellar to get out of the winds!"

They waved, until the sounds of the words were dim.

"A good man," said Tess soberly. "And Mrs. Grantly —I do hope we will meet her again."

"That would be pleasant," said Morgan, though secretly he thought the chances would be remote. The Grantly family was going much farther south, to Barbados, and he had looked at the Captain's map. Maybe a thousand miles away! The islands were scattered over the blue Caribbean, like so many creamy, green gems scattered with a lavish careless hand.

His thoughts were turning toward his own plantation, anxiously. Would it be fertile? Could he manage forty slaves? Would he and his wife and brother-in-law be safe there? And what about Judson, who thought he could take over the empty plantation? And could they make a living at it? Could they survive the fierce abrupt storms of the area?

He had thought to come alone, to survey the situation. If he liked it, he would remain. If he disliked it, he would shrug, pick himself up and go on elsewhere, to apply for work, do something. But now he had a wife, and a brother-in-law. People depending on him! He was not so free as before, not so able to pick up and leave. He must consider them as well.

He drove the first carriage with Tess holding on to the carriage rail at her side. Her small slippered feet were set sturdily on the carriage floor, the tips of her slippers sometimes just meeting the floor. She was a small girl, for such spirit and courage.

Vincent drove the other carriage. Morgan had watched him sharply as he had helped the blacks fasten the horses to the reins, and to the carriage spokes. He did seem to know horses. They would rear up a bit, and he would haul them down; though slim, his arms were strong. He would soothe them softly, his voice crooning. One horse, spirited and dark, his eyes rolling, listened to him and gentled in a few minutes. The blacks had watched him keenly, nodding approval.

They had loaded all their gear, trunks, valises, hat-boxes, leather bags, into the backs of the carriages, and were off before ten o'clock. "You'll be there by one o'clock," the store owner had encouraged them. He had drawn them a crude map, with trail markings. "No road, but you can't miss it. Just follow this. And you'll find the plantations laid out in cane, higher than the carriage and your heads. Follow the paths between the cane, but for God's sake don't try any shortcut through the cane. You'll be cut to pieces, and the horses also!"

They followed his directions, Tess pointing to them with her fingers eagerly, the map clutched in her left hand. "There's the stunted pine, and the rocks piled up," she said once. "And look! There's the seacoast on our left. We follow this about ten miles, then turn inland where the grove of palms clusters."

Morgan followed her directions without question. She was a smart little girl! He enjoyed seeing her face shine, her eyes sparkle with pleasure in the beautiful scenery, her eagerness to reach "home," as it would be.

They turned in, along a long dusty lane lined with coconut trees. They could look up and actually see the small round balls of coconuts! Imagine, Morgan thought, thinking longingly of the taste of fresh coconut as he had known it in his brief previous island journeys. How good it had tasted—and the juicy pineapples, freshly cut. And the mangoes when they were ripe and rosy red inside. Having fresh limes with a rum drink—

Tess gasped, and her eyes went wide. She pointed, speechless. Morgan looked, and pulled up the reins sharply.

A man in a white suit sat on a horse, in the midst of the sugarcane. The scene had been hidden from them until they had turned into the lane toward the plantation house.

Now they could see. The man in white was waving a pistol in each burly fist, and now he shouted at the blacks bent over in the field. "You damn lazy slaves, you get to work! I want the rest of this field cut today! You ain't getting one drop of water until you finish!"

Two grinning white men with whips stood near him, and the whip of one cracked as he spoke. The blacks cringed.

Tess whispered, incredulously, "But those blacks, they are only children—and one old lady!"

Morgan touched the pistol in his belt, said tersely, "Tess, get the rifle out of the back and load it like I showed you. Sit here. I'll tie up the horse."

He pulled up. The white men had turned sharply at the sounds of the two carriages. Behind him, Vincent reached into the back, got out his rifle, and loaded it calmly, as though he had often done it, though his pale face had turned so white that his freckles stood out.

Tess was loading a rifle casually with her small hands. The man on the horse looked them all over; his pistols seemed to waver in their direction.

"Hold on there!" Morgan called, his voice cracking like a whip. "I'm Morgan Hamilton, new owner of Last Hope Plantation. I think, sir, that you are on my land!"

They all stood paralyzed. The black children straightened up, and backed into the tall waving fronds of the sugarcane. The elderly woman groaned a little, and sat down where she was, her dirty white dress gathered about her bare legs. Her hands were bleeding from the cane and the sharp machete she tried to hold firm. She watched with dull curiosity.

"I'm Caleb Judson, owner of the next plantation," the man on the horse finally spoke. He drew his horse forward, then paused, looming over Morgan, looking at him from head to foot. "Who did you say you claim to be?" His tone jeered.

"Morgan Hamilton," Morgan repeated. He and Tess and Vincent were alone in this, and he felt the loneliness keenly. No regiment to follow him over the hill! "I am the only known living relative of one Thomas Hamilton. The solicitors in Glasgow told me I was named in his will, and I have the papers with me."

"Took you long enough to get here!" Caleb Judson

was about forty, not so tall as Morgan, with light brown stringy hair, small dark eyes. He looked muscular for all his potbelly, thought Morgan. Mean in a fight, probably, by his belligerent stance. "What took you so long? I bet you just found out when you landed that the plantation was without owner! If you think I'll fall for a stupid story like that, you don't know me!"

"I came from England," Morgan said quietly. "I came with my wife and brother-in-law. We aim to settle here, peacefully if possible. Where are all the slaves?" he added. "Are there just these?" His wave indicated the children and old woman.

"Went up in the hills a month or two ago," Judson said. His eyes were watchful. "I aim to burn them out! They hang out with some pirate mulatto, he's a vicious one! Got to watch out for them! They'll stab you in the back. I left one I thought I could trust to burn the cane and start the cutting. Then he up and left too!"

Morgan heard him out with a deep sinking feeling. He knew enough about sugarcane to know that he would need many slaves for the cutting. It would take at least twenty able-bodied men and women to cut the cane, take it to the mill, grind it, watch over the molasses and see the process through. And now they had fled to the hills! What if they never returned?

"They'll come back when they get hungry enough," Judson said, answering his thoughts. "When they do, I'll hang one or two of them, and whip the rest! That'll settle them down!"

"I believe they belong to me now," said Morgan quietly. "I'll handle the matter. I appreciate your looking after my place while I was coming. When did my uncle die?"

Judson's eyes flickered at this smooth change of subject. "Last fall, he died," Judson said, shrugging. "Had

95

a fever, couldn't help him. The doctor don't know everything. Buried him beside his wife and children, that was what he always said he wanted. When did you hear?"

"Not long ago. I was discharged from His Majesty's Navy after Waterloo. I went up to Scotland to see my clanspeople, and heard the solicitors were looking for me. They told me in Glasgow about the plantation; I decided to come out."

Judson's look flicked at Tess, then settled, thoughtfully. His gaze was that of a lascivious man, burning, looking her up and down. Morgan stiffened, and brought his attention back.

"I appreciate your watching over the plantation," he said, pleasantly enough, but coldly. "Now, I expect your own work is calling you. Don't let me keep you. I'll manage from now on."

"Just like that, is it?" Judson jeered. "I don't know you from Adam! Reckon you think you can fool me and take over! Well, you just go back to Glasgow, and tell them lawyers they have to have proof that you get Hamilton's plantation! Meantime, I watched over this cane, and I'll harvest it, for me!"

At the challenge, the overseers stiffened, and came to attention, one on either side of him, watching Morgan, and also Vincent, with the rifle in the background.

Morgan said softly, "I have papers with me, all I need. They are attested and signed. Also, folks say I resemble my uncle markedly. Captain Dillon said so, he met my uncle years ago. Captain Dillon of the *Marietta*, who brought us here."

"Huh," said Judson. "Fat lot of evidence that is!"

"If you'll come to the house with us," said Morgan, "I'll show you my papers."

"Papers can be forged!" Judson shot out.

Morgan brought up the pistol easily, aimed it. "Then I'll show you my loaded pistol. Maybe you'll believe that!"

He had done it so suddenly the man had no chance to lift his own pistols. The overseers shifted uneasily.

Vincent called, "I have you covered, so don't try nothing!"

"Now, I didn't come to make trouble," Morgan said, in a pleasant tone, but with the pistol still aimed straight at Judson's chest. "I don't want trouble with neighbors. But if you aren't off my property—say, in about ten minutes, starting right now—I reckon I'll have to blast you off!"

The challenge was flung recklessly at the man. He flicked his eyes, and turned his horse.

"Oh, all right. I'll come over—another day—and see them papers," he grumbled. "But I reckon you owe me plenty for looking after your place!"

Morgan did not answer him. He thought, I'll see you in hell first! But did not say it. He watched the man gallop through the sugarcane, where a path lay between the rows, and his overseers grudgingly followed him on foot.

He turned to the black children, and addressed the oldest boy, about eleven.

"You understand English?"

The boy's eyes were wide black velvet. He nodded slowly.

"You go to the hills," Morgan said slowly. "Tell people to come back. I will not whip, I do not hang. I want work done and will provide good food, good water. You will tell them?"

The boy stared at him, then nodded again timidly. At Morgan's smile and nod, the lad took off through the cane, running lightly and easily.

Then he turned to the elderly woman. "You will not work in cane," he said slowly. "Work in the house, work slow. Can you cook?"

She nodded slowly.

"Good. Tell children to come home, come out of hot sun." He pointed up at the blazing hot sun of noonday.

The woman nodded again, and spoke sharply to the small children in a language he did not know.

They followed her through the cane. Morgan drew a deep breath, went back to the carriage, untied the horse's reins from the brake, and got into the carriage.

Tess was letting out her apprehension in a sigh. "Oh, Morgan! I thought that horrible man would shoot you!"

He grinned down at her. "I reckon he counted on collecting all our cane, sweetheart," he said, and chucked at the horse. Vincent followed them along the path, until they came out from the welcome dimness of the palm-lined lane into the open.

Morgan gasped, as did Tess, and Morgan pulled up, to stare.

Before them sat a large gracious plantation home. It faced the sea, the Atlantic Ocean, sitting up on a hill overlooking the creamy sand beach and the palms.

It was a two-story house of gleaming white and pink coral construction, with a wide wooden veranda all the way around. The beautifully carved wooden doors were closed. Large French windows with real glass were set all along the front veranda, and out on the veranda were set large wicker and bamboo chairs, dusty and rain-drenched, but there, ready for sitting.

They tied up the horses at the porch railing, and got down. Morgan lifted Tess down. "Welcome home," he said, unable to keep the exultation out of his voice. It was so much better than he had dared to hope!

"Morgan, it is so—huge!" she breathed. Her blue eyes sparkled like the sea. With her hand in his, they climbed the wooden stairs onto the veranda, and felt the cool wind from the ocean blowing over them, the shelter of the veranda roof making the sun's rays less stark.

They pushed open the massive doors, and went inside. At once a breeze gusted through the wide hallway, clear to the back door which stood open to the stable yard. Vincent followed them inside curiously.

It was all open on the first floor. The only separations of the various rooms were the huge pillars which supported the walls and the roof and second story. On the right was a living room, with dusty rose sofas and chairs, large glass cabinets with some porcelain bowls and other table service in them. On the left was evidently a study where the master did his accounts, for the huge mahogany desk with its chair looked as though someone had just left it. Books stood on the desk, and in two bookcases nearby. They walked on through the hallway, glancing to left and right, at the mahogany and cedarwood cabinets, tables, carved chairs.

Tess tugged at Morgan's hand, pulling him imperiously. Her face was ablaze with excitement. "Morgan! There—that portrait," she panted, and they came to a halt before it. It stood in the huge drawing room, and they stood with dusty shoes on the parquet floors and gazed up at it.

It was the portrait of a man, done about twenty or more years before, for the man wore the garb of about 1790. He had a strong imperious face, vivid blue eyes, and gray red hair in unpowdered arrangement. He stood before a mahogany desk, that of the study room, with one hand on an open ledger, the other with a quill pen.

"He looks exactly like you, Morgan!" breathed Tess. Vincent, behind them, agreed.

"It must be your uncle."

"Yes, Uncle Thomas Hamilton, I saw his miniature years ago," murmured Morgan. "I had not realized how much we looked alike. Well, that should prove it to Judson!"

"I think he knew when he looked at you," said Tess wisely. "He would have put up more of a fight, maybe.

But he knew Thomas Hamilton, and your looks must have shocked him."

"I wonder if this was his wife, and the children who died of a fever?" Vincent had gone ahead to look at the matching portrait on the other wall. He gazed up at them critically. "Gee, she looks sad. Maybe she didn't want to leave her home in the Carolinas."

Tess moved on, Morgan followed her, to gaze up at the portrait of the dark-haired slim woman, sitting in a rose-colored armchair. Three children clustered about her, one standing at her right, a fine dark-eyed boy. The other two were girls, one in blue, the baby in pink.

"And they all died of a fever, how sad," murmured Tess.

Morgan felt a catch at his heart. If Tess—and their children—died of a fever—could he ever forgive himself? He crushed back the thought. They would be careful, he would make sure the doctor came often. They would take pains to be healthy, to eat the right foods—

Vince had gone on. "The dining room," he marveled. "You just walk right from one room into another."

They crossed the parquet floor around several rose-covered chairs, and into the dining room area. The table was a huge polished oval, now dusty, and around it were ten matching chairs, all of shining cedarwood. Tess ran her hand lovingly over the hand-carved surface. Morgan watched her eyes, she could scarce believe this was their home.

She caught his look, and shook her head in wonder. "And I was a-working in a bar," she said simply.

"And me in the stables," croaked Vincent, half laughing, half sobbing. "Is this all going to be our *home?*"

"Looks mighty good to an ex-sailor," grinned Morgan. "Let's look at the upstairs."

A winding stairs from the dining room area led upstairs, into another wide hall. "That's for the wind to sweep through off the ocean," said Tess suddenly. "With the windows open at both ends, you'd get a fine breeze through."

They walked reverently on the beautiful parquet floors along the hallway, peering into the bedrooms on both sides. There were three on a side, six in all, with small bath areas in some of the rooms, with little iron tubs sitting in them, ready to be filled with hot water carried up in buckets.

"The master bedroom," pronounced Morgan, as he looked into two rooms toward the front. The middle bedroom was huge, with a massive four-poster bed and canopy with mosquito netting hanging from the silks. In the front room overlooking the front doors and veranda was another huge bed, this one with a dainty rose canopy and white mosquito netting, and smaller furnishings, fit for a lady. A pair of tiny white slippers were set in front of a dresser, and on it were some brushes and combs, a pin box, a faded mirror that needed resilvering.

"This must have been hers," murmured Tess, picking up the slippers. "All that time, he kept them here, all those years."

Morgan noticed the silence then, all was so still. The breeze blew in from the opened windows which he and Vincent had unbolted and thrown wide. But otherwise all was quiet.

No slaves, he thought. All in the hills. How could they run this vast house, to say nothing of the sugarcane plantation, without help?

Would they return?

They went back downstairs again. "What about food?" asked Tess, thoughtfully. "Where is the kitchen?" She looked about in puzzled fashion.

"It is usually separate from the house, so the fires there won't set the house on fire," Morgan said. They went out the back, onto the shaded veranda, and looked. Sure enough, there was a cookhouse, all neat with fireplace, cranes for pots and pans, and all manner of cooking utensils, from huge kettles to spoons and knives.

Beyond and on the left were small huts. Slave cabins, set on coral foundations off the ground, simple huts with dirt floors, a single room, a thatch roof. Beyond the cookhouse, at a respectful distance, stood the stables, which were empty now.

"I'll take the horses back there, once we unload," said Vincent. "And I see some chickens there. Shall I get one for luncheon, Tess?"

"Yes, if I can manage this fireplace!" she said ruefully. "I've been spoiled with a stove and all."

Morgan got the fireplace going, Tess plucked the chicken, and got it to boiling in a medium-sized kettle. Vincent returned from caring for the horses, with his hands full of vegetables.

"I don't know some of these, but they were all growing in the garden patch. I reckon it just takes some cooking." He puzzled over the objects.

Morgan recognized some, Tess others. She cooked the ones they were sure of, and soon they sat down to the hastily dusted dining table to a meal of chicken and vegetables. Tess looked weary, and it was three in the afternoon, the hottest time.

Morgan thought, the slaves must come back. Tess cannot cook for us alone, it is too hot for her. She must live like a lady. Through the opened windows, he glanced up to the line of hills beyond the sugarcane fields. The slaves were up there; hungry? without water? They must come down soon. But how would they come? As slaves, workers, shyly friendly?

Or as enemies? He thought of the machetes, the huge curved knives in the hands of the children as they cut the cane. If the men had those, and were fearful and full of hate, the three whites would not live long.

7

Odette lay on her stomach in the thick grass, on the top of the hill. She looked longingly toward the waving fields of sugarcane; beyond were the outlines of the plantation house. It was noon, the hottest part of the day.

She was hungry, thirsty. None of the slaves had enough to eat these days. But starvation was preferable to the harsh and cruel whip of Caleb Judson. Odette knew he had his eye on her. Before the death of Mr. Thomas Hamilton, her master, Odette had been protected.

Mr. Hamilton had known her since her birth sixteen years ago. He had been kind to her mother; in fact, he had been kind to all the slaves. His sadness after his wife died had reached out and touched them all. Their master had become more gentle. And sometimes they saw him sitting on the veranda in his cane lounger, staring out at the sea for hours.

Malkia, the oldest slave, who had come from Africa when she was a very young girl, had said then, "He won't want to live. He just work, work, think, think. Nobody means much to him no more."

It had been true. Mr. Hamilton had gone down and down, until he was a thin shadow of himself. He had kept up the work on the fields, made rum and sent it overseas; he had kept them busy and happy. He had let them sing and dance evenings, despite the disapproval of Caleb Judson, who now vented his rage on them. Oh yes, Odette thought, Mr. Hamilton had been good to them.

Bernardo was lying beside her on the grass. He ran a teasing finger down her spine to her rounded buttocks.

"Now, Bernardo," she said mildly. She tried to ignore the thrill of his touch, but she liked it. He was a little older than she, and he had no other woman in his life.

"I want you now," he whispered in her ear.

She rolled over, and gazed up at him, her dark eyes soft.

He was tall and broad and muscular, a handsome black. They had been lovers for only a short time. Odette had thought carefully before letting him come to her. Malkia had warned her, "Choose your man carefully, pretty Odette! He must be able fight for you! Many men want you for body, but you take man who will protect."

She had listened, but her heart was already inclined toward Bernardo. He was patient, gentle. But he was strong and could fight and kill. For her, she knew he would.

She smiled, and reached up her arms to him. When he came down eagerly on her slim body clad only in a thin white cotton frock, she whispered in his ear, "Be with care, my man. I don't want baby now. Not now. Maybe sometime."

"I'll take care," he said passionately. "But oh, I

want you so much, my sweet Odette! You're like molasses, thick and good. Oh! How I want you!"

As he kissed her slender throat, Odette tried to wipe out the memory of the time Judson had caught her. He had kissed her brutally on the very place where Bernardo was now placing gentle kisses. Then he had torn her dress to get at her young, rounded breasts. She recalled those thick sucking lips! She had fought him then, with claws and kicks, which had no effect. When he had been about to take her, Mr. Hamilton had come along, and raised hell!

"You let that girl go, Judson!" he had said. "She is a maid here! You cannot have her!"

He had had to lay a whip to Judson's back before the man stopped. Odette shuddered in the light breeze as she remembered the deadly menace in Judson's eyes. He had risen from the dirt, where she lay panting, trying to cover herself with the torn dress.

"I'll get you one day!" he warned Odette, and stalked away.

Mr. Hamilton had been understanding. "It's too bad, Odette. Stay away from that man and get another dress from the storeroom. A pretty one. But remember to hide when Mr. Judson comes calling."

She had thanked him, tearfully, and he had patted her shoulder like a father, his blue eyes sad. Then Mr. Hamilton had died.

Bernardo knew something about it, his face got hard when it was mentioned. Now Judson came often to the plantation, talking of taking it over. Bernardo would kill Caleb Judson if he ever tried to take Odette again.

Bernardo groaned over her, bringing Odette back to the pleasures of the present as his hardness pressed against her body. His hand caressed upward over her light brown thigh, his fingers went eagerly seeking her soft, moist warmth. She opened for him, smiling up at him, her gaze blurring with the pleasure she felt.

They writhed in the tall grass, playing, teasing each other, to draw out the happy time. His mouth went over her, expertly, drawing a groan from her. Her legs drew further apart and he pressed himself to her.

She felt the blaze of glory-pain through her as he came in. He rubbed his wide dark chest against her tender bared breasts, and she felt thrills all through her body.

"Ooohhh, honey, love," she moaned, clasping him more tightly to her. Her slim hips revolved rapidly as she lunged up at him. She had learned quickly the love-movements of pleasure. Bernardo groaned aloud, echoing her voice.

When she felt he was going to explode in her, she pushed at him swiftly. "Pull out, pull out," she said, suddenly in panic. She did not want a child yet!

He obeyed the sharp push she gave to his shoulders, and pulled out just in time. His seed spurted over her lower limbs. They lay back, gasping with the delight and relief of release.

Languidly she pulled the dress down to cover her lower body, and lay in his arms in the grass, half asleep. Bernardo slept on her breast, his tightly curled black hair against her lips. She pressed her lips to his forehead tenderly. Like a babe in her arms, she thought, nuzzling closer. Maybe she would one day have his child. A woman wanted the child of her man.

The lazy spell was broken when her stomach growled. She had eaten nothing but berries today, and yesterday they had had only long pieces of sugarcane to suck. There was little water, just what the men had brought up in buckets. She felt dirty and longed to bathe in the beautiful blue waves that she could just see from up here in the hills. She and Bernardo had a favorite cove where he had taught her to swim, naked, and she delighted in it. He had come as a boy of eight from the West Coast of Africa, and he knew the waters as a friend. Some of the others feared the water, and would not go into the waves.

How long could they stay up here, she wondered as she swallowed, trying to alleviate the dryness in her throat.

Maybe they *could* go to Quintero's plantation and beg for work there—Bernardo had suggested it several times. Their friend Louis Abaco had nodded gravely, agreeing it would be better than Judson. But the overseers of the Quintero plantation did bad things behind the back of the Spaniard, and the kindly man did not know it. No, it was better to wait a while.

A sound crackled in the underbrush. Odette sat up sharply, moving Bernardo from her. She saw Louis Abaco stalking toward them from the brush of the hill.

His dark eyes saw her, he smiled a little ironically. She flushed, and looked down at Bernardo. She shook him, to waken him. He rolled over and sat up quickly, immediately on the defensive until he saw who stood there.

The ex-pirate was a mulatto. He was tall and handsome in his navy blue shirt and pants, the red cummerbund about his waist. He had a gold ring in one ear. His feet were bare, as usual. Louis wore his sandals only when going down in the valley among the sharp cane.

"What is it?" asked Bernardo. "Has Judson come?"

Abaco shook his dark head. He was very tall with thick muscular arms and legs from years of being at sea. Odette despised herself a little for letting her eyes run over him like this. He was a fine figure of a man, but she had given herself to Bernardo, she reminded herself sternly, and she meant to be loyal. When Abaco turned his gaze to her, she knew she was desired. Yet he made no gesture toward her.

"Gamba says come. There is a meeting. White men have come."

"What white men?" Bernardo asked. "Has Judson come again? Up in the hills?" He looked about for the cane knife never far from his side, and picked it up menacingly. "I'll never go back to him!"

"Come and hear," Abaco said with good humor, his gaze lingering on them both. He knew what they had been doing, Odette thought. She tossed her thick black hair defiantly and reached out for a red hibiscus on the nearest bush, and plucked a blossom. She put it behind her ear. Louis Abaco's look approved, lingered.

They followed him back to the small clearing behind the wind-bent coconut trees. If the coconuts had been ripe, they could have eaten them. But it was not good to eat too many of them alone; and besides, men would have made strong drink from the milk, fermenting it, thought Odette. Then there would have been no peace.

Gamba stood in the center before them all, his haughty body erect, his arms folded. He had come over when he was sixteen. He never forgot he was the son of a chief. Beside him was young Alfred, whose black velvet eyes were blazing with excitement. He had stayed behind with his grandmother, old wise Malkia.

When all had gathered and waited, Gamba spoke. It hurt his dignity that he had to speak in broken English, but they did not understand his African language, nor each other's, usually. Their only common tongue was English, as taught to them on the plantation. Some were Ibo, some Hausa, some Yoruba, a few Kikuyu, and Gamba was from Zimbabwe.

Mr. Hamilton had let drop the fact one time that the planters deliberately mixed the slaves on their plantations. They wanted no tribal loyalties, no chief bringing them together to speak their native language and plan treachery against the master.

Gamba spoke. "Boy Alfred says, white men come. Two men, one woman." He said it slowly, searching for the words. "I say, go down, kill, take land."

He looked about them haughtily, his eyes flashing. Odette felt a thrill of apprehension.

Louis Abaco stood leaning against a tree, as though apart. He was really apart, though. He was no slave, but a free man, who had escaped from a pirate ship to hide in the hills until the pirates, cursing, had departed. He lived in the hills, crept down to visit them and get food, then came back to the hills again. Sometimes Judson tried to capture him and make him work, but Abaco insisted on being free, although he was part black.

Bernardo said thoughtfully, "Who are these men? Where did they come from?"

Gamba frowned. "No matter. Kill them."

Odette spoke up bravely. "Is one from England?"

Gamba hesitated. Alfred finally spoke up as they looked at him. His childish voice tried to sound adult. "One man has red hair, looks like Mr. Hamilton. Maybe Mr. Hamilton come back alive!"

"Red hair?" Bernardo muttered. Odette had felt a shock.

"Back to life?" Louis Abaco growled. "Nonsense. Never saw that. Maybe he's a relative of Mr. Hamilton, come to claim the plantation. What did he look like, boy?"

"He look like Mr. Hamilton," said Alfred positively. "He tell Judson go away from my land!"

"Ahhh," murmured the crowd of some forty slaves. You could hear the sighing wind of their thoughts sweeping through. Mr. Hamilton had been kind, he rarely whipped any slave. He had worked them hard, but fairly, and they ate well, and slept in their own huts. He let them go down to the sea and get fish on Sunday. He laughed with them sometimes, and let them have drink if they stayed on the plantation to enjoy it. But no running about to other places or to town, not with drink in them! That would be dangerous, he warned them sternly.

"Mr. Hamilton's son come?" one woman ventured.

"He has no son," said Bernardo. "His only son die."

"Maybe another chief in his place?"

"Red hair?"

"He looks like Mr. Hamilton?"

"He send Judson away?"

The questions were coming more eagerly. They were sick of hiding in the hills, of starving and being thirsty.

"What does Malkia say?" asked Odette. Everyone respected the old wise woman except Gamba who was jealous of her power.

"She says come back to the red-haired one." Alfred told them this positively. He related the whole story again, he had never felt so important. All the older men were hanging on his words. He described the way the two carriages had driven up, how the red-haired man had held the pistol on Judson, how the words had flown between them, and how Judson had gone away.

"And there is a little woman with him, his woman," said Alfred. "Her hair is like the jasmine. Her eyes are the blue sea. She held a rifle and loaded it like so." His small arms flew to demonstrate. "She smiled at me," he added thoughtfully.

"And the other man?"

Alfred pointed to his own hair. "Hair like the ripe cane. He held the rifle steady, and calmed the horses."

"Sounds like a family," Abaco said quietly. His gaze sought Odette, who nodded in agreement.

"Maybe some of you should go back first," Gamba said reluctantly, unwilling to have the decisions taken from him. He sensed how they felt. "Bernardo, you go first and see how goes the new man of red hair. Alfred take him back. Women go later. Odette go with Bernardo," he said with distaste.

"Yes, Odette is smart. She will know if he is good man." Abaco nodded.

That was not what Gamba meant. He meant that since Odette had chosen Bernardo instead of himself, she might as well be of use, and go with her man!

Late that afternoon, Bernardo, Alfred, Odette and several others crept down out of the hills, walked carefully through the lanes between the sugarcane, and returned to the plantation.

The big house was silent. Maybe they were asleep, Odette thought.

She peeped into the kitchen. Someone had been cooking, and had attempted to scrub out the kettle. She sniffed at the smell of chicken. But the three of them had finished that chicken. Some vegetables sat on the ledge, still muddy from the field.

Bernardo went more boldly up to the back door of the house. He peered into the hallway, dubiously, just poking his head inside. Odette followed him on her silent bare feet.

They both blinked at the rifle that poked at their noses. A tall slim blond-haired man came to his feet, and said hoarsely, "Who are you?" His blue eyes were wide.

He gave a shout, and a red-haired man got off the sofa in the drawing room, and padded on stocking feet to the back hall. He gazed at them, and they stared back.

"Mr. Hamilton," breathed Odette. It looked like her own Mr. Hamilton, only with bright red hair, not gray. The same bronzed face, the same blazing blue eyes. Then the man smiled, and it was Mr. Hamilton. She beamed at him. "You same Mr. Hamilton?" she asked fearfully. Had he returned from the dead? She would be glad to greet him, yet it was a shocking thing, to return from the dead.

"I am Morgan Hamilton," said the red-haired man. "Thomas Hamilton was my uncle, and left the plantation to me. You have returned! Good!"

His voice was different. His voice had a blurred sound to it, a softer lilt. Odette drew a deep breath.

"You like son of Mr. Hamilton?" she asked more boldly.

"Something like a son," the man smiled, and deep creases made his face pleasant and good. He gazed down at Odette, but not with desire. He gestured to Bernardo slowly. "You have come back to work? You must be hungry. I saw pigs outside. If you will kill the two pigs, we'll have a feast. How many will come?"

He spoke slowly and they understood him.

Alfed sidled up. "Some will come, master!" he piped. "Others wait in hill!"

Morgan smiled down at him, and patted his head kindly. "You let them know everything is fine," he said. "We will have a feast tonight. Tomorrow we work again!"

Odette relaxed. He did sound like Mr. Thomas! "You have missus?" she asked hopefully. "I am a good maid!"

Morgan turned his blue gaze on her. "That's fine," he said. "I have a missus, a nice lady. She does need a maid. You be good to her, I will be happy."

Malkia came from her hut, smoking her old briar pipe. She looked satisfied. Odette went to confer with her in low tones.

Malkia said, "The missus is good, she smile, she give food. The others come back, we all work again. No Judson!"

Her hands had been bleeding, she had put salve on them. Odette crooned over the poor broken flesh. Malkia watched her indulgently.

They had a feast that night. The pigs were killed, and Morgan ordered vegetables brought from the ground and cooked. Bernardo and another man went to the sea, and brought back some fine fish, and they cooked and ate those also. They laughed and sang, beating the drums so the sound reached the hills.

More men returned the next day. Gamba was the last to come. Suspicious to the last, he was sullen and dark of face. But he set to work also.

Bernardo liked the man, who looked so much like Mr. Hamilton.

"I will tell you of the cane," he said eagerly.

It took several tellings, but he took Morgan Hamilton first to the fields. He showed him how the cane was cut. He told him about how the strong men and women were set to work in the cane.

The bigger boys and the old slaves weeded before the cutting. Then they helped do odd jobs, weeded the vegetable gardens, fed the chickens and pigs.

Odette followed the men around the grounds of the vast plantation, quietly listening. She wanted to be sure the big red-haired man would be good to them. He listened carefully, treating Bernardo with kindness and respect.

Bernardo took him next to the tall windmill, just as the first cart of cane arrived. There were three heavy rollers set in a trough under the windmill. "You let men roll the cane, Mister Morgan?" Bernardo asked anxiously.

"Yes, but you'll have to show me how it is done," Mr. Hamilton said. "I'm new to this. I was a sailor," he added.

Ah, he had been a sailor. Odette approved. A sailor, like Louis Abaco!

Two men took the canes and thrust them through one set of rollers then back through the second set. The king roller was in the center and set to turn the opposite way of the two smaller rollers, one on either side. They had turned on the windmill, Gamba proudly climbing up into the top of the mill to set them. He liked this important work.

"It is turned to the wind," Bernardo explained, gesturing toward the windmill. "Then the canes go through the rollers. Juice comes down here—" He motioned to the trough. The juice was then piped into a cistern in the boiling house.

The juice was poured into the largest of four copper kettles which hung over a blazing furnace. Impurities were ladled off, then the juice was ladled into the second copper, the next smaller one. The process was repeated until the thick ropey and dark brown molasses was poured into the smallest of the four kettles.

"What do you do with this?" Morgan motioned to the kettle full of the ladled-off impurities. "Throw it away?"

"No, no!" Bernardo was shocked. "Save to make rum!"

He showed Morgan how rum was made after setting men to ladle the boiling coppers. There was a still house with a pot still in it, a worm and receiver. Molasses, the last of the cane juices, and skimmings from the boiling coppers were set in a large vat and allowed to ferment.

"It boils up itself, it takes about one week," Bernardo said.

"Fermenting." Morgan nodded, peering into the still.

"Yes, Mr. Morgan, sir. After one week, we boil it with fire. Then it's rum. We put it in barrels and leave it one year, maybe two, maybe three years."

"Ah, I recognize the process," Morgan said. "This is what the Honorable Billy described."

Bernardo looked puzzled, but Odette understood. Someone had told him about rum.

"Rum sells well," Bernardo said. "Sugar sells well too. You sell sugar?"

"Yes, we'll make and sell the sugar to a sea captain, to take away," Morgan said. "I'll try making the rum, but we'll hold that in barrels for one year, maybe three. All right?"

The man understood! Odette gave a sigh of relief, and scurried back to the big house. If her mistress had missed her, she might get a whipping! She went in cautiously in the back cool hallway, and was shocked.

The little blond-haired missus had a cloth and a feather duster, and was dusting the furniture in the drawing room!

"No, no!" Odette cried. "We do that. Not the missus!"

"Don't worry, I can do this," Tess said. She smiled sweetly, Odette thought.

Odette took the cloth and duster gently from her, smiling down into the lovely face. She was so small, and so determined! "We do," she said firmly. "I'll get another girl to help. You sit and be a lady."

The little missus laughed, and her laugh was a pretty high lilt, like a bird, Odette decided. Her hair shone from brushing, she looked like the jasmine flower, but softer, paler. Like the rare, silver jasmine, thought Odette. She longed to touch the shimmering hair, and that gave her the courage to speak: "You need a maid," she said positively. "I, Odette, will be your maid."

"Me?" Tess laughed. "I don't need a maid! I have always worked hard."

Odette shook her black head. "You write in book, you read books, you sit on the veranda," she said. "I will get another girl to dust, someone to cook, and I will be your maid!"

Before the lady could protest, Odette ran out to the cane fields to gather up her workers. Boldly she appointed Wamuiru to be the housemaid, and led her from the cane fields. Since Mr. Morgan had no white overseer—Bernardo was doing that—she would take the workers they needed for the house before Mr. Morgan realized.

Wamuiru was about to protest, her lips sullen. "The house work is good," Odette told her firmly. "The house is cool, not hot like being out in cane! You will come, foolish one!"

She pushed and shoved her reluctant helper to the house, gave her a cloth and showed her how to work. She was pleased that the missus did not stand over them. The little blond lady was sitting at the big master's desk, looking in the books where Mr. Hamilton used to write.

Odette found another woman to cook, the best cook among the slaves. Malkia watched over them indulgently, and approved.

"Yes, good, get everything all fixed up. Not go away, not get tired of plantation," Malkia said, nodding her gray head. She was sitting on her own front stoop, smoking her pipe. "These are good people, we will be happy here. They are not like Judson, or Quintero!"

Yes, thought Odette. We will get all fixed up the way we like. We will work hard and the master be pleased. She had seen the fond way he looked at his wife. If they pleased the wife, they would please the master, she decided.

Amused at the way Odette took over, Tess kept an eye on the girls, and noticed that Odette knew the ways of the house, and was teaching the two others. She was looking over the books when Morgan came in with Bernardo from the fields.

He was tired and dusty, but beaming, his blue eyes alight. "It looks good, honey," he said. "We'll have it all organized! Bernardo will be overseer, he knows all the work just fine."

"That is good, Bernardo," Tess said slowly, clearly. She motioned toward Odette, who was coming toward them with a tray laden with a pitcher and tall glasses. "You'll have the fieldwork done, and Odette will manage the house."

Bernardo seemed very happy about that, she noted. He sat down on the edge of the veranda, and spoke to them from there. Tess and Morgan sat down in the loungers that Odette had dusted vigorously.

"You stay. We are happy to work for you," he said. His black eyes gleamed. "We will work hard!"

Morgan asked him questions about the work. Bernardo responded readily. The carts were taken to the fields as soon as they were unloaded, and more cane cut. The cane must be put through the mills as soon as cut. Any delay, and the sugar dried up, he explained. Usually Judson kept his men cutting the cane all through the day and night. But Mr. Hamilton spaced the work, and let them rest at night. He did not have such huge cane fields. They were usually finished cutting in a field by dark, and two men kept the fires burning in the boiling room through the night, and slept the next day.

Vincent came from the stables and stretched out on a lounger beside them.

"That one man, Gamba," Morgan said, getting out his pipe. "Gamba has stripes on his back. Who beat him?"

Bernardo looked at the ocean, his brow crinkled up. Tess watched him sharply. "Did Judson beat him?" she asked.

Bernardo finally nodded. "Judson beat him. Then we all went up into the hills."

"Does he beat his own slaves?" Morgan asked.

Bernardo nodded.

"What if they leave him?" Tess cut in. "Why don't they go away?"

Bernardo hugged his knees and shuddered, his face pale. "If a slave runs away, Judson hunts him down with dogs. He'll find a slave anywhere he goes. The dogs find."

"Well, what then?" Tess urged. "Does he beat them?"

"Tess, don't go on about it," Morgan said sharply. "It won't be pleasant, I know these islands a bit."

She shook her head. "I want to know why everyone is so afraid of Judson," she said. "Why, Bernardo? What happens to a slave then?"

Bernardo swallowed. He whispered, "After he's hunted down by the dogs, he lets the dogs have him—they tear him up in little pieces."

There was a long silence on the veranda. Tess had her hand to her throat, she felt sickened.

"I can go now?" Bernardo asked fearfully. He felt their anger, and did not know if he had offended them deeply.

"I had best go and see if the boiling house work is going smoothly," Morgan said, rising.

"I'll go with Bernardo," Vincent said jumping up. "You've been working with the cane all day. Let me go and learn about it also. Come along, Bernardo."

"Yes, Master Vincent," Bernardo said, and gladly went away.

"Feel sick, my dear?" Morgan asked gently, when they were alone.

She nodded. "Oh, Morgan, how can people be treated like that?" she burst out. "Torn to pieces by dogs!"

"You know Ryder," he reminded her. "And I know some mighty mean sailors. They will whip and beat up another under them. With some, power means complete control over a man's life. And a cruel man can find pleasure in . . . such actions."

Tess shivered, then abruptly changed the subject. "I have been looking at the accounts, Morgan, as you asked. I think in the past three years, much money has been made by rum. It seems to be more profitable than sugar, though good money is made by that."

"Splendid. I'll have a look at the figures tonight. I wonder where the money is," he added thoughtfully. "You looked in all the drawers, and so did I, and there was no strongbox about. I don't think the slaves would have taken it, they can't spend a large sum without having some hard questions asked."

"Do you think—Judson?" asked Tess. "I should not accuse him, but I cannot like the man!"

"I think he would do it, if he could, and get away with it." Morgan said wryly. "I'll try to figure out how much is missing, and ask around. There might be a bank in St. Michael's, it's a larger town in the south. Hopefully, he banked it."

"That could be," Tess said. "According to the figures, he made about four hundred pounds last year alone."

"Four hundred! Clear?" Morgan asked in amazement. "That would mean a fortune can be made from the plantation! I never imagined—"

"Nor did I," Tess said. "That is after the stores had been paid off, more provisions bought, and Mr. Hamilton had evidently sent for some more rifles and gunpowder."

They were silent, thinking about that. Odette came quietly to the door. "Missus, do you want to change? Dinner will be ready real soon," she said hopefully.

Tess turned to smile at her. "I have a maid, Morgan. This is Odette."

"Odette, yes," Morgan said. "You take good care of my missus!"

"I will take good care of her, yes, master," Odette said, smiling with a flash of white teeth. She had found a pink hibiscus for her bushy black hair, and looked very pretty, with slender limbs, oval face and beautiful black eyes. There was white blood in her, that was evident by the lighter coffee color of her skin.

As they went upstairs, Odette said, "I will heat the

iron, and I will press the dress like this flower," and she touched the flower in her hair. "I brush silver jasmine hair, yes? Put flower in hair."

"Silver jasmine," Tess said jokingly. "My hair is that color?"

Odette touched the soft golden curls lovingly. "Yes, like jasmine in moonlight," she murmured. "Silver jasmine. We call you that in our speak of you."

"Silver jasmine," Tess murmured again. "I never even saw a jasmine flower before!"

"I will get one for you," Odette said simply. "We will put a pink one in hair tonight, no other flower would do. It will match your dress. Then, up in hills, I will get a silver jasmine for pretty lady."

Tess shook her head in bewilderment, as Odette helped her to wash and change, then firmly sat her before the mirrored dresser. The brush went softly through the curls, again and again, as Odette brushed her hair. It was as though the girl loved to touch her hair, and she fashioned it deftly into a smart order, with curls fastened in a chignon in back, and in a couple tiny frivolous curls at her ears. The pink dress had been ironed to perfection, every ruffle set in place.

Tess could not believe it—a bar girl, scrubbing out the bar, floors, working like a slave—and now had a maid! She could not believe it!

Some people seemed born to be waited on, and lie in idle luxury, like some of the grand ladies who had come briefly, disdainfully, to the inn, with maids to pick up a handkerchief, wash out their underclothing, brush their shoes. Some had seemed born to wait on others, to work hard, to get on their knees to scrub.

Tess had always thought she was one born to work. But here she was, sitting before a faded silvery mirror, with a dark girl behind her, brushing her hair. A girl not much younger than herself, beautiful, with dark well-brushed hair, sweet-smelling with a flower in her hair, and grace in her movements.

The blue gaze met the black velvet gaze in the mirror. Tess smiled. "The dress looks lovely," she said. "Thank you, Odette."

"I make you a good maid, missus," Odette said quietly, in her soft drawling voice. She tucked a pink hibiscus like her own into Tess's golden curls, and patted the flower down. "There, now you are all ready."

Bemused, Tess made a last check of herself in the mirror, then went down to have her first meal as the official lady of the house.

8

The dawn wind fluttered the misty white mosquito netting. Morgan stirred, and stretched lazily as he opened his eyes. He looked up in brief bewilderment at the rose canopy over the large mahogany four-poster bed, at the netting, then relaxed.

He was in bed with his wife, on his own plantation! And only a year ago he had been preparing for battle with his regiment, not knowing whether he would live or die! What a twist of fate! He chuckled silently to himself, stretching again luxuriously. Things were working out.

It was Sunday morning. All was silent. He had told the slaves through Bernardo and Odette that Sundays they could do as they wished. Bernardo had hinted that he liked to go fishing on Sundays.

"Good idea. Take Sundays off, you work hard through the week," Morgan had said. "All slaves will take Sundays off. Have church services if you wish." At the blank look, he figured they did not know what church was. There were probably no missions around here. Morgan would have to remedy that. He would like to go to church himself. Maybe he and other plantation owners could start a mission, build a church, and get a man from one of the other islands to come once a month. If there were enough people about, they might even hire their own pastor and build a house for him!

The slaves had worked hard that week. For twelve hours in the cane fields, the huskier slaves cut and slashed at the sugarcane, loaded it on carts, and took it to the mill. There the process went on. It was necessary to keep two husky slaves working at the boiling coppers even today, but he would see they got other time off.

A note had come from another plantation yesterday, inviting them to luncheon and to spend the day, and signed "C. Quintero." Morgan had told Tess to send back an acceptance. They would set out about ten o'clock.

So they would have a peaceful day also, with neighbors. And all within a week of coming! He felt quite satisfied with himself.

Tess stirred beside him, and her blue eyes opened. She blinked as he bent over her. Sometimes she looked startled on wakening, as though she could not remember they were married. She was not used to him yet, he thought, as he put his hand gently on her cheek and turned her face to his. She slept sometimes with her arms up over her head, like a baby girl.

He ran his fingers through her mussed curls. "Morning, sweetheart."

"Morning, Morgan." She yawned, and he could not resist. He bent and pressed his opened lips to hers. "Ohhh," she said, against his mouth.

Desire rose hotly in him. The breeze cooled their

bodies, the dawns were always delightful here on the island, since the house faced east. It caught the morning wind, and the morning dawn with the sun a soft pink, before the day reddened it.

He threw off the cotton sheet, and ran his hand over her slim body in the white cotton nightdress. She raised her hand, and touched his bare chest, tentatively, and he caught his breath. She rarely touched him of her own will. He kept his hand stroking over her waist and thigh, watching her face as she touched his body curiously.

He wore nothing to bed, it was such a relief after the cold nights on the ship when he often went to bed with most of his clothes on. He wore only cotton pants to work. One of the women had made sandals for him, and in the evening he took off his heavy boots, and put on the sandals with no stockings. He felt so free now. Free of the sea and formality. Free of England and those painful ties. Free of being subject to orders from above. Here *he* was master . . .

He smiled down at Tess. "A whole new life," he murmured. "Do you like it, Tess?"

"Parts," she said soberly. "I think—Morgan, I think I don't like it, that the black folks are slaves. I would hate to be a slave."

Her words startled him, but he had another thought on his mind now. He bent to her, and began kissing her cheeks, her sensitive earlobes, down to her chin, and over then down to the soft hollow of her throat, where a pulse beat. He kissed it softly, feeling the beat increase dramatically.

He took one of the small hands and placed it on his back. She hesitated, then ran her hand slowly up and down his bronzed back, over his spine, tingling it deliciously. He drew back the cotton nightdress that was loose about her body, and his mouth went to her breasts.

His lips pulled at the delicate, pink nipple gently, and

125

he felt her response. Her hand played more frantically over his back, down even to his thighs. Gently he removed the nightdress, and flung it toward the end of the bed. The husks of the mattress rustled as he moved to lie over her. His hand moved to her thighs, and he smiled as he found her almost ready for him. She was learning rapidly, his petite wife!

He had found passion in her, and he enjoyed it. He moved deliberately against her, and she squirmed and moaned a little. The sound came from deep in her throat, and her eyes were half-closed. He pressed himself against her, then drew back. He would tease her a bit, until she responded passionately.

He moved back and forth between the yielding lips, even as he kissed the breasts and the pink hardening nipples. His hand went under her thighs, and he held her still as she would have withdrawn from him. He thrust a little, gently, then pulled back again. She murmured, "Oh, Morgan—ohhhh—"

"What, sweetheart?" he teased.

"Ohhhh—Morgan—"

"This?" He pushed gently to her.

"Uuummmmm—"

He smiled and gently thrust inside. She was so small, that he had to be careful with her. But once inside, how tightly she held him! It was marvelous. He went in further, enjoyed the clasp of her. She had stiffened, then both arms went about him, and she snuggled up to him, and kissed his throat. He felt the timid touch of her lips, and rejoiced. She was learning to please him, and herself.

Then he began pumping up and down, carefully, not to go too deep. Just as much as she could accept. She was gasping, and the blond curls tossed on the pillow. The bed springs creaked, the husks rustled as he moved faster and faster. The wind cooled his back as he bent over her.

It was so good, so honey-sweet, so think and sweet like molasses from the sugarcane— Wild thoughts went through his mind. She tasted like flowers, like sugarwater, like honey—

He paused again, to enjoy her fully, gazing down into the dazed little face, at the closed eyes. As he stopped, she moaned and tossed her head. She pushed up imperiously at him, unconscious that she did so, he believed. He waited, half-inside her, waited.

She pushed again, her hips coming up to him, arms clasping tighter around his back. She rubbed herself against him, like a kitten seeking warmth. A moan broke from her lips, they were parted, pink as the hibiscus she wore in her hair in the evenings.

He bent to kiss her, coming closer to her. She caught at his shoulders, and her fingernails dug into his flesh. Suddenly she cried out sharply, as his lips left hers. He felt a tremor shivering through her, and held her more tightly. Then she was shuddering in ecstasy, her insides quivering, and holding him, clasping again and again. When he felt the quivering die down, he pushed up again. The trembling started again, although this time it was lighter.

He was driven by his own passion then, unable to control himself. He thrust again as her shivers drove him to frantic passionate desire—mindless, unable to stop. He held her little body close to his, and held high in her as he came to a climax and his hot seed ran into her.

He lay back with a quivering sigh and held her still close to him. A tremor ran through her again and again, as she lay limply against his big chest. He stroked over her lightly with his palm, feeling the fine film of perspiration on her body. He drew up the cotton sheet to cover her against the breeze.

They both slept for a time then, worn out from their

passion. When they wakened, she could not meet his eyes, blushing hotly. He laughed a bit, and kissed her.

"Not be ashamed, Tess," he whispered. "It was beautiful! You are the prettiest wife a man ever had!"

She turned her face away, her cheeks flaming. "I don't know what I did . . ." She murmured.

"Whatever it was, I enjoyed it!" Then he took pity on her embarrassment. "I'm going out for a quick swim. I'll send Odette to you with hot water for a wash."

"Oh, she has the day off," Tess said. "I'll get up presently."

But when Morgan had put on his pants, and gone out, he found Odette waiting patiently on a wooden settle in the hall. She beamed.

"Missus awake? I bring hot water. For you too, master?" Her quick black eyes assessed him.

"Not for me. I'll swim, but bring water for missus."

She frowned slightly. "Tell Bernardo, he'll take you to the cove where there is no coral to cut your feet."

"Fine," he said, and ran lightly down the backstairs, humming. He was a happy man. He found Bernardo waiting patiently near the back steps.

"Good morning, master! Good day!"

"I thought you would be fishing, Bernardo!"

"I fished good! I have five big fish! Feast today! You go to Quintero?"

"That's right. Odette says, you know a cove where I can swim?"

"I will show you. You come with me now?"

They went down the path, around the front to the creamy sands. Bernardo led him past where the ocean waves beat against the rocks and coral reefs, to a quiet cove hidden within a rock formation. He pointed.

"You can have a good swim out as far as that big rock," he said as he pointed. "But no more and don't put your feet down out there. The coral will cut. Only swim to the rock."

"Thanks, Bernardo!" Morgan shed his pants, and slid gingerly down into the water. He found it unexpectedly cool, and shivered, until he became accustomed to it. Then he splashed out happily. The big waves did not come in here, only the tides rose to fill the cove. He could go as deep as he wanted. As a sailor, he had learned to swim, and enjoyed it, more than most Englishmen and Scotsmen did, mistrusting waters.

Morgan was splashing about in the gentle surf when he caught sight of a tall man coming down to the beach of the cove. When the man saw him, he hesitated, then turned and strode away.

Morgan frowned. The man was clearly not a slave, he was too light-skinned; he was as tall as Gamba, but was dressed in blue with a red cummerbund. In fact, Morgan realized, the man wore the clothes of a pirate. Out on the high seas, he had had a few encounters with fierce fighting pirates, and he wanted no part of them—on the sea or on land!

Morgan cursed himself for a fool since he had come without a weapon, or anyone to stand guard! He waited until the man was out of sight, then came cautiously out of the water, put on his pants, and raced back to the house. Bernardo was waiting patiently, sitting on the steps of the veranda.

He got up when Morgan ran near. "Master, what happened?" he asked in alarm.

"I saw a man dressed like a pirate. A mulatto. Do you know him? Could pirates land here?"

Bernardo's broad face took on a guarded look. "Pirates don't come here now. Maybe before they did, sometimes. Maybe you saw Gamba."

"It was not Gamba. Who was it?"

Finally Bernardo admitted it was Louis Abaco. "He is no slave, but a free man," he hurried to add. "He was once a pirate, but he got away from his ship. He hides in the hills."

Morgan thanked Bernardo for the information and went into the cool shade of the house. He went up to his bedroom thoughtfully, and dressed in white trousers, a white ruffled lawn shirt and polished, gleaming boots. He would take a jacket, and see if the other guests were dressed so formally—it got darn hot during midday. When he came down, he found Tess waiting with Vincent, looking at the books in the tall, glass-doored bookcases in the library.

Vincent looked handsome and smart in his white cotton trousers and white shirt. He had filled out a little, and looked less nervous. Tess looked beautiful in the blue muslin she had so carefully made, with her blue bonnet ready to be set on her carefully brushed blond curls. Odette proudly hovered nearby.

"You should have jewels," Morgan sighed. "One day I will be able to afford them. Although your beauty needs no adornment."

Tess blushed prettily and looked down at a book she had in her hand.

"Jewels!" Odette cried. "Master hid the jewels!"

They all turned to her then, to see her black eyes sparkling. "Where?" Morgan asked. "Where are the jewels? Where is the money the master hid?"

"In the safe," she said, and put her finger to her beautiful red lips. "I will show you. You will tell nobody?"

She went over to the painting of Hamilton's wife and three children, and slid it aside. Behind it was a small door, with a combination lock on it.

Morgan came over and stared. "Well, by God! Here all the time. Did Judson try to find?"

She nodded, her gaze suddenly fearful. "He did not

130

find it, he looked through all the drawers and books. He didn't find, though. And I'd never tell him!"

Morgan looked down at the lock in dismay. "Well, I can't open it. Maybe we can find the combination written down somewhere—"

"Five, twenty—forty-two—eleven—nine—" Odette smiled proudly as she repeated the combination. She put her fingers to the little round knob, and twirled it. They heard the lock click. 'I won't open until you say, Master."

Morgan was staring at her, then he nodded his okay. Odette could have opened it anytime, he thought, and evidently had not! He reached inside slowly, and found a bag heavy with coins, a smaller bag of coins, and several leather cases. Odette watched eagerly.

"Sapphires," she said, indicating the cases. She pointed to Tess's blue dress. There is a blue sapphire on a chain. You will like!"

He opened the three cases he had drawn out, and found one contained pearls, one emeralds, and the last case had lovely sapphires. Tess's eyes were wide as could be and Vincent gasped. Morgan took out the single large sapphire hanging from a thin filigree chain with shaking hands. He slipped it over Tess's head, and settled it on her throat.

Tess let out a whooping, quite unladylike cheer and they all laughed.

They started out in the carriage soon after. Vincent drove, Tess and Morgan sat in back. They had taken rifles and cartridges, and their thoughts.

"Odette could have opened the safe and taken everything and escaped. No one would have known," Tess said finally.

"She still could," Vincent said over his shoulder. "But Morgan, you walked out and left it all there!"

Morgan had been thinking. He had been just behind

Odette when she had opened the safe. He had been thinking then about jewels and money. But now he remembered.

"You know, Odette has a tinge of red hair in her hair," he said slowly. "I wonder, I just wonder if she was Thomas Hamilton's daughter by a slave woman?"

Tess gasped. "If she—oh, Morgan!"

"It could be. It would explain her devotion to him, and how he protected her all those years. She had been treated well, taught to be a house servant, not to work in the fields. And he trusted her with the combination to his safe!"

They were all silent, thinking about that. Then their attention was caught by the sight of more cane fields, and a splendid stone plantation house set high on a hill.

"Is that Quintero's?" Tess asked.

"No, that is Judson's place," Morgan said shortly. "I wonder if he'll be there today." He frowned. "I suppose we are all neighbors and have to be friendly. But it sticks in my craw, that he tried to rob me of the place, and take the money."

"We'll take it as it comes," Tess said philosophically. "Mother always said, take each day as it comes. I hope the Quinteros are nice. Did you say they have two daughters? Maybe they'll be my age!"

They drove on for another hour, along the creamy sand beach, for there was only one little path through the cane, barely wide enough for a horse and carriage. The beach was hard in places, evidently used frequently as a road. Finally they came to a wide path up through the cane. They saw a house about twenty yards up the hill.

Vincent turned in, and they trotted up the wide path beneath shading trees, palms and pines, until a turn in the path revealed fully the house where they were going. Tess gasped, "Oh, my goodness—how beautiful!"

They all stared. Morgan had seen such houses before,

but in Spain, not on the islands. It was one story, with wide verandas hugging the main building. The white coral stone shone, and above it was a red-tiled roof, overhanging the verandas. All about were beautiful blue pots with flowers planted in them, and a splendid garden of strange flowers, in vibrant hues of red and pink, orange and blue.

A man came out from the veranda, beaming. He wore a tall white wide-brimmed hat, such as Morgan had noticed on the Spanish men in the peninsula. He took it off and waved it exuberantly as they drove up. A slave ran out to take the horses. Two ladies came out on the veranda and waited demurely, one dressed in red and one in pale blue.

"You'll be Morgan Hamilton! I'd know that red hair and that face anywhere." The man beamed. "Christopher Quintero, at your service, sir! And this will be your beautiful wife, of whom I have heard much!"

"News travels fast," Morgan said dryly, clasping the man's bronzed hand.

The other man chuckled, and gallantly helped Tess down. Vincent jumped down, his gaze going to the ladies on the veranda.

"Come inside, come inside and have a long cool drink! I will introduce to you my daughters!" From his tone, they knew he was vastly proud of them. He led them to the veranda, after meeting Vincent, and heartily shaking his hand.

The girl in red came forward, while the one in blue hung back.

"Señorita Florencia Quintero, my eldest," Quintero said. She smiled with a flash of white teeth and held out her hand. Her red dress set off a voluptuous form. She was a bit taller than Tess but much more full of body. Florencia had blue black hair, and large black eyes that

133

seemed almost purple. She fluttered them boldly at both the new men.

"And this is my little Inez," Quintero said tenderly, and held out his hand to the younger girl. She came forward obediently, and bowed her head gracefully to the guests. She was slimmer than her sister with a gravely innocent face, framed by dark hair parted in the middle. Her dark eyes were the same color as Florencia's, but gentler, and her face had a madonnalike quality.

Florencia took in the gold ring on Tess's finger, and the blue sapphire on the chain around her neck. "Ah, you have found the Hamilton jewels!" she exclaimed. "How did you do that? Mr. Judson and Papa searched for you!"

Oh, so innocent! Morgan smiled warily. "I am glad they did not find them," he said dryly. "It gave us the joy of discovery! What a pleasant surprise to find all intact!"

Quintero gave a grimace, and sent for some refreshment. "You can scarcely blame us," he said apologetically. "We did not know Thomas Hamilton had any heirs, and Judson wanted the plantation. We planned to split the money and jewels between us—if no one showed up, of course."

"Of course," Morgan said, and turned the conversation away from a topic which so obviously made his host —who seemed an honest man—uncomfortable. "That horse is a splendid one," he said, indicating the horse being led around the corral.

Quintero's face lit up, and he discoursed enthusiastically about his horses. Next to his daughters, they were the pride of his life. Florencia had evidently given up on Morgan, as being much too married. She had turned her charms on Vincent, who was sitting there silently. He looked dazzled, thought Morgan.

Inez was directing the maids, shyly, but efficiently, while her elder sister flirted with Vincent. Morgan, his eyes somewhat opened to women during his sailor years, thought the younger girl much the sweeter, more like his own Tess. He might put a bug in Vincent's ear one day, but for the present, let the lad have fun.

Long cool drinks were brought in beautiful tall glasses. Tess tasted hers cautiously. "Rum?" she questioned.

"Yes, Mrs. Hamilton." Inez said softly, in her pretty melodic voice. "I mix lime and lemon, and sometimes other fruit juices in season. Add some brown sugar, then you shake with care. Then add some rum and cool the drink in the cooling house. Do you like this?"

"It is very refreshing," Tess said, still sipping cautiously.

Morgan drained his glass, and was brought fresh drink immediately. He felt a slight buzzing in his ears. "Your own rum?"

Quintero beamed. "Yes, indeed! This is from my six-year-old stock! My best product. Is it not delicious?"

They talked about rums, and Quintero gave him some more tips about making it, agreeing with what the Honorable Billy had told them. Morgan told them about the earl's son, and Quintero nodded, his face shadowing.

"So many from good stock coming out here. Some are ruined by too much laziness and drink. Others straighten up and make good. One hopes he will be of the latter."

Presently another carriage sounded along the wide path. Quintero said, "I invited Mr. and Mrs. Judson, they longed to meet you informally. I understand you had something of a clash? He isn't a bad sort, and his wife is most beautiful!" He was standing then, and Morgan stood also, tightening a bit with anticipation. He had brought the rifle in with him, casually; so had Vincent. Quintero had politely ignored that fact.

The carriage rounded the turn. Judson was driving

himself, and beside him sat a vision in purple, with purple bonnet and sunshade. Quintero went out to meet them, as did Morgan and Vincent. Morgan was nearest to the lady, and so helped her down.

He got the first battery of attack from beautiful large velvety black eyes. "So you are Mr. Morgan Hamilton," she smiled from melting red lips. Her hair was dark, long and curly, to her shoulders. She sounded French, with a slight delicious accent. "You look the image of your uncle, Mr. Hamilton!"

"Yes, ma'am," he said. "Thank you. Pleasure to meet you."

Quintero kissed her hand gallantly, it seemed to please her. She was smiling as she met Vincent, and then swept up to the veranda.

Judson came around the other side of the carriage. He wore light formal garb, cream-colored trousers and jacket, white ruffled shirt and white stock. He was grinning.

"Well, we meet again, more happily, Mr. Hamilton. No hard feelings left, eh?" He held out his hand. Morgan took it briefly. It wouldn't pay to be a bad neighbor until he had very just cause, he reminded himself.

"I don't believe you have met my brother-in-law, Vincent Pritchard. He is helping me get a good start at the plantation."

They shook hands. Morgan thought Vincent bore himself well, quiet and straight, looking a man in the eye. He was not very tall, and seemed almost fragile at times. But his body was sturdy from hard work, and he was willing to try anything.

Morgan found himself next to Mrs. Judson at the dining table when they went inside at noon to the cool room. The arrangement inside the Quintero home was different. There were huge open rooms for the breeze to come through, but all was built around a central patio, in the Spanish style. The dining room was open to the patio, and a cool fountain trickled in the center, watering flowers set about it. And the floor of the patio was not dirt, but blue and green tiles from Spain.

"How beautiful!" exclaimed Tess, seated next to her host. "I have never seen such a garden!"

He beamed at her praise. "I brought it all out on the ship with me, Mrs. Hamilton. I was determined to plant a bit of old Spain in my new home. This is the way we arrange our homes in Andalusia, around a central courtyard. In the evenings we sit on the patio, and I play the guitar, and remember my old home."

"Now, Papa," Inez murmured, her dark eyes soft on him. "We are all happy here."

"Speak for yourself," muttered Florencia, her mouth turning down in discontent. "I wish we had settled on a larger island! Or we could live in St. Michael! It is much bigger!" She turned eagerly to Morgan on her right. "St. Michael has over a hundred houses, two churches, and so many beautiful stores! And it is also on the sea, but the leeward side, where there are not so fierce storms. Someday we will live there!"

"Now, Florencia, patience," her father said, but his expression was indulgent. "Your papa is getting older, but he is not ready to retire and live an idle life! Wait until I have worked some more years, and have more money in the bank at St. Michael before you begin to plan our move. And is it not beautiful here? Do you not love our beautiful home?"

Florencia was about to begin an impatient reply when Morgan interrupted. "You say there is a bank at St. Michael? I should like to go there one day, and set up an account."

"Oh, you will do that," Quintero said. "You will find your uncle has a large account there," he added innocently. "He spoke to me of it. Is it not in your papers?"

Was there a sly look in his eyes? Morgan was not sure. Judson was watching him sharply.

"Probably. I have not examined them all. Tess does much of the bookkeeping," he added with a smile. "I have quite a smart wife, who is accustomed to reading, and writing, and doing sums. She kept the books in an . . . establishment of her stepfather's before our marriage. So we shall do the accounts together."

"You are to be congratulated, señor," Quintero murmured, with a gallant bow to Tess. From his seated position, that was quite a feat, Morgan thought sourly. "A beautiful wife, with eyes like the sea, and hair like gold, and so smart also! What a very—lucky—man, you are, Mr. Hamilton!"

Antoinette Judson interrupted with a sultry smile directed at Morgan. "When a man is tall, very handsome, very smart, he does not need so much luck, no? He finds the luck comes to him, is that not true?"

Morgan glanced at Judson, thinking he would be furious at his wife's blatant charming ways. Instead the man laughed. "My wife is correct. A man makes his own luck! When he is handsome, and attractive to women— and has money—he has luck, also!"

Then Judson turned to Tess. "Speaking of money, I meant to make you an offer, Mrs. Hamilton. You have one slave that I would like to have as a maid for my wife. I understand she is quite experienced at tending the needs of a lady. Antoinette has been after me to offer for her. I refer to Odette. How much will you take for her?"

Tess stared at him, at first in disbelief, then her blue eyes darkened as she grew furious and outraged. She almost spit at him. "Sell her? Never! I would not sell any slave! And certainly not Odette!"

Morgan said smoothly, "The girl Odette is very

nice, she and my wife are friends already. She is my wife's maid, and does well. We will not part with the girl. She is not for sale."

Judson's eyes had narrowed, but he still kept smiling. "Well, we'll talk of it later. You'll find her a sullen piece, when she doesn't get her own way. When you tire of her, we'll talk again of selling and buying. I want the girl—for my wife, of course," he added hastily. Too hastily, Morgan thought.

"Well, I may not need the girl, darling," Antoinette drawled to her husband. "If we move from the country, which does not suit my health, to St. Michael, I shall not need her. I shall get a much smarter girl!"

Her black eyes defied him. He had lost his grin, and his small eyes blazed at her. Then he laughed, but it was not an amused sound. "My wife is from Martinique, and accustomed to French society there. But she will accustom herself to the country, and come to enjoy it, especially now we have such splendid neighbors, eh, my dear Antoinette?" His eyes gleamed with warning.

His wife bent her head down toward her plate. Finally in a subdued manner, she said, "Yes, of course, my dear husband."

The uncomfortable silence grew until Florencia hastily changed the subject.

9

Morgan went out to the kitchen behind the house, where Tess and a couple of maids were working. She was showing them how to mix dough for bread, how to roll it out.

She glanced up when he came. He noted that her blue eyes were wary sometimes, when he came on her unexpectedly. Yet he thought she seemed calmer now, not so high-strung and nervous as she had been in the Last Inn. Tess was enjoying it here, so far. She was not yet accustomed to marriage, but she found these tender bonds less irksome than her former work, Morgan hoped.

"I'll be on my way, Tess. I'm going to Judson's today. He will show me around his plantation, and then we'll talk over lunch."

She nodded, and her shining golden curls bobbed about her smooth throat. She wore one of her simple white muslin dresses, and Odette had woven a blue ribbon about the golden curls. The maid seemed to take great pleasure in her work, and Morgan had watched in some amusement as the black girl had brushed and brushed his wife's hair.

He bent and kissed her cheek, and put his arm about her shoulders. The maids stared frankly, giggling behind their hands. Tess blushed, and bent her head back to the dough.

"Vincent is working with the horses today, and supervising the slaves in the cane," Morgan added. "If you need him, just ring the bell. He'll come running."

"Yes, he told me when he left. And Bernardo will be working nearby," she said soberly.

Malkia came to the door, gazing at them with her wise old eyes. "The missus will be fine today," she said, taking her pipe from her aged lips to speak. "We will watch, master."

Morgan smiled at her. "Thank you, Malkia. You take good care of my missus, eh?"

She gave him a grin revealing half her teeth gone. "We will watch missus, yes. Take good care of her."

He still felt hesitant about leaving Tess and Vincent without him on the plantation, yet he didn't want her in the fields at Judson's. This was a working visit, after all. He gave Tess a final hug.

"Don't work too hard, and rest in the heat of the day, sweetheart," he told her. "You aren't used to this hot sun. And don't go out without your bonnet any time, all right?"

"Yes, I know. It gets terribly hot," she said. "I'll work on the accounts from two years ago, and get some totals for you by the time you return."

"Good. I wonder how mail and parcels get here, and

the gazettes?" he added absently. "I would like to get some news at times."

"A man comes St. Michael," Malkia said unexpectedly, removing her pipe again and waving it. "He come, one, two times, one Sunday, maybe three."

"A man comes out when mail comes by boat?" Morgan tried to set the timing right.

"Yes, when a big boat comes in, the mail comes. Then a man comes. You pay him a little bit." She grinned at him, pleased at giving information.

"That's splendid. Maybe we'll have something in the next ship, Tess!"

"It could be, though there's nobody to write letters. Still, he might bring out gazettes and books."

Just the idea of a visitor seem to cheer her. Morgan was thinking of that as he set out. It was a lonely life for Tess and Vincent. They were accustomed to being in a busy inn, seeing the sailors come and go, being able to go out to shops and restaurants, watching the ships, talking to travelers. It must seem very quiet and he wondered if they would get restless. He must see to it that they visited the Quinteros frequently. He liked them better than the Judsons, and Tess seemed to take to Inez quite well. The girls had had their heads together for quite two hours the Sunday of their visit, talking of housekeeping, cooking, training maids—something *quite* new to Tess, after all.

On the way along the road, riding slowly on horseback, looking over his cane fields, Morgan noted a large signpost he had not seen before. It was half on its side, and the paint was faded. He paused to study it, thinking he must get a slave to nail it up straight. How quickly he had come to the idea that the slaves did all the labor, he realized, not pleased with the thought. After all, as a sailor, he had put his hand to any kind of work.

The faded sign said, in firm black letters now gray with age and the rains, Last Hope—T. Hamilton.

He rode on, thinking about that. Last Hope. He would like to change that name. Hamilton, his uncle, had been bitter and angry about having to leave the United States after the Revolutionary War with Great Britain. His home in the Carolinas had been beautiful, Morgan had heard, and comforts had been many. To come here, make a new start, struggle with the new work of the sugarcane fields, with different slaves added to his own household—it must have been very difficult for such a proud man. And then to have his beloved wife and all three children to die of a fever—that must have been the final blow to him.

But Morgan and Tess were making a new, hopeful start. They must change that name, he resolved. He thought, "Beautiful Hope," "Paradise," "New Scotland," and smiled. Well, he would talk it over with Tess.

Thinking of Tess again, he considered that he must make plans to keep her happy here, and not working too hard. There would be neighbors to visit, surely there were more beyond Quintero's. And as soon as he felt in firm control of the slaves, and could trust them to continue the work of the cane and the mill, he wanted to go to St. Michael, visit the bank, find out how he stood financially, and when ships docked.

He would not leave Tess and Vincent so long alone either. They must come with him. One could replace burned cane fields, or a looted house. But not such a wife!

His mouth grew tender as he thought of his Tess. How sweet she was, still shy and nervous with him, yet some nights so yielding and passionate. He would teach her to love him! And to trust him, for he felt he did not have her trust.

Only the other day, she had said idly, "If we leave here—" to Vincent. Vincent had started, looked grave.

144

Tess had not seemed to notice, but Vincent had stared toward Morgan. Vincent was settling down, accepting the life, and seeming to enjoy it. Didn't Tess like it? Or did she still have that wild idea that Morgan would tire of her? He must convince her otherwise!

All too soon, he came to Judson's plantation. He turned the horse in the lane, and studied the house as he reached the top of the hill. A fine stone and wood house, much like the Hamilton mansion, yet somehow not so attractive. He wondered what it was, then decided it was the lack of flowers and the straggly look of the bushes.

He came up to the veranda as Judson came from the interior of the house. "Ah, good morning, Mr. Judson," said Morgan. "Am I too early?"

The man was red-eyed, yawning. "No, no, I was just late abed," he said, with a sly smile. "Forgive the non-appearance of my wife! She still sleeps."

Morgan ignored the innuendos, and said, "Shall we go directly out to the fields then, before the day grows hot?"

"It's hot already," Judson grumbled, and yelled, "Here, Jim, bring my horse, you lazy no-good slave!"

Morgan stiffened. A boy appeared from around the house, leading a handsome black horse, saddled and ready. Judson swung into the saddle, and thrust his rifle into a fine sheath on the pommel. "All right, let's go. The west fields today. We'll be home for lunch," he said curtly to the boy, who nodded.

The boy had not said a word. His eyes watched alertly for any gesture and word of Judson, but he said nothing.

They rode off. "Doesn't the boy speak English?" Morgan asked idly.

"He spoke too damn much!" Judson growled. "Had to cut out his tongue! He talked all the damn time and neglected his work. Well, it was a lesson to the others. Damn inconvenient for me though. He can't tell me a damn thing!"

Morgan was so shocked he caught his breath. Judson noticed it and grinned.

"Not used to slaves yet? Eh, they take a deal of lessons! You have to be hard with them, or they'll run you! Give them an inch, they'll take the island! I keep them in order!"

They went on out into the fields. Morgan was listening to Judson's lecture on how to plant the cane in the autumn months, after a summer of weeding and hoeing. He seemed to know his work, and Morgan took mental notes of everything he said. Some fields would reseed themselves, so that ratoon cane could be harvested in about a year. But others were plowed up, cleaned, and cleared, so that fresh cane could be set down in narrow trenches in September and October. You cut the cane lengths about a foot each, with one or two "eyes" on them. These would sprout, and take about sixteen months to grow. These were the best.

"You can't count too much on ratoon cane, or letting the fields reseed themselves. Every two or three years, I reseed the fields, rotating them," Judson explained. "That makes the best cane, and I make my best sugar and rum from those fields. The rest is cut and kept separate, for sugar in the house. I sell my best stuff," he added casually.

As they rode slowly along the fields, the hooves of the horses sank into the creamy sand of the beach. Judson pointed out the fields of ratoon cane, and Morgan could see the difference: it was shorter of stalk, and not so wide. Then the fields of new cane were pointed out. Some stalks were two or three inches in width.

"Better sugar, and so better rum," Judson said. "I let these fields ripen until May and June, and cut them last.

We're doing the ratoon cane now, and that will be our sugar supply for a year. Molasses is good enough for the slaves too. Feed them molasses and let them fish, and grow their own vegetables, that's all the food they need."

They turned into the cane, then, along the narrow path between two fields, and rode to the west. There Morgan saw the slaves working, with great slashes of their machetes, to cut the cane a little higher than themselves. Sullen eyes glanced briefly at the two men on their horses. The white overseers came hastily to meet Mr. Judson.

"Coming along all right today, no trouble, Mr. Judson," one of them said respectfully.

Morgan happened to be looking at one burly slave who moved slowly from one clump of cane to another. He had heard a strange rattle. He caught his breath in audible shock. The man had chains on both legs! They were so short they permitted him only to hobble from one short step to another.

Judson followed Morgan's glance. "He tried to run away into the hills. Damn fool! I didn't cut off his foot, the way I should have. I put him in short chains; he's a good worker when he's whipped enough!"

The man worked without a shirt, and the stripe marks were clear and red across his bronzed back. He did not turn his woolly head, but kept his attention on his work.

"Sullen beasts," Judson said, and turned to another worker. "How is he working today?"

"Better, Mr. Judson. He seems better, not so sick."

The man was a queer greenish color under his tan. "Ate something he shouldn't, probably," said Judson, and lost interest. "They're always fishing, and trying out stuff from the sea," he told Morgan.

"He said it was the salt pork," said one overseer incautiously.

Judson turned on him, and half raised his whip; the

man shrank, his hand to his face in fear. "Shut up. Who asked you?" he snarled at the man on foot. "Why did you give him salt pork, anyway? Put him on bread and water for a week!"

He wheeled, and they rode away, Morgan following automatically. He felt half sick as they came across other slaves working. Most bore the marks of the whip and lash, some were chained as the first man had been. Even one woman had chains on her.

Judson rode wildly, until he seemed to have ridden off his temper. He drew up, to permit Morgan to ride beside him, as they reached the sugar mill.

Judson was thorough, Morgan granted him that. He followed closely as Judson explained how his mill worked, how to turn the great wheels to turn the sails to the wind. Then they went to the boiling house, where great copper cauldrons were steaming with molasses. Two burly slaves were skimming off the impurities and putting the ladles of brown gooey mass into another barrel. The first barrel was full.

Judson sniffed at the first barrel, pointed to it. "This barrel is fermenting fine," he said. "If it doesn't go good, you can put in yeast, but it's better if it starts off by itself, though—makes better rum. You let this boil by itself for a week . . ."

He explained everything that Bernardo had told Morgan about making rum. He had his slaves working two shifts, one day and one night, at the crushing and the boiling. They would work that way until the work was finished in June.

Back at the great house, he was beaming and full of good humor as they sat down to an elaborate luncheon. Antoinette Judson, in a stunning green silk dress, an elaborate hairdress, had been waiting for their return with tall glasses of rum punch ready. They sat down to huge platters of fresh fish, then plates of sliced roast beef, indifferent vegetables, and a beautiful dish of fruit to finish. Judson cut his tropical fruits—papayas, limes, an orange—into a dish, and poured rum over it from his own six-year stock. "Makes the fruit taste good," he said grinning.

Mrs. Judson was silent through much of the meal, to Morgan's surprise. She seemed equal to any situation, he had not thought her shy. She directed the maids sharply, rebuked them for any mistake, then finally relaxed over the fruit. Morgan peeled a papaya and ate it.

"Tastes good to me. I remember this as a sailor, coming in to a Carib port," he said.

"A sailor, eh?" said Judson, though he knew it already. "Tell us about where you fought."

Morgan shrugged. "It seems a long time away. Forgive me, not today. I would rather hear about how to make rum! You seem to be an expert at it, judging by the taste of this!"

Judson's chest swelled. "I'm the best around," he bragged. "My rum sells on other islands of the Caribbees as well as in London and New York City! I'll tell you what it is. Keep close attention to it, and let it age proper! No one-year rum can be as good as two-year, and no two-year as good as six-year! That's the principle. Don't be afraid to keep it on hand until it's good and aged."

He talked intelligently about mixing the ingredients, what kind of barrels to buy. "And use them over and over, they just get better!" He talked about charring the barrels, and the kind of rum that produced. He was as smart about it as the Honorable Billy.

Morgan almost enjoyed that afternoon, around the table, then later relaxing on the veranda. Antoinette put in a few smiling words about how intelligent her husband was, and how much he knew about rums, and how respected he was. Judson grew more and more mellow with the afternoon.

He did know his stuff, Morgan felt. Yet there was such an atmosphere of sullenness and fear among the slaves, and even with Mrs. Judson, when her husband was about. How hated he was, and how feared. Was that the way to treat slaves, and keep them in line? Judson was sure of it. "Only way to treat them," he said, when he spoke of having a slave whipped.

Morgan rode home thoughtfully, and told Tess something of the day. Tess's eyes were wide and horrified as he spoke. "Odette said he was mean and cruel," she said. "But, oh, Morgan! I cannot believe such treatment is necessary. It is not—not human! It is beastly!"

"That's what I think," he sighed. "Well, I'm going over to Quintero's plantation on Thursday. When the Spaniard heard I was going to Judson's, he got jealous at once, and said he knew as much or more about sugarcane. So, to keep peace among the neighbors, I'll be going there. Was everything all right today? No trouble?"

She shook her head. "Bernardo came in and out, he and Odette wouldn't let Gamba come near the house. You know, I think they are really protective."

Gamba. Morgan frowned over his pipe. Judson had mentioned Gamba especially. "You got to watch that fellow, Hamilton," he had said. "You'll have to whip him to keep him in line! He's trouble. Over from Africa not long ago, and thinks he's a big chief!"

Morgan decided to warn Vincent about him, and Tess. "Keep rifles close. We'll use the case in the living room, and when you're in back, it would be best to keep the front doors locked and bolted. The French windows also. There's a pirate in the hills, also. If he comes down, he might make trouble."

Tess looked frightened. Morgan was sorry, but it was better to be aware.

"Just think of them as sailors in the inn, sweetheart," he said. "You had to look out for them too, didn't you? Well, just be alert and wary."

On Thursday, he went over to Quintero's. The aging Spaniard, lounging on the veranda, insisted on having a long cool rum planter's punch before they started out. So it was after eleven before they went to the fields to talk about the sugarcane work. Morgan was a little amused, but at least, he thought, Quintero had no slaves in chains! And they were more cheerful, they smiled when he spoke to them and nodded their heads.

Many more of his fields were in ratoon cane, Morgan noted. Made alert by Judson's comments on the necessity of reseeding the fields often, he asked casually about that. Quintero shrugged.

"No, Judson is a fanatic about it; so was Hamilton," he said. "I see no need for it. The cane reseeds itself, and comes up for eight or ten years! Not as high, but still good."

Morgan said nothing, politely, but he rather thought he liked Judson's fields better. He broke off a piece of cane and tasted it, as Quintero watched him. Morgan kept his face expressionless. It did not taste nearly so sweet and there was not so much juice in it as there had been in Judson's new cane yesterday, and in Morgan's cane fields.

The sugar mill was operating rather slowly. The slave had not turned the windmill to catch the wind that morning. Quintero scolded the overseer mildly, and the man caught up his whip. "Now, no need of whipping," Quintero said. "Just tell him to change the sails. He knows how, he just needs reminding."

The overseer nodded, and they went away. Morgan glanced back, and saw him coil up his whip and strike the slave's back. Quintero had not turned, and did not see it. They rode on, Morgan thoughtful.

The boiling house was not as neatly organized as Judson's, and the cauldron was less than half full of juice. The furnace had not been lit that morning. "We'll light it again next week," said Quintero cheerfully. "This lot isn't enough to bother with. Have to dump it. Next week, we'll have more."

They returned to the beautiful Spanish quinta, where Inez was hostess. She apologized for Florencia, the sister had a bad headache, she said. Quintero frowned.

"But we have guests," he said sternly. He turned to Morgan. "My sincere apologies, señor. My daughter is given to headaches, it is the heat which she finds unbearable. But she should not so insult a guest! I hope you will understand, and forgive."

"Of course. Pray, give her my sympathy," he said to Inez. "A bad headache can be troublesome."

"You are most kind, señor," Inez said, her large dark eyes a bit troubled. Her cheeks were flushed as she quietly ordered the maids to bring the first course.

Morgan found himself wondering if Florencia did have a headache, or simply didn't want to trouble herself to get out of bed for a married man! If Vincent had come —he grinned to himself, wondering. It was evident that the younger Inez had the household reins in her hands, and Morgan was satisfied that his initial judgment of the two sisters was correct. Little Inez was worth ten of her sister! More like his own Tess.

The food was delicious, but not strange to Morgan. It was Spanish—a fish course, but the fish was cold, chilled in the cooling house, and served with a tart sauce of lime. It was followed by an immense platter of brown rice, herbs, greens, sausage and chicken. Morgan helped himself eagerly.

"Paella!" he exclaimed. "I have not had it for almost two years!"

That brought on a discussion of the war with Spain under Napoleon, and Quintero's grief about his relatives who had fallen in that war. Morgan was induced to speak of his experiences, and Inez was a most flattering listener.

"Was your—brother-in-law—was he there?" she asked. She blushed a little.

"Vincent? No. I did not meet him until the war was over," said Morgan. "He would have been a bit too young, however, thank God. We pray that no such war will come again, now that the monster Napoleon is safely imprisoned."

"Just so he does not escape again!" Quintero shook his graying head soberly. "What a horrible shock that was!"

"Aye, and led to Waterloo, and all Europe in turmoil," said Morgan, and they talked of politics and economics some of the afternoon, pleasantly, on the veranda.

Inez brought them drinks made with her own hands, from her father's best six-year-old stock. Morgan tried tasting from little sips that she brought in small glasses on a tray, trying to guess which ones were new rums, which ones older. Quintero was visibly pleased whenever Morgan guessed right.

"Yes, yes, you will learn quickly!" he exclaimed. "One tells you are most quick of mind, señor!"

The man was so spirited, so gallant, so Spanish in his exquisite courtesy, that Morgan left with an even better impression of him. He might not run his plantation as effectively as he might have done. Yet Morgan much preferred his methods with the slaves to Judson's, he thought with a profound shudder.

Yet—the overseers did not hesitate to use the whip. Was that the answer? Did one need to whip the slaves, to make them work? Bernardo and Odette did not seem to need it. Yet the time was short so far—he must wait and see.

He had much to think about as he rode home that late afternoon, with Quintero's parting remarks in his ears. "Come again soon, señor, and your lovely wife and fine brother-in-law! I am so pleased that it is you who have come to Elysia!"

10

Several weeks later, Quintero had sent another note to Morgan, inviting him to his home for the afternoon and evening: "I am this afternoon mixing some of my rums in barrels, and would show you the process. It is an experiment, which has resulted in some fine dark rum liqueurs. Pray come, and I will reveal a few of my secrets!"

It was flattering, and Morgan thought he could profit by the experience. It would mean coming home after dark, but he felt more at ease now on the island, and knew his way. At first, he had been very cautious to travel only in the daytime, watching warily for the pirate from the hills, and unusual movements of any slaves. Now, he felt much more confident.

It had been a very instructive afternoon and evening. Quintero was even more friendly than usual.

"I have come to like you, my friend, as much as I did my old friend, your uncle, Thomas Hamilton," he had confided, as they worked in the cool whitewashed still-room. "I am sure he would approve that you carry on my work. You see, I have two beautiful daughters of whom I am most proud, but I have no sons to carry on my plantation. When I retire, I may have to sell the place to some-one. And who will know my secrets of the rum? No, they will die with me," he said sadly, with a dramatic flourish of his white-clad arms.

Morgan thought also that the man was lonely. They had few visitors from town in this season of the year, their busy time. He worked much of the day in the cane fields, supervising that work, went from there to the mills. He had overseers, but it was Quintero who knew the whole process, and all that must be done to insure care of the final product. He might be a bit lazy and superficial in his overseeing, but he enjoyed fine rums, and had pride in his reputation.

Now he showed Morgan how to mix the rums. He took a two-year rum, measured it out by the gallon, then mixed it with a five-year rum. Then to Morgan's surprise, he took out a bottle of some opaque white liquid. "Smell it," he invited.

Morgan did so cautiously, not knowing what to expect. It was unexpectedly fragrant and delicious in scent.

Quintero nodded, his dark eyes sparkling. "Coconut essence, liquor distilled from the coconut, aged a year. Now—I mix it with my rums—"

Morgan watched in great fascination as the man deftly mixed all in a huge kettle. Quintero showed him the proportions, told how he also made liquors of limes, some of lemons. "But none is so delicious and refreshing as my coconut liqueur," he confided. "Everyone wants to know my secret." He put his finger beside his nose and winked. "Keep this a secret, my friend, and make your fortune, long after I have departed this earth."

"But this is your invention," Morgan protested, nevertheless keenly interested. "I would not deprive you and your heirs—"

"Nonsense. I trust you! You will make some fine liquor, and who knows but you may improve on my formulas! I have wished to experiment with the fresh coconut juice, the milk of the coconut mixed with crushed pulp. However, I have not yet done this. You might wish to try it. Years!" he said impressively. "One can work years, trying and testing, to make the perfect liqueurs! You may achieve greatness, my friend!"

They worked much of the afternoon into the evening. Morgan mixed rum with orange under Quintero's supervision, and then helped ladle the resulting mixtures into freshly washed and boiled bottles. They used large metal ladles, and spouts, stuck into the necks of the bottles. Then the bottles were corked and laid tenderly to rest on a shelf, on their sides.

"Next year, we shall have some fine liquors," Quintero smiled. "Ah, now come and taste some from last year!"

They washed up, put on their jackets, and stepped out into the cool evening. Morgan saw with a shock that dusk had come, and the island was rapidly becoming dark. The sky had purpled, and soon it would be velvety dark but for a few stars and a sliver of moon.

"I must return home," he protested. "I had not realized we had worked so late!" They had worked by candlelight in that dim room. Quintero told him he did not like to use oil lamps, they might give an unpleasant odor to the resulting rums.

"No, no, you must first taste last year's coconut

liqueurs," said Quintero firmly, seeming hurt by Morgan's abrupt departure.

Morgan was forced by good manners and consideration for his host, to sit down on the veranda while Inez brought trays of fresh chilled coconut liqueurs. He had to admit they were both delicious and refreshing.

However, he firmly refused her cordial invitation to dinner. "My wife will grow anxious. I am never away so late," he smiled. "Perhaps we may come on Sunday—or you will come to us! Let me consult with my wife about this."

Morgan enjoyed saying "my wife" so often. For so many years, he had been a loner, an outsider at the marital scenes—and glad to be when they were full of quarreling and disloyalty. But now, he was married to such a lovely wife, so sweet and passionate, that saying "my wife" brought back sweet memories to him, and made him long to be with her again.

He asked for his horse to be brought about. After some joking and teasing at him to remain longer, Quintero finally sent for the fine black stallion, and Morgan mounted to return home. It was full dark now, and he felt a bit unsteady after all the "tasting and testing" they had done that day.

He rode out, down the long winding lane, and onto the creamy beach. He could follow that path clearly, it shone under the slim moon. He hummed to himself, then broke out into a sailor song, grinning at himself. He felt really good tonight! Full of delicious rum, and the satisfaction of a growing friendship.

He rode past Quintero's dark cane fields, and on past Judson's. He recognized landmarks now, the dark clumps of pines, the bent coconut trees, a thin lining of tall majestic royal palms. Here were the thick bushes of sea grapes, growing tall and green. And around the bend was a clear stretch of beach, on his own property, near the cove where he sometimes swam.

Out of the thick cane came a rush. He was too bemused to be alert. One man struck him on the head with a machete, and it was deflected only by Morgan's horse, shying away wildly at the closeness of the man's body.

The blow went slicing down the back of Morgan's head, and struck his back and left shoulder. He cried out, and reached for his rifle stock, blindly. But too late— another man was at him on the other side, striking at him with a pole or a rifle butt—

Morgan lashed out both boots, freeing them from the stirrups abruptly. He kicked out at one man, and the man groaned as he went down. The horse veered, and started on, jerking at the reins. Morgan was dizzy, partly with the rum, partly with the blow. His feet were out of the stirrups, he lost his saddle—He was out, and striking the beach, flat out.

A man was bending over him, grunting with pleasure. Morgan used his fists and hands. He was fighting blindly, he could scarcely see for the dizziness. The years of soldiering made him fight by instinct. Use any blow, any chop, any means—only fight, fight, gouge for the eyes—

The horse neighed and raced away, reins dragging. Morgan could not think of that. He was fighting for his life. One man groaned, bent over on the sand. The other was fighting him ferociously. He reached out, grabbed for the man's hair as he butted Morgan's stomach.

Both were out of breath, grunting for breath. Morgan pulled and yanked viciously at the short hair, felt the slickness of some oil in it that made him lose grip easily. He gripped again, yanked the man's head up, kicked up with both knees, and connected. The man groaned as Morgan's right knee contacted with his chin. His head snapped back, and he fell to his side in the sand.

Morgan was up and running. The first man was standing, and after him. Ahead of him Morgan saw the glint of the water. He did not hesitate. Most men could not swim.

He plunged into the water, feeling the chill and heaviness of it as booted and fully clothed he went in. He stepped out over the sharp coral to where he could sink into the water chin-deep.

The man stood uncertainly on the sands, staring out. He had a rifle in his hands. He lifted it, hesitated. He probably didn't want the sound to carry, as it was. Morgan rested under the shadow of a rock, afraid to move, though the water was seeping into his clothes, pouring into his heavy boots, keeping him from moving easily. He watched.

The man moved away, lifted his companion, they muttered something to each other, then limped away in the darkness. Morgan waited, he closed his eyes, shook his head.

He must wait for a time, until he was sure they had left. They might think he had drowned. Cautiously he lifted one hand to his head, and winced. He explored, found a deep cut there, and something sticky that hurt when he touched the area. He knew the stickiness, that of blood.

He could not wait long, he felt faint and dizzy. That rum—damn it, he should not have drunk so much! Had Quintero planned it? Morgan's teeth gritted. If he thought that the Spaniard had done this on purpose, he would go back and publicly horsewhip him in front of his daughters! Damn poor hospitality!

But no—why think that? It must have been that mulatto pirate up in the fields. Judson had said he was a fierce wild fellow. But why attack Morgan?

He could not think straight; he was so tired, he wanted to go to sleep here in the cool water that chilled his overheated body. It was dangerous. Could they be gone, could he risk staggering from the water? Those men had not been badly hurt, and they might be lurking in the thick bushes of sea grapes, or the deep cane fields just beyond the beach . . .

Tess had been busy that afternoon and evening, getting out some of the beautiful silver bowls from the glass-fronted satinwood cases. She and Odette had sat at the dining table, with the silver spread out, and polished and cleaned busily. Now as they were finishing, she said, "Have you lived long here, Odette?"

A look of wariness came to the girl's pansy dark eyes. She finally nodded. "Long time, missus."

"All your life?"

Odette looked puzzled. Tess thought, and said again, "Were you born here?"

"I was born here in this house," said Odette, gesturing about the large airy gracious home.

Tess thought of Morgan's guess, that the girl might be the daughter of Thomas Hamilton. It figured, the mother might have been a housemaid.

"And your mother?"

"My mother was African," she said proudly.

"Did she live here?"

Odette nodded, her gaze discreetly on the silver bowl she was shining industriously. "There. It's fine, yes, missus?" She held it out for inspection.

"It looks good," Tess approved, and Odette smiled in pleasure. The smile lit up her beautiful face. She was a very attractive girl, Tess thought. No wonder Judson wanted her.

They dipped the last bowls into the sudsy water, washed and dried them, and began returning them to the glass cases.

"Very beautiful," said Tess. "Have you polished the silver before?"

Odette nodded. "I helped in the house when I was a small girl—like this high." She measured her hand down to the height of a small girl.

"Mr. Hamilton liked you. Liked you to work in the house and help him." Tess looked at her questioningly.

"Mr. Hamilton was very sad. He just sat in his chair and rocked and rocked." Odette demonstrated with her slim rounded body, and pointed to the veranda. "He looked out at sea for hours, with tears in his eyes. I would bring him a drink, and sit on floor. He would read to me. It would make him happy."

Tess understood. The man had found some consolation in the presence of this small charming girl, probably his own daughter, after the deaths of all he had loved.

She hesitated to say the next, but forced herself to do this. "Sunday, we will go to Judson's," she said carefully. "Mr. Judson says he wants to buy you."

Odette's face was transformed by sudden, abject fear. To Tess's surprise, she flung herself to the floor at Tess's feet. "No, no! Please don't sell Odette! I will work hard, work my fingers to the bone! Please don't sell me!"

Warmhearted Tess could not endure this. She knelt beside her, and put her arms about the trembling girl.

"I will not sell you, Odette!" she said firmly. "Missus will never sell Odette! I promise!" Tess raised her up, held her firmly by the shoulders, made the girl look at her. "I promise never to sell you, Odette! You belong to me!"

Odette collapsed in sobs, and Tess soothed her. "He's a bad man," she whispered to Tess. "Judson's a bad man. All time he wants a girl. All the black girls are afraid of that man! He just want more slaves! He just wants to make babies with his slaves!"

Tess was shocked. "Is that why he wants you,

Odette?" she asked, stroking back the thick black hair tenderly. "He said, he wanted you as a maid for his missus."

Odette shook her head vigorously. "He doesn't want a maid. He has a maid. She make many babies for him. Three, four, five babies. He uses slaves. Many slaves!"

Tess shuddered, then drew Odette to her feet. "I will never sell you," she repeated. "Calm down, Odette. You shall not leave Hamilton plantation. This is your home, we are your people. Do you understand?"

Odette wiped her eyes on her sleeves, and nodded, her smile coming out like sunshine after rain. "You are a good missus," she said passionately. "I will never leave you! I belong to you!"

Tess nodded and repeated the words soothingly, sorry she had brought on such a storm. Yet it had cleared the air, the girl had shown how she felt. They were finishing putting away the silver bowls, when Vincent ran in the back door.

"Tess! Morgan's horse returned—saddled—without him. And blood on the saddle!"

"Oh my God!" Tess whispered; her hands went to her throat. "Vincent!" She was swaying.

"I'm going to find him," Vincent said, with determination. He went over to the rifle case, unlocked it, and took out a long shining rifle, and the bullet pouch and powder flask. "I'll take the carriage, in case he is hurt—"

Odette was watching with wide eyes. "You take Bernardo!" she urged. "Take men!"

"I'll come," Tess said, and snatched down another rifle. She had conquered her momentary dizziness, and her blue eyes blazed fire. "Come on, Vincent! We'll go after Morgan! If he has been hurt—killed—" she choked on the words. "I'll kill whoever did it!"

Odette ran after them on her slim bare feet. "Take

Bernardo," she urged in agitation. "Take men with knives—"

But somehow Tess did not trust anybody but herself and Vincent. They had supported each other through the years, and fought for each other. "No, just us. Odette, you stay inside, and get Bernardo to come here. Have blankets and hot water ready, and bandages," she added.

She did not stay to see the orders carried out. She ran out to the stable. Bernardo was hitching up the horses to the carriage, Vincent was throwing blankets into the back, his face set and hard. He had grown older since they'd left the Last Inn, thought his sister. Vincent had indeed matured.

She ordered Bernardo up to the house to help Odette, climbed into the carriage, and Vincent swung up beside her. He took the reins, and chucked the horse. They set out, down the path to the beach.

"He always rides along the beach, it is clear and he can see his way," muttered Tess, her hands clutching the heavy rifle, her gaze swinging from one side to the other nervously as they turned onto the beach road.

"He was out late," said Vincent grimly. "I was worried when he said it might be dark when he came back. And now this!"

"If he's hurt—"

"Do you think Quintero—"

Tess shook aside that question. "I don't care now! How will we find Morgan if he's hurt?"

Vincent was driving slowly, peering into the darkness. The slim sickle of moon did little to light their way. Tess looked fearfully at the dark fields of cane. Anyone could hide there, a dozen slaves, a hundred men.

"I'll shoot the rifle," decided Vincent. "If the men are still about who attacked him, it might scare them off. If they have gone, it might warn Morgan we are coming."

He stopped the horses, Tess held the reins firmly as Vincent loaded and fired the rifle. The shot echoed and reechoed through the fields, and seemed to rebound against the hills. They waited, no sound came but the rustle of the fields of uncut cane.

They went on, slowly. Tess called out, "Morgan . . . Morgan . . . Morgan . . ."

Vincent did not stop her, though both knew it might bring an attack on themselves. Tess was so frantic, she thought only of finding Morgan.

She paused to listen, called again, "Mor-r-r-r-gannnn!" She had a clear high voice. She called, pausing between the sounds. The hills echoed her voice.

There was a rustle to their left, as though a big fish splashed in the waters. Tess jerked to attention, Vincent brought up the rifle instinctively.

"Morrrr-gannnnn!" she tried again.

"Here!" came a weak voice. "Here—in the sea."

Tess jumped down from the high carriage, tearing her dress, but uncaring. She ran down to the edge of the water. Vincent paused to tie up the horse, then jumped down, to stand with rifle alert, watching the cane fields, as Tess knelt on the beach. Morgan was dripping wet, soaked, even his heavy boots sloshing with water.

"Oh, Morgan," she whispered, and stroked back his wet hair. Her fingers came on the sticky bloody patch, and he groaned.

"It's my—head," he managed to say. "Dizzy—Got the—carriage?"

"Yes. Can you walk?" She helped him up, he leaned so heavily on her slight shoulders that she thought she would be crushed. But she held him up, and he managed to walk, unsteadily, to the carriage.

He half fell into the back part, and seemed to pass out. She covered him with the blankets, and got up on the planks, to sit beside him, tensely, the second rifle in her hands where Vincent had tossed it to her. He got up, and chucked at the horse, and managed to turn the carriage in the thick sand of the beach.

Tess was watching alertly, fiercely. If anyone tried to attack them now—

But no sounds came from the cane, no body came forth to attack them out of the darkness. Vincent whipped up the horse, and they flew along the beach, and back up the path to the stables.

Bernardo ran from the house, another man came from the slave huts, and others gathered to watch in silence as they lifted Morgan down. Malkia came, to push some aside, and come with them.

The two slaves carried Morgan into the house, dripping water, sagging between them. They laid him down on a wooden settle in the back hall. Bernardo tenderly removed the boots, which seemed to weigh him down. Tess bent down to study the wound anxiously.

Malkia bent beside her, her pipe forgotten.

"Salve he need," she said briskly. She ran her thin aged hands over his head, then down over his shoulders and body. "Head bad, and shoulder. Get him in dry clothes, put in bed. Malkia bring salve. We will bandage."

They obeyed her unquestioningly, even Tess, deferring to the old woman's judgment. They stripped Morgan of his clothes, wrapped him in a dry blanket, and the two men then carried him in their powerful arms up the stairs, to the middle bedroom in the master suite. Morgan seemed unconscious, only groaning a little as they set him down.

Tess sat beside him, holding his hand as Malkia worked with the salve Odette had run to fetch for her. Another maid brought bandages. Tess realized dimly that Vincent was there, so were a dozen blacks, crowding the halls and stairs. She thought of what Judson had said,

"Don't trust the blacks. Don't let them in the house." Yet they seemed the only friends they had, the only ones she could trust!

Malkia finished with the head. "Head cut open," she said. "Shoulder cut open. We fix. Watch for fever. Mister Morgan, how long in water, he?"

Morgan finally opened his eyes. "Seemed a long time —left Quintero's around nine-thirty."

Tess glanced at the big old clock ticking in the corner. "Eleven," she said, in a strained hoarse voice. She felt as though she had been screaming for hours. "It takes about an hour to ride back from there . . . He was maybe in the water half an hour, Malkia."

"Half hour. Hum. Night cool. Keep him warm. Dry. Watch for fever. I will bring medicine."

She went out, briskly important, to return with a glass of rum and a powdery mixture in a piece of paper. Tess looked at it, worried. Should she trust the woman?

"Not more rum," groaned Morgan. "I drank so much at Quintero's, he showed me how to make some liqueurs—"

"Malkia will make you well, master," said the old woman, looking pleadingly at Tess. "Do you trust Malkia?"

She finally nodded, and the old woman's face relaxed. She poured the powders into the rum, stirred them, and made Morgan drink it. Then he lay back, sighed, and went to sleep.

"He will sleep much," said Malkia. "Feed him meat broth when he wakes. Make him rest much."

Tess nursed Morgan back to health, but it took weeks. Vincent took over for him in the fields, riding from one cane field to another, anxiously coming for advice when Morgan was awake. Gamba was proudly in command at the mill, Bernardo had another man working in the still.

They kept on with the work, just as Morgan had told them to do, and came up for orders, twisting their hats in their bronzed hands.

Tess ignored completely the advice not to let the blacks in the house. Even Gamba came up, with Bernardo behind him. She felt Bernardo did not trust Gamba, so she did not. The others she felt she could trust with the helpless man in bed.

Tess nursed him, with Malkia changing the bandages daily, dosing him with her powders and herbs, ordering his meals. Her advice always made sense. They fed him light chicken broth, and meat broth, some teas, at first, then gradually added bread sops, later on meat and fruits.

Judson came the first week, and insisted on coming up to see the invalid. He shook his head over Morgan. "I told you not to trust the blacks," he scolded. "Never go out alone at night, keep your rifles about at all times."

"Yes, you told me," said Morgan, weakly, leaning against the pillows. There were dark shadows under his eyes.

"Want me to take charge of the cane while you're laid up?" Judson asked, leaning against the fine-carved bedpost. "I don't mind, my overseers are capable of taking charge of my fields for a time."

"Vincent is doing well," Morgan said. "Thanks very much for your offer, Mr. Judson. I appreciate friends." He spoke with great effort, and Tess gently intervened.

"Thank you for coming, Mr. Judson. I must ask you to leave, as Morgan is not strong yet. Pray, give my kind regards to Mrs. Judson." Somehow she got him out of the room and down the stairs again.

Bernardo hovered about in the back area, Odette had disappeared, and was not about when Judson was there. Judson glanced about the rooms. "Well, everything

168

looks beautiful, the way it used to," he said. "You have worked hard, Mrs. Tess."

"Thank you. We try hard. I'm used to hard work," she said calmly. "Do come again in another week or two. We mean to return your hospitality when Morgan is up and about."

Judson went away. Quintero called on them, much distressed and anxious over Morgan. Tess received him, but he did not insist on seeing Morgan. He left two bottles of his best six-year rum and one of his coconut liqueur, "for when Mr. Hamilton is recovered," he murmured.

A stranger came one day, and Bernardo appeared from the stables. "He brings the mail," said Bernardo, as the man rode up on a sweating tired horse.

Tess was delighted to receive the man, an older graying white man who rode the routes regularly, he said. He was glad to take lunch and a drink, while she wrote a hasty letter for Morgan. He promised to deliver it to the bank in St. Michael, and unwrapped the parcels he had for them—a dozen gazettes which Morgan had ordered before leaving England, and a couple dozen books and magazines.

Tess paid him the amount that Odette indicated discreetly to her. "Mr. Hamilton always pay this," she indicated the coins she pushed on the table with her slim fingers. Tess thanked her, and paid the man, who seemed pleased with it.

When he had gone, she ran up to report to Morgan. "He says he will come again when the next ship comes in, there may be more in April, and many come in May," she said happily.

Tess started reading aloud to Morgan during one hour in the morning and a couple hours in the afternoon. She noted Odette sitting in the hallway, but thought nothing of it. The girl was quick to serve, quick to see when drinks would be welcome, quick to send for Malkia when the old woman was wanted.

"Oh, look—no, listen to this," she said, scanning one gazette. "The British Parliament had ordered slavery to cease in 1806. Did you know that, Morgan?"

He shifted uncomfortably in bed, and she rose to adjust his pillows. "Parliament abolished trade in slaving then, Tess," he corrected in his weary voice. "But that didn't stop the traders. It is illegal, however, to bring in more slaves in British ships. And I think the next step one year will be to free the slaves that we have."

She was scanning the editorial. "This says that the islands in the Caribbees depend on slavery too heavily, with their sugarcane fields—that's us, Morgan! And they ought to turn to other occupations, and free the slaves. Or free them, and start paying for their services, in wages, like free men! Oh, Morgan, I wish we could do that!"

"Would they stay and do that hot work?" asked Morgan. "That's the argument. Planters say that slavery is the only way to work the cane. No sane man would stay and work at it, if he didn't have to."

They discussed it for a time, and she read out other parts of the gazette to him. It was marvelous to have "fresh news" from England, though it was by now a month old.

Presently Morgan said, in a whisper, "Want to show you something. Send Odette for a drink."

She nodded, curiously, and sent Odette downstairs for a chilled fruit drink for Morgan. She returned to the bedroom, to find Morgan reaching out unsteadily for the little table with a drawer next to the bed.

"Let me—" she said quickly, and opened the drawer.

"The ring," he whispered.

She took it out, and handed the signet ring to him. He did not put it on. She gazed at it, remembering the wedding ceremony, when he had pushed the heavy too-large ring onto her finger and kissed her.

"Look at it," he said. He held it up. There were some hairs sticking to the signet, cut in the form of a crest. "Hairs," he whispered. "Judson said I was attacked by slaves. Ever know a slave with thin brown straight hair?"

Tess stared at the hairs, touched them, and a chill ran down her spine. "You mean—"

"I caught the man who attacked me by the hair, we fought in the darkness. His hair was straight and oily, I could hardly hold on to him. Some hairs caught in the ring—I saw them when I began to recover. I put the ring in the drawer, to show the hairs to you later. Judson has hair like that, I saw it again when he came. Quintero has graying black curly hair. The overseers—I don't know—"

"It must have been Judson!" said Tess fiercely. "It would be like him! That hideous man!"

"Maybe. Maybe it was Judson, or maybe an over-seer. I never saw them, it was just too dark. Quintero has a couple shifty men working for him, but I didn't notice particularly what color their hair is." He leaned back wearily into the pillow. "Anyway, it isn't from a black."

They heard Odette's light footsteps, heard her speak to someone in the hall. Morgan whispered, "Put the hairs in a bit of cotton cloth, save them."

Tess nodded, and put the ring and the telltale hairs in her apron pocket. Odette entered, with a tall chilled glass of lime and orange juice on the tray, a shy smile on her lips.

"You are much better, Mr. Morgan," she said, with satisfaction.

11

Vincent stirred restlessly on the veranda, and glanced again at the darkening sky. He had come over to Quintero's again and then again, on the man's cordial invitation. Since Morgan was not yet able to get about, though he was recovering, Quintero was lonely.

But Vincent had a strong suspicion now that the Spaniard had a different motive for his interest in Vincent. He liked to talk, yes, and he had been kind in showing Vincent around, giving him advice, even teaching him about his precious liqueurs just as he had taught Morgan.

Yet——Vincent was too aware of the young girls who came out demurely as the two men sat on the veranda.

Inez usually came with a tray of drinks, and some fresh bread she had baked, or some cakes. Florencia strolled out after her younger sister, languidly waving a fan, dressed in some striking dress. Quintero would watch both his daughters with proud indulgence, then glance at Vincent.

"Am I not the lucky man?" he demanded again. "To have such beautiful daughters! No, I am not modest, I am most proud!"

Vincent smiled weakly. This was a far cry from the way he had been treated in the inn, on the wharf, he thought, with wry amusement. Then he had been "Boy! Get the horse! Boy! Bring down my trunks, and be quick about it. I haven't got all day! Boy, bring fresh drinks, boy, bring hot water!"

It would be flattering to be treated so anxiously by the wealthy man and his beautiful daughters. But Vincent reminded himself, that it was because he was the only single man in this part of Elysia! Not that Quintero saw him as a son-in-law.

He thought Quintero wanted companionship for his daughters, especially Florencia, who grew bored easily, and was always begging her father to move back to St. Michael, or even to Barbados, or another more populous island. She was desperately impatient with the lack of amusements.

Inez seemed to like it here. She would sit quietly in her rocking chair, her little black-slippered feet scarcely reaching the porch floor, and rock, her gaze on the sea in the near distance, or the flower beds. Or she would be up in a moment, moving into the cool house to order a maid to bring more drinks, or to fix them herself. They had begged him to come early for luncheon, and had served him so splendidly that he had been sleepy all afternoon.

"I must go, I don't like being out too late. Tess worries," he said, rising finally. He glanced at the sky, it was growing orange and streaked with pink in the west. Within an hour, it would be dusky lavender, then purple as night came.

Quintero sighed, and stood. "Yes, you are right, my friend. After what happened to Morgan—" He shook his graying head, and his face showed more lines graven on it.

"No, no, don't go yet!" urged Florencia, reaching up to catch at Vincent's hand. She succeeded in catching hold of it, behind her father's back, though Inez frowned worriedly at her sister. "Stay for dinner, we will escort you home! Yes, that would be a splendid idea! We'll have one of the men hitch up the carriage, and we will all escort you—"

"Nonsense," said her father abruptly, more coldly than his wont to his daughter. "You shall not be out at night, Florencia! It is much too dangerous. You know my rules about that!"

"And you are correct," said Vincent, smiling, and managing to get his hand free. He was red with embarrassment, hoped that Quintero would attribute his complexion to too much rum. "I must be off—I cannot thank you enough, sir, for sharing your secrets with me. I'll tell Morgan all about it. We mean to experiment with this next year, when our rums are more matured."

Quintero nodded. Inez stood, and said good-bye very gravely, her dark eyes lingering on him. Florencia pouted, and said her farewells abruptly, then rushed into the house.

Quintero accompanied Vincent to his horse, and said in a low tone, "My daughters are spoiled, forgive them, Vincent."

Vincent smiled weakly. "They are always most kind, and cordial in their hospitality," he managed to say.

Quintero seemed gratified. "You are a fine young man," he said, more cheerfully. "You will come again soon, eh? We will talk again, eh?"

"Most certainly. And Morgan wished me to say to you, he is most grateful for all your kind gifts and expressions of goodwill on his health."

Vincent had said it before, but he didn't think it would hurt to keep on. Quintero beamed at him, and clasped his hand before Vincent mounted. He waved in farewell.

Vincent rode down the dark lane, glancing uneasily at the crimson sky. An hour's good ride before him. With the remembrance of Morgan's experience vividly in his mind, he clucked at the horse, and lifted the reins.

"Mr. Pritchard! Vincent!" The girl's voice came pleadingly from his side. He reined up abruptly, startled as Florencia dashed from the thick trees and bushes.

Her hair hung loose, she looked wild and disheveled. His first thought was that she had been attacked. He pulled up his horse to a halt, and swung down, reaching for the rifle in the saddle stock.

"No—no, not that," she panted. "I must—speak to you!" Her breath came in great heaves, which made her all the more attractive. Her deep blue gown was low-cut, showing the white full breasts rather more than he was accustomed to seeing. Had she drawn down the bosom? He wondered.

She came close to him, and clasped his arm with both hands. He could feel her pressing against him, her warm body in the thin dress pushing at him. His back was to the horse, he could not back up any more.

"What is it?" he asked uneasily, still glancing about. "Someone has attacked you? I will take you back, and inform your father!"

"No, silly!" She shook his arm in her impatience. Her dark eyes glowed with fire, in the magnolia white alluring face, and her mouth glowed red, as though she had bitten the full lips. "I had to speak to you, alone!"

"What is it?"

"Don't you know?" she pouted. "Are you not . . . attracted to me as I am to you? Do you not comprehend

176

what has happened between us? You come often to see me, you glance at me, but are too shy to speak!"

Vincent was stunned. No woman had ever spoken to him like this. At the inn, he had sometimes been looked over by some brazen females, but never by a good woman! "Miss Quintero, you should not say these things!"

"Pooh! I am Spanish! I feel deeply—here!" She caught at his free hand, and pressed it boldly to her bosom. He felt the heat and the curves of her flesh, and in spite of his unease, something made him hot. "I knew as soon as we met that we were destined to be—more to each other." She breathed.

"How can you say that—" he was stammering, when she reached up, and put her hand behind his head. She pulled him imperiously down to her, and put her full red mouth on his. He weakened, he put his hands awkwardly to her waist, and pulled her close to him. His mouth met hers again, and he felt the shock of it racing through his thin body.

She was rounded, curving sensuously. His hand slid to her hip, she curled herself against him frantically. Her mouth opened against his, she moaned to him, "Do it again, oh, Vincent, I have so longed—"

He kissed her again. The heat in their bodies was burning him up. He gulped for air, raised his head. His horse was moving uneasily. Was that a crackle in the bushes? He tensed, and all desire slid from him, like an ill-fitting cloak.

"Florencia, what was that?" he asked.

She stiffened also, and released him reluctantly. Her head turned like a startled deer; she listened, her great eyes darkened.

"You must go back, I will take you back to the house," he said sharply.

"No, no, it is just some small animal, maybe a lizard," she said impatiently.

"I have to go. You should not be here," he said, more firmly. "Go. I will watch you from here, if you do not wish your father to know——"

She said coyly, "Papa knows how I feel about you," she murmured. "You will speak to him about me, yes?"

With a jolt, Vincent realized what she was saying. No, he thought, no, and again no! "I am not able to plan further ahead now," he said firmly. "I owe much to my brother-in-law. He depends on me. I cannot marry—for years!" he added. "I have no money of my own."

"Papa will help us! I know he will help us!"

"Florencia, you must go!" he said, and gave her a hard push.

She gave him a desperate look. "You will come again soon?"

"Soon," he promised, vowing to make it later than sooner. What kind of a trap was this? He had no wish to marry!

He was about to volunteer again to escort her back to the house, when she smiled, blew him a kiss through voluptuous lips, and raced into the trees. She was gone in an instant. Frowning, he remounted, searched the trees with his gaze, saw nothing, but still felt uneasy. He went on down the road, to the beach.

It was quite late now, and dusk was settling. His horse was fresh, and wanted to run. He let the stallion out, and they fairly flew along the hard-packed section of beach, past Judson's place, where lights blazed along the path and the house.

Judson must be back from St. Michael, Vincent thought, with a corner of his mind. He and Mrs. Judson had gone for a few days on business, leaving his overseers in charge.

He arrived back at full dark. Tess scolded him, worry in her tone. "I was getting so anxious about you, Vincent!"

He felt hot inside, and his cheeks burned, at thought of how Florencia had detained him, how she had kissed and pressed her full ripe body to his. "I'll try to leave earlier the next time," he said. "Quintero wanted me to stay and stay. He is hard to leave."

"And the girls?" asked Morgan with a smile, giving him a shrewd glance.

Vincent flushed, and shook his head in despair.

A few hours later, he was still lying in bed, wide-awake. He could not sleep. He gazed from the bed, through the misty white mosquito netting, out the windows, pegged to catch the night winds. How she had hugged him! He had rarely touched a woman, he had been kept so busy and weary at the inn. Now—now something was weakening in him, something coming awake too—a manhood, a desire for a woman. But not Florencia, he thought. He grimaced. Somehow her boldness repelled him. Had she kissed other men like that? She seemed so experienced, her ripe lips knowing just how to press.

Or did he do her wrong? Could she have fallen desperately in love with him? He tossed and fretted, and wondered, and when he slept he had dreams about a woman in his arms.

Morgan went out with Vincent the next day, assuring Tess he felt much stronger. Vincent talked to him about the rum experiments; they discussed it earnestly.

Bernardo overheard them. "You make them this year, master?" he asked hopefully. "Liqueurs sell well, the old master said."

"We don't have the six-year rums," Morgan said patiently. "We need a lot of rum. Six-year rums, five-year rums. We need coconut liqueur mixture."

Bernardo nodded his handsome head. "Yes, yes, you do have rum, master! It's under the house!"

"Under the house? Buried?" Morgan asked, puzzled.

"No. I'll show you!"

Beaming, delighted to show them, Bernardo led the way to the house. They had noticed the slanting doors, placed so they lay almost flush with the ground. He lifted up one, and fastened it back, then the other one, revealing stairs.

He lit a lantern and led the way down into a musty darkness. He held up the lantern, and Morgan, following him, gasped in shock.

Barrel after barrel stood against whitewashed walls. They stood on the planks which had been laid on the earthen floor of the cellars. "Master keeps the rums here, good ones," Bernardo said, proudly, indicating the barrels. He pointed to one side, "These are two-year; these three; four-years are over here; five-years; and these are the six-year. The old master sold all the older rums when the ship captain come. He paid good money."

"Well, I'll be damned," Morgan said slowly. "There's a fortune here in rum!" He moved about in growing excitement, tapping the barrels lightly. The way they sounded, they were all about full, as full as could be allowed for the fermenting.

Bernardo indicated a couple shelves built against the far wall. "Coconut liqueur," he said of one set of milky white bottles. "Orange liqueur, and lime, and maybe there is also mango. He told me not to tell the black folks. They would get drunk if they found it."

"I wonder why Judson didn't carry them away?" Vincent asked, shaking his head in amazement.

"He had no space for them. He said he'd get them when a ship came in." Bernardo beamed at them happily. He had surprised his new master, and master was joyous.

Morgan was tiring, and all this was too much for him. He returned to the house to find Tess looking preoccupied and worried. She had a note in her hands, and was reading it sitting at the large desk Thomas Hamilton had used.

"I have news for you, darling," he said excitedly.

"So do I have news for you," she said, more grimly, waving the perfumed letter. He caught a waft of it.

"Your news first. Is that from Florencia Quintero, wanting us to come over?" He was teasing a little, thinking of Vincent.

He was startled at the change in Tess's face: she looked shocked; then stared at him, her face closing in coldness.

"No. Actually, it is from Mrs. Judson."

"Oh, what does she say? Read it out loud." Why did she look like that, suspicious, and rather sad. Didn't she want her brother to have fun?

Tess looked down at the note—he noted that her hands were shaking a litttle—and gripped the paper tightly.

"My dear Mrs. Hamilton," Tess said in a colorless voice. "We have but returned from a short visit to St. Michael. Just think, we met a close friend of your husband there, and Caleb and I have invited him to stay for a good long visit! You shall be surprised when you meet him! Do come over for dinner, all three of you. May I suggest tomorrow evening, about five?"

Morgan frowned. "A close friend of my husband? Who could that be? Do you suppose Captain Dillon? No, he would not stay for a long visit."

"Or Mr. and Mrs. Grantly?" Tess suggested. "No, she does not mention a couple."

"The Honorable Billy!" said Morgan, still frowning.

"Although I don't imagine he would leave his plantation so soon . . ."

They were still trying to guess as they dressed for dinner the next afternoon. Morgan didn't particularly want to go, but he was curious. And he did feel a lot better these days, though his head still ached abominably at times.

Tess seemed curiously quiet. He wondered what was going on in her mind. She seemed remote, moving about her bedroom and speaking quietly to Odette. She had not shared his bed since the injury.

Morgan finished dressing in the white trousers and white dinner jacket. It felt strange to wear a ruffled shirt once more, and he hated fastening up his throat in a tight stock. He left it more loose than the fashion, preferring to be comfortable.

He found Tess waiting for him in the downstairs hall when he was finally ready. She looked charming in her mother's blue silk with the blue sapphire at her throat. Odette beamed at her proudly, she had dressed Tess's hair in a beautiful Psyche knot with little flirtatious curls wisping around her face. Tess carried a blue sunshade against the hot sun, and a shawl for the cool evening when they returned.

"You look beautiful, my dear," Morgan said.

"Thank you, Morgan. You look—very handsome."

Vincent came before Morgan could question Tess as to why she looked unhappy. Maybe it was because they were going to the Judsons. Tess disliked them as much as he did.

Vincent also wore a white suit. Tess and Odette had made it for him, and though it was not quite so crisp and tailored as Morgan's, it was handsome. He drove them in the carriage, and Tess sat silently in the back with Morgan. She was more than unhappy, she was deeply apprehensive.

She did not trust men. All she knew of men were those in her life. Her father had left them for years, and then died on some battlefield. His picture in crimson uniform was all that remained of him.

Her stepfather had been bullying, cruel, lazy, and at the last frightening, when he had callously gambled her away, like a slave at auction to the cruel and lustful Lord Tweed.

Judson—she shuddered at the thought of him. Even the Honorable Billy on the ship would not have been adverse to a little flirtation with her.

Morgan had bullied her at first, forced her to accept him in marriage, forced himself into her bed, carried her away on a ship, been furious when she secretly got Vincent on board. It was only her newness, she thought, and the fact that she could work hard, that held him at her side.

Tess had seen the looks women gave Morgan. The Quintero girls, even Inez, gazed at him longingly. And Mrs. Judson! The woman was brazen in her attentions, patting his hand at times, clinging to his arm. And Morgan seemed to lap it up!

She did not trust Morgan. Oh, he wanted her now. But one day, sooner or later, he would discard her, she thought. He would go back to sea, tiring of the hard work on the plantation. He enjoyed the free life of the sea, she knew that from the stories he told her and Vincent.

He would toss her away when he decided he'd had enough. And she would have to go back to a life working in a pub or restaurant; some hotel or inn. She wondered how she would feel then, cast from "honored" wife to chambermaid once again, prey to any man who came along and wanted a woman for the night. A discarded woman was any man's prey, she knew that from the waterfront.

Would Vincent help her? Or would he be long gone? She had seen the way the Quintero girls looked at him.

Close as they had once been, it was no longer so. Vincent, her brother, was a man now. Yes, Vincent also would leave her. Men were like that.

Her fingers clenched in her lap. She must be strong and uncaring, grow claws again, and learn how to fight her own way in the world. Her blue gaze went over the beach, the creamy sands, the turquoise sea as it lapped the coral reefs. She would remember this as the bitterly happy time of her days. She knew it would soon be over.

Vincent turned in at Judson's house, and clucked at the horse to pull the carriage up the slight rise of the hill. Tess could not see ahead, but Vincent could. He let out a gasp as they came closer.

"Oh—my God in Heaven!" he said, under his breath. Tess sat up alertly.

"What is it?" Morgan asked sharply. "Shall I get out the rifle?"

"Depends," Vincent said oddly. "Look at the veranda. Look who the surprise guest is."

He turned the carriage, bringing it to a halt beside the wide veranda. Tess, feeling cold with apprehension, glanced toward the veranda. She saw first the graying Quintero and his two daughters, Florencia radiant in green and Inez, in rose. Then she saw Mrs. Judson in a scarlet silk gown cut low at the bosom.

She saw Caleb Judson turning to laugh up at a man, towering over him, a tall man with ash blond hair, a smartly cut gray suit, a crimson and gold waistcoat, ruffled shirt . . .

"It's Tweedy," Vincent said flatly. "Lord Tweed. My God, what does he want?"

Tess sat still in the carriage, numb with shock. Her mind raced about frantically. Morgan got down slowly, and reached up to help her down. She had a wild feeling

184

that she ought to pick up the reins from Vincent, and race the carriage away. Run, run, hide, hide!

Morgan saw the look on her face, said softly, "He can't hurt you now, Tess, don't be afraid."

She shook her head; then blindly, she allowed herself to be lifted down. A black boy came running to take the carriage, and Vincent got down also. With a man on either side, Tess approached the veranda.

The men stood up to greet them. Mrs. Judson had an odd look on her face, a set smile. Judson was grinning, his teeth yellow in his red face. Quintero was smiling politely as always.

Lord Tweed had an odd look on *his* face, but it was the gray eyes that drew Tess. That hot hungry look, that horrible lustful look, as his gaze went up and down her slim body in the blue silk dress that clung to her rounded form.

"Well, Tess, my dear," he said, and held out both hands to her. She shrank back against Morgan, and did not take the hands. Morgan shook hands briefly.

"Lord Tweed," he said with cold formality. "Well, this is the surprise Mrs. Judson mentioned. You are in Elysia for a visit?"

"I have property in St. Michael," Lord Tweed smiled, his gaze flicking back at Tess. "I was talking to a gentleman at the bank, when who should greet me but Mr. Judson. I had been inquiring if any knew of your whereabouts, Mr. Hamilton, and he heard me speak. We met, had a drink or two, and he was so kind as to invite me to stay with him—indefinitely—at least until I decide what to do with my land. Was that not most cordial of him?"

Vincent merely inclined his head toward the man. He wouldn't shake hands with that man under any circumstances. He moved closer to his sister.

Tess could not speak, her throat had closed up.

Judson set a chair for her and led her to the seat, Antoinette offered her a tall cool drink. Inez Quintero settled beside Tess, and her low-toned comments were soothing.

The Spanish girl must have sensed some shock, some fear. Her little hand patted Tess's arm gently. She spoke quietly to Tess of a Spanish dish that Tess wished the recipe for.

It got her past those first moments. But the shock was horrible. Why had Lord Tweed come way up here, away from the entertainment he enjoyed? Why, indeed, had he chosen this time to come to visit his properties in St. Michael? She was afraid, afraid. Tweed had sworn to have her—he had sworn passionately—would he be so mad as to try to come after her?

The gentlemen talked, Morgan was blandly calm when Judson spoke of his injuries. "He was attacked by blacks," Judson said. "He hasn't learned to be careful yet! His own uncle was attacked by some slaves, strangled to death."

Tess jerked sharply. They had not heard that story!

"Really?" Morgan asked calmly. "Do you know which ones?"

Judson smirked. "That one in the hills, for one, that pirate. He's a dangerous fellow! I told you about him, Louis Abaco is his name. Ex-pirate, they say! All I know is, he's an escaped slave, and a big fellow."

They went on about it, until Mrs. Judson stood up. "I see that dinner is ready, we have it so early in the tropics, my lord." She smiled at the Marquess. "The dinner is usually hot, and then we cool off with cold drinks on the veranda as the night draws the cooler airs to us."

"Splendid," he drawled, looking at Tess.

"Since you are old friends, you must take Mrs. Hamilton in to dinner. You will sit on my right"—Mrs. Judson arranged them—"and Mr. Hamilton on my left. We have so much—in common," and she flirted her long black lashes up at Hamilton.

Tess glanced instinctively at her husband. He was smiling, his teeth showing, not angry at all. That was distinctly odd. She shrank when Lord Tweed offered his arm to her. He took her trembling hand and put it in his, and marched her in to dinner in the large mahogany-paneled dining room.

"What a long time since we last met, Tess," he said, seating her, and managing to touch her bare shoulders as he did so. "How very beautiful you look, even more lovely than when I last saw you!"

He seated himself beside her. Tess had thought Morgan might make some token protest, but instead, he gave Lord Tweed only a dark look, then turned to his hostess. He had seated her, bending quite close over her, Tess thought.

Tess was so horrified and so tense, she did not taste the excellent dinner. She ate mechanically, a few bites of each dish. Lord Tweed kept bending to her, murmuring to her, in intimate fashion. Morgan was kept busy talking to Antoinette Judson.

Vincent was next to Morgan, with Florencia on his left. Judson was at the head, had placed Florencia on his right, and Inez on his left, and paid attention flatteringly to both girls. But Florencia was talking mostly to Vincent, her great dark eyes gazing up into his. Tess would look at her brother, begging for help, but he seemed to be looking down into Florencia's face, engrossed in her talk, staring at her beautiful red mouth.

All the men had deserted her, Tess thought, in dismay, leaving her to this lustful beast. Quintero was on her right, but Tweed gave her little opportunity to talk to the Spaniard.

He seemed happy enough, eating and drinking of the

host's excellent six-year rum. Tess shrank again as Tweed leaned to her. "How different you look, my darling, from the little mouse in gray, running about, trying to escape from me," he whispered, close to her ear, grinning. "Still the mouse inside, though, eh? There is no escape, my love! I mean to have you! Your husband does not care, does he? He has—other interests!" And Lord Tweed laughed aloud.

The dinner was an unending nightmare. Course after course, with a different wine or rum drink for each. Tess dared not touch any of the drinks, they were so potent. Tweed did, though, enjoying them all, tossing them off easily.

Morgan, Tess noted, also drank his, all the while leaning to gaze into the black eyes of his hostess. What were they saying? She was smiling up at him, flirting with her eyes, with her pursed red mouth.

Tess caught a few words, "One I can trust . . . neighbors . . . so pleasant to have you near . . . Mr. Judson likes you, is concerned about you . . . must come often. . . ."

Come often, Tess thought savagely, feeling beaten before she had scarce started her wifely existence. Morgan had forgotten her already! That was the way of it. They were legally married, yet here he was, gazing attentively into the eyes of another woman, smiling down at her, even touching her hand on the table.

They finally left the dining room and the party and retired to the veranda until midnight. Tess was numb with despair. Nothing would save her, nothing but her own wits! She would run away, she would go mad, she would jump into the sea!—anything! But she would not endure for Morgan to give her up to Lord Tweed! Never.

It was very late when Judson finally permitted them to call for their carriage. Vincent was silent as they drove home, his rifle cradled in his arm. Morgan was quiet for a time, then, turning to Tess, he murmured, so Vincent could not hear, "I am worried for Mrs. Judson."

"Worried?" she asked blankly. Was this going to be his excuse to desert her?

"Yes, I am sorry for her. She lives a hard life. They married her off to Judson when she was but seventeen, and he blames her for the fact that she does not have his children. He wants a son badly, she said. She seemed so— pitiful, I thought."

"Too bad," said Tess, blankly again. "She is getting older," she added spitefully. "She had best hurry—"

"She may not be able to have children," he said gravely, reproving her with his tone. "And she longs for her home in Martinique. She has not seen her family for three years."

He sat back, smoking his pipe, thinking of Mrs. Judson, and Tess could have screamed and hit him. She had had a miserable evening, she was frightened to death of Tweed, and her husband was dreaming of another woman and her desire to have children!

He would be no protection from Lord Tweed, not this time, Tess realized. She must rely solely on her own wits. She could trust no one else in the world.

12

Tess glanced up from the desk, to gaze worriedly down the lane leading from the beach to the house. The morning sunlight blazed along the line of trees. She saw the blond-haired Lord Tweed on the high black horse, and terror gripped her.

She fled back through the wide halls to the stairs. Odette, padding in on bare feet, gazed at her in blank surprise.

"Missus?" she whispered, apprehensively. "Is it Judson?"

"No, no. Worse! That man is bad," Tess said. "I will not see him. Tell the gentleman I am ill and cannot receive him. Tell him I am most sorry." She ran up the stairs, dropped a slipper in her haste, retrieved it, and fled along the front to her bedroom. She closed the door and tiptoed to the window, standing behind the curtains to watch in cold anxiety. Her hands gripped tightly together in her fear, her nails cutting the palms.

She saw Lord Tweed draw up, call out to Odette. "Is your missus home, girl? Tell her Lord Tweed is here!"

"Very sorry, master," Odette said in soft, but clear tones. "Missus is sick. She had a late night and is sick to her stomach. She's not receiving guests today."

Lord Tweed frowned, he glanced up at the windows. Tess shrank back in the shelter of the cotton draperies. She had a feeling he saw her, or knew she was there.

"You are sure missus sick?" he asked smoothly. "I would see your master then."

"Master is at work in cane fields somewhere. I do not know where today," Odette said.

Odette lied so easily, it scared Tess a little. But Lord Tweed did not frown now, he smiled. He turned the horse.

"I will come back another day," he said. He lifted the reins, and trotted off.

Tess was shaking from the memory of that cruel man. "I'll have you, girl," he had said to her more than once at the inn. "I'll have you, girl! One day, I'll have you . . ."

And he had come all this distance! Oh, God. Tess shut her eyes and pressed her hands to her face. Odette's knock at her door startled her.

Tess went to open it. Odette stared at her, at the white face and shaking body. "Missus, are you sick?" she asked fearfully.

"That man," whispered Tess. "He is a bad man, Odette, very bad. He followed me here from England. Oh, God, I am afraid!"

"We will tell the master," Odette said, daring to put her hands on Tess's shoulders, and to stroke them sooth-ingly. "The master will whip that man."

"No! He would not dare. That man is powerful,"

Tess said resignedly. "That man would kill . . ." she emphasized once more.

Odette nodded, her face somber. She probably had much experience with such men, Tess thought, and knew what it meant to be helpless.

"I will bring you some hot tea," Odette said, and ran lightly down the hall and down the stairs. When she returned, Tess had sunk onto the lovely rose silk-covered sofa, and buried her face in her hands.

Tess was in complete despair. She felt numb with fear. And Morgan—he would not even care! He had had his way with her, no doubt he was ready to discard her. In her torment, she felt sick with the knowledge that no man was strong enough or cared enough to help her.

Odette set the cup of tea beside her on a table, hesitated, gazed down at the little blond missus with a troubled look. Then her own warmhearted nature took over. She sat down on the sofa beside the smaller white lady, and took her in her arms. She rubbed her shoulders, as though the lady were a child. She whispered soothing words.

"There, there, it will be all right. Don't cry, missus. We will keep the bad one away. There will be no trouble, no trouble for pretty missus. We will take care."

"Odette, he will get me," Tess shuddered. "He said that one day he would get me. I am afraid. Oh, God, he chased me all the way here——"

"You will tell good master?" Odette said again, hopefully. "You will tell good Master Morgan, yes?"

Tess shook her head wearily. Another thought had come to her: what if she did tell Morgan, and he cared enough to fight for her? What if they did fight and clever, deadly Lord Tweed beat him with sword or pistol? Then she would truly be lost! She would lose her husband completely, and be in the possession of a man without mercy,

193

without compassion. Lord Tweed thought only of his own wants and desires, and if denied he would not hesitate to whip or kill.

"That man might kill him," Tess explained. She searched for words. "That man is quite good with a gun, or a sword. He has killed men. Odette, he is a very bad man. If he wants woman, he takes her."

"Even a white woman?" Odette asked, drawing back to search Tess's miserable face.

Tess nodded. "Not just black woman are taken by men," she said grimly. "White women can be taken too. Men are strong, Odette. And cruel."

She thought of how Morgan had swept her along with him, how he had taken her that first night of their marriage, without compassion, regardless of her pleading, her tears.

Odette murmured, shaking her head, "White women, too." She patted Tess on the shoulder in sympathy, as though saying they were sisters in trouble. Her dark lovely face was beautiful in its compassion. "I will help you, missus," she promised, and took Tess's hand and put it to her rounded breast. "I will help you, missus, I swear to God!"

Tess was a little shocked at her language and her passion, but obviously this expression meant much to Odette. Tess smiled weakly, and rested her head against Odette's shoulder. "Thank you, Odette. You are good to me. Thank you."

There was a new bond between them after that. Odette hovered about protectively, morning, noon and night, directing the maids with Tess. She must have told Bernardo of the situation, for now he was often lingering about the stables, especially in the mornings.

About three days later, Lord Tweed came again when Morgan was out in the cane fields with Vincent. He looked up at the house, and when Odette told him Tess was sick, he called out, "Tess, I know you're there. I must talk to you!"

She shrank back in the room, her hands pressed to her heart. She dared not answer. He waited, then called again, louder, "Tess, I have something I must tell you alone! I learned of it in England. I must talk to you."

It was a trick, Tess thought, after he had ridden away. Yet she found herself worrying about what he had found out, turning it over and over in her mind.

The next morning Morgan had gone to the fields and Tess was sewing on the veranda. It was a beastly hot day, and there was not a breath of wind, which was unusual. She wore her lightest white muslin gown with just one petticoat. Odette brought her hot tea, which she assured Tess earnestly was best thing on hot day.

"Cool drink will curl up your stomach," she said, moving her hands expressively on her round stomach. "It will make you sick, today. Drink hot tea with herbs. That is good for you!"

Tess smiled and thanked her. She drank the hot tea. It made her feel warm for a moment, then she felt refreshed again. She picked up her sewing, bent her head over it. She was making a new white shirt for Morgan, he needed quite few changes of clothing in the hot tropical weather.

The voice behind her startled her into pricking her finger.

"Tess," the voice said gently.

She stiffened with fear. Lord Tweed strode around the veranda to face her. He was smiling, his whip twitching in his hand. "I walked from the beach," he said genially. "I must talk to you, Tess." The smile disappeared as he saw her fear.

"I have nothing to say to you, my lord," she said.

She glanced about for Odette, but no one was in sight. He had come so silently, right up behind her. She gripped the arms of the cane rocking chair. Her mind numbed with terror.

"Now, Tess, I have always worried about your welfare," he said gravely. "I know that you are frightened of me, my reputation. But I have wished you well. What I learned of your marriage sent me posthaste on the first ship out here."

"About . . . my marriage?"

"May I sit down?"

She stared at him, her mind unable to function. He seated himself gracefully in a chair near to hers, where he could face her. She could scarcely look into that reddened dissipated face, those hot gray eyes that stared up and down her body. Oh, God, where was Odette? Dared she run into the house? Dared she run for the house bell? Would he follow her? Perhaps she was safest on the veranda, in the open.

"I will ring for drinks," she said, and reached hastily for the bell which was always on the table beside her. His hand grabbed it first, he took it and put it down on the floor beside him.

"No, I don't care for a drink," he smirked. "We will talk first. Then perhaps we will have drinks later, eh? Are you not curious—about your marriage?"

"Not particularly," she said coldly. Her hands gripped tightly together, she watched him warily, not meeting his gaze though. She feared that look in his eyes; she hated to see it there. It made her feel dirty, unclean, in danger. "We were married by a parson in the house next to a church—"

"Ah, were you indeed? The house was *next* to a church, yes. But you were not married *in* the church!"

"No, of course not. There wasn't time—" she began, stiffening. What was he getting at?

"No time. No. No time to call the banns as required by that church," he said softly, watching her face. "No time to get a proper license. No time to make sure the man was a real parson. You just accepted the word of that—that crude sailor, is that it? He wanted to carry you off, and the simplest way was to make you think you were married to him!"

Cold chills ran down Tess's spine at his words. She stared at him incredulously. Her mouth opened to refute his speech. She could not.

Yes, Morgan had carried her off. He had said he had a license, but she had never seen it. And the parson—she had taken Morgan's word that the man was a parson. She remembered seeing him slip money into the man's hand, when he had protested about marrying them.

They were not really married! Tess thought suddenly. Morgan had carried her off, making it appear legal! And she had believed him, struggling, fearful, yet so anxious to escape Ryder and Lord Tweed that she'd never doubted him. Morgan had been furiously angry when he found out Vincent had been smuggled aboard, and was sailing with them. He didn't want her to have a protector around!

It all began to add up. Lord Tweed watched her sharply as she shook her head in a daze.

"Now do you see, my dear?" he asked softly. "You are young, just seventeen, are you not?"

"Seventeen," she agreed, still thinking about the false parson, the imaginary license—Morgan had tricked her! He had abducted her, doubtless meaning only to keep her until she bored him.

"You are not even of age," Lord Tweed said. "There was no one to give you away. Ryder said he was not asked to the ceremony. He is a smart man, he would have questioned the ceremony and the license. No, the sailor would not have risked that! You poor child, your virginity's been taken, no doubt your usefulness to him is ended. He will probably discard you when he finds someone that takes his fickle attention, eh? I saw he was much attracted to Mrs. Judson."

Tess shuddered, and paled further. She put her hand to her head, she felt dizzy.

"Poor child," he said. She felt him put his strong hand under her elbow. He lifted her from the chair. "Come for a walk under the trees, it is cooler there. It's beastly hot on this veranda. Let us walk a bit. We will talk when you have recovered yourself. You must take time to think about this."

Before she knew it, he had half lifted her down from the veranda. With his strong arm around her, his warm body pressed to hers, he forced her to walk with him along the path. It was cooler under the trees. She pushed her hair back from her forehead, and stared across the dazzle of white beach with an unseeing gaze.

They walked slowly along, his arm around her. Maybe he was being protective, she thought. Maybe he had meant kindly by her. After all he had come all the way from England to tell her what had happened.

"You are still shocked. My poor Tess," the smooth cultured voice said above her head. "My poor small Tess! You are such a child about the world! I should have understood that. You were brought up in an inn on the water-front, I thought you knew more about men and the world. Instead, you are so naive, so innocent—I wish I could help you."

"You are—most kind," she said automatically. Her misery made her numb to everything but the thought, I am not married to Morgan! I am not married to Morgan! He tricked me, deliberately! I am not his wife!

"I want to be kinder yet," Lord Tweed said, a faint triumphant note in his voice. His arm closed more tightly around her. He drew her farther down the path toward the beach. "I'll tell you what—let's return to the Judsons', and ask their help. They'll tell you about Thomas Hamilton—he was a tricky character, let me tell you! His nephew seems to have been the same type."

Tess roused from the daze. It was dim under the trees, the arm around her made her uneasy. She tried to halt, he pulled her on with him imperiously.

"I must think . . . I must think . . . Please, my lord, do not pull me along. Let me think—"

"My dear, I have a horse here, he'll carry us back. You won't need to bring a thing with you! I want to protect you always, shower you with everything money can buy! What a hard life you have led!" His smooth voice was in her ears, coaxing. "I want to dress you like a queen! Jewels on your throat, and in your tiny ears!" He bent his head, and touched her cheek with burning lips.

Tess stood motionless under his touch. She was still thinking of Morgan, hating him for deceiving her, feeling desolate at the loss. The touch of Lord Tweed's lips meant nothing to her, she scarcely felt him.

Made more bold, he drew her against his body. "Tess, you have missed me!" he said passionately. "Let me show you how much I love you . . . adore you . . . want you . . ."

She shook her head, as though she shook off a fly. "No," she told him, with dull tones. "I must talk to Morgan. I must ask him why he did this, what he means to do. I must talk to Morgan."

Lord Tweed was impatient, and pulled her further under the trees. "Don't think about him, forget him! He is only a stupid seaman. I am a marquess," he said arrogantly. "I'll marry you, Tess! I promise you! Marriage! You can be beautiful when you are dressed up, and you speak well. I'll fix it all! Marriage to me! Think about it!"

She felt only a weary distaste. She hated men, and she wanted no more of them, or of marriage.

She tried to push him away. She felt his hard chest under the silk of his shirt. Shocked, she gazed up at him, saw the burning hot gray of his eyes. "Let me go, Lord Tweed," she said stiffly. "I must return home, and think on this matter."

"Think? Forget it! I want you," he said harshly and pulled her down abruptly on the grass under a sturdy pine. He yanked her dress up to her knees. Tess cried out in surprise, startled from her own deep worries into the recognition of her danger.

"Stop it! Stop it at once!" she cried out, and began to pummel him. He laughed, in a snarling sound, and bent his head to her soft round breasts. He pulled the soft muslin from them, and greedily his mouth pressed to her body. Tess cried out again, caught his hair in her hands and yanked. He was too aroused to pay attention to the pain.

His mouth bit crudely at her nipples. She cried out again, squirming under his long hard body. She beat at him with her fists, yanked at his hair, but he did not deviate from his purpose. His body lay on hers, his fumbling hand found the opening of his trousers, and for a frightened moment she felt the hardness of his flesh on her chemise.

He was pushing at her, panting in the heat of his rough desire. Tess tried to wriggle out from under him. What a fool she had been, coming to this deserted spot with him. His attack had dazed her.

"Let me go! Odette!" she screamed. "Odette! Get Morgan!"

Lord Tweed clapped his hand on her mouth. "Shut up, you fool, he's far away! I'll kill anybody who stops me."

His snarling tone was a far cry from the smooth coaxing tone of moments ago. He fell on her again, and tried to force her to his will.

Suddenly two tall shadows loomed over them. The flat side of a machete struck deftly at Lord Tweed's head. He groaned, and fell from Tess.

Bernardo yanked Tess to her feet. His face was murderous with rage. "Are you hurt, missus. Are you hurt?" he panted.

"He tried—tried—" She began to weep, shaking.

Another voice intervened. "Come away quickly. He will awaken soon." A man swung her up into his big arms, and began to carry her through the trees. Tess stiffened, staring with wide blue eyes up into the face above hers.

She had never seen the man before. He was not one of the slaves, he was lighter, taller, tall as Gamba, but not like him. He had a golden ring in one ear, his hair was short and black and curly, but he was not all black. His eyes were dark, his features strong and scowling just now.

He glanced down at her briefly. "You are foolish missus," he said bluntly. "Never go into dark woods with a man like that!"

"He said—he said—" Tess's face crumpled up, and she began to weep. Everything had been too much. She should fight this man, carrying her away with him. Yet she felt strangely like a small child, being scolded and carried.

His face relaxed. "He's clever with words, sly like a snake," he said. He nodded to Bernardo. "We will take missus to Odette."

Bernardo said something in another language, and the man answered him curtly, anxiously. Bernardo bent his head, glanced over his shoulder. The big man carried Tess through the trees, as lightly as though she had been but the child she felt.

"Who are you?" she asked nervously, trying to sit up straight.

He hesitated a long moment, but Bernardo snapped something at him, and the man shrugged.

"I am Louis Abaco," he answered her.

"Oh, you are not a slave."

His teeth gleamed suddenly, revealing a rather charming wry smile. "No, I'm no slave. I was a pirate! But I hid in the hills until my ship left. I'm no pirate anymore."

"Oh," she said blankly. He sounded complacent, calm.

This had been an incredible day. She had fallen for Lord Tweed's smooth talking. And Morgan—she was not married to him. And the men—

In her own trouble, Tess had forgotten, for her very relief had made her forget it. The two black men had rescued her, but Abaco had struck a white man a hard blow to do it. And white men did not permit that!

No black could hit a white man and go unpunished, no matter what the cause.

"Oh, dear God," she said then. "You will be in serious trouble. You hit a white man!"

Louis Abaco's face altered. "Yes, bad trouble," he agreed simply.

Bernardo had paused, turned to look back nervously over his shoulder. "That white man just got up," he said. "He sees us." There was desolation in his tones.

Tess shuddered. "Is he coming after us?"

Bernardo watched. Abaco turned around, Tess still cradled in his hard dark arms, and looked also. The marquess gave them a long stare, his hand to his head. Tess could see him, the white face pallid in the shadow of the trees. She could imagine the malignant promise of those hating gray eyes.

They had deprived him of his prey, and had struck

him. He would know them again—and he would not rest until he had his revenge. And had Tess also.

Abaco said something sharply to Bernardo, Bernardo shrugged, and answered in another language, his voice gloomy, his shoulders sagging. Abaco shook his head, then turned once more and began to carry Tess to the wide veranda of the plantation house.

She shuddered wearily. She felt sick and so very tired.

13

"Tess! Tess! Where are you! Odette, did you see where she went?" Tess heard Morgan calling her frantically.

He raced out to the veranda then halted in profound shock. He glared at Louis Abaco as he carried Tess up to the veranda. He took in her ripped white dress, her tearful face.

"My God! What have you done!" he shouted. "Put her down! I'll kill you! Are you insane?"

Louis Abaco let Tess slip gently down from his powerful arms, then turned to face the stunned white man, his arms folding before his broad chest.

"A white man came and led missus into the trees. When she screamed Odette came to tell us to go get missus," Bernardo tried to explain.

Morgan raised his fist to strike Bernardo, but Tess

cried, "No, Morgan! It's true! It was Lord Tweed. He tried . . . he tried . . . they saved me." She began to cry.

"What?" Morgan's arms had closed about her automatically, and she pressed herself tightly to his chest, forgetting for a moment her doubts about him as she sought protection in his powerful arms. "What happened? Lord Tweed was here? Why didn't you call me?"

"There wasn't time. He crept up, left his horse on the beach . . . This is the third time he has come . . ." Tess was nearly incoherent as she tried to tell him what had happened.

Odette had come out to the veranda, and slipped her hand through Bernardo's. Somberly, she watched Morgan and Tess.

Tess tried to compose herself. She drew back from Morgan. "They saved me," she said clearly. "Morgan, this is Louis Abaco, the pirate we have heard about. He struck Lord Tweed on the head when that man. . . . He tried to rape me, Morgan, and Bernardo helped get me away."

Morgan flushed, then paled. He ran his hand over his newly aching head. "Saved you? My God. That monster! Are we never to be rid of him? I'll kill him!"

Tess shook his arm urgently. "You'll do no such thing. Morgan, do you realize that Lord Tweed was struck by a *black!* And I know he saw them both. If he sees them again—"

"Even if it was that scum, it's bad," Morgan said, his thoughts calming. "What can we do?"

"Odette will know." Tess turned to her maid instinctively. "Odette, what can we do? Can we hide the men?"

She nodded gravely, her mouth drooping. "They will be killed. Judson will bring his dogs. They must get away now!"

"I reckon we best hide up in the hills, master," Louis Abaco said to Morgan, with a slight drawl in his deep

206

voice. He bowed respectfully, his dark eyes veiled. "With your permission, we will go."

"Wait," Morgan said. He put his hand to his face. "Let me think. Yes, you had best hide, for now. We will deal with him, but for now, you'll be safer away. That man won't stay forever. We'll gather some food, I'll give you some money to see you through."

They turned back into the house, with Tess still held tightly in Morgan's arm, as though he could not bear to let her go.

"Odette, you find cloth bags. We will fill them with food," Morgan said, his voice sure once more. "I'll get some coins. Tess, stay with me!"

"I'll help Odette gather the food," she said, slipping away from him, though he scowled after her. She went out to the back, and through the back door to the kitchen, followed by Odette.

Odette took down some cloth bags, and said, "We will put in bread, some sugar and salt, dried meat. That will be enough for time. Maybe some tea?"

"Yes, yes, tea, and some tin cups and a small pan to cook over a fire," Tess said. They filled the bags. She turned, to find Louis Abaco leaning in the doorway.

She gazed up at him, half frightened, half grateful. He stared down at her enigmatically, then at Odette. "We thank you for food," he said simply.

"It is for me to thank you," she said impulsively. "I will never forget how you saved me from that—He is wicked! Very bad!" She handed the cloth bags to him; he accepted with a slight smile and a graceful bow.

She had to remind herself that he was a pirate. He had manners, he had some gentleness behind that tough face and the keen dark eyes.

"You be careful, missus," he said quietly. "That man wants you. He'll be back."

Tess shivered, and her face paled. "He came all the way from England," she whispered, her voice shaking.

Louis Abaco watched her keenly. "Then he wants you bad."

Tess rubbed her cold arms, where the goosebumps had come up. She nodded, biting her soft mouth. "He swore he would get me."

Morgan came up behind them, watching them suspiciously. He held out his hand to Louis, and gave him a small bag that chinked. "There is a little money in here. More would make men suspicious of you. I will try to come up in hills with more supplies soon. How do I find you?"

Bernardo frowned and turned to Abaco. He was evidently fearful of being found by any white man. But Louis Abaco gave Morgan his slight smile. Tall as Morgan was, his red head was not so tall as Abaco's black one. "Come by the path through the middle of cane," he said stepping outside and pointing with his long arm. "There, you see the path? Cut through the cane to the hills. We will see you and come to meet you. Just ride out on your horse as though you were judging how high the cane is. Do not ride straight to us, okay?"

"Yes, I see."

"Good. We will meet you," Abaco said, his face impassive now. His hooded gaze met that of Tess and he bowed slightly. "Missus, you be careful. Stay in the house, yes?"

"I'll try to be very careful. Thank you again, Mr. Abaco."

She held out her small white hand. He looked at her in amazement, then at Morgan. Morgan did not speak. The callused hand finally took hers gently in his. He pressed it lightly and let go.

She held out her hand to Bernardo. "Thank you also, Bernardo, for saving me. I am most grateful to you."

He gulped, touched her hand briefly, in embarrassment, then shrank back, as though afraid he might be struck by Morgan. Instead, Morgan also shook their hands, wished them well.

"And hide carefully!" he added. "Cover your tracks."

The men nodded, and slipped away into the cane. Odette stared after them, her pansy dark eyes wide and wistful. Tess put her hand on the taller girl's shoulder.

"*You* got them, didn't you, Odette?" she asked gently.

Odette nodded. "I was afraid for you, missus."

"Thank you. Thank you."

Tess's voice faltered, she was shaking again, thinking of that horrible moment when Lord Tweed had her under his hard body, and was trying to—to rape her, as he had always wanted to do! She would have killed herself, she thought. She would have been so dirty, so shamed—

Morgan took Tess's hand, and drew her to him. "Darling, why didn't you tell me Lord Tweed had come? Three times, you said! Why didn't you tell me?"

"I thought I could hide from him," she evaded.

He moved them back to the house. In the large dining area he paused. He put his big hands on her cheeks and kept her face upturned to his, while he looked searchingly into her eyes.

"Darling, didn't you trust me?" he asked tenderly.

Her gaze slipped from his. "I thought . . . he might kill you," she faltered.

"I'll kill him first!" Morgan burst out wildly. "Daring to come here! Trying to rape you! Why did you go as far as the trees with him?"

"It was something he said," she finally blurted out. "I'll tell you sometime—"

"What did he tell you?"

209

"Later," she said, hoping he would forget about it. She wanted time to think. Should she tell Morgan she knew they were not legally married? Should she confront him with the truth? The little trust she had for him faded completely. "Morgan, who will oversee the slaves now? Bernardo might not return from the hills until—"

"Oh, I guess Gamba is next in line. He's smart, but too arrogant," Morgan sighed, turning his attention away from the other subject, just as she had hoped. "I'll go out and see him now. Odette, you stay with missus!"

Odette had followed them into the house, and stood near the doorway, her bare feet awkwardly together, like those of a child, one rubbing the other. Her velvety eyes were worried.

"Don't trust Gamba," she finally whispered. "He's a good worker, but don't trust him. He came from Africa where his father was a chief. Don't let him in house, master."

It had taken an effort for her to speak these words. Morgan looked at the girl thoughtfully. Tess caught his arm.

"Believe her, Morgan, Odette has been good to us! Use Gamba in the fieldwork, but don't let him in the house. There is no one we can trust, is there?" she added in desolation.

"Trust Malkia," Odette said, nodding. "She is a wise, good woman. Malkia will stay near the back door, all right?"

"All right," Morgan agreed. "We'll have Malkia stay near the house. But I think Vincent and I will take turns remaining nearby also. We can't both be in the fields at the same time. That bastard Tweed will probably come back."

Reluctant to leave Tess, Morgan finally went out to

instruct Gamba in his new duties, and see Vincent. Tess sank down into a sofa and looked up at Odette.

"Shall I mend your dress, missus?"

Tess looked down at herself in disgust. Lord Tweed had torn the skirt and the bodice of her pretty white muslin. "I had best change. And I want to wash all over, Odette. I can still feel his horrible hands!"

"I will bring you hot water," Odette said, and went off to the kitchen to heat some water. Tess went up to her room, to strip off the white muslin and her petticoat and chemise, and find another dress to wear.

Odette brought up buckets of water, some hot and some cold, and tenderly helped Tess into the tin tub. Tess felt much better when she finally climbed out, and let Odette wrap a huge white towel about her. She had even washed her long blond curls. They were much longer than when she had worked in the inn—just two short months ago! she thought. She had kept her hair short there, in short curls. It made her look younger and more childish, and the sailors did not pay so much attention to her. Also they had been easier to keep clean than longer curls. She could wash her hair hastily, and have it dry by morning.

Odette helped her dress then in the pale pink muslin gown. She threaded a ribbon through the blond curls, and patted the hair with gentle satisfaction. "You look very pretty, missus," she murmured. "And don't worry. We won't let that man come back."

When they went downstairs, Tess found Malkia installed in a cane rocker near the back door, placidly smoking her pipe. She smiled timidly at the old woman, and received a toothy grin in reply. No one could escape that keen gaze, and she was seated where she could see from front door to back, down the path to the sea, and in back out to the cane fields.

Morgan came in with Vincent from the fields for a late lunch. "We'll take turns staying near the house," he said brusquely. "We can't let Lord Tweed or Judson come close—they aren't to be trusted. Lord, that poor Mrs. Judson, having to live there! She is a nice woman. Imagine being married to that brute!"

Tess's mouth tightened, and she glared down at her plate. So Morgan was sorry for Mrs. Judson, was he? And attracted to her? She was silent during the meal.

Morgan did not seem to notice, chatting with Vincent about the work in the fields, instructing him to work closely with Gamba without seeming to check up on him. "He is sensitive and arrogant about his work. Give him responsibility, and watch that he does it right. But be careful in correcting him. Suggest, don't demand. As a son of a chief in Africa, he is probably used to having authority."

Morgan stayed in the house all afternoon. He went over some of Thomas Hamilton's account books, and came across a volume that described several experiments with different rum mixtures. He studied the results carefully.

He read some out loud to Tess, who was sewing nearby.

"Listen to this, Tess, he experimented with proportions. You take one gallon of two-year rum, and add six-year rum in a proportion of two to one. Then you let it ferment with the addition of some lime for a week. . . ."

She half-listened, smiled and nodded, while her mind went on its own track.

"Not so good," murmured Morgan. "He had to throw out that lot, the fresh pineapple turned it bad. Hmm. Wonder how he managed with the coconut . . ." He leafed through the volume, glancing at the pages.

He seemed to have forgotten that morning com-

pletely, Tess thought resentfully. He obviously cared little what happened to her. She wondered if she and Vincent should go off to St. Michael and look for work in an
inn? Would Vincent come with her? Or was he too en-
amored of the Quintero girls? Maybe he would decide to
remain with Morgan, live a life of chasing the available
women, and turn into another unpredictable, untrust-
worthy Man!

"Missus, have you planned dinner?" Odette murmured. She had appeared silently in front of Tess, dis-
tracting her from her dark thoughts.

Tess set down her sewing and went out to the kitch-
en. She looked absently at the choices and finally decided
on a small beef roast, some fresh greens for a salad, tiny
new potatoes which Odette assured her were very good
though yellow. For dessert, Tess decided to mix some
sliced papaya, mango, coconut, and orange, with a little
rum added. The men seemed to enjoy that.

She was back at her sewing when Vincent came in
looking tired from his work in the fields, but he also
seemed satisfied. "All is going well," he declared and ex-
cused himself to go upstairs. In his bedroom he relaxed
in the tin tub the maids had brought up. When he came
down, he looked dapper and fresh in his white suit. They
sat down to the lovely dinner Tess had chosen.

"Going courting?" Morgan teased with a laugh after
they were finished.

Vincent flushed. "Where, to Quintero's? No, I'm not
going near there!"

Tess glanced up at him in surprise, as did Morgan.

"Why not?" Morgan wanted to know.

Vincent shrugged his shoulders uncomfortably.
"They're so bent on marrying, it makes me sick! They
just want to get away and go back to town. And I'm
staying here!"

Tess could easily believe that of Florencia, but Inez? She thought the demure Spanish girl enjoyed her life here in the country.

Morgan did not ask further about that. He turned the subject to rum mixtures, and the two men talked about it.

Vincent patted Tess's shoulder as they left the table. "Are you all right now, Tess?" he asked anxiously. "You had quite a scare this morning. You shouldn't have gone out with that Tweed! He's a bad one, I thought you knew it."

Tess smiled weakly. "Yes, I know." She did not want to admit what had happened to shock her so much that she had lost her wits.

Morgan had not forgotten however. When she was in bed, he came in carrying a candle, and set it down beside the bed. He sat down beside her, and looked at her thoughtfully.

"Well, Tess?"

"What?" she asked, closing her eyes as though tired.

"You know damn well what!" Morgan said shortly. "Why did you go down the path to the beach with that man? You detest him! What did he say, how did he persuade you to walk that far with him?"

She was tempted to lie, but as she hesitated, he pounced: "No, don't make up a story! I want the truth!"

Feeling as though fate had caught up with her, Tess sat up in her rose-canopied bed, and stuffed pillows behind her back. It did not help when Morgan leaned over and helped her push the pillows into place. It brought him too close, his lean hard browned body, his red head that had lain on her breast many a night, the scent of his masculine limbs, not perfumed like those of Lord Tweed . . . Just clean male scent, the sweat of his body washed away by a bath, but smelling of masculinity, hard work, just himself, she mused.

"Tess?"

He thought she was going to evade again, and his tone was stern.

She sighed. "He came up behind me while I was sewing on the veranda," she began. "I reached for the bell to ring for Odette. She had been hovering nearby. But he grabbed the bell, and said he had something to tell me—about our marriage."

Morgan's brow crinkled in puzzlement. His eyes were shadowed by the dimness of the room, she could see only the outline of his strong cheek and jaw in the candlelight.

"What about our marriage?" He did not sound upset or wary.

"He said—" she hesitated again, then plunged. If Morgan sent her away, it might as well be sooner as later. "He said our marriage was not legal!"

"What? He's crazy!" Morgan said with conviction. "Or leading you on. Our marriage was legal—and still is."

Tess was surprised. Lord Tweed had been so convincing, had so many facts lined up.

"What did he say, Tess?" Morgan asked again. "Come on, what else did he say?"

"Well, he said that I was seventeen and that someone should have signed for me. And he said the man who married us wasn't a parson, and the banns were not called in church. The license you said you had—I never saw it —wasn't legal because you cannot get on so . . . so fast—" Her voice broke then and Tess stared up at him with wide-eyed fear. Would he be furious at being found out?

Morgan turned his head and drew a deep sigh while

215

Tess went rigid with fear. Would he beat her now? Would he stop pretending to be nice and kind?

"Tess, do you remember the night when we were gambling? Your stepfather, Lord Tweed and I?"

She nodded dumbly. How could she forget that horrible night?

"I was going to protest the way they treated you—like some piece of property," he went on, his voice incredibly gentle. "Then—I had another idea."

"What?" she quavered. He put his hand on her clenched hands, and it was big and warm and somehow reassuring.

"Well, I decided that you were not being treated well there. I admired your spirit and your—your beauty, Tess," he added softly. "I had been talking to the captain of the *Marietta,* Captain Dillon. He had mentioned something to me about going to the islands with a wife, that the life was lonely and hard, and I would miss having a woman. Some men turn to the slave women, and live a lazy licentious life."

She was silent, sitting stiffly, holding his warm hand.

"So, I knew I was sober, and the others were not. I got a damn good hand,"—he smiled in reminiscence—"and decided to gamble on the fact that they were drunk and excited. I kept quiet, and let the play go on. And I won you. I got up from the table, saw you and your brother to the stairs, and went out. I found a lawyer, and he instructed me what to do: we roused a law clerk, and he made out the license. It can be done, when a sailor is going to sea."

"Ohhh—" she breathed in doubt, not sure whether or not to trust him. "Lord Tweed said—and he is one who deals in law—"

"I trusted *that* lawyer," said Morgan firmly. "The next morning, I guessed you would try to escape. Your free wild spirit had intrigued me, and somehow I knew you and Vincent would make the attempt to get away. So I came down early, and found you in the stables," he ended with a chuckle.

"I could have got away!" Tess's blond head tossed defiantly. "If you hadn't got up so blamed early!"

"Are you sorry, sweetheart?"

She was silent, not wanting to make him furious. Yet—she wasn't sure. If she had gotten away, it would have been to another hard job of work, long hours, cold lodgings, and more lustful men to fend off.

"Well anyway, we went to the parson's. He looked over the license, decided to accept it and some money for a fee to overlook the delay of several days—"

"So it wasn't legal!"

"Of course it was," Morgan said growing impatient. "It is up to him whether to accept our word that we are free to wed, or to wait for several days to see if there is any just impediment. I was sure you weren't married, and I knew I was not!"

"Oh," Tess said, meekly now.

"Is that everything? Oh, the fact that you were seventeen. Ryder was probably your legal stepfather. But he was no thumping great shakes of a father," Morgan said with contempt. "And besides, I had a paper saying he would give you to the winner of a gamble!"

Tess didn't know what to say. She didn't know whether he was telling the truth, or whether he could spin as good a story as Lord Tweed.

"Do you believe me, Tess?" Morgan asked softly, putting his arm about her. "Move over, sweetheart, I want to come to bed!"

Yes, that was all he wanted, she thought bitterly. She moved over reluctantly, and he lay down beside her, drawing her into his arms. "Still have doubts?" he asked gently.

She nodded reluctantly.

"Well, how about this? We cannot leave now for St. Michael. However, I must go there soon. After the cane harvest which should be done in early June, we'll go with Vincent to St. Michael. We will need to pay bills, stock up, see what uncle left in his bank balance, buy you some dresses and some suits and shirts for us—and we'll get married again."

Tess gasped. "Get married again?" she asked, in a small voice.

"Sure. They have a grand cathedral there, folks tell me. Anglican. We'll stay a couple of weeks. I'll tell the priest there that you don't feel married because it wasn't in church. We'll go to a lawyer, get a proper license with engraving and all, and have a church ceremony. Might be fun, at that!" he chuckled.

She was silent, really dazed and bewildered now. Was he making fun of her? Or did he really mean it? Would they actually go to St. Michael and have a cathedral wedding? Or—did he mean to take her there and discard her publicly?

What was he really like? She wished she knew.

He rolled over, to try to search her face in the dim candlelight. "Tess? If that doesn't satisfy you," he said, laughter in his voice, "we'll get married every damn time we go to town! I'll marry you over and over again, until you're blasted certain I mean what I say! All right?"

"Oh, Morgan," she said weakly, and he bent to her swiftly. His mouth pressed on her opened lips, and he gathered her right into his arms.

Gradually her doubts drifted away, under the feel of his hard urgent body pressed to hers, his hands moving over her, the lips that searched for her cheek, her earlobe, the pulse of her slim throat. He groaned, and lifted off the nightdress that covered her to her knees. He flung it to the end of the bed, blew out the candle, drew down the mosquito netting, and lay back.

"Oh, Tess, I want you so much," he said softly.

"I want, I want" said all the men in her life. Selfish, thinking only of their own desires. I want— I must have— I want!

Her bitter thoughts were being drowned out though, by the hard arms about her slim body. His lips roamed from the soft white throat, down to her rounded breasts. She could not even think now of the way Lord Tweed had tried to take her, how his greedy lips had clung to her flesh.

Morgan was there, holding her tenderly, his mouth moving lovingly from arms, to shoulder, to breasts again. He touched her red pointed nipple, and tugged at it softly. She felt the now familiar weakness in her thighs, the burning desire flaring up in her in response to his urgency.

Morgan drew back a little. His hands caressed her hair, he threaded several locks through his hand. "Your hair is silver in the moonlight, and you are sweet as jasmine," he whispered.

She started, her eyes opening in surprise.

Morgan smiled down at her tenderly. "Odette pointed out the jasmine bushes near the house. Have you seen them? I smelled their fragrance, I think she put some in your bath water, darling. I know they call you silver jasmine—my lovely darling. It suits you—"

Then he had bent to her again, and his lips burned a line from her throat to her thighs. The sheet was flung aside, they did not need the covering on the hot night.

She felt his lips and fingers go here, there, all about her. He kissed and caressed her ardently, and she felt herself melting under his gentle attack. He kissed down to her ankles, then up again inside her thighs to the softly vulnerable places.

Tess could not restrain a moan, and her knees came up. Morgan settled himself on her, and pressed to her warm body. "My darling, my lovely silver jasmine . . . oh, you are so fragrant and beautiful," he whispered against her mouth. He kissed the silver blond hair, light in the moonlight on the white pillow, kissed the dark eyes closed in passion.

She felt him come to her, slowly, deliberately, easy with her, yet an urgency driving him. She wanted to struggle, yet something inside her was pushing her up to him instead. Her hips rose and met his, and they came together with a rush. She was all soft and open for him, and he came in, and held there—

"Ohhh, darling, sweetheart . . ." he whispered, and rained hot kisses on her throat as they came together again, again. "I can't hold back—oh, darling, are you ready also?"

He was big and hard-muscled, and at first she had fought him, the first nights with him. She had called him brute and bully. Yet, now she wanted him! Wanted this closeness, wanted him inside her!

What was the matter with her? Reluctantly, as he pressed himself to her, she began to admit to herself. She was coming to love him. Love? What is that? This strange hot need, this anguish for his body to be hard on hers, this desire that would not be satisfied until he had drawn her with him into a blazing fulfillment?

Love? How could she love him? She could count all the reasons she should not love him. Yet, she was beginning to love him, to need his body next to hers, to think of him when he was not there, to miss him and want him.

And in moments like this, when his body plunged to hers, and her hands gripped at his broad back, and he moaned in her ear, and said fierce love words to her—she wanted to answer him. She wanted to please him. She wanted to fight for ecstasy and release as he did. She felt the tremors begin in her, and she shifted uneasily. He followed, relentless and mindless, his hands held her hips, and she had to take him again, and then the waves began in her, beating higher and higher—

They finished together, and it was like fireworks, glowing in a dark night sky, it was blazing hot candles shooting off in all directions, it was red fire behind her eyelids and a burning in her thighs: quenched by the slowly pulsing need of him, the quickened throb of his desire.

They sighed back to earth together, and she found herself lying half across his body as he gasped for breath. "Oh, my pretty love," he was murmuring. He said something in his own Gaelic tongue, some words she had heard before. They meant darkly beautiful things, and he had told her once what they were.

She lay silently on his quickly rising and falling chest, and her hand stroked over the wet thick hairs of the chest and down his thighs. He was her man, whether they were legally married or not, and she had a desolate feeling that she was his—as long as he kept on wanting her. She would not be able to tear away. It would be like tearing her own flesh.

14

Antoinette Judson arranged the silver carefully on the long dining table. Never before had such a high ranking person visited in their home. She wanted everything to look perfect and had set out her best china. Although Caleb liked the heavier flowered china, Antoinette remembered the way it was at home on Martinique, and wanted to re-create an elegant effect. Hence she used the best French bone china. It was pure white, lined with a thin rim of silver about each plate and cup.

The tall silver candlesticks with the red beeswax candles were waiting to be lit. The red hibiscus flowers were floating in the low silver bowls at each place. The tablecloth was white silk. It was fringed with lace, as were the matching napkins. She was satisfied that the red, white and silver created the sparkling clean look she wanted.

The maids were shuffling in with her bath water

when she went to her bedroom upstairs. Antoinette looked with veiled contempt at her maid, Leonie. The plump girl was her own age, but after five children—by Caleb—she appeared an old woman, her body thickened, pendulous breasts hanging loose under the thick cloth wrap of gaudy flowers.

Antoinette poured some perfume into her bathwater. It was the last of her favorite lavender. She sighed. She *must* go to St. Michael, or go mad! Would Caleb take her there on his next business trip? It scared her to death to be left alone in this huge echoing house with dark slaves shuffling about. The overseers did not really have them in control, and all Caleb's whipping just produced more sullen looks and blank faces.

She shivered, and put the thought away. The Marquess was charming when he wanted to be. Imagine, having the Marquess of Tweed in their home. He stared at her sometimes, paid her compliments while Caleb glared and tried to smile complacently as though the compliments were for his taste in choosing a wife.

Men, thought Antoinette. Their possessions, their slaves, their wives, their jewels, their money, their cane. It all belonged to the man. Children were for bartering for the best marriage, the most dowry; just like slaves.

Her mouth twisted bitterly, she sat idly in the cooling water, thinking of her girlhood on Martinique. She had gone to school for five years, learned to read and write, to draw and play the piano. Men came to their house, praised her beauty, stared at her. And how she had preened! She had begged for more beautiful dresses, more daring costumes for the balls, not knowing why she was on display—until Caleb had bought her.

What she had endured since then! From being a favored, petted, spoiled child she had become a wife at seventeen. And when she was nice to Caleb, he gave her presents, more clothes, perfumes, jewels. When she tried to cross him, he whipped her like a slave. She had soon learned not to cross him, not openly.

But she had not given him a child. They had tried again and again. She had lain stiffly on the bed, enduring the grunting and painful entry to her soft body. But he had not been able to give her his seed in such a way as to start a child. In a perverse way, she was glad.

She didn't want to please him!

He had given Leonie five children, five little babies only a year or two apart. The girls were the same age, Leonie had been given to Antoinette on her marriage.

Six months later, she had discovered Leonie in her husband's bed. When Antoinette had screamed at him, he had laughed. "She pleases me more than you, missie!" he had sneered, his flushed face smirking.

Antoinette got out of the tub, a little maid helping her. She was chocolate brown, wide-eyed, young, slim. "What is your name?" she asked idly.

"Bettina, missus," murmured the little girl, with a shy smile.

"How many years have you?"

"Thirteen years, missus," said the girl.

"I don't remember seeing you before," said Antoinette, puzzling her brow in a frown. She seated herself gracefully before the mirror, shaking back her thick dark curly hair. "Leonie? Where did she come from?"

"Master buy Bettina in St. Michael," said the heavy voice of the maid. In the mirror Antoinette caught a quick glance of triumph from Leonie.

She let them brush her hair, first Leonie, then Bettina, stroking the long thick locks until they lay in shining order. Then Leonie rolled the curls deftly into the six thick sausage curls from the top of Antoinette's head, dangling to her shoulders. She showed Bettina how to do it; the little maid was absorbed, her face shone.

Antoinette was wondering about the triumph in the usually blank face of the maid she had known all these years. She caught a glimpse in the mirror of the thick unlovely body, the double chin, the pendulous swing of the breasts. Caleb never wanted Leonie anymore, he sent her back to her cabin, to the children, at nights.

He sent her back—He didn't want her—Antoinette almost spoke aloud with her shocked understanding. Leonie had done this on purpose! She had deliberately let herself get terribly fat so the white master would not desire her!

The Frenchwoman stood up, allowed Leonie to draw the purple muslin gown trimmed with purple velvet over her head, and down over her slim rounded form. She felt the fingers deftly fastening the buttons down her back. She was a good maid, quick, smart.

Very smart, acknowledged Antoinette gravely. So smart that she had realized what to do to make Caleb Judson stop wanting her. She had five children, they took up much time, she wanted no more—and she hated Caleb Judson. So she got fat.

Antoinette sighed a little as she walked down the winding stairs to the ground floor. She checked the table once more, replaced a drooping hibiscus of flame red with another one. She nodded to the kitchen maid coming in with a tray of drinks.

"I'll take them to the veranda," she said, and took the tray from her.

"You want drink, missus?" asked the girl softly.

"Bring me a drink of lime, no rum," said Antoinette. She wanted a cool brain at all times. She pretended to match Caleb drink for drink, but the maids had orders not to add rum to her drinks. She drank much fruit juice, and that kept her cool in the tropical weather.

She put a smile on her red mouth, then moved out to the veranda. "Drinks, gentlemen?" She smiled, and set the tray between them on the small table.

The Marquess rose languidly to his feet. Caleb made no pretense of getting up. "You look charming, Mrs. Judson," said Lord Tweed. "That shade of purple suits you." His bold eyes admired her, his back to Caleb Judson.

"Thank my husband for his good taste," said Mrs. Judson. "Shall I join you also, or are you talking business which you believe would bore me?"

She glanced toward Caleb, he nodded to a chair curtly. She settled herself in a chair beyond them, nodded to the maid to take away the empty glasses.

Her look went to the cool trees, the straggly garden. It looked a mess, but she did not care. She longed only to leave this horrible place. She had enjoyed it at first, being mistress of her own home—until she realized that no one was really mistress over Judson: he was the master, the brute, the bully. Gradually, she began to give up all pretense of interest in the gardens. If it looked bad enough, maybe they would go back to St. Michael.

With a start, she realized that Caleb and the Marquess were not only drunken, their speech was wild. "I'll kill him," said Lord Tweed. "Daring to have his slaves strike me! I have wanted to get my hands on him—"

Her dreaming thoughts stopped abruptly, she listened intently, sipping idly at the lime drink, and gazing at the trees and the beach as though all her attention was on the cooling evening.

"I looked him up in St. Michael. He is heir to Thomas Hamilton, all right," said Judson grudgingly. "The solicitors have sent all the papers, and the bank is just waiting

227

for him to come in, before turning over all the money there."

"You said they had jewels hidden away?"

"Yes, and money, I'll be bound. Didn't bother to search for it after Hamilton's death, I thought I had plenty of time, damn it! I wanted the cane harvested, I had to round up the slaves from the hills and whip them back to work."

"And the little slave girl—you got her?" asked the Marquess silkily.

Antoinette was straining to hear their low voices, pretending not to, as she sipped. She felt herself tense and excited. Things were going to happen now! She felt it in the air, like the tense feeling before a storm of thunder and lightning, when the harsh winds whirled all around them.

"No, damn it! They hid her until Hamilton came. That Odette—" The yearning in Caleb's voice would have made Antoinette smile contemptuously, but she did not dare. He was a fool about women! An absolute fool! He thought himself so virile that no woman could resist him. But little Odette had evaded him for all this time. "She grew up here, I watched her grow into a beauty. Round form, beautiful face, big eyes. I want her! I offered to buy her from Hamilton—he cursed me, damn him!"

"Maybe the sailor has his eye on her," suggested Lord Tweed thickly, gulping at the glass of cool rum and lime.

"The sailor? No, I meant his uncle, Thomas Hamilton. Stuck-up man! His nose in the air most of the time, his voice so haughty. I could tell you a thing or two about him. After his wife died, he stayed to himself, but I know—" The voice lowered, Antoinette strained to hear. "I know he had a slave mistress! And I think Odette is their child! She is part white, and she was born on that land."

Lord Tweed whistled in surprise. "That Hamilton? Well, he had an eye for a pretty piece. But did he want his own daughter as well?"

Caleb Judson shrugged. "Probably," he said.

Antoinette sickened. The men took it for granted that any woman was theirs—even a daughter! Her throat felt tight.

"Well, you and I can manage together," said Caleb, after a pause. "We are agreed then? We'll kill Morgan Hamilton. Vincent Pritchard will be no problem, he is a thin thing, a poor excuse of a man," and the contempt in his voice told his feelings.

"Right. Then I'll have Tess, you can have Odette."

"I want the whole plantation and the slaves," said Caleb, eagerly. "You don't want them, do you?"

"What would I do with a damn plantation on an island in the middle of nowhere?" asked Lord Tweed. "No, I'll take some of the jewels and money—and Tess. That's what I want."

Antoinette was trying to catch her breath after this, when a maid came out on soft bare feet, and tried to catch her eye. She nodded, and rose to her feet, holding to the back of the rocker for a moment.

"Gentlemen, may I interrupt your discussion? I believe dinner is ready."

She saw Caleb's black look at her, and added hastily, "But it can be put back if you would like another drink." She smiled with an effort.

"I for one am hungry," said Lord Tweed. He rose to his feet, staggered, and caught at the chair before proceeding to the door, to offer his arm to his hostess. "Come, Mrs. Judson. What have you for this evening? I swear you manage well to provide in this desolate wilderness."

"I thank you, my lord, you are most complimentary," she said nervously. They proceeded to the dining room. Caleb sank down into his chair, and put his hand to his head. He must be very drunk.

She thought they scarcely tasted the delicately prepared filets of freshly caught fish, followed by the sliced roast pork and orange sauce. She was the only one to have fruit for dessert, a slice of mango glowing ruby red in its thick green rind. She ate it slowly; they were drinking again, wine this time.

Her mind was whirling all through dinner. Did they mean it, or was it drunk talk? To kill Morgan Hamilton, and his brother-in-law. Lord Tweed to "have Tess." Did they think they could get away with this?

The men rose from the table. Antoinette left the rest of her fruit, and rose with them, hastily. She hesitated at the foot of the table, uncertainly.

Caleb glanced over his shoulder at her. "Bring a bottle of brandy out to the veranda, Antoinette, and tell those blacks we don't want to be disturbed. Bring three glasses."

"God, it is hot as Hades in here," said Lord Tweed, mopping his flushed face with his handkerchief. It was then, as he turned, that Antoinette saw the blood red scar, a fresh one, on the back of his neck.

What could have happened? The men had been talking all day, into the night last night, then again this morning and afternoon. Lord Tweed had been white with rage at times, and Caleb had soothed him with a sort of triumphant tone.

Antoinette took the full brandy bottle from the cabinet, and locked the fine satinwood cabinet once more. She set three bulbous glasses on the tray, and told the maids, "No bring drinks, no come, until I ring. Understand?"

They nodded, their wide dark eyes wondering. She went out to the veranda, and set the tray down. The other tray, the glasses and bottles had disappeared, the maids had wiped all down fresh. A cooling breeze had come up from the sea, and it was comfortable sitting on the veranda, with the air flowing straight through the opened hallway from front to back.

The men were silent for a time, as she kept refilling their glasses and pretended to drink from her almost empty glass. She hated brandy. Her father had drank and gambled; that was how he had lost most of their fortunes, she had learned after her marriage. Her older sister had married well, a banker on Martinique. But when Antoinette came along, the money was almost gone, and her brother-in-law coldly refused to throw good money after bad, as he expressed it. No, her father could bail himself out.

Caleb Judson had come along, and for a price, he had bought Antoinette, and Leonie, and taken them to his plantation. He wanted a hostess, he said, and she was beautiful. And young and stupid, she thought bitterly. She had not liked him, and had tried to refuse him. Her father had struck her and said, "You'll marry the man I tell you, missie!"

"Mrs. Judson will have a lovely little part to play in our drama," Lord Tweed said unexpectedly. They had turned their chairs as they had come out, and now all three sat in a semicircle, where they could see her face in the dusk.

"Drama?" she asked lightly. "It sounds—amusing." Fear was in her heart. Caleb was grinning in the way he did when he was excited and about to whip someone, or rape a girl, or perform some other atrocity. He enjoyed violence against a helpless person.

"I have started the play moving," said Tweed, laughing a little, his gray eyes blazing hotly. "I have told Tess Hamilton—as she is now, poor child!—I have told her she is not legally married. They married in haste, as I told Mr. Judson, and she is but seventeen. So she readily believed me, she is so naive and young."

"So the next move is to make sure she knows Morgan Hamilton is interested in another woman—you, my dear Antoinette," said Caleb Judson, grinning at her. "You will flirt a little with him, you will stroll in the garden alone with him when he is here with his pretty wife. I want her to see you together."

A cold panic struck her. Antoinette managed to smile. She had learned how to hide her emotions rather well, but sometimes the hate shone from her dark eyes, and she could not keep from showing how much she hated for Judson to touch her. When she flinched from him, he snarled, yet he enjoyed it also; "conquering" her, he called it. It made him the more violent with her.

"Flirt with Morgan Hamilton?" she asked, as though idly, her finger running about the rim of the thick brandy glass. She hoped they would both get so drunk they would fall asleep fast, and allow her some peace tonight and tomorrow morning. She wished she dared ride out alone, on horseback, as she had ridden with her sister years ago along the beach, feeling the wind blow through her loosened thick hair, feeling alive and wild and free.

"That shouldn't be hard for you to do. Mrs. Judson admires Mr. Hamilton," sneered Caleb Judson to the Marquess. "They have their heads together, confiding secrets half the time!"

"That boorish sailor?" asked Lord Tweed in vast contempt. "It must be truly boring for you, madame, if you are driven to admire such a crass fellow!"

"But he is not! I find him gentle and understanding," said Antoinette quickly, then saw her mistake.

Her husband's grin was humorless, a mere stretching of his mouth. He glared at her, with small eyes narrowed so she could scarcely see the pupils. She felt cold in the night wind.

"Ahah! You are attracted already!" laughed Lord Tweed, glancing from the woman to her husband, his mouth cruel. "It should be an easy role for you to play, then!"

"I would prefer—not to flirt—with him," said Antoinette, desperately. "What is the purpose? I do not—even like him." She saw her mistake again, fear driving her on. "I mean—he is courteous enough, but he is only a sailor, as you say. I try to make myself polite to everyone who comes to our home—as Caleb wishes—"

Lord Tweed laughed. Caleb smirked.

"Nonetheless, you will play the part," said the Marquess, tossing off the brandy, and reaching for the almost empty bottle. He filled his glass, careless of leaving any for his host. "This is the plan. You flirt with him, draw him on. One night you will make an assignation with him, your husband will find you together—in bed? As, no, my friend," and he laughed again at the expression on Caleb's face. "No, not so intimate! I think it will be enough to find them—say, in the gardens? In the moonlight? We shall make sure it is light enough for your bullet to find its mark. Then, the brother-in-law, Vincent—for he will come running, I am sure, to find out what is happening. Thus we will be rid of both of them." He shrugged, and drank the rest of the glass of brandy.

Antoinette felt frozen. She could not do it, she must warn him. Her glass went automatically to her mouth, to try to hide her face, which was not always in control. Oh, God, these beasts, she thought. These horrible beasts!

Presently she rose, and smiled. "Well, the hour grows

late for me. Shall I send out another bottle of brandy for you?"

Her husband got up tipsily, and reached for her arm. "You have not said you will do as I said, Antoinette," he growled. His arms were hard, as always, his fingers closed about her wrist so that she felt the blood stopping. He always had his way. But she hated him so, she detested him—

The words left her lips. "Why not? I will flirt with him—only how far shall I go, Caleb?"

"You will flirt with him, draw him into the gardens, as I said! Little fool, don't you understand?" he raged. Lord Tweed was laughing in a drunken fashion.

"Oh, she is not averse to flirting with the sailor!" crowed Lord Tweed. "She likes the man, it is evident! Let us find them in bed together! She might as well have some pleasure from it—and he also, before he dies! And no one would blame you for killing him then!"

"You want me to bed him?" snapped Antoinette, her patience going. "You want me to do that? Well, whatever you say, my dear husband! I will obey you as always! Gladly!"

"You little slut!" he snarled. She saw the hand rising, but he held her with the other hand, and she could only turn her head. He struck her hard, on the side of her head, and she fell as he released her.

Her head struck the veranda post, and she slumped to the wooden floor. She knew no more for a time.

She came to consciousness, a vast pain in her head, an ache in her shoulder, and water dripping down her face. She finally opened her eyes wearily, not recalling what had happened. Was it Martinique, her wedding night?

She saw Leonie's broad face first, the face blank and calm. She was bathing Antoinette's head, gently, the cool cloth moving over her face and throat. Beyond her, Antoinette saw her husband, standing with legs apart, a sort of gloating curiosity in his stance.

"She's awake," he said over his shoulder, and tossed off the brandy glass. "I'm to bed. What about you, my lord? Another drink?"

"Lord, no, I've had enough to sink a battleship," he said. "I'm for bed if I can find it!" And he laughed, and weaved his way to the staircase, hanging onto the railing as he lurched upstairs.

Antoinette put her hand to her head. It throbbed and burned, it had been cut open. She began to remember what had happened.

"Leonie," said Caleb. "Send that Bettina to me tonight. I've been watching her, and I want her—tonight. Wash her and send her up."

He went to the stairs, without stopping to find out if he would be obeyed. She heard his heavy boots thumping up the stairs.

"Bettina?" whispered Antoinette. "That child? Oh, Leonie—what can we do?"

Leonie shrugged her heavy shoulders. "Send her, washed and ready," she said tiredly. "I go to her now."

"But she is only thirteen—so young, so innocent—"

"Master want her. You all right, missus?" Leonie got up off her knees and looked down at her. A flare of pity shone briefly, then sparked out, as though she had no time for emotion. "I go then."

Antoinette lay for a while longer on the sofa. She heard the movements of the house, the heavy boots flung aside as the men prepared to retire, the low rumble of voices, the respectful tones of the menservants. The two black men came downstairs and left the house by the back, as always.

Leonie came in, dragging Bettina. The girl was sobbing. Antoinette could not move. She heard them go up-stairs, a door open, voices, a door closing.

And then she heard the screaming begin, the pleading. She put her hands to her ears, but the screaming of the girl came through her hands, through her ears, through to her aching head. She bit her lips until they bled, thinking of the scene above her head.

"Thirteen," she muttered. "Oh, God, God, punish him! God, hurt him, as he has hurt others! Oh, God, is there no end to this?"

The screaming finally stopped, she heard the creak of the bed, the violent creaking sound. She got up unsteadily, and went out to the veranda. She sat on the rocker stiffly at first, until the coolness came to her and dulled the throbbing ache of her head. Finally the house was silent. Still she rocked there rhythmically, trying not to think, trying not to feel, trying not to feel pity. A woman without emotions was safer, she knew that.

When the moon had dulled, and the night birds had ceased their calling, she crept up to her bed in the room next to Caleb Judson's. The door was closed between the rooms; she thanked Leonie for that, she knew the maid well.

She did not sleep well, because of the throbbing pain of her head, the wild thoughts. She lay awake, staring into the distance, through the white mosquito netting, and her fists were clenched, until they finally relaxed.

She must watch and wait, be obedient, be careful. One day, one day, she would find a way, and she would escape from him. She must escape, or go mad. She could not endure this all her life. There always must be a way to escape.

15

The week passed very slowly. Morgan was worried and could not hide it. The Marquess of Tweed lingered, and Morgan had caught glimpses of him riding a black stallion on the beach, rather close to Last Hope.

No word came from the Judsons. Caleb Judson would be glad to find something against Hamilton, only what would he plan? How far would he dare to go?

He hoped Bernardo would have sense enough to remain in the hills, and not come down to fish or swim in the cove. Or try to see Odette. He had seen the girl staring at the hills, her mind far away, her face dreaming. The two loved each other; he knew they had a small hut together.

His worries drove him to action by the end of one week. He gathered up some dried meat, salt, molasses, tea, and a few coins. He told Tess, "I'm going up in the hills to see Louis Abaco and Bernardo. Vincent will stay close to the house today. Don't go out, please, Tess, and be careful. Tell Odette to stay with you all day."

Her frank blue eyes showed her worry. She might not love him, but she was concerned for him, and that comforted him a little. If she was wary of him, she had reason: the long years at the inn dogged her, had taught her to distrust all men. He realized that, yet grew impatient that she could not trust him.

He adored her; she was so lovely and so genuine. She worked hard, he could not stop her from driving herself. But she bloomed now even more than she had in England. There was a light golden tan on her blond face, her hair shone more silver than gold from the sunlight, and her blue eyes sparkled with health. She had gained a little weight, because he kept her from any hard physical labor. He had told Odette not to let the missus do any heavy work, and Odette had agreed, smiling.

"Missus is lady," said Odette. "She should work less, yes? Maybe she shouldn't come kitchen?"

Morgan simply groaned. "Is she *still* cooking? Well, so long as she doesn't get too hot and tired, all right."

But Tess bloomed both in work and leisure, and Morgan fell a little more in love with her every day; enjoying the nights when she lay quietly in his arms, not trying to fight him. He loved to caress her, to hold her, to make love to her, enjoying the small body under his lean hard one.

At long last, after many hard years, he had a home, a wife, a farm. One day he would even, God willing, have a son. However, he must remain on guard. He did not trust Judson, not for a moment. And he did not entirely trust Quintero. If they ganged up on him, he would have to jump quick to defend himself.

He went out, spoke to Vincent earnestly. It seemed

that he had matured quickly in the weeks since they had come. He accepted responsibility, was eager though shy with recommendations for improving the rum and the molasses, took over willingly any job Morgan designed for him. And the slaves seemed to like him, warily, as they liked Tess; and Morgan hoped that they liked him.

Some slaves, such as Gamba, held aloof, their faces blank and their black eyes watchful. The field slaves took a lot of direction and watching. The house servants seemed gentler, more amiable, yet even they seemed to watch carefully to see what kind of master they had.

Odette sometimes chatted away to Tess, and Tess was able to communicate with her more easily all the time. They sewed together, cooked together, and Morgan had even caught Tess reading to Odette from some books of Thomas Hamilton, and from the gazettes. Tess had been rocking on the veranda, Odette sitting on the porch steps nearby, her dark gaze fixed on the blond girl's animated face, as though she drank in the words.

"I'll stick close today," said Vincent. He pushed back his blond sun-bleached hair, and blinked in the sharp sunlight. "What if—what if you don't get back by dark, Morgan? Shall I come looking for you?"

Morgan frowned. He half trusted Abaco, and he trusted Bernardo as much as he trusted any black. Still— "Get Odette and Malkia to take Gamba and try to find me. You stay with Tess. Don't leave her alone. Lock yourselves in with rifles and pistols, no blacks with you, and wait. Don't come for me. I'll get myself out of any jam."

Vincent shook his head in doubt. "We have to stick together, Morgan. I can't see Tess staying behind locked in the house if you're out here in trouble. She's too crazy about you."

Morgan's heart leaped. He wanted to demand, How do you know that? What proof have you? Do you really think Tess loves me? But he stopped himself. Vincent knew only that they slept together often, that they were married. Maybe he just assumed that Tess did love him.

But he felt lighter and happier as he got out the black stallion and prepared to ride into the hills. He put the food in the saddlebags, and went out into the cane fields. Remembering Abaco's warning, he rode this way and that, casually, always making for the foothills of the blue hills in the west.

It was late in the morning when he reached the foothills. He had come to the far edge of the sugarcane fields. He had passed his own blacks working in the cane, with Gamba standing over them directing, ordering the carts to proceed to the mill.

"Good work," he had said to Gamba, and the man almost smiled. But not quite. The dark suspicion of his eyes never ceased.

A couple of other slaves looked up from their work, paused, and grinned at his shouted greeting. One even waved. Morgan waved back. "Remember! Party at end of cane!" he shouted to them.

"Cane party?" one asked of Gamba.

He had promised them a cane party, the same kind that Thomas Hamilton had always held. When the cane was all cut, the last ground in the mills, and the last cauldrons of molasses bubbling, all work ceased for several days. They ate, drank rum, danced, sang all the nights and days, Bernardo had said, his teeth gleaming with a big smile of pleasure at the thought. The big cane party was looked forward to by white and black alike.

It was the big celebration of the year, bigger than Christmas. For it meant the end of the long, exhausting, hard work of the harvest. They could pause in the work, they could rest and be merry, rejoicing in the huge harvest. The master gave them new clothes to replace those torn and worn by the hard work of the fields. He gave them a few coins to chink in their pockets. Sometimes one man was allowed to go into town to buy sweets for them all, or the master would bring back special goodies.

After that, they would rest. Sometimes the master went to St. Michael to arrange for the shipment of his molasses and rum, or the purchase of new barrels, or just to get away from the plantation for a time. He would leave his overseer in charge, and they had permission to sing and dance in the evening, and to sleep late mornings, and to go fishing. It was a good time, after the end of cane in June.

With the master's return, and the late summer coming, the work began again. The cane fields had to be cleared of weeds and loose stalks, the rows dug, the cane stalks laid down to grow into more cane. The watering must take place if the season was dry. By autumn, the cane was growing, there was more weeding between the rows, and the work increased. The chickens were taken care of, vegetables grown, pigs bought; maybe some cows bought for slaughter and the meat dried over hot fires.

At Christmas, there was a brief celebration, the master gave parties for the white neighbors, and a party for his own slaves. He gave them nice gifts, presents.

But it was not like cane harvest: singing, dancing, drinking! Hopefully, Bernardo had carefully explained it all to the new master. They all wanted the new Mr. Hamilton, Mr. Morgan as they had come to call him, to carry on the traditions of old Mr. Thomas. And with nice missus, Silver Jasmine, at the house, they had hopes of this, for with her smile and gentle words she had won some of their hearts. She was nice, not cruel; she never ordered whipping.

Morgan rode more warily now, searching all around. Abaco had assured him they would see him coming, and come to meet him. But maybe they simply drank and slept.

So suddenly that the horse jerked at the reins, a form loomed up in front of Morgan. He pulled the horse to a stop. The two men had come out of the bushes and stood still there, shadowed by the short trees and bushes, and a couple taller mahogany trees of great girth and height.

"Mr. Morgan, you came," Bernardo said eagerly. He looked thin and anxious. "That man, he came for me?"

"No," said Morgan. "Nobody came, we watched. I brought more food for you. Did anybody come up in the hills?"

"Nobody came up hills," said Bernardo. He caught the horse's reins and patted the long black nose affectionately as Morgan swung down. "I miss horses, work," he said. "Everyone at house is healthy?"

"Yes, all are well. We miss you, Bernardo," Morgan said quietly. "Odette looks for you, with her eyes to the hills."

The man bowed his head, pleased, his eyes shining. "Thank you, Mr. Morgan," he whispered.

Morgan turned to the taller man in dark blue. His head was arrogantly erect; he was about six feet four inches, Morgan estimated; as tall as Gamba.

An object in the tall man's hand caught Morgan's attention. It was a long black spyglass like those used by sailors.

He nodded at it. "Was this how you saw me coming?" he asked.

Abaco nodded, his teeth gleamed briefly in a smile. "Abaco sees much from hills," he said significantly.

Morgan hesitated, then nodded. "I would go with you up in hills, and talk," he said. "We are too near the edge of the cane, someone might see us. I do not ask to see where you hide," he added quickly.

Louis Abaco nodded briefly, and led the way up a dim path into the thick undergrowth. A few tall trees grew, mahogany and satinwood, bamboo and flowering flame trees, the ones they called flamboyant, with their scarlet tops. But most of the growth was small, bushy, some flowering.

Bernardo paused as he led the horse, and pointed to one group of bushes. They had small white flowers with tiny yellow dots in the center.

"Jasmine," he said. "Like the missus," he added eagerly.

Morgan bent to smell the flowers. It had the same scent he had smelled on Tess's fragrant skin after a bath. Odette must be putting the flowers into her bath water.

"You call her silver jasmine," said the pirate, watching and listening, his lean face intent. "Why is this?"

"Odette says this," said Bernardo. It seemed to give him great pleasure to speak of Odette. "Odette says new little missus is like jasmine, with hair like silver in moonlight. Small but strong, the flowers are like perfumes from city." He pointed to the bush. "Nobody destroy. She grows strong. Everybody likes."

"I see. Silver jasmine." Morgan nodded. He drew another deep scent, thought of Tess, so small and sturdy, gentle yet tough when she must be, her little face determined when she learned how to load the rifle.

They moved on up the hill, the going tougher now. His heavy boots crushed the bushes and small plants. They wore sandals of woven grass, moving along silently.

He felt more than a little uneasy as they moved into the shade, and paused to rest under a towering mahogany tree. Before him was a clear view of the valley below, and Last Hope plantation. He could just make out little dots of figures moving in the cane. He looked across the shorn fields, and the few fields still being cut with green tops waving in the breeze, to see the outlines of the white house under the flowering trees.

Abaco handed him the spyglass. "Look with this," he said quietly.

Morgan took it with a murmur of thanks, and began to scan the fields. He adjusted the long glass, and began to make out the features of the blacks who worked. He saw Gamba, his dark features intent, point to the fields and wave his arm at one man, evidently directing him to the new area. Then he walked over to a laden cart, inspected it, pulled at the ropes that held the cane, and nodded importantly to another black, who began to tug it from the field.

Morgan looked further, at the white house. He made out a flash of scarlet skirt, thought Malkia was moving about near the back door. Then there was a lighter color, and he adjusted the glass, and saw the blue muslin dress and the face of Tess, as she came out the back door. She moved to the kitchen, Odette just behind her. The girls were talking animatedly, waving their hands, and then Tess laughed. He could almost hear the clear ringing of her laughter. And Odette laughed with her. Then they disappeared into the kitchen.

"A strong glass," said Morgan, pleased as he handed the glass back to Abaco.

"Abaco sees much," said the man slowly, giving him a significant look. "Sees much in two years here."

"They tell me," said Morgan, settling himself more comfortably on the thick grass and flowers, "that you rode a pirate ship."

"Pirate," said Abaco definitely. "Captured in Spain. I rode much, fought, earned money. But the captain's whip. Always the whip."

Morgan waited but the man said no more. Morgan said hopefully, "I rode ships in England's navy. We fought the French. In Spain, France, down near Egypt and Africa. There was much fighting, there were bad times."

The pirate's eyes gleamed, he sat up straight. "Did you fight much? Good, good. One must fight."

"Why?" asked Morgan. "Caleb Judson?"

Bernardo sat up anxiously, looking from one to the other. But he did not interrupt them.

"Yes, Judson—a very bad man. He smiles, while shooting you in the back. A bad man."

"Who did he shoot in the back?" asked Morgan. "Slaves?"

"No. For his slaves: the whip, the dogs, chains, beatings." Abaco's face twisted. "He tried to chain me! I said no, not a slave: free man!"

"He chained Abaco," said Bernardo, "and made him work for him. But Abaco got away! Not a slave, but a free man! He escaped from pirate ship, hid in hills until pirates went away. Mr. Hamilton talked to him: 'you are free, no man shall chain you.'"

"He took the chains from my feet." said Abaco, staring firmly at Morgan. "Mr. Hamilton said, 'You are a free man.' I am *free*. Black, but free. No man shall chain me!"

"Were you a slave in Spain?" asked Morgan.

"No! A free man. My father was white, Spanish. He freed me."

"And on the pirate ship, were you a slave or a free man?"

"Free man! I shared in booty," said the pirate proudly. "I fought equal. Captain was mean, but he said, 'You are no slave, you have part of gold.' He gave me gold. No chains!"

"Then you are a free man," concluded Morgan, nodding his head. "I agree with my uncle. You are not a

245

slave, and no man has the right to chain you and make you a slave."

Abaco's face glowed, Bernardo beamed at him as proudly as though he had freed the man himself. There was silence for a little time. Abaco seemed to be pondering some question.

Morgan was about to get up and go back home, when Abaco spoke again.

"I will tell you truth. Judson killed good man, Mr. Thomas."

Morgan jerked. He looked at the man in shock. "What did you say?" he snapped.

Abaco nodded. "I watched from the hills, all the time. Never want to be captured again. Watch. See Mr. Hamilton come from house, go into fields at evening. He talks to men, comes out of fields, goes back to house. I see Mr. Judson ride up on horse. He ties horse to tree, creeps up in cane. I watch."

Morgan caught his breath. "What—did you see?" He had seen for himself how far the spyglass could reach, how clear it was to see to the house.

"I saw Judson creep up, Mr. Hamilton going to house from that side." Abaco pointed with his arm straight and the finger pointed, as a slave would never dare to do. The slaves pointed with their fingers in a downward motion, not daring to point straight out. He pointed to the side toward the Judson estate. "He took a rifle, I heard shots. One, two, three shots. Mr. Hamilton fell down, then slaves running; Mr. Judson, back on horse, riding like crazy home."

Morgan pushed his hand through his red hair. It was cool in the shelter of the trees and bushes, but he was sweating. "Why? Why did Judson shoot my uncle?" he burst out. "He had no reason! They both had big plantations, all they could want—"

Bernardo interrupted, "Judson wants Odette!"

Morgan stared at him incredulously. "Odette? He wanted her so badly, he would kill—?"

"Judson wants Odette," repeated Bernardo. "He said to Mr. Thomas, 'I want Odette. Here: take money, jewels.' Mr. Hamilton said 'No, no, she is dear as daughter to me.' Mr. Judson said, 'She *is* daughter to you!' He called Odette names. Mr. Thomas said, 'Go away, or I whip!' Odette cried, Mr. Thomas touched her head: 'No sell, no sell, no sell.'"

Morgan looked toward Abaco, the man stared back impassively. "You know this?" he asked.

The pirate shrugged. "Only what I hear. Odette is part white, I know this. Whose child she is—" His shoulders lifted again. "What does it matter? She is a slave. But Mr. Thomas was good to her, and Judson hated him. I saw him shoot."

"What happened then? When was this?"

"Before Christmas," said Bernardo. "We planted, we weeded, we worked in the fields. Mr. Thomas talked about going to St. Michael to get presents for Christmas. But he got bullets in the back first."

"Bullets in the back!" exclaimed Morgan, his mind whirling. "Judson told me Hamilton was strangled by slaves!"

Bernardo shook his wooly dark head vehemently. "Not strangled by slaves! We liked Mr. Thomas, good man! He said 'No sale, no sale,' to Mr. Judson. We didn't want to go to Mr. Judson!"

"Then what happened? You worked for Mr. Judson?"

Abaco said gravely, "A long time hidden in the hills, afraid. Odette came up, crying. 'Hide me please, please!' We hid her. Mr. Judson said we would all starve, he yelled from cane fields. He said to come down, work. Some came, worked. But he hurt them, he whipped; but

247

he fed good. Malkia said to work hard and keep mouth shut, maybe a new Mr. Hamilton come. But all the time, whip, hurt. Some blacks said it's better to die in hills than work. They hid again. Judson cursed. Then Mr. Hamilton came, the new Mr. Hamilton." Abaco did not hide his satisfaction with that event.

Morgan sat thinking, his chin on his knees. The other two watched him for a time, then politely turned to gaze out over the valley below. He noted how strong and sure of himself Abaco was. No, the man was no slave, he had lived free and wild, not like a hunted slave.

He was handsome too, tall, with the dark blue garb on him, the red cummerbund fresh and wide around his thin waist. His hair was neatly trimmed, his beard short. And his eyes were keen. He kept himself well, though he probably did not eat too lavishly.

That reminded him of the food, and he was hungry. He got up, opened the saddlebags, and took the food from them. "We will eat," he said. "It grows late in the afternoon. The sun is high."

"Come up in hills more," said Abaco, and led him to a small clearing. There were the little pans and a fire, burning among some cleverly arranged rocks. Abaco set out a tin to heat the meat in water, while Bernardo filled the pot to heat for tea. Morgan took out the fresh vegetables and peeled and washed them, and arranged them on a tin plate.

They sat down together and ate hungrily. They gave Morgan one cup of tea, and shared the other tin cup. When their hunger and thirst were taken care of, Morgan had decided what he wanted to do.

Morgan thought the ex-pirate was honest, but he wanted to be sure. Judson told quite a different story, a story that could be true: that Thomas Hamilton had been strangled by slaves. The body had lain in the earth somewhere for more than three months. It would not be pleasant, but Morgan had witnessed death before, and burial.

"Where is my uncle buried?" he asked finally. "Is there a graveyard with his remains and that of his wife and three children?"

"Judson sent slaves to bury Mr. Thomas near cane," said Abaco. He looked at Bernardo. "That's all I know."

Bernardo offered, "Malkia say, Mr. Thomas went to St. Michael to put flowers on graves of wife and children."

"So Thomas Hamilton is buried here, on the land?" Morgan brooded. The pirate might be right. If the death had been natural, by illness, or by strangling by slaves, the man would have been taken to St. Michael for burial near his wife. He had probably purchased a plot there, and it would have been normal for officials to have been sent for, and the body taken to the St. Michael's plot for burial. But Judson had not wanted officials to see that body! So he had probably buried him, and made up some story to satisfy the officials when he reported the death. He would have had to report the death, the man would be missed, the neighbors would talk, the bankers in St. Michael would have sent to inquire, and Judson would not want that.

"Can you show me his grave?" asked Morgan.

Abaco nodded. "I know. I marked it with a few stones."

They went down the hillside again, and Abaco pointed out the place. It was near the cane fields, not far from where Morgan had left them to go up in the hills. He studied the plot. No marker, no headstone, even of wood.

"We will need shovels," he said thoughtfully. "I will get shovels. Will you help me?" he asked.

Bernardo stared, Abaco nodded. "We will help," he said.

Morgan rode back to the house, got the tools he needed from the shed, and told Tess briefly that he had an errand that might take a few hours. "Don't worry about me, I may be back after dark, but don't worry. Lock yourself in with Vincent."

He rode back with the shovels and a pick to break the hard ground. The three of them worked at it. Morgan had taken off his jacket. Dusk had come, and it would not be easy for anyone to see them from a distance.

He had also brought a lantern, but left it unlit until they had dug deeply enough to find the body, wrapped only in a blanket. Bernardo went down into the grave, and handed it up gently, for the blanket was falling to pieces, and the body had rotted.

Controlling his nausea, Morgan bent over the remains. Abaco lit the lantern and sheltered it with his body. Morgan turned over the body. The flesh had fallen away from the bones.

Bernardo crawled out of the shallow grave. His face was gray, he shuddered and crossed himself, muttering something. He did not like this task.

Morgan didn't like it either, but it had to be done. He searched with his eyes and with his hands until he found the things he had been searching for. Two bones were shattered, and the small black bullets still lay in the remains. Three bullets, and one had broken the spine dead center in the middle of the back.

"Three bullets," said Morgan somberly. He showed them to Abaco and Bernardo, then put them into his pocket. He wrapped the remains, with Bernardo's help, in a fresh blanket, and they lowered the body back into the grave, and threw in the remains of the old blanket after it, before shoveling the earth back in.

"Was a service said over him?" he asked.

"No prayer," said Bernardo somberly. "No words."

"Then I'll recite the service of the dead. I did at sea," said the ex-sailor. He and the ex-pirate and the slave bowed their heads, and Morgan recited solemnly the service of the dead, commending the body of his uncle to the earth and into the hands of the Lord.

It was finished, and he had what proof he needed. He did not know what he would do with the proof: he would ponder that.

He thanked the men, and they departed for the hills. Morgan went back to the house, but felt he could not enter it. He felt filthy, his flesh crawling with what he had done. He asked Malkia to have two men bring down his tub and fill it with water. Then he washed himself thoroughly on the back veranda and splashed water all around, before drying himself and putting on fresh clothes.

His mind was racing with all the possibilities. His uncle had been murdered by a man who had been his neighbor for years. Morgan could go the same way, and Vincent, leaving the women to the sadistic pleasures of a lying murderer.

He went in the kitchen and looked at the food. He didn't know if he could eat.

He went upstairs by the back way, and lay on his bed for a time. Finally Tess came up. "Morgan?" She stood in the doorway. "Are you sick?"

"Sort of," he said.

"Can I get you something to eat or drink?"

He groaned. She came to the bed at once. He had scrubbed his hands and nails to get the dirt out, but he still seemed to feel those light fragile bones in his hands: all that remained of a man who had been living only a few months ago.

He had the problem of whether to tell her or not,

and decided not to. Tess was so open and quick of temper, she might immediately say something to Judson, before Morgan was ready.

Reluctantly, Morgan got up. "Just tired, honey," he said. "I'm coming down now."

He made himself put on soft grass slippers and come downstairs to the dining table. Resolutely he put from his mind the scenes of that day and evening. Vincent was watching him curiously, anxiously.

He could not make light talk, but he made himself eat a little, and drink some one-year rum, and comment on the work of the day. Vincent took over, and discussed what to do with the new barrels of rum they had, and where to place them in the cellars.

It was only during that night that Morgan found release, in the dreams and nightmares from which he woke, sweating. But his mind felt more at ease. He was alive, and the whole incident was a terrible warning to him—not to trust Caleb Judson.

16

Vincent had been very quiet at breakfast. This was not unusual, he didn't talk much. And in the morning, they all thought of the day's work, the problems, as they drank coffee and ate fried pork and eggs, fresh bread and jam. Tess had prepared some ripe mangoes, and they enjoyed those also, digging into the ruby flesh of the delicate fruit.

Finally Vincent spoke up. "I had a note from Mr. Quintero yesterday," he said awkwardly. "He said he misses our visits. He realizes we are busy, but—he wants me to come over today."

He glanced questioningly at Morgan. Morgan looked back at him with a little grin. "Are you willing to risk it?" he joked.

Vincent blushed under his tan. "Well, I do miss them," he said frankly. "They are always nice to me, and they're gentry. I mean, at the inn, people that had their rank—they wouldn't have looked sideways at me, would they? But they are really friendly and kind."

"At the inn, you worked far below your position," said Morgan, understanding him. "Ryder had you and Tess working like servants, which you are not. I'm damn glad I got you both away."

"You wouldn't have taken Vincent," burst out Tess, her blue eyes sparkling with anger, "if he hadn't got aboard ship, and signed on!"

"Are you still holding that against me?" Morgan asked her furiously, rather hurt.

Vincent said at the same moment, "He didn't know me, he didn't know we were close, Tess. You can't blame him—and he has been darn good to both of us!"

Tess sulked, which she rarely did, her lip curled. Morgan felt in despair that for every step forward there was a step backward, where their relationship was concerned. He would think they were getting close; then she clammed up, or pushed him away when he tried to make love to her.

Well, he didn't have time to figure her out today. He said to Vincent, "Why don't you go over for the day? But take your rifle and watch out. Ride clear of the trees, and be sure to start home long before dusk."

Vincent grinned boyishly. He was an attractive lad, and just growing up, Morgan thought. He worked hard, and deserved a day off. "Thanks, Morgan. I'll be careful. I thought I'd take one of our bottles of coconut to Quintero, and see if he thinks that has fermented enough."

"Do that, and get his advice on it. He's a smart man about rums. You haven't told him about the barrels in the cellar, have you?"

"Not I! He doesn't need to know about that," said Vincent indignantly.

Tess said, "Quintero and Judson probably both know about the barrels. That was part of why they were so eager to take over the plantation, wasn't it?"

Morgan told her, "I think Hamilton kept it quiet, how much he had. They probably knew he had some, but Bernardo seemed to think the cellar stock was a secret. He never took guests down there, nor ever went down when guests came here."

"Is the stuff that valuable?" asked Vincent curiously.

Morgan said cautiously, "Probably come to some money in England or the United States. However, I think I'll sell off only the six-year stuff and get the best prices. I think it's worth it to save the rest, and age it here; and then get a really good price for it when it reaches six years. I want to experiment with the liqueurs also."

They talked about that for a time, then Vincent went out, to saddle up and go over to Quintero's. Morgan decided to remain near the house, since he didn't trust the silence from Judson. The man was probably planning and plotting something, it would be like him. The Marquess of Tweed would not remain on the island of Elysia forever, and he would be smarting for revenge before he departed for more lively places.

Morgan wished he would hurry up and go. Judson was enough to bother about. The man was older, and if he had once been a good neighbor to Hamilton, that time was long gone. He had gotten greedy, wanting money, jewels, and all the slaves, especially Odette. Probably nobody had thwarted him for so many years, that the man had gone into a rage when Hamilton refused to sell Odette to him.

Morgan was looking over the shorn cane fields near the beach, from the line of pines, when he heard horses' hooves on the soft sands. He glanced up, his hand on the pistol at his belt. His mouth tightened as he recognized the big stallion of Judson, but he relaxed again as he realized the rider was not Judson. The rider was a woman, riding sidesaddle, gracefully, her veils flowing out from her head and shoulder.

She drew nearer, raised her hand and called, "My dear Mr. Hamilton! How are you?"

It was Antoinette Judson, startling in a purple riding habit and violet veils over her dark curly hair. She drew up beside Morgan, and smiled down at him, her scarlet mouth beautiful. He could smell her strong perfume— gardenia, he thought it was.

"How are you, Mrs. Judson?" he asked.

She gave a little grimace. "Well enough," she said, and gazed off to the sea. Her dark eyes grew sad. "I wish—I wish I could talk frankly to—to someone like you. I am so mixed up—"

Morgan immediately felt cautious. He knew Judson probably mistreated the woman, but it was not his concern. "Have you parents?" he asked casually. "Why don't you go to visit them?"

"My mother is dead, long ago," she said, in a low reproachful tone. "Father—sold me to Mr. Judson when I was seventeen. He was deeply in debt, and Caleb offered to pay off some of the debts in return for—me—I learned of this later, of course." She gave a deep sigh.

He studied her lovely face warily. He felt sorry for her, yet—would Judson use his wife for a trap?

"May we not talk for a little time?" asked Mrs. Judson, wistfully. "I am so weary, my mind goes round and round, and I cannot think. I have not slept well—" There were indeed deep shadows under her eyes.

"Of course." He looked about. "At the beach near the rocks there? We could tie up your horse to that stunted pine."

She smiled, and he helped her down. She seemed to

half fall into his arms, and that made him more wary. He led the stallion to the small pine, and tied it securely. Mrs. Judson had followed him, her booted feet soft on the sands.

"Oh, this is beautiful," she breathed. "I think this is the loveliest stretch of beach along the coast, on this side. Of course, the leeward side is much lovelier, with more beautiful sea. Do you ever go over there?"

Morgan continued with his caution. "We landed there, that is all we have seen of it. It seemed quite attractive at the small port of St. John."

"Oh, St. John! That is deserted——" She waved her hand gracefully. "I thought of St. Michael, and the beautiful beaches there. Much more civilized! They must have more than two hundred houses there, a splendid cathedral. I long to go again. We have dear friends there."

"You should go and speak with them," he said significantly, as she stood with feet slightly apart, to gaze out dreamily at the sea. "They could advise you."

She shook her shining dark head. She had pulled off her violet veils impatiently, and they hung from one hand. Her dark curly hair hung about her shoulder, a few curls wisped on her forehead. She was not so carefully groomed, so sophisticated as she seemed when a hostess in her own home. Today she looked younger, less reserved, more eager.

"No, no, they are really Caleb's friends. They drink together, we discuss the sale of rums." She grimaced. "But they are pleasant, and we laugh, and they hold a dance for us—it is very gay. But I have not seen them for a year."

He waited for her to get to the point. She turned from her contemplation of the sea.

"Oh, Morgan—I am so unhappy," she said in a low tone. Tears had come to her dark eyes. "Caleb is so—so brutal. And he is drinking very much these days. Lord Tweed encourages him, and laughs when I try to stem their drinking. I am afraid of them both. They—talk and plot together. I have heard them—"

"Oh, what about?" he asked. "How to get the Hamilton land and slaves?"

She caught her breath, her eyes went huge. "You know?" she breathed in a wispy voice. "You know what they—". She put her fist to her mouth. He could not tell if she was acting, or if her terror was genuine.

"I would imagine anyone could guess," he said dryly. "Judson is after all my slaves, he was working them when I arrived. And it was with difficulty that I—persuaded—him to leave my property. And he wants young Odette, we all know that. Why? Why is he after her so strongly?"

"He is very lustful," said Antoinette Judson in a low voice. She gave a delicate shudder. "He has seduced most of the women and the girls he owns. It gives him pleasure to be—the one who chases—to pursue a girl. You understand?"

"Not really," he said bluntly. "I'm but a poor sailor-man. I know some chaps who would chase a girl when in their cups, who have been to sea for a year. But someone who chases women all the time, who cannot be satisfied with a beautiful wife—no, I cannot comprehend that. Is he mad?"

To his amazement, she nodded. "I think so. I think he must be mad. He is so brutal, he gets no pleasure from —having me—unless I scream—and fight—" She shivered, and pressed her hand to her face. "You do not know what I have endured—in these seven years," she whispered.

He did look at her with some pity then. "I can imagine, ma'am. However, you should not be confiding in me. I advise you, return to your father, or to some friends on Martinique. Tell them of your belief that your husband is mad. It may give you some protection under the law."

To his horror, she came to him, put her hand on his chest, and gazed up at him with brimming eyes. "Cannot you help me, Morgan? Cannot you aid me? I am so afraid of him! Would you hide me?"

He gulped. She seemed to sag against him, and as he put out one hand to steady her, she promptly put her arms about his neck. "Now, ma'am," he said. "Now, ma'am! You must not do this!"

"Oh, help me, help me! I feel faint at times for worry of my life!" and she began to cry. She pressed her face against his chest, and her arms clung tightly, frantically. "You must help me, you are the only strong man I know!"

In spite of his doubts, he could not but be flattered. "Ma'am," he said, "you must go to Martinique to your family. They will assist you. Do let me go!"

She lifted her face. It was lovely even when streaming with tears, her dark eyes seeming to melt as she gazed up at him. Her beautiful blue black hair fell over his arm, and the scent of her strong perfume was overwhelming. In spite of himself, he felt sadness for her, and even a little desire. She was so beautiful, so appealing. He put his arm around her and stroked her back. She shivered, and drew closer to him.

"You will help me, won't you?" she whispered. "I cannot get away even to St. Michael. Judson watches me like a hawk, like a cruel falcon. If he even suspects what I feel—about you, how I long to rest in your arms—he would whip me as he does the slaves!"

Morgan was shocked, yet stirred. "You cannot feel anything toward me," he began.

"I do, I have from the first. I felt that you were a man who would be strong but gentle, firm and sheltering, yet so sweet. Oh, Morgan, kiss me—" She put her hand behind his head, raised her lips to his, and before he knew it, their lips were meeting in a long kiss.

He felt as though he were going under the waves, a wave of perfume, a wave of desire, a wave of compassion and need. He met her kiss with his own. His hand bent her back gently, and he kissed her throat as she frantically kissed his cheek, his ear, any part of him she could reach.

Then he remembered Tess. His wife! Tess. He shoved Antoinette Judson from him, though she tried to cling.

"You will shelter me, you will help me get away," she whispered, her eyes shining.

"I cannot, ma'am. Send for friends, your family. Beg their aide—" he said.

Her dark eyes reproached him sadly. "Judson opens all my letters, should I be so foolish as to try to seal them before he has read them," she said. "Oh, Morgan, pray help me."

"I must go, I must return home," he said. "The sun is high. You will be missed also. Come."

He tried to turn her to the horse. She clung to his arm, she begged him. "Do not push me away, dearest Morgan. Oh, promise that you will aide me, so that I may rest with that thought—"

"I'll help you if I can," he promised, seeing she would not depart without some assurance. "But I can't say what—"

"Thank you, darling," she whispered, and grabbed him about the neck again and pressed her lips to his passionately. He felt a weakening sensation in his hard lean body as her slim rounded form pressed to his. She was so perfumed, so soft, so sensuous—

"Now, you must go!" he said, and pushed her to the horse. After he had helped her up, she smiled down at him, and dashed away the tears from her face.

"Thank you, Morgan. I knew I could depend on

you. You will come to the house—sometime soon? Or shall I come to you?" she asked softly, her dark eyes glowing.

"No, do not come," he said harshly, reality returning. "You must not. Do you want your husband to kill me?"

"He must not know about us," she said, her face paling. "If he knows of our love—"

"We are not in love," said Morgan desperately. She only smiled down at him, and touched her hand to his cheek in a tender caress.

"Until we meet again," she whispered. "I know you will save me—I know it!"

She took the reins from him, and turned the horse. In a few minutes she was galloping along the beach back toward her plantation.

"Whewwwww," sighed Morgan. He went to the water and scrubbed his face and neck. He saw the red gloss on his hands, and grimaced. She was a powder keg ready for a match, he thought, and he didn't want to be in the vicinity. She was trouble waiting to happen.

Yet—so pretty, lovely, even beautiful, with the soft light in her eyes, her thick dark hair falling back from her face as he kissed her, the desire in her mouth, the warmth and looseness of her in his arms—

Tess was on the veranda, sewing on some white stuff, when he came up the path slowly, among the trees. She did not look up at him when he came. Her face was hard, she sewed in angry little jerks that threatened to break the thread.

"Hello, Tess," he said, attempting to sound at ease. "Ready for lunch?"

"At eleven in the morning?" she snapped. "Hardly. Something got your appetite up?"

He stared at her guiltily. "What's on your mind?

Worried about Vincent?" He stood in front of her and took the sewing out of her hand. "Come inside, and talk about it."

"No," she said, and tried to snatch the sewing back. Her face was flushed, her blue eyes blazed with anger. "I saw you down at the beach. I was walking down to talk to you about something. I saw you, Morgan Hamilton. Don't try to lie about it. I can smell her perfume all over you too!"

"I told you not to leave the house alone," he said without much conviction.

"And now I know why!" she snapped. "Do you meet every day, or just when she can get away?"

"Are you jealous?" he asked softly, a little pleased in spite of his guilty feelings. "I bet you are, Tess. You're jealous of her—that woman is married to another man—"

"Doesn't bother her much, does it?" Tess asked. She stood up, and stalked into the house. "I'll see about lunch. A man is always hungry for food—and other things!" she called back over her shoulder.

He followed her in and flung her sewing down on the desk. He grabbed her shoulders. "Now, Tess, I'm going to explain, and you're going to listen! That is the first time I have ever met Mrs. Judson on the beach—"

She stood rigid under his hands. Her nose crinkled. "I can smell her perfume, it makes me sick," she said.

He shook her in some exasperation. "Listen to me! She is scared stiff of her husband—"

"After seven years of marriage? Does she want to leave him for you?" asked Tess, a dangerous softness in her tone. Her blue eyes blazed up at him. "Go to her, I don't care. Vincent and I can get jobs in St. Michael, easy enough. I can cook and sew and scrub, and tend bar, like I did before. Don't let us stop you!"

He gazed down at her, loving her for her sturdy spirit

and unwillingness to be daunted. Her blond curls tossed, her eyes sparked fire.

"I'm crazy about you, Tess, I won't ever leave you," he told her gently. "I love you, I guess I did from the first. I won't ever leave you, don't fret about that—"

"Who is fretting?" she snapped. "Not I! Marriage is just a form of slavery for a woman! I'd rather be free! You just let me go, Morgan Hamilton, and see who frets!" She struggled to pull free of his hands.

Angered, he yanked her closer to himself. Her words stung. A form of slavery! Was that how she saw their marriage?

"I'm not letting you go!" he yelled at her, though she was pulled close to his body. "You just get that out of your little head! You belong to me, and I'm keeping you! I married you—"

"Not legally!" she shot back.

"Oh, yes, it was legal!" he cried. "Damn it, are you going to believe that drunken lord before me? Tess, I tell you—"

"Tell me nothing," Tess yelled right back. "I think all men are liars! They want, they want, and they get and get, and they lie and lie! I don't believe a one of them!"

That did hurt. All the months of trying to build up her confidence and trust, and she could still yell that at him. He picked her up bodily in his arms, and made for the winding stairs in the back. She kicked and yelled at him; Odette peered inside, put her hand over her mouth, and disappeared again.

Morgan carried his little wife up the stairs, into the hallway, and back to his bedroom, while she kicked and yelled at him all the time. He was glad Vincent wasn't around. Her brother might have tried to stop him, and Morgan was in no mood to be halted.

He carried her into his bedroom and shut the door

with his booted foot. He took her to the bed, and dropped her. She bounced on the husk mattress, and flailed her arms and legs, her face pink with rage.

He fell down on top of her, and held her down, when she tried to get off the bed. "No, you don't. You're staying right here until you say you believe me."

"Then I'll be here until hell freezes over!" she shouted, and said several more words she had learned in the Cornish bar.

"Shut your mouth!" he said severely. "No lady talks like that." And he pressed his mouth to hers hungrily. She had such a pretty pink mouth, with no lip gloss to smear all over him.

"I'm no lady!" she cried, as soon as he let up. "I told you—I'm no lady! I'm a bar girl, I'm a bar girl! And you made a bad mistake when you fooled me and took me on that ship. You'll be sorry, you'll be mad sorry you carried me off. I won't be a lady—you'll have to go to your nice-nicey Mrs. Judson for that—with her dainty fingers pouring tea, and grabbing at you!"

Morgan shut her mouth again in the only effective manner he had ever found. She yelled and squirmed when he let her up, so he kept on. He rolled over with her on the bed; she was on top, and pounding at him with her fists. He warded her off, caught her fists in one of his hands, and rolled her over on her back again.

Her dress came up, he yanked it up further, and opened his trousers. He was so wild for her, he could not be gentle. The desire that had welled in him when Mrs. Judson pressed her soft body to his had set him off. He had to be satisfied, though Tess squirmed, and yelled at him, and cried out when he entered.

Morgan held her steady under him, and pressed to her. He found her soft for entering, in spite of her fighting words. He pressed tighter, and held her, and pressed his mouth against her slim tanned throat. The pulse was racing there, and he moved his lips over and over it, loving the feeling of her, and the soft smell of her jasmine-perfumed body.

How pretty she was, so soft and dainty, and little, his little Tess, his fiery little Tess. He pushed again and again, breathing heavily, and finished in her, and rolled off. His arm was over her, and his booted leg.

When he had caught his breath, he leaned up. "All right, Tess?" asked hopefully.

"Go to hell!" Her voice was muffled against her arm, she had her arm over her face. He scowled down at her uncertainly. The encounter had drained his anger and passion. He felt at peace. Why couldn't she feel the same?

"Tess?" He tried to pry her arm down. He was stronger than she was. He got the arm down, and a glimpse of flashing blue eyes, and a tear-wet face. Then she scrambled up, and past him, and off the bed. "Tess, you come back here!" He got up, realized his trousers had come half off, and he was trapped, hobbling.

She paused in the doorway to her room, to send one more blast. "Haven't you had enough for now? Are you just like Mr. Judson?" She slammed the door on his startled face.

That did sting. Like Judson! Morgan scowled at the closed door. He could go in there, there were no locks on the bedroom door, but now he didn't feel like it.

Ruefully, he grimaced. He had messed that up! Tess would surely be furious with him now for a long time. After all his efforts to be gentle and careful, to make love to her carefully, and now he had done this!

He went to the washstand, and scrubbed his face. He felt hot and flushed and weary.

He pulled up his pants, and fastened them again,

and put his shirt back on. It had gotten torn off in their struggles. He found more of Antoinette Judson's lip gloss on the shirt. He ripped the shirt off, flung it to the floor, got out a fresh shirt, and fastened it.

Damn it all, women did play havoc with a man's life!

17

Vincent whistled a little as he rode. He looked about alertly and kept the rifle on his arm, yet he felt light and happy that morning.

It was a beautiful day. The Atlantic Ocean rolled and rolled in blue and white waves against the creamy beach. The green palms waved against the vivid blue sky. Stark rocks carved by the ceaseless pressure of the water made outlines of curious shape. It was a beautiful place, the island.

Some said the other side of the island was more beautiful, and Vincent had noted eagerly the turquoise and purple of the Caribbean waters. Yet this was wilder, untamed, not so placid as the Caribbean side, and he liked it. He liked the wind in his face, the splash of the salt water when he rode close to the edge of the ocean.

He rode past the Judson plantation, keeping a watchful eye for anyone from there. But all seemed quiet. In the distance, he caught a glimpse of men working in the sugarcane fields, slashing at the cane with their machetes glinting in the sun. He saw Judson there, waving a whip at one man, shouting, then going on to another place. He sure wouldn't care to work for Judson, slave or free man.

Morgan Hamilton had been damn good to him, thought Vincent happily. It had been a big stroke of luck when the ex-sailor had appeared at the Last Inn, and taken Tess away. You might have thought he would be furious with Vincent for coming along, and Vincent had thought he might have to stay with the ship. But he had been angry only for a little time; then he had calmed down.

Now his brother-in-law treated him as a friend and partner. He talked over matters with him, even asked his advice. Vincent glowed at the thought. He was but nineteen, and Morgan, an experienced man of the world, would turn to him and say, "What do you think, Vincent? Shall we go ahead in this field, or do the best cane first?"

He liked the work, hot and tired though he got. He felt that he was really a man now, supervising other men in the cane and at the mill, and watching over the bubbling cauldrons of molasses for the right moment to ladle the hot syrup into the final cauldron. He liked working with the rum mixtures, and deciding when to bottle, and when to let it go on fermenting a bit longer. That took skill and judgment. His experience in the bar was not wasted, he thought with a grimace.

He turned in the dark lane leading up to the Quintero villa. He had not been here for some time, not for several weeks, and he wondered if the girls had missed him. He had been uneasy with Florencia; she was a bit brazen, he decided. But Inez—there was a nice girl.

Florencia was on the veranda when he rode up. He

bowed, and took off his sombrero to her, and she flirted with her fan, standing up to greet him. A boy came running to take his horse.

"Rub him down good, will you?" asked Vincent slowly, and the boy nodded and beamed.

"Rub down good, give water later," he said, and led the horse away proudly.

Vincent came up the steps, and took Florencia's hand awkwardly. She liked to have her hand kissed, but he didn't know how, though he had watched the other men keenly. He just shook it and let it go quickly. It felt hot in his palm.

"How are you, Miss Florencia?" he asked.

"We have missed you, señor Vincent," she murmured, flirting her long lashes at him. She was so small and short, she made him feel big and strong though he wasn't nearly so tall as Morgan.

"Thank you. We have been very busy with the cane," he said. "Working up till nightfall, like you have, I guess."

She motioned to a chair. Before sitting down, he looked about. "Your father about?" he asked.

Her mouth went into a thin line. "I will send for him presently," she said, but just then her father came from the cool villa. Vincent jumped up, and shook his hand heartily, in relief. He had no wish to be alone with the brooding-eyed, red-mouthed Florencia, with her hungry look.

"Ah, señor Vincent, how good to see you," beamed Mr. Quintero. "Ah, you have the bottle with you—is it coconut liqueur?" He took it, uncorked it, and smelled it deliberately. "Ummmm," he said.

Vincent watched him anxiously. "Is it fermented enough?" he asked.

"Too much, I fear, my friend." Christopher Quintero sighed, and motioned him into the villa with him. Vincent

269

followed, forgetting all about Florencia. "Two glasses, my dear Inez," he said to the girl moving about the dining area.

"Immediately, Father," murmured Inez, and bowed to Vincent and greeted him. "You are welcome to our poor home, señor."

She was formal today. He eyed her anxiously, wondering of a sudden if Florencia had told of their meeting in the trees.

The glasses were brought on a tray, and Quintero poured out some of the liqueur. He swirled it about, sniffed at it delicately, like a cat with some strange dish. Then he took a sip, savored it in his mouth, shook his head.

"Too long, my boy," he said, and patted Vincent on the shoulder. "Never mind, next time you will know. Inez, there is a bottle of my coconut liqueur in the credenza?" He pointed to the sideboard, and Inez nodded. She moved gracefully in her blue gown and small black heelless slippers to the sideboard, and took out a white smoky sort of bottle.

She also brought a tray of glasses and a glass bowl. Vincent's eyes opened wide as Quintero spat accurately into the bowl.

"One does not drink it all down, or one loses all sense of taste," said Quintero. "Be seated, my friend, and old Quintero will teach you something of the art of tasting. Inez, the orange liqueur and the plain rums, also a loaf of bread for cleaning our palates."

She brought them with a slight smile, as though she had done this many times before. Seated at the dining table, Quintero instructed Vincent to take a small sip of one liqueur or another, roll it about on his tongue, then spit it out. They would drink a sip of water, or eat a bite of bread, to cleanse the palate, then try another sip of rum. Quintero talked learnedly about the various rums, and by words and example, Vincent began to realize the differences.

The slightly sour taste of the coconut liqueur was not evident in Quintero's liqueur. His was smooth, creamy, sweet. "You see—not much fermenting for this. Better not to ferment longer than eight hours," he said. "Quick, quick, then mix with the six-year rums, for the best results."

Inez deftly set the dining table, placing the white lacy mats near them, setting out silver and a wineglass at each place. Vincent found himself watching her easy movements, the low direction of her voice and hand to each maid who helped her.

Vincent felt eyes burning into his back, but he would not turn about. He knew by the perfume that Florencia had come into the house, and stood near to them. Not helping Inez, just watching, watching, like a big cat, he thought.

Inez arranged some flowers in a glass bowl, and set it in the center of the table. He liked to watch her small fingers, and she had directed a maid to bring in white frangipani and white jasmine, and three scarlet sprays of hibiscus. She set them together beautifully in the bowl, arranging them just so.

"That is really lovely," said Vincent, in appreciation. He glanced up at her, the dark-fringed eyes were sober.

She bowed slightly. "Thank you, señor," she murmured.

She was really formal today. He bet that cat Florencia had talked and bragged to her sister about their embrace. He fumed to himself. Did she know how her sister had chased him? Probably. There wasn't much to talk about here on the island, for the women.

Luncheon was served, and Vincent talked mostly to Señor Quintero. They discussed the progress of the cutting of cane, and he told the señor that Morgan was going to give a cane party for his people at the end of harvest.

Señor Quintero beamed. "A cane party!" he exclaimed. "Splendid! I shall do the same! I thought I had not the heart for it this year, with my old friend Thomas Hamilton gone. But if Morgan Hamilton will do it, so shall I."

"Will Mr. Judson?" asked Vincent curiously.

Quintero shook his graying dark head. His spirited face showed distaste. "He never does. I reproved him one year, I said, how do you expect to keep your people content? You never give them gifts, or parties to sing and dance. People need to sing and make music, I told him. He said, the lash sings, the whip makes them dance! I cannot like the man as well as I should like a neighbor."

Vincent shivered. "No, I cannot like him," he admitted in a low tone. "There is something—evil—in the way he likes to cause pain. A good man does not take pleasure in causing pain to others."

Inez looked at him strangely. Florencia rippled a laugh. "But they are slaves? What do they matter?" she asked. "If they are not contented, they must hide it. It is their duty to do what the master and the mistress tell them. Their happiness is not important. It is the happiness of the master that is vital. Otherwise, the master will leave the land, and the slaves will starve. Is that not so, Papa?" She smiled at him.

He looked troubled, Vincent tried to hide his shock. That she should be so callous! Tess thought it was important for everyone to be happy and contented. "They work hard; one must praise their work, give them enough food to eat, and new clothing sometimes," she had said once.

Vincent said, "From my own experience, I would say that even a servant has feelings, and can know hurt and pain. If I ever have a servant of my own, I shall make sure he knows that I care about his pain and griefs. Never will I let a man under me experience what I did!"

Quintero gazed at him in surprise, as did the girls. "You speak with strong conviction, my friend," said Quintero slowly, sipping at his rum punch, with the slice of lime to sharpen it. "Do you mind telling us something of these experiences?"

"I should like to do so," said Vincent, flushing a little under his tan. "You think I am a gentleman because I came with my brother-in-law to this island. However—" He hesitated, deciding not to bring Tess into this. "When I met Morgan, I was working in a bar, scrubbing the floor, taking orders for drinks, mucking out the stables, tending the horses. My mother had married again after the death of my father. . . ."

And he went on bravely to explain the position he was in, how his stepfather had taken advantage of them to make them work. He left Tess mostly out of his account, saying merely that she did the bookkeeping and kept accounts for Ryder. "I must tell you, I carried buckets of hot water up to the bedrooms for ladies and gentlemen. I endured their cursing when the water was too hot, or not hot enough. I kept my mouth shut when they kicked me in their drunken rages. But I felt. Yes, I felt! A servant can feel, and know anger, though he must suppress it."

"So you were not a gentleman," said Florencia, with some distaste, her red mouth curling.

Quintero gave her a grim look. "You should know, my daughter, that the quality of a gentleman shows through, whatever tasks he may have to perform!" he said sternly. "I have known great gentlemen who were pressed

273

off the streets and forced to serve before the masts. I have known gentlewomen who were forced by poverty to become governesses and even maid-servants, who retained even so their gallantry and courage! A man's circumstances do not alter his essential character!"

"Yes, Papa. I am sorry, Papa," said Florencia meekly, but her dark eyes were flashing anger.

Inez gently changed the subject. "Your brother-in-law, Morgan, seems to have made some success of his new work, señor," she said to Vincent. "He takes to it well for a man who has been a sailor and officer for the British navy, no?"

"Yes, he likes the work." Vincent turned to her in relief. "I think between us we shall make a success of it. I am proud to say he confides in me, and we work together well. My sister Tess manages the household, and Morgan has said he will divide the direction of the plantation with me. We shall both learn all the work, from the cutting of the cane and the working of the mill, to the mixing of the rums. He is most generous to me."

"Truly, your fortunes have taken a turn for much better," smiled Quintero gallantly. "I am happy for you, my friend. You shall learn much, and who knows? One day you might manage a plantation of your own."

"For one who was this time last year scrubbing the stables and taking care of horses, and putting drunken sailors to bed, that is a change of fortunes indeed," grinned Vincent, glad to have that behind him. He didn't like to pretend, and he wanted Quintero to know what kind of person he really was.

They had a pleasant luncheon. Florencia seemed thoughtful, gazing at Vincent from time to time. Inez was busy directing the maid, seeing the plates were kept full, the rum glasses filled. She served them delicious fried chicken in a dish of herb-laden rice, the best rice Vincent had ever eaten, very light and fluffy. With the chicken came the dish of vegetables from their garden, beans and maize, and a plate of baked breadfruit.

For dessert, she had concocted a dish of mixed fruits, papaya, mango, oranges, limes, bananas, and shredded coconut, all with a delicate light rum.

Vincent complimented Inez on the luncheon, knowing better than to say anything to Florencia about it. It was all too evident who was the housekeeper in that family, he thought. "You serve most delicious dishes, señorita Inez." He bowed on rising from the table. "I know my sister will wish to ask for your recipe both for the chicken and the dessert."

"You are most kind, señor," she murmured, with an answering bow. She turned shyly to the maid, and directed her to take a tray of drinks to the veranda. It was about three o'clock in the afternoon. Vincent glanced at the sky.

"I must be certain to leave early, señor Quintero," he said, and found the "señor" and the "señorita" coming easily to his tongue. "I promised Morgan to start home early, he was anxious that I return home before dusk."

"Ah, yes, you must do so!" Quintero's face was grave. "One does not know what to expect in the dusk these days," he added with a sigh. No one said Judson's name, but it quivered in the air between them.

Florencia went before them, waving her fan. Vincent turned deliberately to Inez. "I do not have much time, señorita Inez. I wonder if you would stroll with me in your beautiful gardens? I wish to learn the names of some of the flowers."

Florencia's back went rigid, her fan snapped. Quintero stared, then began to grin and wag his head slightly. Inez went the color of a pink rose, her eyes were wide and dark.

"Me—señor?" she faltered.

"Yes, señorita Inez," he said gently. He offered his arm in the white coat. "If you will be so kind?"

She glanced uncertainly at her sister, then at her father. He nodded, beaming at her. "Thank you, señor. I will be happy to—to show you our flowers," she said gravely.

She put her hand on his arm, and he felt proud and happy. He also felt when they walked past her sister that darts of pure fury were going right into the middle of his back! But let that be. He liked Inez, and she was a pretty gentle creature, not a hard selfish one like Florencia. He could not forget what she had said about slaves not deserving or needing to be happy!

If Florencia Quintero had come to the Last Inn, she would have looked haughtily past the boy who took the horses, the boy who brought up the hot water. She would have complained of slow service, of the food not being hot enough, or anything she chose, not worrying about the effect on the boy, if he might be whipped for it.

Inez would have been kind, giving a gentle smile of encouragement, as she did to the hesitant maid. She would have been a lady, courteous, though aloof.

They walked in the garden. Vincent would point out a flower, solemnly, and Inez would pronounce the name in English. She knew the Spanish names of some also.

"That is a jade vine," she murmured. "That? A form of orchid, señor. Is it not lovely, that violet color? Ferns, around the base of the breadfruit tree. Ginger; Mexican heather; and the vines? They are called bougainvillea—is the color not splendid?"

They paused to admire the reddish purple of the flowers on the vine that splashed its magnificence along the side of the villa. The white of the stuccoed house, and the bright red of the tiles set off the flowers set lovingly in the gardens about it. It was peaceful there, strolling along the shaded paths, bordered by pines and coconut trees and royal palms.

Inez pointed out a flower like that of a silver dollar, another of small red and pink and white blooms. There was a large yellow bloom she called "allamanda," and a bunch of bright orange daisies. He tried to remember the names for Tess.

"Tess wants to build a garden such as yours, when she has time," he confided. "My sister has never had such a house to manage, and it takes much time to manage all. But one day, we too shall have a fine garden. Mr. Thomas Hamilton had a small one, but it is overgrown with weeds and needs much attention."

"I would be happy to aid her, if she wishes it," Inez murmured in her soft musical voice. She had a trace of a Spanish accent, but her English was clear and well-pronounced: she must have gone to an English school.

Vincent asked her about that. "Did you attend a school in St. Michael?"

"Yes, señor, for five years; then Papa hired a governess to teach us at home. He was not happy with the teaching of the ladies, who wanted us to learn English manners and the writing of political pamphlets. One lady in particular was for the vote of women, imagine that!" Her dark eyes were wide, gazing up into his. He thought he could have melted in that dark liquid look.

"Imagine," he said soberly, scarcely taking in what she said. He was content to hear her speaking, she spoke so seldom.

"I think I would like to vote," said Inez. "But I would have to vote the way Papa said, wouldn't I? So maybe it is just as well that I do not," and she gave a little sigh. "One English lady was a spinster, and she said she would never marry. She did not wish her money to be spent in gambling by a husband!"

"Obviously she had had bad experiences of men," said Vincent. "Did you disagree with her?"

"Oh, not to her face," said Inez quickly. "But I would like—one day—to marry—if I could find someone like Papa, someone gentle and kind and good, someone honorable and noble. But Papa would not make a marriage for me, unless he finds a man like that, I know it. He has promised Florencia and me that we shall marry only when we find a man to like and respect."

"Does not any father feel so?" Vincent asked.

"Not the father of Mrs. Judson," murmured Inez; then she put her hand to her mouth. "Oh, I should not say it! But she was weeping one day and came over here to cry to me, that she wished she was dead! It was wicked, it was against religion and faith and hope! But I understood how she felt, I would feel so, married to such as—as Mr. Judson!"

"He is evil," said Vincent gravely, nodding his head. "You can tell by the way he treats his slaves, and I imagine he is not much better to his wife. Poor woman."

"Poor indeed. For she has many jewels, but her heart is not content."

Vincent drew a deep breath. He had not thought to come so far with Inez today. Indeed, he had not realized he wanted to speak of marriage to her! Yet think how far he had gone, that they walked, talked, spoke of what they honestly believed, and had discussed marriage! He was making fast strides!

Inez looked at the sky. "It will be dusk before long, señor Vincent," she said, worriedly. "Did you not say—"

"Oh, Lord, yes," he said. Then he apologized, "I did not mean to swear, señorita Inez! Forgive me, the words come much too easily, after my years in an inn."

"It is forgiven," she said solemnly. "I try never to take the names of the Lord and Our Lady in vain. But I can understand how one would say so. And indeed, I pray so, with their names."

"Are you Roman Catholic?" he asked. He had not thought of that.

"I was baptized so," she said. "But we never get to the cathedral anymore, and Papa does not bother to keep up a chapel. I do have a prayer stool in my room at which I pray. It seems to help me."

He smiled down at her. He had no religion at all, but for brief services when he was very young. He thought it must be nice to have a faith in some great power. He called it luck, that Morgan had come to the inn and found them. But maybe it had been someone higher, a Power.

Quintero came out to the garden, and behind him a boy led Vincent's black stallion. "I am sorry, I do not mean to speed you, lad," he said anxiously. "But it is past five o'clock, and your brother will be angry with me for keeping you."

"No, no, he likes you, but indeed I must depart." Vincent took the reins, and looked down once more at the glow in Inez's face. "May I come again, perhaps on Sunday?"

"Please do, señor," she said softly. He thought her pink mouth was like a flower, and longed to touch it.

He shook hands with them. Florencia was not in sight, she was probably furious with him. Or maybe she had wiped him off her list, because of his early experiences in the inn. He hoped so! He mounted, and waved good-bye again as he rode down the darkening lane of trees.

After the curve of the trees, he could see down to the beach. He glanced back, the house was gone but for the red roof. He lifted the reins, prepared to ride on more rapidly; then he reined abruptly.

Florencia stood in his path, her hands on her hips.

Her red dress glowed like a flame among the dark trees.

"So—you are taken in by my little sister," she smiled, but there was a nasty wild look to her eyes.

Vincent did not dismount. He didn't want to get caught in any situation with this girl again. "What do you mean, señorita Florencia?" he asked cautiously.

Florencia tossed her dark hair, and her hands clenched on her hips. "She seems so meek and sweet, doesn't she? And only I and her maid know how she sneaks out to meet Pedro!"

Vincent went cold. "Who is Pedro?" he asked.

"One of the overseers, the young handsome one with big ears," Florencia sneered. "He is always creeping up to her window and giving a whistle, and down she goes to him! When Papa finds out, he will be wild, but he must agree to the marriage when she gets enceinte."

"What is that?"

"When she makes the baby!" flared Florencia wildly, her Spanish accent getting stronger in her fury. "She is a bad girl, hiding her wickedness under the sweet goody ways!"

Vincent lifted the reins. "I am sure you should not be telling me about this, you should inform your papa," he said, quietly. "Now, good-bye, Miss Florencia!"

He moved the horse on, and she had to get out of the path of the big animal. She shouted after him, "You will see, when her stomach gets big! You will see! She is a wild wicked girl, she likes the men, all the men—she is bad, bad—"

He went on faster, and put the horse to a gallop. The breeze cooled his face, he was sweating.

He could scarcely believe it. Gentle Inez! To be playing about secretly with the overseer. He vaguely remembered the two Spanish overseers, big and grinning and dark-eyed. With no white women about, except the daughters of their boss!

Inez—to go out, sneaking out to meet that man! He shuddered, and the horse flew along the stretch of beach. He scarcely noticed the shadows of the pines and palms, he went so fast, the sands tore up under the feet of the horse.

He drew in as he approached the Last Hope plantation. He was wet with sweat, and yet chilled by the breeze. Dusk was closing in after the hour's ride.

He went in the back, and let the boy take the horse. "Rub him down good, and feed him when he is cooled," he directed. The boy nodded proudly, and took the horse. He was doing well, but Bernardo had been much better.

He went up to his room, and Tess sent a maid with a bucket of hot water for him. He splashed in the basin, and put on a fresh shirt. When he had cooled down, he sat on the edge of the bed to try to think.

Would a girl who talked of praying to God and Our Lady, would she sneak out and meet an overseer, a crude tough man, secretly? She had spoken of marrying only a man she could respect. Did she, could she, respect Pedro?

And would she lie to her father, when her every tone in speaking to him was not only respect but deep affection?

No, he could believe that of Florencia, with her sly ways and her crimson mouth and her hungry body pressed to his. But not Inez. Inez was shy, and quiet, and dignified.

He went down to dinner. Tess was quiet, Morgan kept glancing at her. He wondered if they had quarreled.

He finally burst out, "Morgan, how do you tell if someone is lying to you?"

Tess raised her head, her eyes deep blue in the lamplight. Morgan looked right at Tess, then finally back at Vincent. He seemed to ponder; then he spoke.

"I guess it is a matter of trust, Vincent," he said slowly. "I know with the men in my regiment, I had to get to know them. Then I always knew if Peters was lying through his teeth if he said he had been writing to his mother. He had probably been off in town. And Thomas, or Watson, when they said they had searched the woods and found no Frenchies, I believed them. They were brave good men, and would do it. But I never trusted Lister to do that. He was such a coward, he would sneak away, hide out, then come back and say he found nothing. I think it is a matter of knowing the person. If he is straightforward and courageous, he will not lie. If he is a coward, a bully, a cheat, he will also lie."

"Oh, I see," nodded Vincent. Then Inez was not the liar, he decided, Florencia must be. But it worried him. What if he did not know Inez well enough, so that she seemed like a sweet girl, but underneath was false and wild?

"Who were you thinking about? Quintero?" asked Morgan.

"No," said Vincent, then blushed. "That leaves only the girls, doesn't it?" he asked wryly. "Yes, I was wondering about them. They seem—so different from each other. I don't know which one to believe."

"Inez," said Tess, entering the conversation for the first time. She nodded her head. "I would trust Inez. But not the other one, Florencia. She reminded me of the grand ladies who came to the inn with their lovers while their husbands were away on business. Remember that woman who caused so much trouble, coming every week on Thursday? We called her the Thursday lady. Her husband finally caught her out."

"I had forgotten that woman," said Vincent slowly. "Yes, I remember now."

Yet he still felt uneasy. Would Florencia, no matter

what kind of woman she herself was, tell such lies about her sister? Maybe they were both cheats and loose women, behind the back of Quintero, who was such a gentleman and chivalrous honorable man.

Or was he? Maybe he also was a cheat! He had admitted that he had tried to find the money and jewels of Thomas Hamilton after the man's death. He and Judson were going to divide the loot between them!

Lost in thought, he scarcely heard Morgan say softly to Tess, "You see, my dear, that is the heart of the matter. Either you can trust a man, or you cannot."

Tess tossed her blond head. He vaguely wondered what they were talking about.

18

Odette lay in Bernardo's strong arms, her hand gently stroking his broad chest. She smiled up into his eyes.

"How lovely you are," he murmured, in the tongue they both knew. He had taught her his African tongue, and words came more easily to him in that language. He praised her loveliness, her beautiful pointed breasts, her grace.

She sighed with contentment. "If only you might return soon. I miss the sight of you, my beloved," she whispered.

"And how I miss you, my beautiful," he murmured against her soft red mouth. They kissed long, and she turned over on her back, drawing him down yet again to her. Their embraces were more frantic now, the few times they could meet.

He moved over her, his long bare legs brushing her

slim ones, finding the sweet places to kiss, hungrily. Louis Abaco was standing guard nearby, gazing out over the valley. He said little, but there was a sympathy and knowledge in his eyes. Bernardo knew they were safe, he said, so long as Abaco watched.

He plunged into her body, she forgot all else but the keen ecstasy of his touch. He was a good lover, he was gentle for a time, building up her feelings, until—explosion, and she would cry out, and enjoy the rapture of his body against hers.

Afterwards, they lay together, letting the cool wind through the trees cool their heated bodies. She gazed up dreamily at the sky, then noted that the sun was casting long shadows.

She sat up abruptly. "I must go back! White mistress is good, she say 'be careful' when I ask for day off. But she worry if I don't come back."

"She knows where you go?" asked Bernardo, worried.

Odette nodded thoughtfully. "White missus know much. She smile, and let me wear her white dress now. She make frill on hem, because I am taller. Look." And proudly she showed the pretty white muslin gown with the single frill along the hem.

Bernardo looked, and nodded, but Odette decided he did not understand fully. Mistress was kind to her, and gave her a dress, and she smiled with soft eyes when Odette asked shyly for the day off. It was a working day, too, not Sunday! But mistress knew that Odette longed for her lover and worried over him.

"I must go," she said again with a sigh, and stood up. Bernardo rose lazily, brushed off the twigs and leaves, then put on his brown trousers. They were dusty and she longed to remain, and wash his clothes for him, and fix a meal. But she dared not stay—not because of her mistress, but because of the danger.

It was growing dusky as the two made their way down the hill. Odette had caught a glimpse of the tall still figure of Louis Abaco, as they went past him. He lifted his hand gravely in response to her wave. His dark eyes were distant. She wondered sometimes what he thought. She believed he looked at her with desire at times, but he made no approach to her. He knew she was the woman of Bernardo.

Could a pirate be a man of understanding and honor? Perhaps so. Mr. Hamilton had been good to him, and sometimes sent food to him in the hills. He had been angry when he saw the chains on Abaco, and had taken a hammer to strike them off with his own hands. Mr. Hamilton had been a good kind man.

They reached the foot of the hill, and hesitated. "You come no further," she whispered, as though the cane would tell stories.

"I see you to the house," said Bernardo firmly. It was darker now.

They walked slowly through the shorn fields. There was little shelter left, most of the fields had been cut here. Hand in hand, they strolled along, looking more to each other than to their path.

On the edge of the cane, she stopped. "Go back now, Bernardo. Take care, my love!"

He nodded, kissed her hard, then went slowly back through the cane. Odette stood to watch him, dreamily.

She did not see the black horse stealing up behind her. She did not see the grim hungry-eyed man who rode the horse, until he was upon her with a rush. She did feel him when he reached down and swooped her up into his arms.

"Got you!" laughed Caleb Judson. "You little devil —got you now!"

Odette screamed out in shock and terror. He clapped

his hand over her mouth and turned his horse, to ride back through his cane fields which met the Hamilton fields on that side. She struggled and fought at him, kicking out with her long slim legs, but he only laughed, in a sort of snarl, and held her more cruelly tight on the pommel of the saddle. The high horn of the saddle bit into her side.

Most of all she feared him. He was always after her, now he had caught her! She had been careless, she had wandered too far from the house alone—oh, God, she thought. Oh, God, that Mr. Hamilton prayed to—save me! And then she thought of her own gods. She cried out to them silently.

They rode like a horrible wind through the cane, which lashed at her bare legs. He had torn her white dress, she heard it rip. She kicked and tried to scream, but the dirty hand held her mouth and chin tightly.

In her struggles, she saw behind him, and cold terror paralyzed her. She stopped her struggles, because she saw Bernardo! He was running after them through the cane, stumbling, wide-eyed, wildly, letting the cane lash at him. He was racing the horse, running with the light stride that was his own. Her Bernardo, coming after her!

Mr. Judson would kill him!

She tried to relax, hoping that Judson would not notice Bernardo. But the pinch of his arm on her body hurt so badly that she could not rest in his arm. And the thought of the hours ahead made her wild.

She fought him again. He paused then, near to his house, and flung her down in the cane. He was off his horse and down on her. "I'll have you now, I'll have you now," he panted, and grabbed at her dress, and ripped it right up to her bare brown thighs.

She screamed out and fought him, kicking, scratching with her fingernails. Judson laughed, and fought her to the ground, pressing down on her with all his brute strength. She sobbed once, then concentrated on keeping her legs closed. His hand went to her thigh, he pulled brutally, so her leg felt as though it would come out from the socket. Would he tear her to pieces? She felt his slobbery lips moving over her bared breasts. And after Bernardo's gentle touch on her——!

Above his head, she saw a dark shadow. Bernardo lifted a rock and brought it down forcefully on Judson's head. The man collapsed like a balloon fish dragged from the water.

Bernardo's teeth were drawn back, he was a man gone mad.

Odette scrambled up from the harsh cane. She felt blood trickle down her back, it did not matter. She caught at Bernardo's arm as he raised to strike again.

"No, no, run away——I shall run also——" she panted.

Judson was stirring, getting up. His face was a mask of fury, his eyes blazed fire. He saw the two of them. Odette screamed and began to run, blindly, as he reached out for her. He must be mad!

Bernardo ran also, in the other direction. Odette thought she was running back to her house, but instead it was to the Judson house. She came out of the cane, on the edge of the flower garden. She paused, blankly. She had run into the area of the enemy! She saw Antoinette Judson on the veranda, in her violet gown, rising in alarm.

"What is it?" asked the languid voice of the marquess. He also stood up, his gray silk suit glowing in the fading light, in the orange glow of the lantern.

"I don't know. It looks like a slave girl," said Mrs. Judson. She raised her voice. "Who are you? What do you want?"

Odette shrank back into the shadow of some trees. She saw Judson race into the clearing, panting, foaming, his mouth slavering like that of a mad dog.

"Get my dogs!" he yelled at the mute boy who came around the house. "Get two of the overseers—get my dogs! I was attacked in the cane—I'll kill that bastard! I'll kill him—daring to hit me!"

"Mr. Judson, what has happened?" One of the overseers came around, smirking, all attention. Odette hung back, fearfully, afraid to leave, she might be seen in the remnants of her white dress.

"There's a girl hiding in the trees," the Marquess pointed languidly, with mild interest. "You chasing her, Judson?" and he laughed.

"Get her," said Judson to the overseer. "You there, bring my dogs! I'm going after that bastard slave that dared to hit me! We'll chase him, get him this time! He hasn't gone far. Move, damn you!"

The dogs were brought. The one overseer had caught Odette by the arm. She felt nothing but a fatalistic knowledge that she was doomed. Those white people would not help her. She could scream, they would only laugh. The overseer dragged her closer to the porch, carelessly tied her with a rope to one of the posts. She saw Antoinette Judson, her violet eyes wide, her hand to her throat.

The dogs had been brought, and were sent out in the cane. They were barking wildly, and were lashed with whips, which sent them farther out. Judson had his horse, riding after them. Odette could only wait, her body cold in the dusk and the breeze, her heart cold, her mind a blank. They would catch him, her Bernardo—

The ropes cut her arms and her waist. Her breasts were bared for any man's gaze. Her head drooped at the way the Marquess was staring at her. She felt shamed, yet it was drowned in the strong fatal feeling—this was the end.

Judson gave a wild whoop, she heard screaming, the dogs were barking wildly. Then Judson rode back through the cane, and on the end of his rope Bernardo was dragged on his knees, on his back, on his belly, any way Judson tossed the rope.

The dogs had been at him already. His head was bloody, his face bled, his hands and arms. Odette longed to go to him, her arms moved; she was tied.

Judson yanked Bernardo back into the middle of the clearing before the veranda. Odette watched with wide eyes, living in a nightmare. The dark gods won. Always the dark gods won. One could fight and struggle, but one was doomed forever.

Judson tied the rope to the porch next to the pillar which held Odette. "Let the dogs have him," he said curtly, and grinned in a slash of white teeth as the snarling dogs were let loose by the overseer and the blacks that held him.

One of the blacks turned away and was quietly vomiting in the bushes. Judson watched every move. Odette watched, because she could not turn away, and could not close her eyes.

Bernardo was screaming, screaming, though much of his face was already torn away. His arms were loose, he had struggled enough to get them loose. The dogs yapped at him, then darted in again. One caught his leg and pulled. The others dared to get in close and eat. They were kept half starved. They had already feasted before on slaves.

Judson watched and laughed. Antoinette turned away, and put her hands over her face. The black girl stood, hanging in the ropes, her body sagging. Bernardo screamed, and screamed, and finally his voice faded.

Antoinette did not want to watch. The Marquess was watching with cold curiosity, his whip striking his legs lightly. His teeth gleamed as he looked at Judson.

The dogs' yapping died away. Antoinette ventured

another look, and shuddered. All that was left of the man seemed like great hunks of black and red beef, and a couple strips of cotton trousers. She swallowed back the nausea.

Judson's trousers and coat were covered with blood. He went over to Odette, and growled at her. "I'll have you now, you little slut! Sneaking out to meet him, huh?" He slapped her cheek when she did not answer.

Antoinette saw the girl was rigid with shock. She made herself go down the porch steps, though her legs were trembling and she wasn't sure her knees would hold her.

She ordered one overseer quietly, "Untie the girl. She is in shock."

Judson hovered close. She could smell the sweat and rum on him, and the smell of blood. She felt so sickened, she could scarcely conceal her contempt and hatred of him. But this poor girl—

Judson reached for Odette again, put his hands on her waist. The girl was rigid, her eyeballs rolling in her head wildly, her arms trembling with the shakes, as Leonie called them.

Antoinette saw Leonie hovering on the veranda; curiosity had brought out many of the blacks. They were staring, waiting, listening. Oh, God, she thought, they will never remain now! They hate us, I can feel the hate around like a cloud.

She forced herself to say coolly, "Caleb, the child is in no condition for your—attentions. I'll take her inside, let her sit down for a while."

Judson scowled, his eyes blazed with lust. "No, I want her," he said, and put his hands on her, pulling her to him.

Antoinette controlled herself with an intense effort.

292

"Before us all?" she asked lightly. "The Marquess will be—most amused, I am sure."

The Marquess of Tweed had not stirred from his idle stance on the veranda. "Yes, indeed, this story will earn me many a drink in the clubs back in London," he said, and laughed. "A man torn to pieces by dogs, his lover forced to watch. Good, eh? I wonder if they will believe me!"

Judson hated mockery. He had killed a man once for mocking him. He glared at Lord Tweed, and his hands fell reluctantly from the slave girl. Antoinette moved the girl, with her hand on her arm, over to the veranda steps.

"Come inside, child," she urged. "Leonie, help me!"

The large woman moved automatically to help her mistress. Between them they moved Odette to the shelter of the living room, just inside the doors. Leonie crooned to her softly in some other language, and Odette fell limply into a chair. Her eyes still rolled, her body was stiff, her legs stuck out before her: she looked like a broken doll.

"Bettina, a glass of rum," ordered Antoinette. "Leonie, give me your scarf."

The woman handed it over without a murmur, and watched with black gaze as Antoinette fastened it about the girl's bodice, so her breasts were covered. Judson had followed them in, and hovered, scowling blackly at them.

"You may wish to change your clothes, Caleb," said Antoinette, lightly. "They are covered in blood."

"I want the girl!" he muttered. "I want her. Leave her alone! She'll come to when I have her. I'll take her up to the bedroom if you don't want a public scene!" he ended with a sneer.

"She is in a terrible state of shock," said Antoinette, and her voice shook. "You must not think—Judson, I beg you. Let the child alone."

Bettina brought a glass of rum on a tray. Antoinette took it, gave Odette a sip, held the glass to her lips, a deep compassion in her. She had never felt this way about anyone, but that scene tonight had torn something loose inside her. What women went through! The lusts of men did something terrible to women. This was a sister-woman, she thought, and wondered at herself. She had held her hands to her ears the night of Caleb's rape of Bettina. Today, she could endure no more.

Judson watched sullenly as the girl sipped. She could not hold the glass, her eyes had stopped the ominous rolling, but they seemed to gaze upward at the ceiling, showing the pinkish whites.

"She's all right now. Leonie, take her upstairs to my room!"

The Marquess had strolled inside, watching idly, as at some dog-baiting, with as little pity or mercy as he would have shown to a wounded dog, thought Antoinette. "Don't think she would be much fun today, why don't you wait, Judson?" he asked. "Looks sick to me. You might catch something if she's been with that black fellow."

Judson hesitated, then shook his head. He hated to be thwarted, he hated to wait. "No, I want her now. Come on, girl!"

As he grabbed at Odette's wrist, she went stiff and began to scream, a high-pitched wailing keen that made the hairs on Antoinette's neck stand up. It shattered her composure completely.

"For the love of God, Caleb!" she cried. "Can't you let the girl go? Have you no mercy in you?" She wrenched at his arm, shuddered at the blood on him, but pulled blindly.

He let Odette go, swung his arm around, and struck Antoinette on the side of the head. She fell like a log, striking her head on the side of the chair, and going limp.

She was not quite unconscious. She knew hate, she knew a bitter rebellion. Odette was a symbol of all that had happened to Antoinette also. The nights of knowing her husband was grunting and lusting and bedding a slave girl in the same master bed in which he forced Antoinette. The shame of knowing everyone white and black knew what he was, how he acted. She had no pride left.

She lay there, unable to get up, her head whirling dizzily. Odette was screaming and screaming, Judson was trying to drag her across the floor. The Marquess watched them all, as at some strange play which amused him, a grin on his face.

"Servants should know their place," he remarked idly. "Wives also. I admire the way you handle women, Judson!"

He was sneering, Judson paid no attention. He was dragging Odette with him. The girl was screaming in some language, then abruptly in English.

"God curse you, God curse you, may His curse follow you to the grave!" she screamed.

It sent a chill down all of them. Antoinette shivered, and pushed herself to sit up.

"God curse—God curse—God curse—" yelled Odette hoarsely.

Judson struck her across the mouth, a thin stream of blood came from her lips, she choked and was silent.

Then they heard the sound of the carriage driving up.

19

Morgan had come in at dusk. He met Vincent near the back veranda, and they went in the house together.

"What are those dogs yapping about?" he asked Tess sharply. "I heard them when I came from the beach."

Tess was troubled. "I don't know, Morgan. And Odette hasn't come back."

"Come back? From where?" he snapped, stiffening.

The dogs sounded louder. He thought he heard the scream of a woman, then it faded, and he heard only the dogs, the sound carrying in the still evening air.

"She—went to meet Bernardo, I think. She misses him," said Tess, her mouth tight. "I said she could have the day off." Her blue eyes met his defiantly.

He nodded, softening a little. Tess could understand the pull and power of love, at any rate. "All right. But I'm worried. Does she stay out late?"

"Not usually. She comes back before dusk. Do you think—" She gasped, her eyes getting huge. "Do you think —Judson—"

They were staring at each other, when Malkia came in, plodding, her head bent.

Tess turned to her urgently. "Malkia, where is Odette?"

"Caught," said Malkia, her face looking pinched and old. "Caught. Big black horse came in cane. I warned that girl, I told her, you stay way from that man. Odette caught."

"Judson caught her?" cried Tess. She was hanging on Morgan's arm, her fingers biting into the cotton sleeve and the flesh. "Did he take her away?"

Malkia nodded. "Through the cane. He picked her up on horse, took her. Bernardo ran after her. They will get him, too." She shook her head sadly.

"Morgan—we must go after them, we must," panted Tess. She shook his arm. "Please, for the love of God—"

He turned to Vincent. "Hitch up the carriage, hurry. I'll get the rifles."

He strode to the living room and unlocked the case of weapons. He took out three rifles. Tess followed, grabbed a huge pistol, so heavy it made her hands sag. He did not stop her. Her face had that kind of determination in it; he knew it would be useless to say anything. Besides, she could shoot.

Vincent was driving the carriage around as Morgan filled his pockets with bullets, and put the powder flask on the belt on his hip. He raced with Tess out the front door, and as Vincent drew up, Morgan swung Tess into the back seat of the light-sprung carriage, and followed her in. He tossed a rifle up front to Vincent, and the lad caught it, setting it between his legs.

Vincent drove like mad through the flying sand of

298

the beach, not sparing the horse for a moment. His face was set and hard.

They reached the dark lane leading up to Judson's. They could hear the wild yapping of the dogs and the screaming, even as they approached. It grew stronger and stronger. Vincent ran the carriage right up to the veranda, where some blacks stood around, their faces blank as they gazed at the white people approaching.

Through the open doors of the house, Morgan could see the Marquess lying back in a chair. He saw someone in violet silk sitting on the floor. He glanced at the slaves.

"Where is Bernardo?" he snapped.

They stared at him in silence, and pointed to the yapping dogs. Their attention seemed to be on the house. He thought they did not understand him. He swung down from the carriage, rifle in one hand, the whip he had been carrying in the other.

"Where is my slave Bernardo?" he asked slowly, distinctly.

Several of them pointed significantly to the dogs. One of the overseers had come to start snapping chains on them again. They snarled at him, yipped, fought to get back to the red meat on the ground. The overseer pointed to it.

"What's left of Bernardo," he said, and laughed. His face was bronzed, shiny with sweat. "He hit the master, and that's what he got."

Morgan stared, sickened. He heard a gasp from behind him, Tess or Vincent. He dared not turn about, to turn his back to the men before him.

Then a woman's shrill scream came from the house. He leaped up the stairs, and went inside. He saw Mrs. Judson first, sitting on the floor, a dull red mark across her white face.

"Mrs. Judson, whatever—" he began.

She saw him, and her face changed. She tried to get

up. He lifted her into a chair, stared down at her. "Just fell," she said, with a grimace meant to be a smile.

"Leave my wife alone," said Judson behind him. He was dragging a black girl in the remnants of a torn muslin dress. Odette was stiff as a board, her eyes rolling wildly.

"What the devil do you mean by this?" asked Morgan, lifting the rifle significantly. "Damn you, let Odette go!"

"She's mine now!" snarled Judson. "Damn you, get out of my house!"

"With Odette," Morgan said steadily. "Let the girl go, damn you, you bastard! Did you put your dogs on Bernardo?"

The silence in the big house seemed to scream at him. The Marquess was leaning back idly in a chair, smirking in amusement. The blacks stood about alertly, away from the white people. Mrs. Judson leaned her head on her hand, looking white and sick and weary.

"He struck me," said Judson. His eyes seemed glazed, his mouth had flecks of white spittle about it. Was he mad? "He struck me on the head. No black strikes a white man, you know that, Hamilton!"

"Did you—put your dogs—on Bernardo?" asked Morgan, again, deliberately.

Odette lay like a broken doll on the wooden floor. Her eyes still rolled, the only sign of life in her. He could not look at her now. Did Judson have a weapon on him? He glanced once out the wide doors. Vincent and Tess were still in the carriage, and their rifles were trained on the blacks and the white overseers, and idly toward the house. Bless them! he thought, passionately, for their loyalty and the toughness they had learned early. He figured those rifles had been loaded. And Tess had the big pistol also, in her lap.

He felt as he had in the days when he stood alone

on a wharf, but knowing that his sailors were behind him, waiting for a signal. They would not fail him.

"Damn you, I'm waiting for an answer!" Morgan said, with a ring of iron in his tone. "Did you kill Bernardo?"

"Yes!" yelled Judson, his nerve going. "I set the dogs on him; No court in the land would find me guilty of anything! He hit me!"

Bernardo. That big, gentle, eager-faced man, who had helped so much, had trusted Morgan, had saved Tess from Lord Tweed. That smiling-faced, honest, big helpful man —that he should have gone down to such a horrible death—

Red blood filled Morgan's vision, so angry, he had to blink it away to see straight.

"You bastard son of a whore! You filthy fucking bastard! You shit piece!" Morgan flung at him every sailor's curse he could remember from his years at sea. Judson shrank from the blaze of anger. The man was a damn coward, and Morgan said that also. "You blasted coward, you mean little shrinking piece of shit! That man you killed was ten times the man you are! He was your superior, by God in Heaven! He was a hundred times what you little—"

Judson straightened, red-faced, mouth opened to shriek his denial of the oaths. Morgan shifted the rifle to his left hand, and let loose with the whip. He caught Judson across the face, deliberately, and the man screamed, his hands flying to protect his eyes.

Morgan whipped him back and forth across the shiny polished floor. Judson screamed and cringed from him. Tess had left the carriage, and stood in the doorway, blue eyes shining with fury, rifle steady on the Marquess. A word, and she would have blasted him from his chair, and he knew it, thought Morgan, in cold delight.

The overseers had disappeared, no black would interfere. The Marquess shrank in his chair, and affected cool amusement. He would not interfere in the affairs of these colonials.

Not with Tess pointing a rifle at him.

Morgan struck Judson again and again, across the shoulders, his brawny arms with the sleeves rolled up. He slashed at him until the shirt was streaked with blood, and half torn from him. He hit again, again, until his arm was weary, and the lash was covered with blood.

Judson fell on the floor, his arms over his head. "No more," he yelled. "No more, damn it. No more, God damn you, damn you to hell, no more—" He was cringing, rolling on the floor, trying to hide behind the sofa. Morgan followed him, lashed until he had satisfied some of the anger in him.

"Enough," he said wearily. "Judson, you interfere with me one more time, and that time I won't bother with the lash. I'll kill you. Get that? You bother me or mine, and I'll kill you."

He tossed his rifle to Tess, who caught it with her free hand. She stood at the door, waiting as he walked over to Odette, picked her up gently, and carried her from the house. Tess followed him, warily, walking backward in gingerly fashion, down the veranda steps out to the carriage, where Vincent stood, rifle trained easily on the doorway.

Morgan put the back girl in the back of the carriage, gently. Then he lifted Tess up to the back seat, and she sank down beside Odette, taking the girl's body in her small sturdy arms. Morgan leaped up beside Vincent. "Let's go."

Vincent turned the horse and carriage slowly, so Morgan's aim could be true if anyone tried to stop them. No one tried. The blacks stared at them blankly, as at some amazing phenomenon, and did not move an inch. The overseers and the dogs were gone, and only blood and dirt lay before the beautiful front veranda with the cane rocking chairs.

Vincent drove back slowly. No need to rush now. Tess cradled Odette in her arms. Morgan heard her crooning to the girl.

"No bad things now, Odette. All right now, my dear. All right now, don't fret. He shall not have you, Odette. We shall soon be home, poor child. Poor little dear, we soon be home."

Morgan's anger cooled, hardened to iron. That Judson should have done such a thing! Captured Odette, set the dogs on Bernardo. He pieced the story together. He had probably taken Odette on her way back from meeting Bernardo. Bernardo must have seen, followed, tried to prevent her rape. Bernardo was a big gentle giant, only fury and fear could have made him strike a white man.

Back at Last Hope, Vincent drove around to the back. Malkia appeared, and Gamba, and some of the others. Morgan told them briefly what had happened, his face dark.

"Judson caught Odette in the cane. Bernardo followed, hit him. Judson put dogs on Bernardo, ordered him torn to bits. Then he tried to take Odette. We came and took Odette away."

Gamba lifted the whip curiously. Dried blood showed on the lash. He showed it wordlessly to the master, his face dark.

Morgan said, "I whipped Judson. It is not enough, but it is done: he has been whipped. He shall never touch me and mine again, or I will kill him!"

Vincent lifted Odette down. "Where shall I take her, Tess?" he asked.

"Into the house," said Tess, and moved to allow him

to pass her. Malkia stopped them gently, her withered arm outstretched.

"No, missus. Take to my hut. I take care."

Tess hesitated. "She is in shock, Malkia," she said gently. "I'll care for her tonight. You tomorrow, all right?"

The old woman stared curiously at her, then nodded, and followed the little procession inside the house. Vincent laid down Odette in the first bedroom upstairs, the guest room they had never used. Malkia opened the windows, brought warm water for bathing the girl. She and Tess gently removed the torn scraps of cloth from her. Odette stared up at them, her eyeballs seeming to be rolled back and sightless. She said nothing.

They bathed her poor bruised body, and put a white cotton nightdress of Tess's on her. She did not move a muscle, so stiff they could scarcely move her. They finally had her comfortable and on the soft bed.

Tess smoothed back the thick black hair, and crooned to her, "You are all right now, Odette. Nobody will harm you, nobody will harm you, you are safe now, Odette." The girl did not seem to hear her.

Malkia said, "Me stay, missus."

Tess hesitated, then nodded. "You stay part of night. Then I'll come, and you sleep."

She brought a soft-cushioned rocker from her room, and set it beside Malkia. From the kitchen she brought a bowl of broth, and some hot tea in a kettle, with a cup and tray. She set them all on a table beside Malkia, as the old woman rocked and smoked her fragrant-scented pipe.

"You wait on me, missus! Oh, no, no," said Malkia, shocked.

Tess smiled, and said quietly, so as not to disturb Odette, "If you wish anything, call me. I will come. Good night, Malkia."

With a last look at Odette, she went to her room. She

undressed, and washed. Morgan, in his room, was silent. She had seen his dark angry face, and knew he would lie awake a long time, fighting out his fury.

Tess lay awake for a long time also, her arms under her head, gazing out through the misty white mosquito netting at the purple black sky and the few stars that shone, dimmed by the bright white moon. Poor, poor Bernardo, loving so much, he could not evade the dark hand of death.

Her own thoughts were in chaos. She had never liked and fiercely admired Morgan so much as today. It had been a brutal scene, but somehow she had gloried in it. She had hated and feared Judson and Lord Tweed so much. And today, she had held a rifle on Lord Tweed, and he had not dared to try to wrench it from her. Because Morgan was there!

And Morgan had taken a whip to Judson, and whipped him around the room like a mad dog! Mrs. Judson had not said a word, she had sat in that chair with the dull red mark across her face, and her dark eyes had gleamed with something like satisfaction, though she had been masklike as she watched.

Oh, what a satisfaction, to see a wicked man whipped and beaten as he had so often whipped and beaten others!

Tess turned over in the bed, thinking of Odette, that poor lovely child. For her beauty, men had wanted her. And how she must feel—if she felt anything after the shocks of today. Tess must be especially kind and gentle to her now, for she had lost the man she loved, in a scene she would never be able to erase from her mind.

Lust—what a devastating thing it could be! The emotion that drove men to demented acts, to horrible acts. And supposedly akin to love!

From thinking of the terrible scenes, Tess went on to think of Morgan, her husband. How she had admired him today. He had not hesitated, he had taken command, he had gone to the rescue, like some red-haired war god! What a fury in battle! How strong and sure and wild he had been!

One could almost love a man like that. Almost, she thought. She smiled a little, dreamily, and stretched out her arms. Love. Could she love a man at all, after all she had seen of them at their worst? Her stepfather, drunken. The sailors, lusting after anything in skirts. Lord Tweed, his hot eyes seeming to tear her clothes from her and look right through.

Then Morgan Hamilton had come, had looked at her coolly, and proceeded to win her at cards! And had stopped her escape in the stables, and carried her off to marry her. Carried her off on a ship to this strange island paradise, inhabited by strange beings.

The first night had been horrible. Any night was, when she fought him; she felt pain. But lately—lately, he had been so gentle, and when she was quiet and responding, he was—was—Tess blushed even in the darkness, and put her hand to her face.

Could she be starting to feel love for him? Was this what love was? Part lust, part gentleness, part wishing to help him, part his helping her?

Only a month or two ago, Tess had been thinking about living in St. Michael with Vincent. Finding a job, when Morgan tired of her. Being independent, earning wages, not having to answer to any man.

But now, she mused how hard it would be to think of a life without Morgan. He was so strong, so sure. He took charge, he took away worries, because she could turn to him and he would do whatever was necessary. What would they have done today without him? She and Vincent would have tried to rescue Odette, but without Morgan, would Judson have given in? Could she have whipped

Judson? No, he would have torn the whip from her and—
She shuddered. Judson would have treated her as he had
been about to treat Odette. No, a woman was not respected, she was shoved about, whipped, struck.

But Morgan did not strike Tess. He was good to her,
he was kind, he gave her presents, he treated her with—
with concern. She sighed deeply, almost asleep. Was this
—love? Did he feel love for her, besides lust? And could
she ever really love him, could she ever learn what love
really was?

She slept, to wake with a jerk. She judged by the
position of the moon that it was past midnight, perhaps one
or two in the morning. She rose softly, and put on a light
robe and her slippers.

She went softly to the room where Odette lay. She
carried a candle with her, and held it carefully as she went
into the open door of the room. Malkia started, jerked
awake from where she slumped in the rocker.

Tess bent over Malkia. "How is she?" she murmured.
"Has she spoken?"

Malkia shook her head wearily, passed her hand over
her face, tried to get up. "No wake up, missus. No drink
water."

Tess took a glass of the water and went to the bed.
"Odette," she said. The girl did not stir. "Odette?"

She put the glass to the faded pink lips, and held
the head in her palm so she would not choke on it. The
girl wet her lips, then drank a little. Tess watched her,
worried. The girl was usually so lively, so quick, it was
a shock to see her like this.

She stroked her hand gently over the cold forehead,
and brushed back the limp hair. "Poor dear child," she
crooned.

Malkia had gotten up, slowly and painfully. "Malkia,
bring hot broth and herbs," she muttered. She went out,

returned in about fifteen minutes with a bowl. Tess held it to Odette's lips, and they both encouraged her to drink. She swallowed about half the mixture, lay back, and closed her eyes.

"She sleep now," said Malkia.

"You go to bed now, Malkia. I will watch till morning," said Tess, and urged her to go. She herself sat down in the rocker, and rocked slowly, her head back. Malkia left, and the house settled to silence again.

The hours passed slowly. Tess kept herself awake by thinking about home, the early years, going slowly through the years of her short life. When her mother had died, the way her stepfather had reacted to that. Grief, then anger that the frail lovely woman had slipped from his grasp. His turning on Tess and Vincent, the way they had worked seven days a week, from early morning to late at night, never satisfying him.

And Morgan had come, and spirited them away to a new life. Not an easy life, but exciting, different, and one that did not crush their spirits.

Her head dropped, she made herself get up, and give Odette another drink of the cooled soup and herbs. It seemed to help her, the black eyes opened and shut, and she seemed cool rather than cold. Tess drew the blanket up to her chin and covered the slim shoulders, as the morning breeze came in to chill the room.

Morgan came in as dawn cut pink and crimson slashes across the paling blue sky in the east. He was in stocking feet. "How is the girl?" he asked, bending over the bed.

"I think she is better, Morgan," Tess whispered. Odette opened her eyes. They were blank, but the eyeballs no longer rolled. She stared at them both, then closed her eyes once more.

One of the other girls came up soon after, to find

Morgan and Tess sitting in watch over Odette. She gave them a startled look, and said shyly, "Malkia send me."

"Good," said Tess. "Help her drink water when she wishes. Malkia will bring soup by and by."

The girl nodded, and sat down carefully in the rocker, as though afraid of the white man's possessions. She was clean and neat, freshly washed. Malkia's doing, thought Tess.

Tess went to wash and dress, as did Morgan. At breakfast, which a maid had prepared, they talked in low tones, but not for long.

"It is over and done," said Morgan. "We cannot think more about it. Poor Bernardo. He was a good man, a decent man."

"Yes, we shall miss him. Always good with the horses, and willing to turn his hand to anything." Vincent shook his head. "Why does such a thing happen to a man like that?"

There was no answer. Morgan and Vincent went out to the fields, Morgan staying in the near fields, with a rifle at hand. Malkia hovered about, anxiously, took soup up to Odette, pattered down with a report later. "She better, she go back to the hut today."

Gamba came, and he and Malkia carried the weak girl out to her hut. It was what she wanted, they said.

The men came in for lunch, rather quiet and subdued. "The blacks are all upset," reported Vincent, with a worried frown. "They don't sing and laugh today, or crack jokes."

"Why should they? One of them was brutally murdered," said Tess bitterly. "They will want to mourn, though there is nothing to bury."

"Don't, Tess," said Morgan gently. "We cannot do anything about that. But we will remember him in our hearts."

They rested in the heat of the day, for an hour, then went back to work. They were anxious to bring in the last of the cane by early June, and it was early May by now. Neither of them had realized it was such a long process, but the cane must be cut by hand. Judson drove his men seven days a week, from before dawn until midnight if he chose, and his cane was almost all cut; there only remained about ten fields. But Morgan had about thirty fields yet to cut.

Tess was sewing in mid-afternoon. She had resolved to make a new white dress for Odette. Startled, she pricked her finger when about four o'clock there came a loud screech.

She started out of the rocker on the veranda, and raced through the house. The sound came again, it seemed to come from the kitchen area. But when Tess went out there, no one was about. She saw one of the boys. "What is wrong? Who cried out?" she demanded.

The boy gave her the blank look that meant he didn't want to answer. But the screech came again.

Tess followed it, out beyond the cabins. She thought afterwards she had been careless, she did not take a pistol or even a knife.

She found a curious sight. Someone had set up an open sort of cabin, with one wall and four posts. Over it was a hastily-erected thatch roof, and there was a wide pole down the center. In the dust of the floor, someone had drawn white beautiful marks, and around the pole Odette danced.

She had changed. There was a taut excited look about her, she wore a cloth about her hips, that was all. Her pointed breasts bounced a little as she danced up and down, and clapped her hands together.

Malkia was seated near the entrance, Tess went over to her and sank down beside her. Curiosity would not let her leave, and they did not look at her. Several other women were there, two played drums rhythmically, with their open palms striking the stretched skins. One woman held two gourds, and shook them with the beat of the drums, so that they rattled and made a pleasant sound.

Another young girl dressed in white jumped up to join Odette in the dancing. As Tess's eyes became accustomed to the dimness of the shelter in the hot sunlight, she saw there was a table set against the far wall. On it were some strange objects: a broken bottle with an unlit candle in it, a calabash with some piled fruit, another bottle with some liquid, a crude wooden painting.

She crinkled up her eyes, puzzled. What were they?

Then Odette began to cry out in a strange tongue. Tess caught some words, but she did not know them. It sounded rather like a religious service, when the worshippers were caught up in a trance. Only the words were not "God," or "Jesus," as Tess had heard them.

Odette cried out to Erzulie, to Baron Samedi, to Ogun, over and over. And she cried to Damballah, which made the women screech, in real or pretended fear, and draw up their legs, and pull their skirts over their knees.

She cried out again, and again, then bent her head back and forth, her long hair flying about her bare shoulders. She cried out and screeched, in an ear-splitting way that made chills run down Tess's warm back. No one looked at her, nor told her to go away, so she stayed.

One of the women had been quietly working in the corner. Now she rose, and bent and bowed to the middle pole of the shelter. Then she held out to the dancing Odette a small doll made of straw and cloth, with a crude face painted on it. Tess felt a jolt, for the crude face was recognizably that of Caleb Judson! And the body was short and squat like his, the clothing, cloth pants such as he wore.

Odette held the doll and danced around the pole, calling out again and again to Damballah. The women watched; some drummed the drums until the sweat rolled down their dark cheeks. The girl dancing with Odette went to the altar, drank some of the liquid, and with a strange, obscene gesture blew it at Odette, so the liquid sprayed over Odette and the doll she held. She did this again and again, the liquid sometimes splashing on the dirt floor.

Tess was so fascinated she did not notice the time passing. Dusk came and the blue sky turned to purple. The dancing quickened, the women were singing something loud and breathless. Then Odette drew from her skirt a long pin, and held it up. The drummers went on drumming, faster and faster, but the singing stopped. In the hush, only the drums rolled.

Slowly, deliberately, Odette lifted the small straw doll. She cursed it, spat at it; then she lifted her other hand, and drove the long pin right through the body of the doll, dropping it to the dirt floor.

The drums halted instantly. In the silence, suddenly aware of a shuffle of feet, Tess glanced about, torn from the trance she had felt as the drums had beaten monotonously, faster and faster.

She saw the black men gathered about, watching in awe and silence. Gamba was there, his tall build standing out from the others. His head was erect, his eyes arrogant as he watched. The other boys and men were standing outside the circle of women.

Then they came inside, Gamba first. They walked to the doll, and each one lifted it, drove the pin inside the doll again, and muttered something. Each in turn, again and again, as Odette watched, leaning against the center pole, her eyes blazing with dark fire.

Each boy and man did the same, until the last one

dropped what remained of the doll at Odette's feet. Contemptuously, she ground her heel on it.

Then they began to slip away, one by one, into the darkness, leaving Malkia and Tess and Odette. Odette was staring down at what remained of the doll. Malkia took the arm of Tess, and urged her in a whisper, "We go now, white missus. You say nothing, yes?"

Tess nodded, and returned to the house with Malkia, leaving Odette there alone.

20

Louis Abaco knew what had happened down there. His mouth tight and hard, he had studied the scene through the spyglass. They were too far away for his interference. He saw Odette captured by Judson, saw Bernardo run after her.

He snapped the spyglass shut, and walked slowly back to his campfire. He sat down, leaned against a tree, and sighed. Bernardo would not be back. He was alone again. Bernardo had loved too strongly not to come to grief.

Yet, Odette was very lovely, and a fine girl. He did not blame Bernardo for loving her. Abaco's mouth twisted as he put his head on his hand wearily. He loved her also. Who could help it? Such a beautiful graceful girl, with a spirit in her of gaiety and charm, a sweetness, an eagerness to please, and—and Judson wanted her.

By now Judson probably had her. Abaco closed his eyes. That bastard was so damn cruel, he would probably hurt her badly.

He could not eat. He finally rolled up on his blanket, ready to move it about himself when the wind came up and night cooled. His rifle was always at hand.

In the dawn, he was aware of sounds. He sprang to his feet, grabbed up his rifle, stuck his knife in his belt. The ashes of the fire had been put out last night; he never kept a fire in the night, no matter how cold he was. It would draw attention against the dark purple sky.

He listened alertly, his head to one side, his eyes half shut. He heard the shuffle of feet, the murmur of voices. He moved soundlessly on bare feet to the shelter of the bushes, and then through them, past one tree, then another, until he came to the dim path that wound up the side of the mountain, the highest on the island of Elysia.

He stared. He had never seen such a sight. A procession of blacks was moving up the hill: men, women, children of all ages, babies carried in their mother's arms.

He recognized some of them by sight, but he had not met them. They were Judson's slaves, most of them. A few from Quintero's plantation.

In the dim light of dawn, they shuffled along the trail, fear in their faces, frequently glancing back over their shoulders as though someone might follow. Louis Abaco silently cursed. The blacks were coming right to his hideout. Must he leave this island? Solitary though he was, it had become his home, and he felt as though he knew everyone up here, in this part of the island. He would hate to leave the shelter of the cave where he hid when the strong gale winds blew, or the rains blustered.

He watched in silence. They did not know he stood there in the shelter of trees and thick underbrush, watching them. There must have been more than sixty of them, more like seventy, counting the smaller children.

He felt some pity in his heart, but also impatience and dread. They would ruin his shelter, white men would follow them, he might get captured as well as they.

They moved on wearily, they must have been walking for several hours to come this far so slowly. Some had bundles of clothing and food, others carried a pan or two, a precious crudely carved statue; some had only a baby or small child by the hand.

Now came the men bringing up the rear, the strong field hands, their eyes alert in haggard faces. They glanced about, and one spotted Louis Abaco.

Before they could challenge him and kill him in their fear, he stepped from the brush, and held up his right hand in the universal gesture of peace. His left hand remained casually on his belt near the long knife. He could throw the knife with either hand.

"Where do you come from?" he asked, though he knew.

The procession halted, fear filled their dark faces, some of the women cried out and shrank from him. They stared at him; some had seen him from a distance. He was not white, nor was he a slave. "You—are the pirate?" asked one of the men slowly.

Abaco nodded. "Yes. I am Louis Abaco," he identified himself. Several of the men pointed to themselves and said their slave names.

"I have shelter up here," he said, with resignation. They would find it anyway, the way they were going. "There is water, cool and pure. A little food. Come."

He motioned with his open palm and fingers, like the slaves did, not like the whites. They looked at each other, murmured, muttered, hesitated. He waited. Finally they gave way, and followed him up the path. He picked up one of the small girls who was staggering with weariness. She shrank from the stranger, but he held her gently and patted her back, soothed her, and she finally cuddled down with a sigh.

They seemed reassured, and some were chattering to each other as they entered the clearing. The men went to the water, flung themselves down and drank greedily. The women waited their turn. Louis Abaco went upstream from the men, filled a pan with water, and brought it back to fill cups for the children. One plump woman seemed to be in charge of five small children. She eyed him keenly, nodded her thanks as she gave water to the children.

He glanced at the sky. "It is light enough for me to light a small fire now. We can cook food and eat together," he said.

They accepted his authority numbly. He knew some disaster had happened, and he thought it was connected with Bernardo. But he had infinite patience when necessary, and he could wait for their story.

He produced what food he had, a little meat that Bernardo had brought, some breadfruit, mangoes, papaya, coconut, bananas. The women took it from him, and cooked it deftly over the fires; they were accustomed to this. They had a meal ready while the men sat and stared at the trees or Abaco; or crouched, with their gaze on the ground, their thoughts gloomy.

They ate, drank some herb tea, and then sat back refreshed. They sat in a little circle, gazing suspiciously at Abaco. He took out his pipe, shook a little tobacco into it. Morgan Hamilton had brought him the tobacco. He was a good white man, thought Abaco, little as he trusted any man.

He waited for them to speak. Finally one of the men

stood up and cleared his throat, and flung back his head. The others sat up in expectation.

"We tell what happened to Mr. Judson," said the man. The others murmured and nodded.

Louis Abaco listened to the story with impassive face. Although he had guessed what had happened, the reality was shocking. The man told of seeing Odette come through the cane; of Judson after her on the great black horse; of how Judson had gone after Bernardo with the dogs; how Bernardo had been torn to pieces.

But there was more. "Big white man came, little white man, and little white missus with silvery hair, called Silver Jasmine," said the man, and his black eyes lit up. "Came with rifles, and with anger. Big white man Hamilton, he asked, 'Where Bernardo?! Where my slave? Where Odette?' He whipped Judson."

Louis Abaco sat upright. The women were murmuring with satisfaction. He noticed the big rather handsome black woman with the five children. Her face was usually blank, but there was a spark in her eyes as the man spoke of the whipping.

He made another man repeat the story. They all agreed, some had seen it with their own eyes. The white man Hamilton had come with rifles, and he had beaten Caleb Judson with a whip. Then he had picked up Odette and taken her out to the carriage. Silver Jasmine had taken her in her own white arms and crooned to her like a mother. They had driven away.

Finally Abaco got to the crucial part of their story. Why had they run away?

The big woman spoke slowly, and they all listened with respect. "I was Judson mistress many years," she said. "Five children. I hate him like devil. He *is* the devil!" They all nodded with agreement. "When he is better, he whip all. He whip us. We must run."

319

"Ah—I see that," muttered Abaco. He knew what they meant. Judson had been whipped before them, he had been humiliated. Now he in turn would whip the helpless ones who had witnessed his downfall. It was like on the pirate ships. When a man was whipped and hated, he would turn savagely on those he could whip in turn. He could not turn on his officer, he must fawn at the man's feet. His captain could not be whipped. But he must whip someone, to restore his confidence, his manhood, his threatening presence.

"He will set dogs on us," muttered one man, and fear flashed in their eyes.

Abaco had thought the same thing. The starved animals were trained to chase slaves. And the thought of having done to them what had been done to Bernardo sent tremors through them. They had finally fled from the cruel master they could no longer endure. But he would be after them.

"If you go back today, maybe he will not whip?" he suggested.

They all shook their heads, and shuddered violently, casting fearful glances behind them. "No, no, we must never go back!" they assured him.

There was not enough food even for today, he thought. They would have to go back, or starve, or be chased by dogs. Unless—unless their minds were set on a rebellion! Had they courage enough for that? He wondered about it, as some lay down to sleep, their children close to them.

They could not stay up in the hills indefinitely. It would grow cold at night. There was not enough food here for one or two men, to say nothing of seventy men, women and children. He noticed that a few of the slaves were set apart from the others.

He questioned them casually. "No, not Judson's. We

belong to Quintero," they said. "He is all right white man. Overseers bad. They will whip. They will hear what happened, and whip. Bad men."

They had eaten little the rest of the day, and settled down for the night stoically, some of the women in the cave with the children, the men curled up under trees. Then Abaco heard other sounds on the trail. He slept lightly, and so he heard.

He went out, and found a dozen more men coming up, but no women and children this time. He spoke to them, and told them who he was.

One of them was Gamba. Abaco was surprised to see the man with whom he had spoken in the past. He was closest to the hills, at Hamilton's plantation.

"Why do you come, Gamba?" he asked.

"Hear about Judson slaves," said the man, his eyes flashing. "Bernardo dead, Odette scared. We came. We will rebel!"

Abaco stared at him thoughtfully, then nodded, and took them back to the camp. He settled them all down for the night, feeling like an unwilling ship's captain who had too many sailors signing on. His pirate crew was a motley lot, he thought, grinning a little ironically into the darkness.

With dawn, and folks stirring and hungry, he spoke to them. "You must go back soon, or dogs will come. Or —we must plan."

"Rebel!" said Gamba, his eyes gleaming. "We will take over plantation. We will fight, we will kill Judson!"

"Do you have guns, do you have rifles?" asked Abaco. "Judson will have many guns."

"Mama, I am hungry," whined one of the small girls, rubbing her little distended stomach.

Her mother hushed her sharply, and gave her water

to drink. Abaco, his mouth drawn tight, wondered how long they could live on water.

Gamba said, "I have a machete," and he showed his long curved knife used for cutting sugarcane. "Cut off white heads with knife!"

"I have some guns," said Abaco slowly. "From pirate ship. We will get them. Come with me. Did you bring meat with you?"

The dozen or so men from Quintero's and Morgan Hamilton's nodded, they had brought food.

"Give it to women, they will fix meal. We will get guns now."

So they divided the work. Abaco led them uphill to another cave he had found and shown to no one. There was now fire in his blood, though his caution wanted to hold him back. He knew the odds against them. White men with rifles and cunning. Black slaves broken to obedience, with only a few muskets, some ammunition, a little gunpowder, and their knives.

They grabbed the weapons, dark faces shining with new hope. "We will kill, take house, take cane," said Gamba. "I am a chief, I will tell all how to work!"

Gamba's words did not sit well with the slaves, there were glances at him, then away. Abaco said, "It is too soon to talk of who will be chief. And what about the other white men?"

One of Morgan Hamilton's slaves said, "Not Mr. Hamilton. He is good white man. He whipped Judson!"

There were nods and murmurs of approval. But Gamba shouted out, his arrogant head high, "Kill all white men! Kill all white men! They would kill us! We must kill all."

Several of the blacks of Judson shouted and raised their knives. Abaco reproved them.

"Yell like that, and we all dead! Keep your voices

down! We must speak clear, think clear." He tapped his head. "Drunken men with rum or words! Think! We must not kill Morgan Hamilton. Or his white missus, Silver Jasmine. Or the brother of Silver Jasmine, he is good, right?"

A few murmurs, and a look of relief from some of the slaves. But Judson's slaves were hot for blood. "Kill all whites!" called one woman fiercely. "All white men are bad! Judson beat, beat! Cut out tongue!" And she pointed to one mute black boy. "Whip, set dogs on us, call girls to bed. Hit, beat, hurt," and she pointed out one young girl, who sat with her head hanging down.

"That one?" asked Abaco. "She is twelve, no?"

"Thirteen. He took Bettina," asserted the woman, and the big woman Leonie nodded. "He takes any girl he wants. Make slave babies, he say! More slaves for him!"

They hated Judson, that was certain. Abaco said nothing more, but polished up an old musket, got out his knife and began to sharpen it on a stone. The other men imitated him, sharpening their machetes, repairing the few muskets they had, and the couple of pistols.

Two nights after the rescue of Odette, Morgan went out to the fields in the early morning. He and Vincent had gone together, they had talked quietly about that. It would be best not to go alone anywhere for a while. The black slaves had been sullen yesterday, quiet, giving them blank looks.

"They may blame all whites for Judson for a time," said Morgan. "We had best stay close to the house, and keep together. None of us alone. I don't think the women would hurt Tess, but they are pretty upset, and it doesn't pay to take chances."

"Hurt Tess? Why would they do that?" asked Vincent, his blue eyes, so like those of Tess, wide in his tanned face.

"Just hatred of all whites, a blind unreasoning hate, because of slavery," sighed Morgan. "And not so unreasonable. Would you like being a slave? I know I hated it when I was first impressed. They kept me in chains until I calmed down!"

"Of course!" said Vincent, thoughtfully. "I sure hated Ryder. I would have killed him if he had hurt Tess—I guess you are right. We better be careful."

They went out to the nearest cane fields, strolling slowly, talking. It took a few minutes to realize there were no blacks about. None of the field hands had come to cut cane. The carts stood where they had been left near the sugar mill, but no blacks were there either. No Gamba, no big sturdy field hands. A few women and children lingered near the cabins, watching with sidelong looks.

"They have all left!" Vincent stared about the cane field incredulously. "I wonder if they have left the molasses as well?"

They went back to the hot steamy hut where the cane sugar was supposed to boil continuously for a week. The fires were out, the sticky masses in the cauldrons untended.

Morgan looked at it grimly. It would be a total loss, he supposed, but that was not his biggest worry. If the tough field hands, including the sullen arrogant Gamba had left, they were in trouble.

He went to the slave huts, and found Malkia smoking her pipe. "Where are the men?" he asked bluntly.

Her wizened face was blank. She lifted her shoulders. "Not know, master," she said.

Odette was in the kitchen, with a couple other maids. He was relieved to see they were all working, Odette rolling out bread dough, the others preparing luncheon meat.

"Where are the field hands, Odette?" asked Morgan quietly.

"I don't know, master," she said dully, her head bent.

He did not bother to ask again. He went into the house with Vincent, and told Tess, "All the big blacks that work the cane and the mill have departed. I beg they have gone up in the hills. I think I'll go after them, talk to them, persuade them to come back."

Her face had gone so white, the freckles stood out. "We'll come with you," she said sturdily.

Morgan hesitated. "No, you cannot do that."

"Morgan, you can't go alone! They know those hills! And that pirate is up there, the one who sheltered Bernardo!" she urged. "He won't know you didn't have any part in his—his murder!"

"I bet they know everything," said Morgan grimly. "They get word to each other plenty fast. Well, maybe you're right. But I can't work on the cane alone."

"I didn't think our slaves would leave," said Tess solemnly. "I mean, I can understand why Judson's would leave. But not ours. Don't they think they are treated fairly?"

"Did Ryder treat you fairly?" asked Vincent, putting his arm about her. "And didn't you figure all men were brutes, after Ryder and the sailors and all?"

She nodded, her mouth rueful, her glance catching at Morgan's, then away again, shyly. "Yes, I see what you mean, Vincent. But what can we do? Just wait?"

"We best lock up the guns," said Morgan. "In case of a slave rebellion, they would head right for the weapons. And we best lock up the house—"

"Slave rebellion!" Now Tess was white again, all pink gone from her cheeks. She caught at his arm, "Morgan, do you think—would they—"

"I don't know. I just figure we had best take care for a time, until they all calm down," said Morgan. He ran his hand through his red hair.

It was bad enough to try to figure out how to cut

cane, make molasses and sugar and rum, all the new things he had had to learn. How to run the slave plantation, how to cope with the hot weather and a new life, and a married life with Tess. And now this!

"What about talking to Quintero?" suggested Vincent. "He has lived here for years, surely he knows how the slaves will act. Maybe they will just go away and, you know —sorrow for a time for Bernardo. Then they'll come back. What do you think?"

"I don't know, but it's a good idea. We'll go to Quintero," said Morgan. "He should know what is going on, we can put our stories together. Tess, you get your shawl and bonnet, the sun is hot. I'll get the rifles, and Vincent—"

"Right—the carriage. We'll go talk to Quintero." Vincent's face had lighted up. He was humming as he went out the back door to the stables.

He was looking forward to a visit with Inez, thought Morgan, wryly as he went to get the rifles. They had just three rifles, and some pistols. He filled a bag with all their ammunition, noting how low it was getting, and brought that along. Tess carried a rifle and two pistols in a large cloth bag. He had his pockets full of bullets, and Tess put the rest in a cloth handbag.

Odette came in the back door as they were about ready to leave. Tess went over to her, her hands full of the weapons.

"Odette, we are going to visit with Señor Quintero and his girls," she said slowly, gently. "We will come back by nightfall. You will stay with Malkia? Yes?"

Odette nodded dully, her dark eyes full of pain and sorrow. "With Malkia," she echoed.

"You will be safe. Hide if—if any men come. Hide safe!"

Odette nodded again, and watched from the front

door, one foot on the other as she leaned against the door frame, watching them leave in the carriage. Tess had set the weapons down, and waved to her. Odette did not return the wave.

"She is still sick with the pain of it," Tess said to Morgan anxiously. "She has scarcely spoken since then."

"Give her time, my darling," said Morgan gently, and put his free arm about her. "Give her time. . . ."

They drove to Quintero's in about an hour, the horse trotting briskly on the loose sands of the beach. Morgan and Vincent kept a keen watch for any of Judson's men. But the Judson house and plantation seemed curiously quiet. They saw no one working in the cane, and the horses and dogs were still.

"Do you think Judson's slaves have left?" asked Tess.

"I have no idea. But if some of ours left, I bet some of his did also," said Morgan.

They reached Quintero's, only to find the house shuttered and still. At first they thought nobody was there, and Tess and Morgan watched anxiously as they approached. But as they turned into the round circle drive at the front of the Spanish villa, they saw the older man seated on the veranda, a rifle across his lap.

The windows behind him were closed and barred, with only the big wooden front door open to the breeze. Behind him a skirt fluttered, and as Vincent pulled up the carriage, Inez came out in a blue gown, her face anxious and pale.

"Ah, my friends, you come!" Quintero got up, and came out to greet them, the rifle held loosely in his left hand, his face beaming. But there were lines of anxiety on his forehead, and his eyes were bloodshot, as though he had not slept much.

Morgan clasped his hand, then turned to help Tess down. A black boy came running to take the horse.

Morgan let out a breath of relief. They had heard of the trouble, but were not touched by it, he thought. But the next minute, Quintero disillusioned him.

"Have some of your slaves fled? About twelve of mine are missing. I'm afraid to send my overseers, because of what I heard about Judson's. Is it true? He set dogs on one of your men?"

"About ten of ours are gone, the field hands," said Morgan gravely. He sank down into a rocker with a sigh, after seeing Tess seated.

"I'll bring some cool drinks," said Inez, after greeting them. She gave them all a shy smile. "Lime and rum?"

"I'll help you, Miss Inez," said Vincent, and followed her closely into the house.

Morgan told Quintero what had happened. The older man sighed deeply, and shook his graying head. "I was afraid of this. Judson treats his slaves worse and worse. He wasn't bad when he first came, but drink and the tropics can wear a man down, he has a strong streak of cruelty in him, and there's no one to stop him."

"What will happen?" asked Morgan. "I am new here. Will they stay away or try to attack us?"

"No, no, I don't think so!" Quintero reached for the tall glass Inez was offering him now. "Don't worry too much. Be on guard, in case of a few rebels. But my guess is, they'll all come back in a day or two. Hunger, you know."

"Hunger?" asked Tess quickly, her glass untouched. "What do you mean, Señor Quintero?"

"There's not much to eat in the hills." He shrugged. "No trees with fruit on them, only stubby pines, a few coconuts. Fresh water from the mountain streams, but little else. No vegetables, no meat, no grain. They'll have to come back."

They discussed the possibilities. Quintero advised

them to keep the house locked most of the day, and completely locked up at night, not allowing any slaves, even the most trusted ones, to remain indoors. "They just might be forced to open up to their men," he said. "A girl can be mighty loyal to her man, even the black girls."

"And they will come back?" asked Tess anxiously. "I don't like to think of them going hungry. Do you know if any of Judson's slaves left him?"

Quintero tasted his lime and rum thoughtfully, then nodded. "One of my overseers told me that they all had left, but I don't believe that. He likes to exaggerate. I am sure the women will stay, they won't leave their children, or take them into the hills. And the men will come back when they are tired of playing, and have their bellies empty. Don't worry, my friends! I lived through another such rebellion some years ago, and nothing much happened. A couple of burned houses, some stolen pigs and chickens, and they all meekly came back. Hamilton forgave his and gave a feast, which I think was a mistake. I let my overseers whip a few, and the others fell at my feet and begged forgiveness, which I granted, of course."

Morgan had been looking absently at Tess as the man spoke, and he noted she was exchanging a look with Inez. He glanced quickly, caught the glance from Inez, a sad grimace, and a shake of her head. Inez knew something more.

"Where is Señorita Florencia?" he asked idly.

"Oh, she is hiding locked in her room," laughed Quintero. "She refused to come out, and Inez took her some breakfast. She is terrified! She is sure we will all be killed. Poor girl. She begs to return to St. Michael, but I think she is exaggerating it all. She would love to go back to town and buy a dozen new gowns," he laughed.

"Perhaps I should have a little visit with her," offered Tess. She and Inez went upstairs, and were gone about half an hour. She returned with a grave look, and was silent the remainder of their visit.

"Well, we must return home," said Morgan finally. "Thank you, señor, for your reassurance. We will keep in touch by messenger. Let me know if anything seems dangerous, and we will come to your aid. And we will notify you when all the slaves return."

Quintero begged them to remain for luncheon, but they refused. Tess seemed uneasy, and wanted to leave. Morgan got them into the carriage, and they departed.

When they had turned out of the lane, and were on the open beach, Morgan said quietly, "Well, Tess? What did Inez tell you?"

She gave him a wide-eyed stare, and began to protest, until he said, "The truth, if you will, my dear. We are all in danger together."

She bit her lips, then said, "Florencia was hysterical, talked about someone named Luis. It seems that he was an overseer at the time of the slave rebellion years ago. They both remember, she and Inez. Inez and I left Florencia, then Inez told me the story. Luis was beaten by a slave, and the slave fled into the hills. Quintero demanded him back. Instead, all the slaves rebelled, and they had several days of shooting and firing the cane. Quintero sent word through Hamilton that all was forgiven, they might return."

She hesitated, her lip trembling. Morgan urged gently, "The rest of the story, Tess?"

She nodded. "The slaves came back, believing them. Hamilton treated his to a cane party, as Quintero said. However—Quintero took the slave who had beaten Luis and had him killed. It was justice, he said. The slaves were sullen for a time, and Luis disappeared. He had gone out fishing alone—and never returned. Inez thinks the slaves killed him, drowned him."

"He never came back?" The story had sent a chill down Morgan's spine, and Vincent, who was listening also, turned away.

"No, never," said Tess simply. "Quintero was upset, because he had the bother of hiring another overseer. He did not seem to suspect anything."

Tess was shivering in the heat of the midday sun. Morgan put his arm about her and held her close, but he was thinking; not seeing the lazy waving of the coconut trees in the trade winds, not seeing the beautiful creamy beach, the splash of the blue waves of the Atlantic against the shore.

Quintero had sort of lied to him—again. Could he ever trust that man? And the slaves—they would remember that time. They would not be willing to trust again, not easily. Oh, God, what a mess, thought Morgan.

A man sowed what he wished, and then he had to reap it. Was there no other way in the dark destinies of mankind? When would man ever learn?

21

Back in the airy plantation house, Tess moved about
in a daze. Odette came in silently to help with the evening
meal. Morgan and Vincent talked at his big front desk,
then moved out to the veranda, where they sat with rifles
near at hand.

The maids cooked a good dinner, and Tess thanked
them. However, they did not beam with shy delight at her
praise. They bobbed their heads and thanked her in a
mumble, and scurried back to their huts when the evening's
work was done.

As the purple dusk fell, and outlined the palm trees
waving along the beach, Vincent and Morgan went about
the great house, pulling the great shutters closed and
bolting them. It made the downstairs stifling warm in a
short time, and they went upstairs to the opened rooms.

"Reckon I'll turn in, or do you want me to keep

watch?" asked Vincent, pausing at the door to his room.

"Might as well turn in," said Morgan. "I don't think trouble will come tonight, if ever. I cannot believe our blacks will turn against us."

"Hope you're right, but I'll keep my rifle beside the bed, anyway," sighed Vincent. "Good night, Tess. Keep your chin up!"

"Good night, Vincent, sleep well," said Tess soberly. She moved along to her room at the front of the mansion. She felt the silence of the house, no voice echoing downstairs, no giggle from one of the girls, none of the men calling to each other as they went down to fish in the night sea.

All silence, ominous silence that made one's heart beat faster and caused one to jump when a bird cried out, or a wind came up that caused a tree limb to crackle.

In her room, she undressed and washed at the basin. Odette had brought up fresh hot water. At least Odette had not deserted them, nor the women, especially Malkia. She had seen the black woman hovering about the back door, rocking in the cane rocker, smoking her pipe, her keen eyes watchful. Would someone like Malkia get caught up in the fever of hate directed toward white people? Was her loyalty to her own stronger than her loyalty to any whites?

After all, thought Tess, she and Morgan and Vincent had not been long on the island, not nearly long enough to build up loyalty from the slaves. Yet they had tried to treat them kindly, with generosity and no cruelty.

But the death of Bernardo had hurt them all, frightened them. And fear did mad things to people. A strong emotion, it could wipe out love, loyalty, devotion, and with the greatest ease, common sense.

She stood at the opened window for a short time, clad in her thin cotton nightdress. Her bare feet felt cool on the wooden planks of the floor. A slight breeze lifted the strands of blond hair, ruffled the curls at her forehead. A whiff of perfumed fragrance came to her—it was the night-blooming jasmine that clambered up the pillars of the veranda, and scented the house deliciously in the evening. White starry blooms with yellow centers, tiny blooms, almost unnoticed, until night brought out their strong fragrance, and the butterflies and sleepy bees fluttered about them. She took a deep breath of the jasmine.

Odette scented her bath water with the little white blooms, and washed her hair with it, crooning over "little white missus" as she did so. Tess had felt pampered and spoiled, delightfully so. She and Odette had conversed shyly, yet openly, talking of the new land, of the island, of the flowers, of love.

And now Odette was gloomy and silent, hurt to the depths of her young body. She had a heart and soul—how could anyone deny that? Tess's mouth compressed, and she sighed, turning to the bed wearily.

She had just slipped into bed, and decided she needed the white cotton sheet over her, when the door to Morgan's bedroom opened and he came in, dark in the shadows. "Tess?" he said.

"Yes, Morgan," she replied, and her heart leaped, and thoughts of sleep fled into the corners of the room. She had been alone and lonely, feeling desperately afraid in spite of her courage.

Now he had come. He moved to the bed, and lay down beside her. He reached for her, and drew her gently against himself.

"I felt too alone tonight, my love," he said simply. "I had to come to you."

"I felt—alone also, Morgan," she murmured, and pressed her cheek thankfuly to his chest. He had worn nothing, and she felt the warm skin and hairy pelt of his chest against her flushed cheek.

His hand stroked over her hair softly, his fingers twined in the lengthening curls. "I used to be alone a lot," he said. "A man can be alone on a ship full of men. I would lie awake, with my hands under my head, and look out the porthole, and wonder if I would die on the next day."

"Oh, Morgan!" It was too close to her own thoughts tonight. She had been thinking subconsciously of death, of terror, of slaves coming with fanatical lights in their eyes, torches burning, terror and fear making them attack the whites, burning, killing, destroying. She shuddered against him, and he closed his arms more tightly about her.

His hand moved from her hair, down over her slim back and thighs, back up to her waist, where it rested. "I thought then, it did not matter if I died. Yet—it felt such a waste." His deep voice was close to her ear. She felt the timbre rumbling through her, as though he spoke to her heart, and the beat of her heart responded to him.

"A waste? How do you mean?"

"I had not lived and loved," he said. "I had not loved any woman but my mother, and that was a different love. I had not taken any woman for my wife, slept with her, had the pleasure of the dream of a child. I was—incomplete. Half a man. Oh, the bachelors would have laughed, they took their pleasures, and forgot the women who gave it to them. But I wanted more: a home, a family, a good woman of my own, sons, daughters. I have wanted a daughter, Tess, a little girl who would wind her arms around my neck, and call me Papa." He chuckled a little ruefully. "Me, a rough sailor, impressed on a ship, fighting my way up, living from one day to the next, half naked in a battle, with a knife between my teeth as we boarded an enemy vessel! Was it not mad?"

"It was good," she murmured to him, thrilling to his

336

words. "Morgan, it probably kept you sane, and fine. And maybe it kept you alive, to think so."

"Perhaps it did," he said, after a minute of silence. "It may be. You are a wise little one, do you know it? I guess the life you had to live made you think. What did you dream about as you scrubbed floors, and ran to bring drinks to drunken sailors, and crept up to your cold room at midnight?"

She sighed, a little luxuriously, at the thought of confiding in someone who cared that she had been cold and miserable, that she had cried herself to sleep sometimes; because no one but Vincent had ever cared, and he had been in trouble himself.

"I was almost too tired to dream at nights," she said, in a little mumble against his chest. "During the day, when I scrubbed floors, especially in the morning, with nobody about—I would wish—I would wish I could go off and do exactly what I wanted. I would go down to the wharf in the sunshine, and stroll from shop window to shop window. I would sit in the sun, and read a book from cover to cover. I would be idle, and nobody would yell at me."

His hand moved on her wrist. "Did you not wish to be with someone, Tess? Did you ever wish for marriage—for children?"

She hesitated, cautious at telling her innermost secrets. But in the darkness, with his voice rumbling in her very being, she finally confided, "I wished for someone—to protect me from others. I wished, that one day I might have a son, strong and fine, like Vincent, good and intelligent, not like one of those drunken louts. And a daughter, and a little house of my own——"

"I can give you all of that," he said eagerly. "You know, I was thinking, Tess, if there is much money in the bank in St. Michael—we could buy a house there. Even a little house, if you wish, or a bigger one, in which to entertain. Several months of the year, we could live there, and have parties and entertain, like Mrs. Judson and the Quintero girls do."

Mrs. Judson again. She stiffened in his arms, and he misunderstood.

"Or do you not wish the care of another house? It shall be as you choose, Tess!" his voice coaxed. "I want you to have what you wish, my dearest. You do not think now of leaving me, do you?"

She had not thought of it for a time. She had come to feel that leaving him would not be relief, and freedom. It would be—a wrenching part of the fibers of her being, a pulling apart of the strands of her heart.

She shook her head against him, but he did not see the movement in the dark. "Tess?" he urged.

"I have not thought so—for a time," she said faintly. "I wish—to remain with you—if you wish it."

"Good," he whispered against her hair, and she felt him relax in relief. "I love you, my little Tess. I want you to be that woman in my life, the wife and mother of my children, of which I have dreamed so many years. I am tired of being lonely, of living a wasteful life with no one to share my dreams."

She felt as though she melted against him, in a warm swimming soft emotion. She put her arm timidly around his neck, and he moved to lean over her, and kiss her mouth. Their lips lingered, softened, hers parted to receive the swift tongue he thrust gently inside. The intimate kiss made her melt completely, and turn hot with desire as he drew his hand over her, from her shoulder, to the soft rounded breast.

He kissed her more hotly then, yet gently, holding her in his big hands which could hurt or caress. Tonight they caressed, because she did not fight him, but instead moved her hands over his naked back, and his chest with the thick red hairs on it. She twined her fingers in the hair, and moved her hand and palm down him, to his thighs. Timidly she found the softer hairs there, and touched him intimately. He caught his breath in a gasp.

"Tess—love," he said sharply, and moved over her. He lifted her nightdress, and his hands went over her hips as she touched him. Some instinct taught her to hold him in her fingers, and she felt the stiffening and hardening of his flesh. "Oh—my God—darling—love—" he groaned against her mouth.

Her flesh felt moist and soft for him, and he knew it now, with his fingers, and then with his hard thighs. She opened her legs, and he came between them slowly, still hotly kissing her mouth with his lips, learning how soft they were, with little nibbles at her underlip. He caught the lip in his teeth, gently, and pulled softly at it, then he moved his head down onto her breast. She felt him nibbling at her breast; then he took one nipple in his teeth and chewed gently at it, and she moaned with the pleasure of it.

She felt a strong taut need in her thighs, a blazing longing for his flesh in hers, that she never felt so wildly before. She took the hard flesh again in her fingers, and put it blindly to her thighs. He said something in Gaelic, as he did when he was nearly out of his mind with desire, and he pushed to her.

She felt him coming in, and she lay back, and her fingers twined in the red wiry hairs of his chest once more. He was moving more urgently against her, and in her, in and almost out, then deeper in. Deeper and deeper, and stronger and bigger, and she took all of him, and did not hurt with it.

"Tess," he gasped once. "Too much?"

"Go on, go on," she urged, and her hand went to

his thigh, and pulled. He came into her completely, all the way, and she felt herself quivering inside, quivering and trembling, then it was out of control.

She was pressing on him, crying out softly, and holding him with damp hands, pushing up to him as he drew out and begging him, "More, oh, more, please—do it again, oh, I am there, I am—ooohhhh—there it is—darling, oh, darling—"

He held in her, and came, hard, the gushing warmth of his release filling her, and spilling over. She was holding him with her soft thighs, holding him inside, and squeezing and shaking with the most intense feeling she had ever undergone.

He came again, again, and then it was over, and he was drawing out, limp and breathing hard. He fell over beside her, his mouth open, breath coming in gasps. She was wet and chilled from the night breeze, but she felt so good, so good, so satisfied and pleasured.

His arm lay across her as he turned to her. He drew up the sheet over them, and lay limply while he regained his breath. "Oh, God, my darling, you are so marvelously sweet—so great, I cannot believe—oh, my little love, so sweet," he muttered against her ear, kissing the lobe with sensuous slow kisses.

She trembled at his touch, her breasts still rising and falling swiftly with excitement. He whispered to her, love words, and praise, and sleeply words in Gaelic then abruptly he was asleep against her, his head butting into her side, his arm heavy across her.

She did not lie awake long, only for a moment, to smile at the wonder and ecstasy of it. Oh, the rapture of his lovemaking! And to think how she had dreaded and feared it for those weeks and months!

In the morning, when she wakened, it was to find Morgan awake, and holding her gently. He smiled down into her eyes when she blushed vividly and tried to turn from him.

"Adored," he murmured against her throat, and kissed her before rising, and stretched his hard body in a yawn. She could not even avert her gaze from the sight of that body, so tall and red-pelted with hair, lean and sturdy with muscles.

He went to his room to wash and dress, and she heard him singing some sailor's song. She smiled to herself. Odette brought a pitcher of hot water after Morgan had gone downstairs and unlocked the doors and unbarred the windows.

The girl was still silent, her dark eyes blank with shock or fear. Tess spoke to her gently, and did not insist on replies.

They lingered over a late breakfast. There was no work to do in the fields, not until the slaves returned. Vincent and Morgan were discussing the situation when one of Judson's overseers rode up and dismounted at the front veranda.

They all three went out to meet him. His insolent, yet somehow secretive, look went over them. He held out a blue envelope to Morgan.

Morgan took it, frowning down at it. It looked like the writing of a woman. He tore it open, and a faint fragrance came from the pages, as though the woman had leaned her arm on it as she wrote.

It was from Antoinette Judson. Morgan read it through quickly. "I'll read it aloud, it is to all of us," he said deliberately, aware of Tess's jealous scowl, and Vincent's questioning eyes:

My dear Mr. Hamilton,
    I am stricken with fear. All of our slaves—all of them, even my personal maid, have departed

from us. We believe they have escaped into the hills, and mean to bring on a rebellion.

My husband and I beg of you—come to us. Bring your weapons, and we can hold off the blacks. Caleb begs you also to forget your differences, and unite with us in this fight. We cannot afford to be enemies at this time. Besides, I have never been your enemy, my dear sir.

Have pity on me, also, dear Mr. Hamilton. I am sick with it all. Hoping to see you very soon, I am,

Your friend and neighbor,
Antoinette Judson

Vincent snorted, then turned away and coughed. Tess stood silent, frowning. Morgan tapped the note, and looked at the overseer, who stood insolently watching Tess's slender form.

"Have all the blacks fled? All of them?" he asked sharply.

The man nodded, and a flicker of fear came into his eyes, glancing over his shoulder as he sat on the tall horse. "All of them. A bad lot, Mr. Hamilton," he said. "Gone the first night, even the babies."

"Well, we must consider the matter. Take word to Mr. Judson that we have his message, and will try to consult with him today."

The man scowled, and his lips went tight and hard. "He wants you now, Mr. Hamilton!"

"I am not under his orders," said Morgan curtly. "Go on, be off, and we shall come if we choose to do so."

The man hesitated, then rode off, watching all about him with fear evident in his posture.

Tess said not a word as they walked inside and sat down. Morgan sat at the desk; Tess sat down on a chair nearby; Vincent on the arm of her chair, his hand on her shoulder.

Morgan read the message again. "I think she wrote this at Judson's dictation. I wonder if it is a trap."

Vincent said, "Probably so. He would like to kill you, I think."

"Maybe not. If the slaves have all fled, they may well expect a rebellion. Those field hands are big and tough, and with machetes—"

Tess spoke up. "I can understand her fear. Perhaps we should go, Morgan. They have experience of rebellions and might advise us. In danger, we may have to stick together."

Morgan looked at her thoughtfully. It had cost her something to say this. "I don't trust Judson, but you are probably right, Tess. All right, we'll all go. But let us go first to Quintero, and persuade him to ride with us. I don't think Judson would attack us, if this is a trap, with Quintero along to watch and report."

So they decided. Vincent hitched up the carriage, again they took out rifles and pistols and ammunition, and locked up the house before departing. They told Odette where they were going. And Malkia was there to hear them.

"Stay hidden," Tess warned them again. "If any man comes, you hide. Do not trust any of them. All right?"

Odette nodded, a flicker of gratitude in her eyes. She reached out shyly and touched Tess's hand. "Thank you, Silver Jasmine."

"You take care," repeated Tess. "We will be back pretty soon."

They rode over to Quintero, keeping a sharp watch on the wide beach road, and found him at home with the doors and windows locked. He was reluctant to leave his family, but curious also. He finally put his two overseers in charge, admonishing them to lock up and remain inside, and then rode his tall horse with them.

"Have any more of your slaves disappeared?" asked Morgan, as they rode down the winding lane.

Quintero shook his graying head. "No, thank God. Just the dozen or so field hands, which I would expect. They have to be watched continually by my overseers. The house servants are much gentler, of other tribes, and amiable in nature. Inez feels she can trust the maids and the two houseboys. Florencia locks herself in her room, and weeps or sleeps!" He grimaced.

At the Judsons', they found them all on the veranda. Judson had his rifles and pistols out, spread on a large table. He and Lord Tweed had cleaning cloths and oil out, and seemed to be getting all in good repair.

Antoinette Judson jumped up when the carriage rolled up. She ran down the steps to meet them. Her eyes were swollen with tears, she looked haggard from sleepless nights. Tess and Morgan got down, Vincent followed and tied the horse to the corner pillar of the house. Quintero was swinging down from his horse, Vincent went to tie his animal also.

"I say, good of you to come, after all that has happened," drawled Lord Tweed, his gaze flicking over Tess.

Morgan came onto the veranda. Tess had paused to speak quietly to Mrs. Judson. "Are all of your blacks still gone?" he asked.

"Gone, the lot of the bastards," scowled Judson. "My wife wants to run into town, but that is a mistake. They would just fire the fields. Brave when they aren't in front of a gun!"

Antoinette turned to him, her hands clasped tightly. "Caleb, most of the cane is in, the rum in barrels. Couldn't we go? It may save our lives! Think of the last rebellion, how wild they were! Oh, God, I am afraid!" And tears rolled down her wan cheeks.

Tess put her hand on the older woman's shoulder. "We must be brave, Mrs. Judson," she said calmly. "I think we must be prepared for the worst, but hope for the best. After all, they are human, they will be hungry and return to work."

Lord Tweed gazed at her curiously. "You call them human? Those animals?" he asked. "They are but a step from being a horse or cow! No feelings, no understandings, no minds."

"That is where you are wrong, sir," she said spiritedly, her blue eyes flashing. "You make the mistake of thinking that people are of two kinds, those born to command and those born to be commanded. That is not so! All men hate chains, and women also. One day, we shall all be free, to make choices and live as we wish, each in control of his own life!"

"Well, well, a bluestocking," he sneered, with a smile that made Morgan want to smash his mouth. "And without a day of schooling! What do you let her read, Mr. Hamilton?"

"She reads what she wishes, Lord Tweed," said Morgan quietly. "She is no slave! She is my wife, my equal, my partner in the enterprise. And I might add—my inspiration!"

"Oh, nobly put!" Lord Tweed laughed cruelly. "What does it take to inspire a sailor? A tot of rum?"

Morgan kept control of his temper with a great effort. "My lord, you but show your great ignorance of women; indeed, of the human race," he said with a grim smile. "I warrant you may pay dear for that stupidity one day. However, that is not the cause on which I come today," and he turned to Caleb Judson.

Judson was standing open-mouthed, at the way

Hamilton insulted a marquess. Antoinette spoke quickly, "We are grateful to you for responding so quickly to our —my—message."

Morgan bowed slightly to her. "We are happy to join with you in trying to solve our common problems," he said ironically. "However, I believe Mrs. Hamilton is correct. We must wait quietly, realize the injustices with which the blacks are burning, and welcome them when they return. I believe what my uncle did was to throw a party for them. I shall plan a cane party, as I have already promised them, should they return peaceably."

"A party!" yelled Judson, his face turning beet red. "I'll throw them a party, all right! I'll make the whip sing! Damn bastards, running out like that! My wife had to fix the meals for two days!"

"I did not mind, really," murmured Antoinette, rather white with apprehension. "It is just that—the cane, you know—you feel it more than I do, Mr. Judson," she said to her husband.

He gave her a hot angry look. "Much you know of it! You cannot be soft with them, Mr. Hamilton," he turned back to Morgan. "What I propose is this," he went on, ignoring his wife. "You bring your wife and brother-in-law here, Mr. Hamilton. And Quintero, bring your daughters and your two overseers here. We'll hole up together, combine our weapons and ammunition. We can fight off the bastards then!"

"Yes, combine forces," drawled the Marquess of Tweed, giving a critical polish to his rifle barrel. "Show them who's master. They'll never run away again." His face showed his eager anticipation of teaching them their lesson.

Morgan did not hesitate in refusing. He did not mind fighting with one or two helpers. What he did not like was fighting with an enemy behind him, anticipating a bullet in his head or between his shoulders.

"No, I thank you. We shall return home to our plantation, and await them there. I think they have fled to the hills. Should they meet with the former pirate, Louis Abaco, he may well talk some sense into them."

Judson and Lord Tweed shot him strange looks. "You have met the pirate?" demanded Judson. "You have talked with him? You are friends?"

"I have spoken with him briefly," said Morgan. "He seems a sensible intelligent man, not a slave, of course." He could not resist the dig. "He is a free man, and with much sense. He may persuade them to return. In that case, I shall welcome them with a party, and assure them I do not mean to have them whipped! I might advise you to do the same, if I thought you would listen," he added dryly.

"One can tell you are new to the islands, and to the blacks," snapped Judson, beet red again, his eyes blazing mad. "You don't know how to handle them! You'll be murdered in your bed, and don't say I didn't warn you!"

Antoinette Judson turned to Morgan frantically. She put her hand on his arm, in spite of her husband's glare. "I beg you, Mr. Hamilton! Do not leave in anger. Join with us, or help your wife and me to go to St. Michael. You wish your wife to be safe, do you not?"

"I'll tell you about Abaco," said Judson, ignoring this. "He killed your uncle, he'll kill you also. Louis Abaco is tricky and treacherous, a dangerous man. Did he tell you he is not a slave? He lies! He is an escaped slave! I had him under my control, but your uncle would not have it. And for reward, for knocking off his chains, your uncle was murdered by Abaco!"

"How was he killed?" asked Morgan smoothly.

"I told you! Choked to death," said Judson impatiently. "Those blacks are strong and dangerous! Think of your wife, if you won't think of yourself!"

Antoinette's hand was still on Morgan's arm, her perfume in his nostrils. Gently he took her hand in his, removed it from his arm, pressed it. "I am sorry, ma'am, I am not going to St. Michael," he said. "I plan to remain at home, and wait for the return of my people. I hope to assure them that they are safe with me, as safe as I can plan for them." And he gave Judson a hard look.

Antoinette gazed up into Morgan's eyes, her own dark eyes blurred with tears. "Do you care nothing for your wife, Mr. Hamilton?" she begged. "Take us both to St. Michael! I implore you—have mercy on us!"

"I do not leave Morgan," said Tess's sturdy voice. She held the pistol in her hand, pointing it to the ground. She looked small, touching, her chin up, her blue eyes sparkling. "Where he goes, I go. I do not leave him."

Morgan smiled at her, and went over to her. "Bravo, Tess," he said in a low voice. "Now, we'll be on our way. Farewell, all. I shall try to send word to you of any news. I hope you will do the same," he ended courteously. "Vincent—if you will bring the carriage—"

He did not want to turn his back to Judson or Lord Tweed, who both had rifles too near at hand. Vincent nodded, brought the carriage, and Quintero, who had been silent and thoughtful, got his horse and came also.

They rode down the lane, and paused, out of sight of the house. Quintero spoke up. "Do not come with me, my friends. I have decided it—I do not trust Judson, nor his slick royal friend. I am going to ride to St. Michael, and beg help of some men there. They will come to our aid, and that is better than depending on such as them—" And he jerked his thumb contemptuously back to the house they had just left.

"That is a splendid idea," said Morgan enthusiastically, in relief. "I had not thought of it—I know nobody in St. Michael. You think relief will come?"

"I am sure of it. And my girls will be all right with our people. The overseers are dependable, and the house slaves adore Inez," he added absently. He lifted his sombrero, and rode off home alone, his erect back somehow gallant.

"He should not leave the girls alone," muttered Vincent, and grumbled a little on the way home. Tess had slipped her hand into Morgan's free hand, and he paid little attention to Vincent.

He kept thinking of her face, her blazing eyes as she had proclaimed that she would not leave Morgan. Was she coming at last to trust him, to love him?

22

They rode home slowly, watching the fields of cane alertly for any approach of slaves with machetes. They saw no one. The waves of the Atlantic continued to roll up over the creamy beaches, large blue green waves, ending in a delightful spume of white spray.

It was so lovely, thought Morgan. A paradise indeed, in which only man was vile. How did man manage so readily to ruin and despoil what he would find unsullied? He found a paradise, an Eden, and filled it with slaves to earn money for him, and enable him to live idly if he chose. He used the whip on animals and other humans made like himself, but with darker skins, and made them do what he wished.

There was something badly wrong here. He said so to Tess. She nodded her curly head, her blue eyes wise.

"I have read in the gazettes brought from St. Michael,"

she said, "that the British Parliament is much disturbed that their colonies continue the slave trade. They have outlawed it, yet cargoes continue to be brought in from Africa. Some come by the Yankee ships, but some, Morgan, some are brought by our own English ships! They enslave the free peoples of Africa, for their own gain! And we use those slaves!"

"How could we grow the cane, and bring in the harvest, and make sugar and rum?" asked Vincent, from the seat in front, where he handled the horse. "How could we continue this, if we did not have slaves? It is necessary!"

"Our stepfather would have said it was necessary to keep us working from dawn to midnight," said Tess ironically. "He paid us no wages, he worked us like—like slaves! And he earned good money at the inn. Was it right then?"

Vincent scowled into the distance, and was silent. Morgan squeezed her hand.

"Tess, what would you have us do? Free the slaves, and let them go? Where would they go? Other men would but capture them, and make them slaves again."

She frowned in thought, and he watched her tenderly. "I don't know," she sighed. "But it is wrong, wrong, that Odette, an intelligent and lovely girl, must be a slave to me! It is wrong that we pay them nothing to work, only their clothing and food and a little crude shelter. Have you seen inside their huts? They have only dirt floors, a stool or two, mats to sleep on, and a thatch roof which they must make. And Bernardo was a good man, a smart man, who taught you much about the sugarcane and making rum."

"If we freed them, would they leave?" asked Vincent suddenly, as he drove more slowly along the beach. "What if—what if Morgan gave them their freedom and *asked* them to remain and work, for pay? I might have stayed at the Last Inn if Ryder had paid me, and let me work decent hours! I enjoyed the horses, and the bar wasn't bad. And if we could have kept the money, the coins the sailors and the gents gave us, we would have done well."

"Did he not allow you to keep any coins?" asked Morgan, appalled.

They both shook their blond heads. "Tess often got good money as a maid, but Ryder forced her to give it all to him, the bastard," said Vincent indignantly. "He was afraid she would save it up and run away, I guess."

"And I would have done just that," she said vigorously. "No, I did not enjoy the work, I hated it, and I would have left. Although I did not mind the keeping of the books, that part I liked."

Morgan thought about it, her small strong hand enfolded in his big one, so one could scarcely see it. She was small, but strong, smart, and so loving in bed when she wished! What a little gem he had found that night at Last Inn!

"I wonder—if we paid the blacks, would they still remain? Would they work for us for decent care, their food and clothing, and a little money to spend?" Tess wondered aloud.

"They would run off," Morgan said at once. Then he frowned. "Or would they? Where would they run? There is no food in the hills. They might go to another island, but at the risk of being captured. No, I try to treat them well. I hope they will return, and work again. We need to finish the cutting of the cane. And there is the rum to make. Some is still in the distillery fermenting. I must look at it when we return."

He sighed, unconsciously, and Tess put her free hand on their clasped hands. "We will help," she said sturdily. "I can come out to the still and help you."

"No, you will not do that work," said Morgan. "You do enough around the house. Vincent will help me, and a couple of the women. Maybe the blacks will be back by the time we return," he said more hopefully, as the horse turned into their lane. He looked with renewed pride at the plantation house as they came up to it.

How handsome it was, with the beautiful pillars and the stone work, the white jasmine climbing to the second floor, the purple bougainvillea on the south wall, the white shutters pinned back against the stonework. The bushes rioted with color and fragrance, the pink and cream and blazing red hibiscus, the yellow allamanda, the pale orange plumeria, the tender blue jacaranda. What a picture it made, with the darker green pines bent against the Atlantic breezes, the coconut trees and the royal palms waving slowly in the winds. His home, his and Tess's home, where they would be happy, and have a child, then another—

Vincent drove around the side of the house, back to the stables. It struck them all at the same time: it was too quiet.

Morgan said sharply, "Where is the stable boy?"

Vincent drove right into the stable, picking up his rifle as he let go the reins. He jumped down to look around. Morgan had left the carriage in a leap, and his eyes had narrowed in the dimness to glance about in alarm.

Tess took up the heavy pistol, and moved to get down. "Stay there," he said sharply. "Let me look about."

Her eyes were wide and blue, but not terrified. She had a sort of sturdy purpose about her, a strength that came from within. She nodded briefly, and stayed where she was, the pistol ready.

He moved cautiously about the buildings. Vincent came from the kitchen, a puzzled frown on his blond tan face.

"The food is cooking, I pulled the meat off the stove.

It is boiling hot," he said. "But not a soul around. Wonder where they went?"

"Surely Malkia is still here, and Odette," said Morgan sharply. He called them by name, and others. No one answered. His voice echoed through the small buildings, against the empty blue sky.

He went back for Tess, and escorted her into the house. Vincent leaped up the stairs, rifle on his arm, and they heard him thumping from room to room. He came down again. "Nobody here," he said blankly. "There is fresh water in our rooms. And Tess's bed has a fresh dress laid across it. There is a dress half cut out in the sewing room at the back. But nobody there."

"Has—Odette left us?" asked Tess, her mouth drooping.

Vincent nodded, and put a comforting hand on her shoulder. "If the others left for some reason, she would have to go also, Tess. They must stick together. Maybe someone came." He frowned in puzzlement. "But who?"

"We were with Judson, all three of his overseers were there," Morgan counted aloud. "Could it have been one of the overseers from Quintero? But they were supposed to remain with the Quintero girls, surely they would obey orders. And why would all our slaves run away for an overseer?"

"Maybe some strangers came," suggested Tess. "They might have been on edge, afraid, and fled when strange men came."

"How would they come?" asked Vincent. "I saw no marks of carriage wheels other than ours in the sand of the beach. And if anyone came from St. Michael, we would have seen and heard their carriage, and their horses."

It was weird and somehow frightening, this silent disappearance, with no clue as to why. "I guess we best eat," said Morgan. "Then we can lock ourselves in the house before dusk. We have had no lunch, this can be luncheon and dinner. Tess, I'll get the food, you set the table. Vincent, guard from the door, and keep watch."

He brought in enough food for them for two days, and several buckets of fresh water, while Vincent stood guard. Tess had set the smaller table in the dining area, and put a couple fresh red hibiscus flowers in a low bowl.

"Did you go out for flowers?" he asked sharply. "I don't want you roaming about—"

She was shaking her head. "No, Morgan. The flowers were sitting in a basin of water near the door. I think Odette must have brought them in. I cannot understand why she left," she sighed. "It looks as though they were preparing luncheon, the napkins were on the table, and the basin was there," she said, pointing.

All the more puzzling. Vincent went out with his rifle as Tess dished up the food into bowls. He came back, reported, "The huts are all empty. Looks like they left in a hurry. Baby clothes spilled about, food on plates half-eaten. Someone must have come, and surprised them into terror. But who would do that."

They were silent at the table, eating because they were hungry and must stoke their bodies against the needs of the day. Tess ate automatically, Morgan scarcely tasted anything. The disappearance had such fear about it, such evidence of terror appearing in the midst of normalcy, that they were deeply puzzled. Tess shivered from time to time, even in the heat of the afternoon.

"We'll keep enough food here to eat tomorrow without going out—if we must," said Morgan, when they had eaten all they could. "The fruit will last, and the meat can be placed in the pan near the window, where it will remain cool tonight. What about the vegetables, Tess?"

"I'll sort out what will last," she said, and did so. She cleared the table, and Vincent escorted her to the kitchens. They rinsed the dishes hastily, and brought them back to the house, then locked all the downstairs windows with bolts and bars. They left the front doors open, with Vincent sitting guard. Morgan and Tess filled the dining table with their motley assortment of weapons.

He had decided to clean them, count the ammunition and be ready. Tess brought out the oil and cleaning cloths, and sat down with him.

She seemed so calm and poised, that he loved her all the more. He said softly, as he rubbed at the rifle barrel, "Tess, you are the best person in the world to have about in trouble. If I hadn't loved you before, I would now."

She gave him a shy smile over the pistol she was rubbing. "Why? We do what we must, Morgan. When trouble comes, you have to face it. It won't go away if you turn your back."

He chuckled softly, got up on the pretense of getting more oil from near her elbow. He bent over her, tilted back her head with one finger on her chin. He kissed her lips, deeply, and then again.

Her mouth was soft and pink, fragrant as the jasmine and more. It had petal fragrance of a flower itself, a rare and beautiful flower named Tess. He breathed in the scent that was her, light and a little spicy.

"I love you, Tess," he said, and waited, hoping.

She ducked her blond head, and he saw only the top of her head, with the blond curls rioting on it. He waited, but her cheeks only grew more pink, and she said nothing. He went back to his place, a little disappointed. But when a girl responded to a man as she had done last night, there was hope! He took out the three machetes he had found in the stables, forgotten or discarded, and began to sharpen them on a grinding stone, and the noise prevented conversation for a time.

Dusk came, but they were not hungry. They drank

some cool tea, but no rum. They wanted their minds sharp and keen. Nobody came. Vincent left his post, they bolted the front doors, and moved upstairs together. Morgan and Tess took the front windows, and watched for a time. Vincent went to the back, moved some blankets, a pillow and sheets to a bed there, and prepared to wait out the night. Morgan had thought they could sleep.

"If anyone comes, and tries to get inside, the racket would waken us," he said calmly. "I sleep lightly. If I hear anything, I will come and waken you, Vincent. No need to go without sleep."

"I have heard people are afraid of the night," said Tess, musingly. "Perhaps they would not attack at night. Do you think so, Morgan?"

Morgan thought of the battles with the French that went on day and night, when one could not see a hand before the eyes, when a sentry was stabbed to death by the enemy. But he said cheerily, "That is certainly true at sea, Tess. Few fight at night. One cannot see in the dark, and one needs to aim true, if there is to be little waste of ammunition. I remember a time when our ship engaged a French ship. . . ."

And he told a little of that, as they went upstairs to their rooms. Vincent had water with him, and a cup. He carried them carefully, set them on a dresser, and prepared to wait.

He could not sleep for a time. He sat up in a chair near the opened window, and looked out the back of the house toward the purple hills. Up there were the slaves, hiding, frightened, yet defiant. Morgan had said they had no food, only water. How long would they last?

There was something ominous, menacing, strange about all this silence. Vincent thought of the blacks as he had met them first. Blank faces, afraid to smile, afraid to show any emotion. Wary of the new white men.

Then gradually, they had opened up. As they worked in the sugarcane, slashing at the cane expertly with great strokes of their sharp machetes, they had sung; African songs, Creole songs, songs with humor that made them laugh and joke among themselves. They had shared some witty remarks with him, shyly at first, then more daringly, as he had laughed and encouraged them, and told them stories of his own.

Damn it, they had liked him! thought Vincent angrily. They had worked alongside him. Even Gamba, the dark menacing fellow with the smileless face, had showed him how to wield the machete to get the most good from the stroke. Bernardo had told them eagerly how to work the sugar mill, which canes to cut first, which cane yielded the most sugar, how to boil the juices in the great copper cauldrons.

And it was Bernardo who had showed them the rum cellar—the cellar he had kept secret from the whites! It did not add up. Odette had adored Tess by the end of a month, and followed her about, talking with her with gentle eagerness. Vincent had heard Odette and Tess talking like old friends, over the sewing and the polishing, the cutting of flowers, the arranging of food on the table. Many of the slaves had been friendly and smiling.

How could they turn like that, and be the enemy? They were now locked in the house, waiting for their own slaves to attack! It was more than weird, it was past understanding, even difficult to believe.

What had happened to them? How could they change in a minute? It must have been but a minute, from the time "someone" came, or something happened.

Could the "someone" have been a slave from the hills, telling the women and children to come with them? His eyes went wide as he thought of that. Had that pirate come, stalking darkly through the few remaining canefields, to tell them they must join the rest in the hills? Would they come then? Would they obey some dark power of his?

Morgan seemed to like the man, even to trust him somewhat. Vincent did not know why. It was something between the two men; they had met, talked, trusted.

Vincent sighed, the darkness was deeper. He was growing sleepier. He glanced up at the dark hills, they showed no sign of fire or smoke. How did they endure the night chill, the cold wind off the Atlantic? It was not like the Carribean side, with caressing warm breezes even at the nighttime.

He lay down on the bed, removing only his heavy boots. He kept his rifle beside the bed, and listened to the silence. How very silent it was.

At the inn it had been noisy most of the time. Only in the small hours of the morning had it grown quiet. Then only the creak of the lantern in front of the inn had broken the silence, or the slow fumbling footsteps of a drunken sailor stumbling back to his ship.

Here at the plantation, there had been sounds in the night: the men talking in the huts; the women giggling as they ate, or fed their children; friendly sounds, warm human sounds. The men going out to fish, or returning with a catch which they would cook and eat then and there, no matter what the time of night.

At dawn, there would be sounds, the men rising to dress and go out to the fields. The women would rise also, and the children would squeal and run about in play. There would be scents also, the smell of fresh coffee and tea, the hot bacon frying on the kitchen fires, good homely smells just like in England.

And always there was the smell of the flowers, even as now. But now there was silence, a silence he did not like. Was it his own fear which brought bad omens in the silence? Perhaps so. Men peopled the dark hours of the night with their own personal demons. What they suppressed in brave show in the daytime came out at night to haunt them, and make them cry out in their sleep.

In the nights past, Morgan had not been alone with his thoughts in the night. Vincent had been aware of how often Morgan went to the bed in Tess's room, and he had been a little envious of the sounds he had heard. The creak of the bedsprings, the rustle of the mattress husks, the soft sounds of their lovemaking, the crying out of their voices in pleasure. A man was not alone, who held a woman in his arms, and loved her.

Vincent was nineteen, and he longed for a woman of his own. Was he too young to marry? Perhaps so. Morgan was twenty-eight now, and had not thought to marry until his time in the wars was over. Women were different, they matured early here in the tropics.

He thought of young Inez, her wise dark eyes, her quiet smile, the soft light and glow of her tawny skin in the afternoon sun. How sweet she was, her slow musical tones, her shy glances up at him through long black lashes. The beauty of her form in the blue or pink gowns. How different from the brazen heat of her sister, Florencia!

And they were alone at the Quintero villa, but for two Spanish overseers. Vincent frowned, and turned over in bed. He did not like the thought of Inez being there with those two men, whose bold black gaze looked through a woman's gown hungrily. He did not believe Florencia is what she had said of Inez. Inez was good, young, innocent! He thought he knew her now—yet—

Inez was alone, but for her weeping sister and those two Spanish overseers. Vincent growled, growing more wide awake and restless the more his mind took over for him. He could not sleep, and finally rose, to sit at the window for a time.

All was silent. His tortured imagination forced him to

listen for the sound of a woman's screams, his eyes sought across the fields for the glare of a flame—

Would the blacks fire a house? Or just the fields? How far would they go? Quintero should never have left the women, even to summon aid. How long would it take for him to ride to St. Michael, tell them of the fears, and return? Would he linger on the way, would he stop to drink and forget the urgency of his mission?

Worry over Inez kept Vincent awake for a long time, long after there was silence in the front room where Morgan and Tess lay together. Vincent finally went back to bed, and sheer weariness sent him to sleep. His last thought was of Inez, in a blue gown, her pink lips parted as she gazed up at him dreamily.

23

Odette was silent as she moved about the dining table. She was worried with her white missus gone. And the two white men she had come to—almost—trust. Mr. Morgan was a good man, he reminded her much of her father, Mr. Thomas. Mr. Vincent was rather nice, with a shy smile, and eager ways. Neither of them pawed at her, or stared with rude hot gaze.

She hated being alone in the big silent house. Most of the shutters were closed and bolted, but the big front wooden doors were pegged open, and the back doors, so that a breeze might blow through and make all cool.

She went out timidly to the bushes beside the house, giving little darting looks around. Most of the men had gone to the hills, the big field hands, leaving the boys and the women and children. She felt contempt for them. They wanted excitement, they did not truly care for their women and children, or they would not have left.

Excitement—fear—rebellion! They talked big, and her mouth curled down. How helpless they were against the white men! They talked, and cursed, in low fearful tones, and glanced about in the dimness for worry the whites would hear them! And when the white man came and said something to them, it was "Yes, master! Right away, master! Me do it, master. Whatever you wish, master!" Bowing and scraping and grinning or blank-faced, as master wished.

No one of the men was strong enough to stand against a white man. Odette had known fear in full ever since her white father had died. Not a night since then had she slept the night through. Deliberately she had chosen a big strong black man as her lover, hoping he would keep the other men from her, protect her even from the blacks.

Her mouth compressed as she plucked the red hibiscus blossoms carefully, held them carefully in her palms, and carried them back to the veranda. She set them lovingly in the basin of cool water, and set the basin just inside the door of the house, where they would not be singed by the hot sun.

Bernardo. Even to say his name hurt. He had been kind and good and loving, she had loved him for his gentleness to her. But his goodness had not been strength. He had died, trying to save her. She was lost, lost, lost, and the word echoed through her mind, in a thin shrill cry of fear that never ceased. Bernardo had held her in his strong arms, and made promises to her: "I shall never leave you, you my woman, you my love."

Poor Bernardo. She shuddered and went stiff again as she thought of those horrible minutes when she was tied to the pillar of Judson's house. Forced to watch her gentle lover torn to bits by growling dogs, while Judson laughed—laughed!

She shook off the memory. She could not think of it, or she would foam at the mouth and run mad. She had thought for days that she was mad. She could not eat or sleep. The nights and days had slipped into each other. Only one memory remained: of gentle hands smoothing the hair back from her forehead, a gentle voice urging her to drink cool water or warm broth.

Caring—protecting—gentle hands.

She moved outside to the back veranda, headed for the kitchen. Surely white missus, lovely Silver Jasmine and her two men would come back soon. Odette felt uneasy without their protection.

She was aware of the silence then.

She glanced about, and her nightmare took on reality.

Judson sat on his black horse, grinning down at her, right in the stable yard!

She opened her mouth to scream, but not a sound come out. Malkia cringed at the threat of a pistol held on the women. The maids stood paralyzed at the door to the kitchen, hands held high. The children sat in the dust, staring open-mouthed and quiet.

Oh, no, no, no, cried her mind. No, no, the nightmare would not come again, it could not come again!

She turned to run into the house. Judson rode the steaming sweaty black horse closer, grabbed her easily by the back of her neck, and swung her up before him, still holding the pistol on the women with the other hand.

"Got you now, and no black will get you from me!" he grunted in triumph. She smelled his sweaty body pressed close to hers, she smelled the vile smell of him, remembered from too many encounters.

She felt like screaming, but not a sound could she make. It was a terrible dream. She must waken—

He rode off with her in the cane field toward his big house. Behind her the women were screaming and running, and the small children crying. She heard the crash of pans, the calling to each other. "We must run, run, white men come, burn—" And they were fleeing blindly through the cane, up toward the hills.

Odette tried to fight the cruel arm about her. But he was so huge, so tough and strong, he only laughed down at her, his eyes blazing. "I like it when you fight," he grinned. "Go on, fight. I'll take you now—"

He slid from the horse, there in the cane field, in the stubble of the cut cane. He yanked her down with him, careless of how he hurt her, how he ripped her clean gray dress. He flung her to the cane stubble, and it raked her back and made her bleed.

Odette tried to fight him, but he held her brutally. Whenever she tried to move, the cut cane remnants bit into into her back and thighs, and she felt blood rolling down her body.

Judson was roused and panting. He fell over her, and held her to himself, fumbling with the dress, ripping it from her thighs. She thought of Bernardo, and his gentle reverent touch, his soft kisses and caresses.

The heavy slobbery lips moved over her bare body. She bit and scratched, and he cursed her. He took both her arms, and held them in one of his, high above her head, stretching her painfully. Then watching her grimacing face, laughing down at her, he pushed himself at her.

She felt the pain as he came inside her, her own body so stiff and unready and fearful that the pain increased into a mighty bubble of blood and fear. She groaned and cried aloud, and screamed out, but he went on and on. Pounding at her, pushing at her, pushing into her tender young body while the blood ran down her thighs.

He finished in a great burst, and drew back, breathing hard. He grinned down at her, his red face running with sweat.

"Hell, I had to have you! Hell, it was good! Worth the wait, you little black witch! I'll take you again, soon as I'm ready. Put your hand here." He tried to make her caress him with her hand. Instead of caressing, her fingernails bit into his flesh, and he cursed her and struck her face and breasts.

"Black devil! I'll teach you," he grunted. "I'll have you crying, and kissing my feet, and doing whatever I tell you! I'll learn you so good, you'll be glad you come to me, I'll bet! No lover like Caleb Judson, you'll see. I'll give you little babies, too, black babies! More slaves for me, blood of my blood," and he flung back his brutal head and laughed.

He had her again, and she was so weak she lay still for him, panting for breath as he covered her with his heavy body. He thrust inside her again, watching her face, his fingers wound in her hair, keeping her head still, brutally.

"Fight me," he grunted. "I like it when you fight me! Go on, fight, wiggle your hips, you little bitch! I bet you give your black lover plenty cream! Do it, you bitch!"

She lay still, fainting in the heat, desperate and lost. She moaned faintly as he came again in her, high and hard and wild. He grunted with satisfaction, and pulled out, and pushed again, in a vain effort to raise his flesh once more.

"Damn it, I come too fast," he grumbled. "I want more!" and he pressed his wet mouth to her high beautiful breasts, and slobbered over her waist and thighs.

Then above him, she saw the dark figure of a man. It was the same nightmare again—Bernardo with the rock raised high over his head. Bernardo—her mouth formed his name.

She blinked away the tears, and looked again. How could it be Bernardo? Her dear gentle Bernardo was dead! Had he come to life again, would the same horror repeat itself?

The rock came down, crashing down on the back of Judson's head. He groaned, and went limp on her. The man bent over her, pulling and pushing Judson from her.

Then she saw him clearly: Louis Abaco, dark fury on his face: the pirate!

He took off his shirt, and gave it to her. He pulled her up, and when her hands shook in weakness, he put the shirt about her, stuffing her arms into the long full sleeves. Now he looked like a real pirate, bare-chested, gold earring in one ear, dark and furious and dangerous.

"Come," he said abruptly, and swept her up into his arms.

"He will kill you!" said Odette abruptly. "The horror again! Run quick, or he will set dogs on you!"

His face gentled a little, he shook his head, and strode with her to the horse, standing with its head down in the cane. He managed to get into the saddle still holding Odette, and lifted the reins. He gave an indifferent look to Judson still lying in the cane, unconscious.

"He never get Abaco," said Louis Abaco coldly. "Never. I kill him first. Maybe kill now," and he seemed to ponder that.

"Kill a white man?" gasped Odette. "If you kill a white man, all white men come and kill you! Never stop until you dead!"

He nodded, and urged the horse on. They rode through the cane to the nearest path, then he chucked to the horse, and kicked at the weary sides of the tired animal, getting him into a trot. They were heading for the hills.

Odette lay back against him, so tired and scared and shocked that she did not care what happened. Yet she felt vaguely safe, vaguely secure, against the hard bare chest of this big man. He had found her, he had taken her from that horrible man—

They rode swiftly up into the blue hills, and were

abruptly in the dim coolness of the trees and thick bushes. He slowed the horse, and let it pick its way easily through the bushes, ever upward.

She did not really care, but she finally asked, "Where we go? Where, Louis?"

"Up to my hideout," he said. "Many come, many. All of Judson's slaves, some of Quintero's, some of Morgan Hamilton's."

His face above her was dark and somber. "What will you do? No food, and they will hunt us down!"

"I do not know yet," he said simply. "But there will be a way. I will think about it. Hamilton is a good man, yes?"

"I think so, and missus a good missus."

He nodded abruptly, his hand gentle on her body where she bled and stained his trousers. "You are much hurt. Get woman to bath you with warm water. Wish I came early. I watched from hill, saw with spyglass that you in danger. Run, but not in time."

He was not her lover, she had never given herself to him, it was not his fight, and now he was in danger. "Why, Louis?" she asked softly. "Why did you come to me?"

He looked down into her small earnest face, and shook his dark head, the ring swinging lightly in his ear. "Why? You ask why, woman?"

His eyes were dark and intent on her. She turned her face away. Did he want to make her his woman? He had never looked at her with desire. She thought his look now was more studying her, but not desire.

They came into the clearing, where she saw Malkia and the others from Hamilton's, weary, with dusty feet and legs, as though they had run through the fields. Louis Abaco got down carefully, not giving her to any of the men, though Gamba strode up and held his arms for her.

"No, I will take care," said Abaco abruptly. Gamba's eyes flashed, and he fell back, insulted.

Abaco carried her into a little shelter, and beckoned for Malkia and another woman. They brought warm water, and bathed her, and put a cloth about her from breasts to hips to cover her. They brought herb tea, and she rested and slept a little time.

When she wakened in alarm, it was to hear the men talking and quarreling. She propped herself up on one elbow to listen.

Gamba was saying, "Hate all whites—kill! kill!" and his voice rose shrilly. "I will lead you! Gamba is a leader, he is chief!"

"We must not kill white men," said Louis Abaco stubbornly, with a weary tone as though he had said it many times. "White men will come after us, kill all. No. We must not kill whites."

"We kill, kill, kill!" said Gamba, a feverish intensity on his dark sweating face. It had turned dusk, and the fires had burned low. The women and children sat around the circle, outside the rim of the tough men, watching and listening.

Odette was conscious of the wide-eyed children, listening to the talk of killing, of the way they leaned wearily against their mothers. There was no food, no drink. No pots boiled on the fires.

Her thighs burned and ached, her whole body burned with the pain of her cuts and bruises, and the forceful rape. She leaned back on the blanket and closed her eyes, but the voices went on and on, as the fires died.

She thought, "I want Caleb Judson dead!" and it shocked her. She had never wished anybody dead in her young life, he was the only one toward whom she had ever felt such fear and enmity. When he had come chasing her, she had known repulsion and dread. As his attacks increased, she had wished him dead. She had stuck pins in the voodoo doll, she had crushed him under her feet.

Yet it was not for her or her friends to kill! The gods would see that the deeds were punished. The gods would make him dead. She trusted the gods, she had prayed fervently to them, she had danced for them, she had begged them and made offerings.

Her hand did not need to lift the knife to kill. The gods would kill. Puzzled, she frowned a little as the voices rose and fell. Men thought differently. They would pray to the gods and swear great oaths. Yet they still felt they must go out and do the killing themselves. Did they not trust the gods to visit vengeance on the evil?

Malkia had taught her much of the gods. She said the gods always won, and those on the sides of the gods won. But—Bernardo had died. What of that? He had been good and kind, and he had died. She opened her eyes again, and stared blankly out into the purple darkness.

Some of the children had gone to sleep. Louis Abaco rose and said, "All fires out, so fire is not seen. We sleep. Tomorrow, we will get some food."

"Tomorrow we kill!" insisted Gamba, his voice thick and furious. "We kill whites! Gamba is chief, you will listen to Gamba."

"We sleep tonight, tomorrow we will speak of this," said Abaco, wearily. "We need food for the women and children. The whites must be punished, but we do not kill!"

"Why not kill? Are you great coward?" sneered Gamba, and the camp fell deathly silent at the challenge.

Louis Abaco was at his full great height, but Gamba was equal in height. Both men stood facing each other across the dying fire. Odette stiffened. Malkia muttered something and drew her small form into a ball.

Everyone thought that in a moment knives would flash, and the two would go at each other's throats.

Instead Abaco spoke calmly. "Gamba, you are a son of a chief, you would be a great chief in your country in Africa. But we are not in Africa. We are in Caribee island. We are on white man's land. White men make the laws. White men look down on us of color. If we kill white man, all whites will raise their hands against us. We will all die."

There was a silence. Gamba stared at him. "You—not kill whites? In Africa, we kill our enemies!"

"Yes, but this is not Africa," said Abaco flatly. "We must think carefully. We must use our heads," and he tapped his head. "There is some way to take revenge, without killing. We must think of this. Tomorrow we will talk again, and decide. Perhaps sleep will bring wisdom and knowledge to us. All sleep now, except the guards."

Gamba turned arrogantly, glad to regain some superiority. He named five of them crisply to stand guard for the first part of the night. They nodded, and went off swiftly, glad the crisis was over.

Gamba strode over to where Odette lay. He seemed about to throw down his blanket beside hers. Louis stiffened, and said, "What about the food tomorrow? Can you steal close to Hamilton plantation? They keep no dogs. We can get food there."

Gamba turned slowly and came back to the fire, which Abaco then kicked to pieces, stamping out the last embers. "I go, I lead men in silence, and get food," he said. "There is much food at Hamilton's. We will bring—for women and children."

"That is good," said Abaco mildly. "Perhaps the horses also, they have two good horses. If we need to escape from the hills, horses will help."

"Yes, I will get food, horses—I go, I lead," said Gamba. While he muttered on about it, Louis Abaco took his blanket and went over to Odette's side, spread it out,

372

and lay down. He did it so quickly and silently that Gamba did not realize until it was done.

Gamba came over. "I will take Odette now," he said. "She has no man of her own now. I am chief."

"Odette will choose her own man," said Abaco. "Tonight she is shocked and ill. All men leave her alone." And he rolled over on his side and pretended to go off to sleep.

Gamba hesitated, grumbling, then moved off in the darkness. Louis Abaco drew a soft breath of relief. Malkia lay on the other side of Odette; he just caught her toothless grin at him.

Odette seemed to sleep. Louis lay quietly, his brain slowly calming. He must keep Gamba calmer. The man was too ready to fire up—

It was necessary to make some show to the whites that the slaves would not take such treatment in silence, cringing. Yet it should not go so far as the murder of white men, which would not be forgiven or forgotten by the authorities. He puzzled it round and round in his brain.

The cane was almost all harvested, only a few fields remained. The cane! He thought of it, coming more wide awake, lying on his back, gazing up at the wonder of the white stars blazing in the purple black sky.

Firing the last of the cane! It would not spread much damage, most of the cane was cut. But it would be a symbol of what they meant. Then, satisfied, the slaves would go back to work. Some would be whipped, they expected it. He himself must escape, perhaps to another island. Let the blacks blame him for leading them. But firing the cane would be a fine gesture, without badly hurting anyone. They could take oil from the plantation, spread it over some of the uncut fields, then fire it. The black smoke would rise and carry for miles.

He was thinking about that, figuring out whether it would work, whether he could keep Gamba and the more belligerent blacks in hand, especially those of Judson, when a small hand came to his arm. He caught his breath, dared not turn.

Slowly his head turned just enough to see Odette's sleeping face with his keen eyes. He saw her, her eyes shut, her body relaxed. The little hand had crept out, and now clutched at his big arm, as though in her sleep she reached for some security.

Perhaps she thought he was Bernardo, sleeping close to her. A stab of jealousy shot through him, he stifled it roughly. Bernardo had died for love of Odette, in a bitter and cruel death.

He had been jealous even as he stood guard so they might make love. He had seen Odette from a distance, and thought she was the loveliest, most graceful girl he had ever beheld. She was young, sweet as the sugar from the cane, ripe as the mango fruit, and born for love. There was no sourness nor evil in her. She was gentle and good and kind. Much bad had been done to her, but it had not turned her to the sourness of the unripe lime.

The hand clutched over his arm, then relaxed, lying there, soft against his hard muscles. He did not move. But he lay awake for a long time, thinking of Odette.

He slept then, and wakened from time to time in the night, listening. Sounds told him more than sight at night. The children moaned or softly wept, for hunger. The women were more stoic, hushing the children brusquely, or bringing them cool water to drink. Tomorrow they must have food. Yes, the Hamilton plantation was best—he did not keep half-starved dogs to give warning.

Gamba came to him late at night, and stirred him gently with his foot. "Time to stand guard, Abaco," he said roughly.

Louis snored, faking sleep. Gamba tried again, but Louis pretended to be heavily asleep. Gamba finally turned away, disgusted, and Louis smiled inside himself. Gamba would like to take Louis's place here beside Odette, but Louis would not give it up!

There were enough men to stand guard, he was not needed there.

Dawn came, and Louis was up, going down to the creek to splash water on his face and arms. Other men came silently, their faces dark with eager purpose and deadly design.

They went back to the fires. The children were stirring, rising, the women took them into the bushes. A baby wailed, the mother shushed it.

Louis, standing before them at the small fire, said, "Gamba will lead five men to the Hamilton plantation. Move quietly through the cane, make no noise. We need food. Go to the kitchens, he will lead you and direct you without words. Bring back food quickly to the women and children, this is necessary. By the time you return, we will be ready to move out to attack."

Gamba said, "We attack! We will kill all whites!"

"No, that would not be wise, and you are very wise, Gamba," Abaco said, in the solemn tone his pirate captain sometimes used. He had learned much from that old wolf of the seas! How to lead men where they would not be dragged, how to fight only as a last resort, how to hoard his strength. "It is better to make a sign to them."

"What sign?" asked Gamba, scowling with suspicion, certain he was being duped, yet unable to put a finger on how.

"The firing of the cane fields. I shall arrange it while you are gone. We shall do much damage, yet not kill. This will show them we are not meek souls, to be set under their heels!" And fire stirred in Abaco's blood, at the way Odette had been treated, at the way Bernardo had died, so slowly and horribly. His eyes flashed. "We will show

375

we are revenged for Bernardo! Judson will know this is why it is done!"

Gamba grumbled, he wanted to kill.

Abaco said, "You choose your men, Chief Gamba," he said, showing respect. "Take the best men, who will move silently, and obey you instantly. Bring back the horses, and much food. We eat, then we will move out. Go quickly, and you can return before the sun is lighting the earth."

Gamba chose his men, and moved out. They were back within two hours, with the two horses, and much food. The women took it eagerly, and cooked it, and gave to them all, feeding the men first, as was the custom. Then the men were ready to move out.

Louis was conscious of the dark eyes of Odette on him. She gestured weakly to him, and he went to kneel at her side.

"You feel better today, Odette? All evil will pass one day," he said gently.

Her dark eyes flashed. "I say—if you must—see that Judson dies! But do not let it be by your hand, or you will be killed. Judson will die by the hands of gods!"

He studied her gravely. He knew she studied to be a mambo priestess of voodoo under Malkia. And the women like that had much power and understanding.

"I will do as you wish, if possible," he said. "Anything else, young Odette?"

He did not know for what he longed, some word of caution for himself, something that would say she liked him and wished him safety. Her dark eyes brooded.

"I would ask for safety of my white missus," she whispered. "She is good woman. No hurt?"

"No hurt," he promised, and she nodded and lay back. Then remembering, she rose up again, and put her hand on his arm. "I would tell you, Mr. Abaco—of the white missus of—of Judson." She forced the words with difficulty. "When—when he did what he did—to Bernardo—"

"Yes, Odette? Do not strain—you can tell me another time—" He put his big hand on hers tenderly.

"*Now* tell. Mrs. Judson, she seem cold. But on that day, Louis—I tell you, she is good woman. She give me to drink, she tell him, no, no, no, not touch Odette. She protect me with her body, though he strike her down! There is good in her, Louis."

"The woman of Judson has some good?" reflected Louis Abaco, frowning. She had reminded him of the loose women of the ports, all bold eyes and too free hands on a man. He had seen her in the spyglass with Morgan Hamilton, and admired the way the man had pushed her away.

Odette nodded. "She is sorry for women. Sorry. Pity is in her, not evil." She sighed, and lay back weakly. He pressed her fingers, and dared to touch his lips to the hand. She looked up at him with her great dark wide eyes surprised. He smiled down at her.

"There is much good in you, Odette. Lie easy, hide with the other women if you hear noises. Be safe, eh?"

She nodded. "Be—safe, Louis," she whispered.

He got up, and went to rally the men. They went down quietly into the valley, and got oil from the edge of the fields, where it was stored. They sprinkled oil on the uncut fields of Judson, the ones near the hills; then growing bolder, they scattered the thick heavy black oil farther into the cane.

There were fields of young uncut cane that smelled sweetly as they came near. Louis compressed his lips. It seemed a sin to destroy such cane, for it meant food for people, molasses in the cold times, sugar for the rare times of feasting. But it must be done, for a sign.

This was the most dangerous time now. They lit torches made of green cane, bound together, and began to run through the oil-strewn cane fields. They started with the fields nearest to the ocean and beach, and ran back through them, to the hills.

They put the oil-smudged cane to the torch, and it caught, flared, and began to burn. The flames shot up into the sky, and black smoke drifted over the cane, the smell of burning, sweetish fire.

They ran on and on, until they were breathless. The torches inflaming the fields, the fires lit up the sweaty blackened faces of the exultant slaves.

"Destroy, destroy!" yelled Gamba, and something else in his own tongue, in a snarling high voice. His tall form dashed from one field to another, distinct even in the tall cane. "Burn, burn, destroy, destroy, kill, kill, kill!" And he put the torch to the fields, and danced before it in his bare huge feet, intoxicated with the smell of burning cane, the power in his hands, the fire he held.

24

Tess wakened at dawn, watched from Morgan's arms as the sun rose slowly in a glory of soft orange that turned to crimson and gold. From the window she could see the beautiful blue waves of the ocean, rolling endlessly from the far horizon to the creamy white beach.

How beautiful it was here, a paradise, if only—if only men were not so greedy and evil. She sighed a little, and stirred cautiously. Morgan did not move.

She put her legs outside the bed, slid out from the circle of his arms. He did not move, he was deeply asleep.

She slid to her bare feet, and stood up, yawning in the white nightdress. She went over to the wash basin and pitcher, then hesitated. She must not be reckless with the water, they might not be able to venture outside for more today.

She poured some water into a cup, splashed some on

her face. She brushed her teeth briskly with a bit of water and a peeled twig, and felt somewhat refreshed. Then she began to dress, pulling off the nightdress, and reaching for her cotton undergarments.

Tess had the uneasy feeling of being watched, and glanced over her shoulder toward the bed. Morgan's eyes were open, and he was looking at her. The expression in his face made her blush vividly. Hastily she pulled on the undergarments, white pantaloons, and a white petticoat, then drew on the white muslin dress she had worn yesterday. It would be hot again today, the sun told her so, and the heat haze was already dimming the vivid sky.

Summer would be much hotter, they said, with July the hottest month. Then August, September, October might bring the horrible big whirling winds and ocean storms. She wondered if they would be there to see those storms, or if something might happen before then to drive them out—or kill them.

Morgan was yawning and stretching, when Vincent came to the door on hasty bare feet. Tess opened the door to him.

"They're coming, five of them, through the cane," he whispered. Morgan got out of bed, pulled on his pants, grabbed his rifle and ran after him soundlessly. Tess paused only to make sure she had the ammunition for her pistol.

They crept to the room where Vincent had been sleeping, the back bedroom overlooking the kitchen. Vincent was loading his rifle, but as he began to point it at the black men creeping through the cane, Morgan put a hand on his arm.

"Wait. Let's see what they're up to—and who they are," he murmured, almost soundlessly. Tess strained to see around the form of Morgan who had moved to another window. He stood against the side of it, his rifle down, watching. She stood half behind him, watching.

Vincent at the other window watched also, fairly trembling with excitement. His eyes were bright and eager after the night of sleep. How could the men be eager for battle, wondered Tess. She dreaded it so much, she felt half sick at her stomach, as though she would faint with the worry.

Morgan's arm was iron-hard against her. He was taut and ready for anything. She drew a deep steadying breath, and tried to be as calm as he was. He had known many battles. He knew what it was to wait—and wait—and wait longer.

They saw the men come closer, throw cautious looks at the closed and shuttered house. They glanced up at the windows, but could not see past the fluttering white curtains. In the lead was an unmistakable figure, the very tall Gamba. Morgan recognized him, Tess knew, by the indrawn breath.

Two men crept to the stables. They came out leading the two horses, but not the carriage. The other three men went to the kitchens, and began to carry out food, pans of meat, bowls of fruit, bowls of vegetables. One carried out a thick sack of beans and tied it to the back of one of the horses.

Tess watched, and knew what they were doing. There were many people up in the hills, and there was no food up there. They were taking food to their families and friends.

Morgan did not move. He waited. The men led the horses away, and carried pans of food and sacks of food with them, all they could carry on the horses and in their arms. They had no weapons but the huge machetes fastened to their rope belts. They were barefoot, ragged and dirty.

They all drew deep breaths of relief when the men had disappeared. They watched a bit longer, but no one came.

"Thank God they just wanted food," said Morgan aloud.

"And our horses," mourned Vincent.

"We'll go down now, get some food into us, and bring fresh water into the house," Morgan decided. "Vincent, keep watch while I get my boots on. Tess, you stay right here!"

It was an order, and she nodded. He disappeared, to come back when he had put on boots and a dark shirt. They went downstairs, waited while Morgan unbolted the back door, and looked thoroughly around outside. Then he nodded to them. Tess scurried to the kitchen, drew water from the well, refilled the pans and basins in the house. She took down a big slab of bacon, and carried it to the house. They could live on this for a time. Vincent brought other foods, more fresh fruit.

Tess prepared the food over the dining room fireplace, moving awkwardly around the swinging cranes and pots. They did not use this often. She had cooked over a fireplace years ago, but at the Last Inn a cook had done this, while Tess used the big stove.

They were eating the bacon and bread, some fresh mangoes and papaya, when Vincent started to sniff.

"I smell molasses," he said. "Do you suppose they have gone back to work at the still?"

Morgan frowned, and moved to the back door abruptly. He gazed out over the land, and his mouth set grimly. "No—they are burning the fields over at Judson's!"

"Oh, God," murmured Tess faintly. She set down her coffee cup, and hurried to look. The black smoke was rising, drifting over the fields. As they watched, they saw more fields fired. The flames rose, then the black sickly smelling smoke came to them as the winds blew from the south.

"Are they burning our fields?" asked Vincent, watching from the window in the dining room. "I can't see any smoke over ours—"

"No, looks like it is Judson's cane. It must be revenge

for Bernardo, then, and hatred of Caleb Judson," mused Morgan. "I wonder if they will stop there? I didn't know all those men this morning, only Gamba was ours."

"I've seen one of them over at Quintero's," said Vincent, his mouth taut. "God—will they go there next? With Quintero away?"

"They might. And they might come here next," said Morgan. "If it is just the fields, and helps them take out their anger, it's all right. But we must be ready to fight, if they decide to attack us."

"How far is it to St. Michael from Quintero's?" asked Vincent. He had lain awake some of the night worrying about that, and almost woke Morgan to ask.

"About seven or eight hours on horseback, if you have a good fast horse," said Morgan. "More like twelve hours in a carriage."

Vincent muttered, "So it depends on how fast Quintero rides, and he is getting old."

"And he might have to stay and talk to people in St. Michael," said Tess. "Will they believe him? And will they care enough to come and help?"

Morgan frowned. "I don't know them at all. They don't know me, they would hardly come for me. Unless they believe all whites should stick together. They aren't a large colony, with a governor to take charge. It's a small place."

He seemed to be musing over the possibilities. Vincent said, "I'd like to go over to Quintero's. I don't think I trust those two overseers much. They would be for saving their own hides first! Those two girls could not fight off an attack."

Morgan was silent, Tess put her hand on his arm. He glanced down at her, his blue eyes somber. She nodded, silently.

"Well, if you think you can get away unseen, and make your way over there without being caught—you may as well go ahead, Vincent. We can hold out here," said Morgan.

"The slaves are heading for the hills, they are going farther away from us. I'll go right off, and they won't see me." There was growing excitement in Vincent's voice, and a gathering determination.

Tess wanted to say "Be careful, be safe," but she knew he would try. They were all in danger, wherever they were. In silence, she put some ammunition in a small cloth bag, and gunpowder in his flask. He took his rifle in hand, gave her a quick hug, and shook hands with Morgan.

They escorted him to the front door. Tess watched from the front window, through a little crack at the side, and nodded. "All clear here," she said, in a choked voice.

Morgan swung open the door enough to let Vincent out. Vincent slipped through, gave another longer look around, then moved down the path through the trees, avoiding the coral crushed on the carriage road.

He slid into the trees, and was gone. He had put on his dark shirt this morning, and with the dark pants he was not noticeable from a distance. Maybe he could make it without being seen by the overwrought slaves, thought Tess.

Morgan slid the door shut quietly, and put the bolt across it. It was getting warm indoors. "We'll go back upstairs. It will be warm, but we can have the windows open," he said.

As they walked through the large house, that now felt so vacant and still and silent, he slid his free arm about her, and the rifle swung from his other hand. "Vincent will probably be all right, he's a smart young man," said Morgan gently.

Tess nodded, her head bent. If anything happened to Vincent, she would be without the last tie to her family, her home. All would be gone, all—except Morgan.

He pressed a kiss lightly to her blond curls. "Cheer

up, it'll be all over in a day or two. It won't go on long," he promised.

"How can you tell?"

"They will grow hungry, and uneasy up there in the hills. They want their comforts, their huts, their food. Even someone to tell them what to do," said Morgan. "I have seen it before, on shipboard. A defiant sailor will give in and beg forgiveness for rebelling, because he wants to return to people from the solitary cell. He wants his mates, other humans about him, work to fill the empty hours. A man needs people, needs work, needs to be useful."

They had come to the dining room, and he glanced at the table. "You haven't finished your breakfast," he said. "You eat, and I'll watch a while. Drink some coffee while it's hot. Go on, honey." And he pressed her gently down into her seat.

Tess looked at the food, thinking she would get sick, but she attacked it slowly. A bite of crisp bacon on bread, it went down after she had chewed it. A sip of hot coffee. Then another sip, and another bite. She ate a mango, it was fresh and cool. The slaves had not taken all the fruit, they could not carry it all.

One or two days, and it would be all over, and life would return to normal. Odette would return, they would finish sewing the dress Odette had cut out and laid on the table in the sewing room. They would talk again, and even laugh.

Was it true?

She finally finished all she could eat. She watched, while Morgan ate, and then he locked the back door and bolted it. He checked all the windows carefully, then they walked up the winding stairs to the upstairs. She hesitated.

"Shall we split up, I'll watch the front?" she suggested.

He shook his head. "I think they will come down from

the hills. We'll both watch from the back bedroom here, where we can get a good view over the cane."

They moved into that bedroom, with rifles, pistols, ammunition, bowls of water, cups. Morgan sat in an easy chair before the window, with the curtain drawn back slightly to give him a view over the hills and the blackly burning cane fields. Most of the fires had died down now, stopped by the fields of cut cane, where nothing was left to be burned.

They talked a little. Morgan said once, "It is interesting how one evil man can spoil things for everyone. It happens everywhere. A crime wave, and all are fearful and must stay indoors, until the murderer is caught in London. On shipboard, a sailor who is sadistic to his men, and must be punished or discharged from the service, before the ship be peaceful once more. Here—Judson."

Tess nodded gloomily. "And I suppose there are many Judsons on these islands," she said. "Where men get power over other men, and use it unwisely, men will rebel. And the slavery system itself is humiliating and demeaning for both the slave and the master."

Morgan turned his head to stare at her for a moment, before returning his look to the window. "For the master as well?" he asked in a puzzled way.

"Yes. To be a master of slaves means to presume he is much better than they are, that he has a right to treat them in a terrible fashion. Even the masters who seem good and kind, like your uncle Thomas Hamilton, even they will take a slave girl and—and have a child of her. Like Odette's mother. What if she did not want to—to be with him? What if she loved another black, and Hamilton insisted on having her?"

"We don't know that," said Morgan, after a pause.

"No, but it does happen. A master has the power of life and death over his slaves, and also the power to direct their work in mean ways. She had no choice at all, did she? Few women do, it seems to me," she added rather bitterly, thinking of her own fate.

Morgan seemed to read her mind. "You mean yourself, Tess? Ryder made a slave of you, you said that once. But women are the weaker creatures, and must be guided and provided for. When I saw you and your situation, I was moved to take care of you. You seemed to resent that bitterly, at least for a time. Do you still feel so?"

He did not turn to look at her, but his tone was urgent. He was gazing absently from the window, watching over the fields.

She thought for a time. "Well, I resented it very much—yet I wanted even more to get away from Ryder. I think I could have fought you and escaped," she said boldly. "I think I could have made the ship captain help me get away."

"Get away—to where?" he asked. "Where would you have gone? To another dingy inn? To even more demeaning work among strangers? Who would have protected you? Vincent was not able to, he was trapped himself."

She was silent, her fingers twisting in her lap. No, a female of her age was trapped, unless she was an heiress. Even then, her fortunes must be directed by parents or guardians. No woman was free, any more than the slaves were.

"You are an intelligent woman, Tess," Morgan continued thoughtfully. "I have traveled much more than you have. I have met and talked with intelligent women who do not marry. They are sometimes called bluestockings. They are usually women with a fortune, or able to earn a living as a school mistress or a writer. But they are few. It might be that one day you would have been able to make your own way. But the path would have been difficult, and wearing for you. You would have been old before your time, and perhaps bitter with the experiences. I would not wish that for you."

She stirred. "I know, Morgan—I thank you," she breathed. She came to sit beside him, on the arm of his chair, timidly. She leaned her head to rest against his, in one of the first gestures she had made toward him. "You could have taken me, used me as Lord Tweed meant to, and discarded me. Instead you treated me honorably, married me, brought me with you. I—think you deserve my gratitude and respect, rather than the angry words I have hurled at you."

He caressed her hand on his arm, and brought it to his lips. "Tess, Tess," he said. "I do not ask your gratitude, though I thank you for the word *respect*. But it is your love I seek. Our marriage was unusual, the circumstances dictated that. But I have come to respect and to love you. Can you not one day bring yourself to love me also?"

He could not see her face, she hid it against his head. In a muffled tone, she said, "I wanted to say that, Morgan. I think—today we might—die. We will fight with courage, I will fight by your side. But we just might not—succeed in living through the day."

Morgan did not contradict her. He pressed another kiss to her small hand. "Yes, my darling girl," he said, "and I would say, that I could choose no other girl to be with, no more brave companion than I have beside me now. If we go, we shall go together, and perhaps—who knows?—we may arrive at that Heaven they say is waiting for us, to stand hand in hand before Our Maker. I can ask no better finish to our time on earth."

"Oh, Morgan—" she said, her voice choked. His head turned, she put her lips to his timidly.

"Of course," he said, more lightly, as she raised her head, "I should prefer, much prefer, to live with you, and know you better, and have children of you. We would live on in this paradise Elysia, and make a good thing of our lives together. I should much prefer that. And there is every good chance that it shall be so. Should you like that, my love?"

She nodded. "Oh, Morgan. I should like that," she told him simply. "I—I love you, I think."

"You think?" His mouth moved whimsically. He put down the rifle on the floor carefully, then moved to draw her down on his knees, and hold her small form against himself. "No more than think, Tess?"

She was flushed and bright-eyed, and his eyes were shining with love. She put her cheek against his rough, bristled cheek. "Oh, Morgan, I do—love you," she said.

"And I love you, my little darling," he whispered against her ear, and kissed the lobe, sending a thrill down her spine.

They sat quietly together in the dimness of the closed room, and waited. They talked a little through the day, and he wanted to hear again and again, that she loved him. She said it more freely, more gladly.

It gave them hope, and fresh courage, to be together, to talk of their growing love, and how it had happened. It made the night to come less fearful. They looked together over the smoky fields of cane, and watched the blue hills, but it did not seem so bad now. They would fight together, live together, if necessary, die together. They were not alone.

25

Vincent moved slowly from one group of thick trees to an open stretch, cautiously glancing about from time to time. There was no one on the beach, the sands were creamy white and unspoiled by footprints or marks of hooves. No one had come here today.

Yet he was still careful, moving like a shadow, his rifle in one hand, ready for action. He had a short dirk in his belt, but it was no match for machetes, he admitted to himself. And how they could wield those long curved knives! He had watched with admiration their long brown arms, sweeping to slice off the cane at the ground, then to slice the green tops from the ripe cane. And those very blows might be directed at him! He would not have a chance.

Shivering a bit, he forced himself onward. He must get to Quintero's without being discovered. He was only one man against thirty, maybe forty husky male slaves. Slave rebellion! He had read about them idly in the British gazettes, and they had seemed remote and strange, something that happened in the tropics, from heat and drink, perhaps. Now—he was here, and it was happening. And not from the heat! It was from the cruel treatment of one man, Caleb Judson, for which all would suffer.

He came to Judson's plantation, glanced up the hill, but could not see the house except for the tops of the roof. He heard nothing from there. Perhaps the slaves were eating, satisfied. Would the burning of a few fields please them, and cool their fury?

He could still smell the molasses scent of the burned cane, as the black smoke drifted over the fields, blown aimlessly by the breezes. He hurried on, it was almost noon. The girls had been alone for a day and a half. He did not trust those Spanish overseers, not a bit. Would they dare molest the girls? That fresh thought sent him hurrying even faster.

He should have gone yesterday, he fretted. Why had he waited so long? He was no man, but a child! He had wanted to go, but had wondered if they would welcome him, or if he should leave Tess and Morgan. He should have made up his mind sooner, and been with Inez last night.

He thought of her worry, her fear, with tenderness. A sound alerted him, and he drew into the shadows, crouched down. He heard voices, white men's voices: the Marquess of Tweed and Caleb Judson. He waited until they had returned to the house. He had no wish to remain with them, and thought they might try to force him to do so.

It was a long hot walk. He forced himself to pace rather than stride, to walk in an easy swinging movement that ate up the miles. He longed for his black stallion that galloped so easily over the sands. But the horses were gone.

He hoped the slaves would bring back the horses, he missed them.

By the position of the sun, it was about mid-afternoon by the time he reached the Quintero plantation. He turned in at the drive, but instead of walking up the crushed coral driveway where the carriages and horses proceeded, he ducked in among the bushes, in and out of trees, noting alertly that they grew thick and straggly. Slaves might hide here, and it would be difficult to see them at night. He saw an especially thick section, where it was well-nigh impossible to walk, it was so overgrown.

He broke out from there into some bushes, and then a grove of coconut trees; and from there, went up slowly to the Spanish villa. He looked about alertly. The downstairs windows and the doors were all shut tight, and he thought they would be bolted.

Then he caught a flutter of a curtain upstairs from a front window. He lifted a hand and waved, watching.

The curtains parted, and Inez' lovely face appeared, radiant, smiling. "Vincent!" she called softly. "Come to the front door—I shall be down at once!"

He leaped up the wooden steps onto the veranda, held the rifle alertly beside the door as he waited. He heard and saw no one. But the slaves were usually barefoot, and could walk so softly that one did not hear them approach. He watched, until he heard the sounds of the bolt, and the door creaked open.

He slid inside, and helped Inez bolt the door again. Then he turned to her. She was weary-eyed, with dark shadows under those great deep eyes of hers. But she was smiling.

"You came—oh, Vincent!" she whispered. He did not hesitate, he drew her into his arms, and kissed her mouth. She blinked, startled, as he held her back and smiled down at her.

"There, Señorita Inez! I have waited long for that," he said boldly. He watched anxiously for her reaction. If she frowned, drew back, acted haughty, he would be miserable, for his cause would be lost.

She smiled, shyly, the lashes drooped. She put one shaking hand on his dark sleeve. "Oh—Vincent," she said again. "Papa is not yet returned. We wait—how are Tess and Morgan?" she asked anxiously.

"All well. Locked inside the plantation house at Last Hope," he said briskly. "You knew the slaves fired the cane fields at Judson's?"

She nodded. "We could see from the upper windows. Pedro and Augusto wanted to go out and shoot them, but I told them to remain here. Papa ordered them to remain with us. And the slaves may not come here."

There was a sound from the back hall. Vincent turned about alertly, saw one of the overseers, the younger one, Pedro, staring at them, with a sly grin at his mouth. He had seen the embrace, thought Vincent.

Then it struck him—Pedro had seen the embrace, and grinned! He had not been possessive, or jealous, as he would have been if Florencia's accusations about Inez had been true! He had been sly, and he was grinning!

Inez' chin went up. "Pedro, you are to watch at the back bedroom," she said sharply, with cool composure. "Have you seen anyone approach?"

"No, señorita, no one comes," he mumbled, as they approached him.

"Then return and watch again," she ordered. Vincent thought she had cool authority in her tone, and some displeasure. The man went upstairs again. She turned to Vincent. "I am glad you have come," she said more quietly. "That man bothers Florencia. I actually found him in her bedroom, and she was crying in fear!"

Vincent glanced down into her solemn face. "Does Florencia welcome his—attentions?" he asked.

Inez grimaced. "You have guessed?" she said. "She was bored, in the past. She used to go out and meet him in the gardens. However, she is betrothed to a man at St. Michael, who is now gone to Barbados for the winter. When he returns, they are to be married, Papa says. He is weary of the constant nagging to go to St. Michael, or to have parties, and so on." Inez drew a deep sigh and shook her head, as though to relieve herself of a burden.

"You are not betrothed to any man, are you, Inez?" he asked boldly, anxiously, detaining her with a hand on her slim arm. She was clad in blue muslin today, and her small form was so pretty, though it drooped with weariness.

She shook her head vehemently, and the dark curls flew about her strained face. "No, no, no, I would not! Papa suggested it, but I do not like any man so much!"

"Not any man?" he murmured.

She colored sweetly, and glanced away from him. "Not any man—who has asked for my hand," she said, and her Spanish accent was pronounced.

"Ah," he said, satisfied. There was a chance for him! "I know one man who wishes to ask one day—when he has more of a position in the world, when he has proved himself a man worthy of you," he went on.

The dark eyes glanced up at him, gave him a quick search, then flick—the lashes were drawn again. "Why would he wish to ask—one day, señor?" she asked demurely.

If she had carried a fan, he thought she would have waved it before her small face! "Why, he is deeply in love," he said, enjoying the gentle flirtation. "He feels madly in love, yet conscious that he is very young and unworthy as yet of her devotion and the care of her. He feels he must wait for a time to ask her papa for her hand."

She turned to the stairs, and put one small foot on the first rung. Above them, Florencia hissed, "Will you remain there all day? Vincent, is that you? Why do you not come up here? Why are you whispering down there! Don't you know the danger?"

Her voice was hysterical and shrill. Vincent said, "I have come to aid where I can, señorita. Be at ease. Can you use a rifle?"

He went up the stairs with Inez to confront Florencia. She wore a rumpled red silk dress, and her eyes were as red as her gown, with tears and temper, he suspected. Nothing so bad had ever happened to her, and she must have railed at the fates that had put her in such a position.

"A rifle!" she exclaimed, shuddering. "Never! I carry a knife, and if needs must be, I shall defend myself with it!" She lifted her hand dramatically, showing the small knife.

He hid a smile, and said seriously, "Well done, señorita. You wait in your room, yes? And you, señorita Inez, where is your post?"

Florencia had to draw back to allow them to come up to the landing on that floor. She listened sullenly as Inez explained, "I have the post in the front bedroom. Pedro waits in the room across from mine. Augusto is at the back bedroom, overlooking the fields."

"And how is your supply of food and water?" he asked.

She shook her head. "The food is gone, the water is low."

"I had to bathe this morning," burst out Florencia petulantly. "I never go a day without bathing! Would you have me filthy?"

Inez flushed. "It was the drinking water, Florencia," she said, patiently. "I told you—"

"Never mind. While it is quiet, let us obtain more. Augusto, come downstairs with me, while Pedro watches. Inez—" But she was already following him down the stairs.

While Augusto watched with rifle alert at the back door, Inez and Vincent went to the kitchens. He gathered up the food that would last—some cured ham, a bowl of vegetables, two bowls of fruit—and they carried that back to the dining room, and set it down.

"Now the water," he said, and frowned down at some kegs and bottles in cases near his feet. He had stumbled over them twice. "Why are these here?"

"They are the rums, and some wines," explained Inez. "Father wished to preserve them. They are his six-year rums. And the best brandies and sherries. The others are locked in the cellars."

Vincent hesitated, then nodded. "Come, let us take them to the kitchens."

Inez opened her eyes wide. "Take them out to the kitchens?" she exclaimed. "Why, Vincent? Papa wished—"

"I'll explain later," he said. He picked up the first keg, and carried it out, and returned with a pitcher of fresh water. He did the same on another trip, and another. Soon the dining room was filled with basins and pitchers of fresh water from the well, and the kegs and barrels and cases of bottles were out in the kitchens.

Pedro scowled down over the bannisters. "Where do you take the rums, señor?" he demanded aggressively.

"I'll explain later," said Vincent again. He had caught the sour smell of rum on the breath of Augusto, and from Pedro's slurred speech he suspected both men had been at the bottles. And he had another reason for wishing the rums and wines out in the kitchens—where the slaves could reach them when they came looking for more food.

He had worked for several years of his life in a bar, and knew the effect of bottles of rum and wine on the sturdy sailors. It blurred their vision, slurred their speech, and finally some of the toughest would be lying flat out on the wooden planks of the bar floor.

He brought in some firewood, and started a small neat blaze in the vast fireplace of the dining room. Inez watched him, then seeing what he did, she began washing and slicing some breadfruit, cabbages and onions, and other greens. While he sliced the cured ham, and added it to the water in the pot, she began washing the fruits. She piled them in a fresh bowl.

Pedro and Augusto came to the smell of meat cooking, and Florencia tripped down the stairs, to sit languidly at the table. Vincent glanced at them ironically.

"Where is the guard at his post?" he asked.

The men glared at him sullenly.

"Augusto, you watch again at your post," Vincent finally ordered, since neither man moved. "Pedro, at the front window. When the food is ready, a plate will be brought to you. Go, now!" he added, more sternly, as they sat still.

"I am hungry," said Pedro boldly.

Augusto started up the stairs. "The food is not as yet ready," he said dryly, and went to the bedroom.

"Pedro? You will do as I say!" said Vincent, in his sternest voice, and glared directly at the man. He held his breath. Would the man accept his authority, or not? Inez was silent.

Reluctantly the man got up, and trudged up the stairs, his boots heavy on the stairs.

"I suppose you want me to watch also," said Florencia, her mouth curling, "so you can be alone with Inez!" There was a sneer in her tone.

"No, you can set the table," said Vincent. "And arrange two plates for the men."

She glared at him, and did not move. It was Inez who moved from dresser to table, set the table neatly at one end with three places, and then took out two metal plates for the overseers, and some metal knives and forks.

Florencia ate greedily, paying no attention to the other two. Inez sat at the end of the table, as graciously as at her father's finest dinner, and served the plates. When Florencia finished, she moved back her chair and left the table.

"You may now take the plates up to the men," said Vincent quickly. As Inez moved to leave the table, he put his hand on her arm and stopped her. "Florencia?"

She glared, hesitated.

Vincent added dryly, "The men will not like it if they are so long hungry!"

Sullenly she picked up one plate. "They are too hot," she complained. "I will burn my hands!"

"The tray is there." He indicated the tray where Inez had left it.

She put the plates on the tray, and whined as she went up the stairs, "So now I am a serving maid!"

Vincent looked at Inez as the older sister disappeared, and surprised a dancing light in her dark eyes, and a smile about her soft mouth.

"Nobody has ever ordered Florencia about so!" she whispered.

"About time somebody started! You do all the work about here," he said shortly, and put his hand on hers. "Your hands should be as soft and white as hers, not red with work!"

"I do not mind that they are red," she said, flushed. "I would work hard—for those I love."

"I also," he replied simply, and together they washed up the plates, glanced around outside, and stole out again for more fresh water to replenish what they had used.

About dusk, Pedro called down, "One rides up the path in front!"

From his slurred speech, he had been at the bottles again. Exasperated, Vincent realized the man must have several bottles stashed away at the "guard post" in the bedroom.

"It is probably Papa," said Inez, without panic. They went to the front window downstairs, and peered out, to see Quintero riding up, his head alert, but his face deathly weary. They opened for him. He slapped the horse away, after unsaddling, and came in. They bolted the door after him, and looked at him expectantly. He did not seem surprised to see Vincent there.

"Papa, are men coming?" asked Inez eagerly, her hands tenderly aiding him in removing the tight riding jacket.

He shook his head. "No, not yet anyway. They detest Judson. When they heard it was he who caused the trouble, they shrugged and said, 'Let him handle it then.' Two of my older friends finally said that if I believed myself in danger, they would organize some aid, and perhaps come tomorrow—or the next day." He sat down in a chair, and put his hands over his face.

Inez comforted him, they fed him, and took up posts again. Quintero insisted on sharing Florencia's bedroom at the front as his post. She was sullen and angry; Vincent suspected she had shared it with Pedro, her lover, and did not wish the arrangement changed.

Augusto took one back bedroom. Inez and Vincent shared the other. Augusto was drinking again. Quintero merely shook his head when Vincent protested to him.

"They enjoy the drink, what matter?" he replied, with some of his old charm. "I enjoy wine also. Where are my wines?" he asked more sharply, glancing about the dining room.

"I moved them out to the kitchens," said Vincent. "If the slaves come for food, they will find rum and wine again. Hopefully, they will drink themselves into a stupor, and with a hangover the next day, they will have little fighting spirit left."

"My best wines and rums!" exclaimed Quintero incredulously, his face flushing red. "My best rums, my six-year rums! How could you do such a foolish thing!"

He was about to go out after them, when a shot sounded from upstairs. Vincent cursed, and went to the window downstairs. He saw the torches as the slaves approached, and now they were shouting and firing.

"I must get my rums!" said Quintero, fumbling at the bolt on the back door. He had the door opened before Vincent could stop him. A lamp outlined his elderly figure.

A shot came out of the darkness, and he staggered back, his face a mask of blood from the cut over his temple. Vincent slammed the door, and shot the bolt, before turning to see him. Inez was bending over him, supporting him.

"On his head, Vincent," she said. He brought a basin of water, she bathed and bound the wound with steady hands, her face pale in the lamplight.

There was more shooting from upstairs, wildly and aimlessly, Vincent thought. He shouted up the stairs.

"Hold your fire! We don't have that much—hold it!"

But the shooting went on, and more shots came from outside. The slaves must have muskets and pistols, he thought, from the echo of the shots.

A smell of smoldering wood brought his attention to the back window, sharply. A torch had been thrust inside the slim slit of the side window, and it burned. He threw water on it, but even as he did so, he smelled smoke from another source.

The house was part coral limestone, and part wood. They would be smoked out, or burned to death in the house!

"We must get out of here," he said grimly. "Get Florencia, Inez. Tell the men to slow their shooting, until we get out, then I'll cover them from the bushes in front."

She ran to tell the men. Florencia shot down the stairs, crying and hysterical, and flung herself at her father. He had managed to stand up, the white bandage about his head. But he staggered before her onslaught.

He got Quintero to the front door, sat him down

nearby, and ordered him to wait. He slapped Florencia's cheek sharply, and she hushed and stared at him.

"Be quiet," he ordered. "Do you want to be killed? Be quiet. I'll be right back. Don't move!"

She stood still, and he ran back for Inez. She was coming down the stairs, a knife in her soft silk belt, a rifle in her hands. "All ready," she said.

He kissed her quickly. "I'll just confirm the arrangements with the men," he said, and ran up the stairs.

He told Augusto, "Fire at the back, to keep them here. I'll send Pedro to help you. I want them to think we are all here. Then after we get out, you and Pedro come down and steal out the opened front door. Close it after you! I'll cover you with my rifle. There is plenty of underbrush out in front, down to the beach. Spread out, hide, and be quiet."

The man nodded, but seemed sullen and afraid. Vincent went to Pedro, frowned as he saw the number of bottles about, and told him the same. He left them firing spasmodically at the back, toward the black slaves who crept up closer to the house with muskets and pistols. He recognized Gamba, by his height. He was standing near the back of the crowd, waving a torch in one hand and a machete in the other.

Vincent and Inez unbolted the front door, and he looked about. All was quiet there, not a leaf seemed to stir. He put Quintero's arm about himself, and told the girls, "Now follow closely, right after me, and not a sound!"

They rushed out, quickly, over the veranda, and down into the bushes. Inez was half holding Florencia, guiding her in the darkness. Florencia was sobbing softly.

"Quiet!" hissed Vincent, impatient with the girl. Didn't she understand the danger?

Quintero was half unconscious already, sagging in Vincent's grasp. Vincent pushed himself and the older man deeply into the undergrowth, and then found a thicker place, where the winds had blown down several trees. He tucked the old man safely in, and whispered, "Stay there! And be quiet."

The man sagged down in the growth, and put his head down. His eyes were shut. Vincent thought he was unconscious; all the better. He would not make a sound.

Florencia was stumbling, she reached out for Vincent as he went back for the girls. "Come on," he said tersely, and thrust her, paying no attention to her wails, into the bushes and thickets. He was careful to lead them through very thick undergrowth, Inez following them closely, away from their father. When he thought they were well away from Quintero, he chose a thick place for Florencia. He pushed her into the bushes, in spite of her petulant protests.

"They are tearing my dress! Vincent, stop that! My hair is caught!"

"Better than being caught by the half-mad blacks," he said grimly, and pushed her firmly inside one windfall. Then he caught Inez by the hand, and drew her further with him, toward the path, but down nearer the beach.

"Wait here," he whispered, pushing her near the bushes. She stood like a statue in the blue muslin. Too light-colored a dress, he worried. He should have insisted on cloaks, but they might have been light also.

He fired at the house. One shot, a second, as a signal. He waited, impatiently. But the front door remained slightly ajar, and no men came out.

Damn the men!

He shot again, and this time some slaves came running around the corner of the house, shooting and yelling. Damn it all!

He caught Inez by the arm, and pulled and shoved their way into the underbrush. They were deeply in one area he had discovered on his way. It was difficult to get through the brambles. She gasped once when one must have caught at her, but she said not a word, just pushing and staggering on with him through the thickest part.

They sank down to the pine-scented floor, on the needles. He pulled the bushes closed over their heads, and laid his rifle over his knees, ready. They must hide until the slaves were drunken and asleep, then get back to Last Hope plantation. The men were wild now, shooting at everything.

If they would just find the rum and drink themselves into a stupor! He cursed the Spanish overseers for shooting too soon. If they had only waited and watched—

He smelled burning cane, and knew they were firing the few remaining fields of cane of Quintero. Then he smelled burning wood, and through the thick brush and trees he caught sight of the flames as the house burned. Tongues of orange flame leaped against the purple black sky.

Inez shivered against him, he put his arm about her and held her tightly against him. He had no coat to give her.

He heard shouting, yelling. Pedro's voice, shouting something in Spanish, the two men screaming. Had the slaves caught him? No, he thought, they are burning—in that house, the smoke smothering them—

They waited, unable to help. He gritted his teeth. If the men had only followed directions! He wondered if this was how Morgan felt in battle, to find someone dead because he had not followed orders!

Then he heard another voice, a hoarse commanding arrogant voice. "Get Judson, get him!" ordered Gamba. "We go get Judson!"

The voice was coming closer. Ahead of them, Florencia screamed, and ran out of the bushes. Two of the slaves caught her easily.

"Quintero woman!" one cried exultantly. It was Gamba. "Take her! Use her as Odette was used! Rape, kill, rape, kill!"

They took her, and she screamed and screamed. Vincent put his hands over Inez's ears. Then as she opened her mouth, to moan, he moved his hands and put them over her mouth, squeezing urgently. She must make no sound. The men were mad, wild with rage and the urge to riot.

Florencia screamed again, and the men were laughing, laughing. She cried to them, begged them, promised them money. They laughed, and grunted. They were about twenty feet away on the coral path. Then her voice came no more.

Someone yelled, "Rum, I find rum! Much rum!" The men left the limp red-clad form, and went back to the house. Vincent heard them roaming about, calling to each other, laughing, drinking, smashing the bottles against the burning house. No sounds came from the house now. The Spanish overseers were deadly silent.

"Get Judson, get Judson!" came Gamba's commanding voice. "Come on, bring bottles, get Judson!" By the sounds of it, he was angry at the men; he hit them with the broad side of his machete, but could not get them to move. Finally he and several men moved off, leaving the others drinking and smashing bottles.

Vincent waited, with Inez crumpled in his arms. He had loosed his hold on her mouth, and kissed it gently, in apology for his roughness. He had not wanted to hurt her.

He waited, with deadly patience, while the men muttered into silence. Then he ordered Inez to remain where she was, and he went for Quintero. On the way he found Florencia, crumpled in the scarlet dress, a crushed flower on the coral path. He felt over her, but there was no pulse, no movement of breath. She was dead.

He found Quintero just rousing in the bushes. He

made no explanation, he just lifted the older dazed man, and helped him through the trees and bushes to where Inez waited. She came to her father's other side, and painfully they made their way through the trees, down to the beach.

They said nothing, the weary three of them. Quintero seemed only half-conscious, sagging between them. They kept to the beach, near the trees, in the shadows, moving warily where the beach was clear of trees.

It took the rest of the night. Dawn was coming when they reached the path to Last Hope plantation. The sun was blazing pinkly, then creamily red across the blue Atlantic waves and the beach, as they turned in at the path. The house was closed and silent, the upstairs windows were opened, the white curtains blowing.

Then the curtains parted, and Vincent saw his sister's startled face. She called nothing, but waved urgently, and pointed to the front veranda. He nodded his head, and helped Quintero make the last painful steps up the coral path to the steps.

As they reached the steps, the door was unbolted and opened. Morgan came out, and Tess. Morgan picked up Quintero and carried him into the house and laid him on the first sofa he came to. Vincent put his arm around Inez and helped her up into the house.

Behind them Tess shut the door, and bolted it again, her rifle beside her on the floor. Another state of siege, thought Vincent, but at least there were five of them—five good ones. He was thankful they had made it so far.

"What happened?" asked Morgan quietly.

"Plantation fired, the overseers dead, Florencia dead," said Vincent wearily.

He and Morgan and Inez sat down at the dining table, and he told Morgan the whole story.

26

Louis Abaco had felt uneasy all night. He roused again and again, to stand with his spyglass, and study the valley below. Smoke and flames drifted against the night sky, he smelled the burning cane.

Then in the distance he saw the other fire. Not a cane fire. A house fire. It came from Quintero's.

He cursed aloud. "Damn that Gamba!"

Odette sat up, so did Malkia beside her. He could just make out the pale lovely face of Odette. "What is it, Louis?"

"That Gamba and some men. They must be drunk!"

Rifle and musket fire drifted up to them, the faint crackle of gunfire, that sounded so ominous. His mouth tightened.

Malkia got up painfully, her bones creaking. Odette stood, to stand beside Louis. He handed her the spyglass, put his hand to her head to show her how to use it. He felt the soft sleepy warmth of her so near his body, and he fairly tingled. He controlled himself. She had gone through enough. He would not act the savage with her. She must have time to rest and recover.

"Is that a house burning?" she asked, puzzled.

Malkia caught her breath. "Them fools! All blacks suffer now! Fools!"

Louis nodded grimly. "It is the house of Quintero. It comes from that direction in the valley. Also it is too large to be the kitchens or huts. I think it better I go see."

Odette put her hand on his arm. "You must go, Louis?" she asked in distress. "If Gamba get trouble, let Gamba take care!"

"They are probably drunken," he said gently. "Men go round and make trouble for all. I talk to them, bring them back."

Her head dropped. She murmured. "Much trouble, much trouble. When ending and peace again? We will all die."

"No, Odette. Have hope and one day you will be happy again," said Louis gently. He put his hand to her neck in a quick caress, then urged them both, "Lie down, sleep again. I will go down and talk to men, talk sense."

Malkia hesitated, glancing about. "If men come back drunken," she said, "no like drunken."

Louis nodded. "Right. We all go." He picked up their blankets, Malkia got a bottle of water and a packet of food, Odette carried the spyglass and rifle. They walked stealthily away from the campfire and the sleeping forms of the other women and children. Louis led them through the brush, and some distance uphill, walking steadily, helping Odette and then Malkia through the rough undergrowth.

He showed them the small cave, just about large enough for the two of them, in a small clearing. "Sleep here," he said. "Daylight come, you see path down to others. If all well, come back. If shooting and yelling, stay here."

He left the spyglass with Odette, and took only his rifle and machete with him, the huge knife thrust in his belt. His thoughts were grim as he made his way lithely down the hill, by the paths he knew so well. He rarely took the same path twice running, but went by devious ways up and down the hills, so the paths would not be clear.

He looked again and again, as he went. The fires had died down at Quintero's. But now he saw men with torches coming through the cane fields toward Judson's. His mouth set grimly. They must be indeed drunken, or they would not dare. To attack the old man Quintero, his two cowardly overseers and two girls, that was one matter. He wondered if Quintero had driven them off, or if all were dead.

They would all pay in blood, he thought wearily, and began to consider how he himself could get away. If Odette would come, he would take her with him in a boat, some small boat he could steal, and go to another island. But the white men might still chase them, and try to kill them. All would be blamed for the attacks of the few, "to teach them a lesson," as the white men said.

In Louis Abaco's experience, few men were so fair and considerate and gentle as Thomas Hamilton had been. He seemed to understand, and he had been good in both word and deed. With his death, all had changed.

And now those foolish ones, probably led by Gamba, would go attack the most merciless foe they could have, Caleb Judson. If he was shot at, his property damaged beyond the cane fields, all would pay in much blood. They would be torn apart, as Bernardo had been, for the man enjoyed tormenting others, and would laugh with pleasure at having such torture for the bodies of black men and women. He would not be pursued by the law, they would say he was "right and just."

In his pirate days, Abaco had met many a sailor who had fled from such righteousness and justice, in terror and horror. They had fled to the sea, submitted to the brutal system of a pirate captain, rather than return to the unequal treatment of wealthy men, white men, "just men and good." Courts had sentenced them for stealing to keep their children alive. Judges had pointed at them, and committed them to horrible torture, for siding with a rebellious duke who had commanded them to do so. The islands were filled with the apprenticed men, the convicts, the poor Scottish and Irish, sent from England as punishment, to live for years under the lash of men who had bought their terms.

In Abaco's life there had been two kinds of justice. One was amiable and gentle, for wealthy white men. The other was for all others: the poor, and mean, and despised, and the men, women and children of any color other than white.

And he knew that when the black men rose up in fury, they would be struck down without mercy.

If he rushed, he might be able to persuade those black brothers of his not to be so foolish, to come back to the hills, to sleep off the rum that made them so bold and reckless with their own safety and those of their women and children. For the men alone would not suffer, but all of them, all.

And as a man, Abaco had best flee, he told himself grimly. There would be no security left on Elysia, it would be paradise no longer.

He strode through the burnt cane, his nostrils dilated by the thick burnt smell of molasses. He walked on and on, his boots crushing the remnants of the cut cane. As he walked, he kept glancing ahead to the Judson plantation. Off to his left was the Hamilton house, still and quiet. He hoped that it would remain so. Food had been taken from there, but no shots had come from the house. He thought Morgan Hamilton and Silver Jasmine understood.

The torches were advancing in wavering lines toward the Judson house. He caught glimpses of them through the thick trees that lined each plantation. If he hurried, he would be in time. But could he head them off? It would be dawn before long; he knew that lightening in the eastern sky, and it was late. With the sun on them, the blacks would not have a chance, the men inside the Judson house would fire with deadly accuracy.

He reached the outbuildings, panting for breath. There were no people in the slave huts, he did not expect it. The dogs were howling, straining at their chains, but no one came to release them. The sounds drowned out any sound he might make. He made his way slowly to the stable, moving cautiously. The blacks were not in sight now, they were still in the trees, or in the remaining cane fields.

He turned the corner of the stable door, and went inside. He stiffened at once, sensing a presence, and his rifle came up.

The horse was being attached to a small carriage. But no one stood there. He crouched at the door, just inside, in the darkness, his eyes becoming accustomed to the dimness.

Then he saw the woman, dressed in a black cloak and black bonnet, her hand to her mouth in terror. It was the Frenchwoman, Antoinette Judson.

They stared at each other. He glanced about quickly, no one else was there. He looked back at her: there was blank terror in the lovely dark eyes.

He remembered what Odette had said of her, that the woman had been kind to her, had prevented Judson from raping her after Bernardo's death.

"You are alone?" he whispered.

She nodded slowly, fear twisting her features. "Go on," she said harshly. "Kill me. Kill me—make it quick, if you have any kindness in you!"

He stared at her, shook his head. His hands moved quickly. He dropped the rifle at his feet, moved around the horse, to finish attaching it to the carriage.

He came to her, as she shrank back against the wall, saw the beautiful white throat as she swallowed back a scream. He picked her up by the waist, lifted her into the carriage, and put the reins in her hands.

Then he lifted the rifle, and ran forward to the bit at the horse's mouth. He heard shouting, knew the slaves were coming.

He came out of the stable, pulling at the horse's bit urgently. Antoinette sat in the seat with a long whip in her hands, holding the reins loosely. Her eyes were wide with fear, but she made no sound.

Louis ran with the horse soundlessly around the corner of the silent house. He could see the slaves approaching, waving torches. But they did not see him and the carriage, not yet. They were looking fearfully up at the big house, the shuttered windows.

A shot came from the house. The slaves began to scream and yell, and jump up and down, shooting off their ancient muskets. He saw Gamba yelling, jumping high in the air, his great height impressive, the torch waving in his long arm.

Louis ran with the horse, the carriage jolting after them. He pulled it along, into the coral path, and down the bending, twisting path in the shelter of the trees. They had gone unnoticed in the shooting and the yelling.

He ran on down the path, the horse working up to a good trot. The horse was restless, his head tossing, hard to hold. He was fresh, and frightened.

Louis moved on, and the woman held tightly to the seat, and her whip and reins. They came out on the beach. Louis turned the carriage to the right, to the south, and ran on with them for a short distance. Then he halted, and released the bit, running his hand along the horse soothingly as he went back to the carriage.

The dawn was lightening the sky, the sun would rise shortly. He looked up at her. "Listen. You going to St. Michael. The horse good. Nobody stop you! Whip them if they try. Understand?"

She nodded, staring at him in a daze.

"Why do you help me?" she asked slowly.

He shook his head impatiently, he had no more time for words. "Go—quick—" He slapped the horse on the rump, and it started up and jolted the carriage forward.

She called back, her voice soft on the morning air, "Thank you—thank you!"

He grimaced, and started back at a run. If he hurried he could stop the slaves from killing each other, and the men in the house. It sounded like the battle had already erupted up there.

He raced back up the path, finally stopped, and slowed, to view the scene cautiously from a screen of bushes. The men from inside the house had used their rifles to good effect. Two blacks lay dead on the path, sprawled out, blood running from them, staining their dark shirts.

Gamba still yelled and jumped, a safe distance out of rifle fire, thought Louis with contempt. He was a good leader! He urged them forward, keeping well out of the fire!

The sun rose, turned hot and bright. The house could be clearly seen. Louis saw the rifles poking from five windows of the house, as he circled the huge mansion, once so beautiful. It was now pockmarked with bullet holes, and burn marks scorched the wooden frames of the windows. One curtain had burned, and lay limply in rags on the window frame.

He went up to Gamba, and put his hand urgently on the man's bare sweaty arm. The man stared at him, black eyes glazed with rum and power and fight.

"Get the men and draw back," urged Louis swiftly. "There is time now—get the men and pull back. Back to the hills!"

"Kill—kill—" panted Gamba. "I am chief. They kill! They kill and burn and rape! Kill, kill!"

"Gamba, two blacks lie dead! Those men can shoot good! Come back to the hills! Hide! We must go to another island!"

His words went unheard. In despair, he withdrew, back into the bushes, and watched grimly, his rifle at his side. One bold slave ran forward, torch high. He flung it, and the burning torch landed on the wooden roof.

It blazed up. The black cried out exultantly, and in the next moment—crack!—a rifle blazed from inside the house. He stumbled, his face went bloody red and masklike, and he fell forward, hands outspread in a pleading gesture. He went down limply.

The other slaves stopped firing, staring at him. The drink was dying in them, thought Louis. He called out, "Retreat! Come back to the hills! Run, run, run!"

Gamba yelled angrily, trying to drown his voice, "Kill, kill, shoot more, shoot more!"

But the blacks were running, running, as the rifle fire increased in the house. The fire was deadly, one black stumbled and went down near Louis. He went forward, picked him up, dragged him out of range. The man had been shot in the leg.

He smelled of rum. Louis cried out again, in his powerful voice, over the rifle fire, "Run, run to hills! Run, all is done here! Run, run to hills!"

And the panic grew. They followed Louis as he strode back through the cane, half carrying the wounded man. They followed him blindly, shooting recklessly back at the house as more shots were fired at them.

"Save your shots," Louis said angrily. "Save bullets! We got no more up there!"

Some listened, and the fire gradually ceased. Wearily, their steps slowed to a slow run, then to a walk, their heads down. They were sick with the rum, and the consequences of their actions were beginning to come to them.

One muttered to Louis, "Where we go now, master? Where we go now?"

"I am not your master," said Louis curtly. "We talk in hills. Come on, now."

Gamba followed them sullenly, disappointed. They had not killed the white masters in the big house, and he growled as he stumbled along. He had one more bottle, and he would pause and drink at it; then muttering, followed the last men up the cane fields and into the low hills.

Louis's thoughts were bitter. Now all would have to flee the island, or be killed. How could so many get away? There must be more than one hundred men, women and children hiding in the hills. All white men would be up against them.

As Louis carried the other black, Gamba caught up with Louis and offered him the bottle. Louis shook his head.

"What happen at Quintero?" Abaco asked abruptly.

"Kill, kill, kill," said Gamba.

"Who kill? Quintero?"

Gamba nodded. "Kill Quintero, shot at back door. He fell back. Kill two men inside house, overseers who whip men! Kill white girl, rape and kill, rape and kill!"

Abaco felt his heart go down to his boots. Grimly

he trudged on. That really did it! Not just burning the cane, not just burning the two plantation houses. They had had to kill whites! And to rape and kill a white girl! That would really close the case against them. No black or mulatto like himself would be safe on the whole of Elysia. They must run! Run and never stop. Another island? Only a stopgap. Wearily, he wondered if he must sign on another pirate ship, the next one coming this way.

Not many pirate ships came along this way, but a few still came. He could raise the black flag, and one might stop, and take him on. Maybe. Maybe. But what about the others? What about Odette? Must he leave her? He could never take her on a pirate ship. The pirates would go mad over her, and tear her to bits between them.

He plodded up the hill slowly, carrying the man, while Gamba raced on ahead, to brag of his exploits to the women and children. He had shown he was a great chief! He had led men in battle!

At the Judson house, the Marquess coughed fastidiously at the smoke. He glanced about, the house walls were burning about them, there on the second floor.

"I say, I think we had best leave," he said to Judson, picking up his flask of powder. "The whole place is burning down."

"Damn it, get some water," said Judson, still peering from the back windows.

"Are you ordering me about?" asked Lord Tweed, in a very polite voice, deadly cold.

"No, no, I meant Hank, there," said Judson hastily. He scowled out the window and raised his voice. "Hank, get that fire out!"

"I tried," said one of the overseers. "The house is burning down, Mr. Judson! We best get out!"

"Oh, hell," said Judson wearily. He frowned at the

416

hills. "All those damn blacks have run, that's good," he said, with some satisfaction. "We best get outside and see what damage is done."

The men scrambled to safety eagerly, racing down the stairs, followed more slowly by Lord Tweed and Judson. Once outside, they heard the burning and crackling of the fire. It had caught hold, the whole roof was aflame, and the wooden sides now. A curtain caught, and blazed brightly.

"Hadn't you best rescue your valuables?" suggested Lord Tweed. "I suppose my trunks will go up in smoke!" And he frowned, disgusted by this whole venture.

"My valuables are in a large iron safe, it won't burn, no matter what happens to the house. And the rums in the cellar are always safe, they are surrounded by coral. That won't burn either," said Judson. He raised his voice furiously. "Why don't you damn fools get some water and throw it on the fire?"

The three weary overseers ran about, throwing buckets and basins of water futilely on the fire, but mostly unable to reach the upper stories. The fire burned sullenly down to the first floor foundations, and finally licked itself out. The house was a ruin, the upper story gone, the furniture in cinders, only the iron safe intact, and the cellar of rum.

Judson went about cursing everyone. It was Lord Tweed who asked idly, "I say, where is your wife? Was she sleeping upstairs?"

"My God, I forgot her," said Judson. "I'll go inside, when it cools, and see if she is there."

"She ran away," said one of the overseers timidly. "I saw her run away in a carriage."

Judson turned on him furiously, and would have struck him, but the man was already seated on the

417

ground, and Judson would not bend down. "Damn you to hell! Why didn't you tell me?"

"We was shooting and yelling, I couldn't see you about," said the man.

Judson went to the stables, finding the horse and carriage gone. He cursed again and again. "That damn bitch, running out on me."

"Saving her own hide," said Lord Tweed idly. "I say, are you just going to let the blacks get away with this?"

"Hell, no, I'll string them all up. Or get the dogs after them. I'm damn tired. Wonder what's to eat?" and he went about grumbling that there was no cooked food for him. They ate fruit and drank some rum, and felt better.

Judson then got an idea. "Say, Hamilton's plantation isn't burned, is it?" he said, turning to one of the overseers who had been posted on that side of the house. "Did you see it go up in smoke?"

"No, Mr. Judson. Just Quintero's went up."

"So—they didn't attack him!" Judson mused, his red-rimmed eyes burning with thought. "Wish I got some slaves left, I'd set them on him!"

They sat on the ground near the slave cabins, and watched the last planks of the house burning and falling with a thud. "It seems a pity that his house is left," said Lord Tweed idly. His gray eyes were hot, however, belying his tone. "I wish the man was dead! I'd take his woman, and burn his house!"

"It will take months to rebuild my house," Judson grumbled. "Damn it, wish I had Last Hope plantation house! Now, there is a mansion!"

"A mansion, is it?" asked Lord Tweed. "That sailor, living in a mansion with his barmaid wife? What a joke! Why didn't the blacks burn him out?"

"Oh, they like him, he's soft with them!" said Judson, contemptuously. "Well, they may turn on him yet. Yes, by God, they'll turn on him—today!"

"And how will you manage that?" asked Lord Tweed, with thinly veiled contempt.

Judson got up, went over and retrieved a burned plank. He moved his brown palm along it, and held up the blackened palm. "With this!" he said. He began to grin, slyly. "We'll blacken our faces, get some torches—and burn him out. And everyone will know it was the blacks!"

Lord Tweed stared at him. "Blacken our faces? Play blacks? I don't know about that—"

One of the overseers began to laugh. "Lord help me, you're a brilliant man, Mr. Judson," he said, with admiration. "That's a great idea! Blacken us, and pretend to be blacks, and burn them out!"

"Or kill Hamilton," said Lord Tweed. "You said the house is fine. Why not go with torches, threaten them, and when they lean out, we'll kill Hamilton and his brother! Then you can have that black girl, Odette, you're so hot for. And I'll have Tess!"

Judson slapped Lord Tweed on the back with his blackened hand. Lord Tweed winced and was about to snap back a rebuke, then he closed his mouth tightly.

"Good idea! Great idea! We'll kill Hamilton, and take his house! Kill that sniveling little brother also! Then the women belong to us—and that house! Sure, I'll live there! It's a better house than mine, anyway," and he gave his burned-out house a bitter look. "We can find the jewels and money, too, and sell his six-year rums, and whatever else we want. I'll get the blacks back, and kill enough to put the fear of death in the others," he crowed.

They went around, found blacking in the planks, and mixed it with the pitch from discarded torches. They blackened their faces and hands, Lord Tweed grimacing with distaste. Judson was racing about, his face grotesque, his tone croaking with the smoke, pausing to drink from a rum bottle at times.

"Best save that for the celebration, or you won't see straight to shoot Hamilton," advised Lord Tweed dryly. "I could do with some meat! Can anyone here cook?"

"No one can," said Judson impatiently. "We'll get some food later! Get Tess to cook for us, and Odette! Eh?" And he laughed and crowed, as they checked their rifles, filled their pockets with bullets, and made sure of the powder in their flasks.

"I always wanted that plantation," said Judson. "This time I'll keep it! No one can come taking it from me this time! I'll kill anybody who tries! Should have done it when that sailor came, claiming to be Hamilton!"

"I wonder if Mrs. Judson went to St. Michael," said Lord Tweed reflectively. "Would she bring back aid, do you think?"

"Who cares?" shrugged Judson. "We can handle them. I ain't waiting for any mouthy judges to fix things up! I'll get Hamilton, take his place, be in possession, take Odette and the others, and it'll be my say-so! When Antoinette comes back, she'll get a whipping before I take her back!"

Lord Tweed was silent, his brow scowling, as though he wondered what he had gotten into. But when Judson led the way through the cane fields, Lord Tweed strode after him, the rifle on his arm, as though he were on a pleasant and unusual hunt.

"The islands surely are an interesting area," he said dryly, as they stalked along. "Nothing like jolly old England. I shall have stories enough to entertain many a host, and all my friends at the clubs in London!"

"London, is it? Too civilized for me," grunted Judson. "Out here, a man can do as he pleases!"

27

Tess and Vincent were watching that afternoon, as the heat haze drifted with the remnants of the black smoke across the fields. Tess sat at the back window, letting the light cool trade winds drift across her cheeks. Would it ever end, this nightmare of terror?

She thought of England, of the cold rainy days, when the Atlantic fog crept in and covered everything with a chilly blanket, and one couldn't see a hand before the face. When the sailors stumbled into the bar, their jackets covered with dripping water, grumbling, calling for hot grog. When Ryder would be cross for lack of business from the gentry. When she and Vincent would have to carry heavy loads of wood to each fireplace, up and down stairs with heavy pails of hot water, working, working, until they collapsed at night with exhaustion.

But England had been home. This was an alien land,

full of heat and insects, of blacks with terrible fear in them, of whites who could be monsters of evil. Yet—the island was beautiful, the fragrance of the white jasmine, the loveliness of the spilling bougainvillea in purple red glory, the blazing red of hibiscus blossoms that dotted the lush green bushes. And ever the Atlantic Ocean, blue and white, lashing against the red and coral rocks.

Tess jerked erect, and rubbed her eyes. Was she asleep? Was she having nightmares, or were men coming through the fields with torches and rifles?

She looked again, then jumped to her feet. She ran to the front bedroom, where Vincent lounged at the window. Inez lay asleep in the bed, and he was glancing down at her, his blue eyes dreamy.

"Vincent, men are coming—through the fields!" she panted.

He snatched up the rifle, bent and touched Inez on the forehead. "Inez? You must wake up now," he said.

"I'll wake Morgan." Tess darted back to his bedroom. He had been asleep such a short time, she hated to do it. But he was not only the best shot, he had the coolest mind, and he was accustomed to battle. She bent over him as he lay sprawled across his bed, his unshaven face buried in the pillow.

As she touched his shoulder, he jerked awake, and turned to gaze up at her. His eyes were red-rimmed, blinking.

"Tess?"

"Men are coming through the fields, Morgan."

"God. I thought it was over," he groaned, and managed to roll to his feet. He yanked on his boots, and tied them quickly, then reached for his rifle.

"Shall I wake Señor Quintero?"

He thought, then nodded, standing up. "Yes, we'll need every gun. What direction, Tess?"

"From Judson's. The smoke over there has died down."

Morgan went to the back bedroom while Tess went to one of the middle bedrooms to waken Señor Quintero. He slept so deeply that she grimaced with pity. But Morgan had said he would be needed. She touched his shoulder gently; he groaned, and finally opened his eyes.

"What is it, Señora?" He was polite even in his grogginess.

"Men are coming, blacks, with torches. Morgan said you will be needed. Can you stand, Señor?"

She helped him to his feet. He staggered, put his hand to his bandaged head, his face was almost as gray as his hair. "Ay, ay, ay," he sighed. "I come, yes, I come. Where is my Inez?"

"In the front room, Señor. She is awake."

"I will watch here, then?" He took up his stand at the window, drew aside the white curtain cautiously about two inches. "Ah, they come across the fields. One—two—four—I see five men," he muttered.

Tess sped back to Morgan, now waiting at the back window. His face was grim, he was loading his rifle, counting the bullets. As soon as she came in, he said, "Tess, tell them to hold their fire, and count their bullets. We are low on ammunition. Tell them to fire only to keep them from coming close enough to burn the house. We have to keep those torches away."

Tess sped to give the message to the other three. They listened, nodded, and turned back to the windows. She returned again to Morgan, watched at the window while he examined her rifle in turn, and loaded it, and the pistol.

The men were much closer, creeping through the burned cane. She frowned. How many clothes they wore, she thought. Boots, trousers, shirts and even jackets, and hats. All wore hats.

"Morgan!"

"Yes, my darling?"

"I don't think—they are blacks," she said slowly.

"What?"

He came to look. "They *are* black, Tess—look at them. You can see—ah!" he exclaimed.

She nodded. "They wear white men's clothes."

"Might have got them from Judson's or Quintero's." He was hesitant, peering out at the men, who were now crouched together in a field, muttering together. Three of them held torches which were burning brightly. The other two were loading their rifles.

"Morgan, one of them is wearing that gray suit of Lord Tweed. It was lined with velvet along the lapels, remember? And their hats—"

They studied the men intently. Tess felt a strange feeling in her bones, that made her shiver. She had a strong sense that they were not blacks; yet they looked black, their faces, their hands—

The man in the gray suit stood up, turned from the others, his arm moved languidly. Tess tensed. That was Lord Tweed, no black carried himself so, with head erect, face arrogant, arm movements so sure and like those of a rake. Arrogant, a very Corinthian—

"It is Lord Tweed," she said.

Morgan was frowning at the small group. They were moving forward now. "Well, blacks or whites, if they try to fire the house, they'll know the feel of our bullets," he said grimly. His rifle came up, he waited.

No shot came from the house, she felt a pride in the ones who waited: her husband, her brother, Señor Quintero and Inez. She thought of what Morgan had said of her. Well, she could ask for no better fighters to be beside her! She would trust every one of them, unto death! And it might come to that. But they would go down fighting fiercely and with cool heads.

One man ran forward, swiftly, torch in hand, while the other four waited. Morgan held his fire; then just as the man lunged to fling the torch, Morgan fired. The man went down in a heap, the torch on top of him, and his clothes began to burn and smolder. He did not utter a single cry, he must have died at once.

The other four moved back, seemingly dismayed. Morgan watched, keen-eyed.

Tess murmured to him, as she handed the other loaded rifle to him, "If they were blacks, they would come for food, they would make for the kitchens. They must be hungry Morgan!"

She worked swiftly at cooling and reloading the rifle he had fired. Morgan nodded.

"Yes. Look at that stocky fellow. The way he moves. I think it is Caleb Judson."

She studied the man through the gap in the curtains. The man moved his arm, pointed to the house, seemed to be urging one of the other men to take his torch and move closer. The man shook his head, cringing. The first man struck him across the face.

"Judson," said Tess positively. "The blacks would not strike each other, I believe."

"Yes, I think so."

They were silent then, waiting. The men withdrew a distance, and seemed to be arguing. A bottle came out of one pocket, they drank, and glared at the house. Later in the afternoon, they moved forward again. But all in the house held their fire, until a man moved forward timidly with a torch. Quintero shot at him from the bedroom, he yelped and dropped the torch, and ran back to the safety of distance and the thick burned cane.

It was hard, waiting, watching. The afternoon wore

on. Tess took cool water around to each one, and talked briefly in whispers to each. Morgan remained at the window, though his eyes were heavy with sleep.

At Morgan's wish, Tess told each of them her suspicions.

"White men Judson and Lord Tweed?" asked Vincent, in surprise. "I cannot see them from here, but would white men do such a thing?"

Inez listened gravely, the pistol beside her on the small table. Her small hands grew weary of holding the heavy weapon.

"I think he would do it, he is a clever man and a cruel one," she nodded. "I think he had something to do with the death of Mr. Hamilton's uncle. I heard our blacks whispering about it, and making fearful faces. I did not question them, for they are afraid of Judson. But it may be true. He is truly evil."

"I wouldn't put it past Lord Tweed to go along with it. Wonder what happened to Mrs. Judson?" mused Vincent. "Do you suppose she is dead? Too bad—I bet Judson wouldn't do much to protect her! He would be all for saving his own hide!"

His tone was bitter. He had blamed himself for not being able to save both the Quintero girls. Inez' look on him was compassionate.

"I think the Lord above makes our fates for us," she said gently. "It was His will that some should live, and some should die. If Florencia had not jumped up and screamed with hysteria, she might be alive. You did your best, Vincent."

Vincent looked gratefully at her, and pressed her hand.

Tess said, "The Lord may make our fates by deciding on our natures for us, one of courage, one of cowardice, one of fearfulness, one of lying, one of murderous will, such as Judson. But I must believe we have

426

something to do with this working of our fate ourselves. We must grasp opportunities, do what we can, struggle to free ourselves from oppression. And if all else fails, we must meet the future gallantly and with head high." She nodded her small blond head with determination.

Inez smiled at her, her dark eyes admiring. "As you do, dear Tess," she said quietly. "I cannot imagine you defeated! You will ever try again! Just as Vincent does. You cannot imagine how he helped us all, and tried to save us. If he had not come, I should be dead, and Father also."

Vincent blushed, and his head lowered. "I would have saved all, had I been Morgan," he muttered.

Inez took his hand in hers, and squeezed his fingers. "Do not continue to blame yourself, my friend! You did all, and more than could be expected. It was so clever of you to hide us, and Father would not have lived if you had not carried him from the house. And I—I owe you my life, my—my soul."

That was pretty strong for a Catholic girl to say, thought Tess, as she went on to Señor Quintero. Tess grinned a little. Vincent was young, but he had become a man, and Inez evidently saw him as very much a man! She could wish no better wife for her brother than this sweet Spanish girl with the large eyes, the gentle candid spirit, the need to help her family and work for them. She was just what he needed, a loving adorable woman, and he looked as though he could drown in her great eyes.

She went to Señor Quintero, and gently told him what she believed.

"White men attacking us?" His very gray mustache quivered with the shock of it. "Attack us? No, no, they must be blacks! Do you mean to say it was white men who attacked and burned my home, raped my daughter— murdered her? My Florencia?"

His voice shook, he put his hand to his forehead

427

under the bandage. She patted his shoulder, she somehow felt motherly toward him in his weakness.

"I am not sure, Señor Quintero, who attacked your house. It could have been the blacks. But look carefully at the men who come toward the plantation house here. Look at their clothes, the way they walk and hold themselves. I think these men are white. The ones who attacked you last night—" She hesitated, delicately. "The ones who cried out, you heard their voices, saw them. Do you think they were white?"

He thought, frowning. "No, no," he said. "I saw them, their naked chests sweaty and dark brown. And their voices, thick and uncultured, using the Creole of the natives. Some were bare to the waist, and went barefoot in the cane as though they did not feel it. They must have been blacks."

She returned to Morgan, and told him what Quintero had said. Morgan listened, his gaze still on the men outside.

"I wonder," he said. "I have been watching them, they move like white men. I don't think any are Gamba— he is too tall for that. And Abaco is also very tall, as tall as Gamba. He is not there." His voice told his relief.

"I cannot believe our blacks would attack us," said Tess, with more certainty. "They liked us, didn't they, Morgan? We tried to treat them well. And I did like Odette. I wonder—I wonder if she is safe?" Her gaze lifted to the hills.

"We won't know until this is over. But it is a puzzle, Tess. Why would the whites attack us like this? If they hate us, as Judson probably does, and Lord Tweed, why come as blacks?"

"So the blacks will be blamed for it," said Tess.

"Ah. As they were blamed for the death of Thomas Hamilton. When it was probably Judson who killed him," said Morgan, nodding.

They waited, through the long afternoon. The men did not come closer, though they often looked at the house.

"Why are they waiting?" asked Tess, impatiently. "They haven't sent for more men, have they? Would anyone else attack us?"

Her voice was full of dread.

"Probably waiting for night," said Morgan. "Look, Tess, you get some sleep. You look worn out."

"I could not sleep now," said Tess. "Morgan—I think I'll creep downstairs and bring up more food and water. If we have food, we won't need sleep so much."

"Good idea. Take Inez with you, and for God's sake, be careful! No looking through the windows, and avoid the places where the windows don't fit tightly."

"Yes, I'll be careful."

She crept away, got Inez, and the two girls, moving as soundlessly on their heelless slippers as possible, brought up cool water. Then they returned for the food, some cooked ham, vegetables, fresh fruit.

The men ate hungrily. Then the girls ate, sitting on the floor in the hallway, out of range of any stray bullets.

"It is the waiting that is so hard," said Inez, wiping the juice of a mango from her dainty chin.

"Yes, the waiting. Morgan has been in many battles, and he says the waiting is the hardest. Men grow impatient, grow incautious, or are tempted to drink rum or brandy. Then it is very bad."

"Our men do not do so," said Inez simply, her dark eyes shining with pride.

"No. I was thinking—I could not ask for finer men, and for anyone dearer than you, to fight along with me," said Tess, reaching out her hand impulsively for the hand of Inez. They clasped hands, smiled, and sat quietly for a time.

Dusk came, and the girls cleared away the tables of any food, set out the ammunition again. The powder flasks were set carefully out of the range of the windows, yet close enough to be caught up by the men who shot. The bullets were counted and apportioned with care. There wasn't much left, as Morgan had said. Every bullet must count. There were four men left out there. The man whom Morgan had shot still lay where he had fallen. They had made no move to come and get him.

The sky turned deeper blue, then purple, and the shadows lengthened and faded into darkness. Tess took up her pistol, and waited at the window next to Morgan's.

It was so dark now, they could not see the men in the fields. Suddenly a shot came out of the darkness, and another shot splintered the window beside Morgan's arm.

He cursed softly, drew back. "They are closer, damn it," he said dispassionately.

He gazed keenly. Then when another shot came, he fired at the flash of the bullet and powder. "Missed, I'm afraid," he said ruefully. "But they may pull back now."

Bullets sounded at intervals. They would just relax, and think the men had settled down for the night, when another bullet would crack out of the darkness and hit the house.

Then in the fields, torches were lit. The four men were standing too far to be hit by rifle bullets. Morgan watched them keenly, sent Tess around with orders.

"If any man comes close to the house with a torch, kill him. We dare not let them get that close," he said. "The roof is dry, so is the upper floor. Don't let them get that close, for God's sake."

Tess darted around, giving the message. They all nodded. Vincent left Inez at one front window, and went to the other side of the house, to the middle bedroom, where he could see along that side. Morgan kept to his post, Tess took the post across the hall from him.

She felt lonely there by herself, with the pistol ready, the bullets and powder flask beside her, a basin of water ready to douse a fire that might start in the white curtains. She did not have Morgan to talk to, though she could see him across the hall in the other back bedroom, ready, lounging near the window, lifting the curtain slightly from time to time to watch.

The torches came closer. Morgan was watching alertly. Then at the urging of one stocky man, one of the others ran forward, glancing up fearfully from moment to moment. The torch was high in his arm.

Night and the shadows made firing tricky. Morgan fired just below the torch. With a yelp, the man dropped the torch and it burned in the grass. He ran back into the cane, holding his arm.

They could hear urges, yelling, cursing, and one man kicked at the two others. Morgan smiled grimly. He wanted to yell at Judson tauntingly. But he must have patience, he reminded himself.

If they were patient, the white men in blackface might drift away. They might go get drunk, and sleep off their fury. Evidently the blacks had burned Judson's house, and Judson had decided to take Last Hope by fire or bullet, or both. Well, he could just think again.

When it was all over, thought Morgan, he would see to it that Judson was arrested for murder. He had caused all this trouble by his treatment of Bernardo. There must be some charge that would stick.

If the courts would not act against a white man, then, by God, Morgan would personally run Judson off the island! It was not right or fair or just that one man could ruin a paradise for everyone else.

This island, Elysia, could be a paradise for them all. The houses could be rebuilt, the blacks pacified, if Judson were removed by one means or another. And Morgan meant to do just that.

Hamilton, his uncle, had found it good, even in his grief over his dead wife and children. And Morgan and Tess could find it good again. She got along well with the slaves, they trusted her, and he thought he himself might gain their trust. It was no wonder they were suspicious of white people. But trust could be earned.

He watched, eyes narrowed, as another man was persuaded to try again. Then when the man grew close, his arm upraised with the torch, Morgan fired at the arm below the torch. Another shot rang out, as Quintero was eager to get into the action. The bullets rang out over the hills, echoing. The man yelled, dropped the torch, and ran back into the cane.

More waiting. Morgan watched, though his eyes burned for lack of sleep, and with the powder smoke drifting about the room. He took advantage of the pause to scoop up a palmful of cool water, and let it drip over his face, disregarding the way it fell on his shirt. Ah, that felt good. Cool water. Bless Tess and her foresight.

Morgan glanced across the room, through the hallway, to the other room, dim and shadowy. Tess in her blue muslin sat near the window, the pistol on her lap, watching. She seemed to feel his gaze, glanced toward him, half raised her white arm, and smiled.

He raised his hand to her, saluted her, his partner, his wife, his beloved.

They would fight and win, he vowed. For she was a wife worth fighting for, worth any trouble and pain. He turned his attention back to the window, and settled down again for another long wait. The night would be a long one.

28

In the hills, Louis Abaco moved about, helping to bandage the wounded men. Some had bullet burns, some burns from the fired cane, some had bullets inside them. Many more groaned and were sick at their stomachs from too much raw rum in their empty stomachs.

They needed food, they could not last long without it. The blacks were kept half-starved on Judson's plantation. The others were in somewhat better shape. Yet they also needed food, and about all they had left was some water and fresh fruit, and not much of the fruit.

When he had made them as comfortable as he could, he glanced about, as though casually. Gamba had jumped up and down, bragged, boasted of his exploits for a time. Then he had fallen over, and now snored drunkenly under a tree.

Abaco had seen the weary disgusted looks of the

black women. They knew him, he had not acted like a chief, hanging back while the others took the bullets and burns. There was not a mark on Gamba. Even the older children eyed him gravely, and some of the men had turned away in the midst of his yelling.

Perhaps in his native country in Africa, Gamba might one day have succeeded his father as chief. He had evidently been spoiled by women in his early years: he was arrogant, insolent, sullen, unwilling to work hard. Yet in Africa, pride and his position might have forced him into the role of leader. He might have done well.

But here, as a slave, his pride and sullenness kept him from any leadership position at all. And he was not a man of great courage, though he was tall and looked dignified. He was not one in whom they would put their trust. They had tried him in their minds, and found him wanting.

Louis Abaco sighed to himself as he looked over the group. More than one hundred men, women, and children of all ages. What could he do with them? They could not all join a pirate ship. The pirates would have howled with laughter, and tipped the children overboard to feed the sharks that infested the Caribbean waters. The women they would have used, then discarded into the water, or one of the notorious ports of the islands. The men—they would have tested, and kept, or discarded. No, it was no future for them all.

Perhaps they could all go to some other islands. They might find work on plantations. The owners were all too glad to get good slaves, now that the British were trying to stop the entrance of any new slaves from Africa. The British Parliament had passed laws that were supposed to stop the slavers from bringing in more slaves. Louis had seen the black slavers sailing, however, and knew more slaves were being captured and brought in.

But the flow was decreasing to a trickle, and the price of a good strong black had gone high.

Yes, they might get work on another island, and if they were fortunate, the owner would not talk. Yet, the word of the slave rebellion would quickly go round, and the owner would know—and he would have to report it. Or gossip would report it for him.

They might scatter among many islands, a few here, a few there. Some men had their women and children. It might be best to divide them into families and small groups, and distribute them, five here, six or seven there, according to the size of the family. Single men let off on one island or another, to make their way as they could. Yes, that might be the best plan.

Louis gathered up a bottle of fresh water from the stream, put some fruit casually in a calabash, and disappeared among the bushes. He strolled casually, until he was sure he was not being followed, then made his way up the hill to the cave where he had left Odette and Malkia.

It was late afternoon, almost dusk. The sun was slithering down behind the hills, slanting rays of light through the branches of the trees, to make a radiant path for him. He lifted his face to the sky, the vivid sky of the Caribbean islands, that he had grown to enjoy so much. He could smell the flowers, the plumeria growing wild and tangled, the bright hibiscus, the subtler scents of purple wild orchids, the small orange lilies, the herbs from which Malkia made her ointments. He crushed one under his boot, a little patch of sage, and the sharp fragrance came to his nostrils.

It was a good land, a glorious land. Why must men fight each other, and kill? He had left the pirate life because he had hated the killing. And he had lived a free life, though chased at times, and continually vigilant.

What must a man do to remain free, to enjoy the flowers and the sweet trill of the birds, to work with his hands in the good earth, to enjoy the companionship of a fine woman, to see his children growing around him?

Was that life such a dream, that it could never be?

The melancholy thoughts accompanied him as he walked slowly up the hill. He plucked a spray of plumeria and put it to his nose, and was not soothed as he usually was. He flung it away, and lifted his head again. He would not give in, he would fight for his freedom, though he must leave this island he enjoyed.

He came noiselessly into the clearing. Odette started violently as the tall dark figure loomed up, and for a moment he saw the stark fear in her beautiful small face. He felt a pang for it. She had suffered much.

Then Malkia said easily, "It is Louis Abaco. All goes well?"

He shrugged. "Some good, some bad." He sat down easily beside them, and set the bottle beside them, and the calabash of fruit.

Malkia reached for the bottle, drank eagerly. Odette studied his face. She had lost the wild look, but she was still stiff with fear, and shivering a bit.

"What has happened? We saw the fires, the houses of Quintero and Judson," she said quietly. She handed the spyglass back to him, and he fingered it, his head lowered.

"Yes. The houses burned. When I got there, Mrs. Judson with carriage, I helped her get away. Gamba yell, 'Kill, kill, kill,' and foolish men follow. Quintero shot, daughter Florencia die of rape and pain. Two overseers dead. At Judson's, no killing of whites. But Henri, young Benny, and Pete, they die. Others injured by bullets and fire."

They all sat thinking about that. Malkia handed the

water bottle to Odette, she drank a little automatically, indifferently. She ate no fruit, though he urged the calabash gently into her hand.

"I heard shots today maybe two hour, maybe one hour." Odette looked at him questioningly. "Where men? All men come back?"

"No, some drunk, lie in cane. They come back later," he said.

"Maybe so, I go down to men, see wounds," said Malkia, eyeing them with her shrewd eyes. "You come later, maybe?" She grinned her toothless grin, and slipped away.

Abaco sat quietly. Odette had undergone much, yet she was still so young, so beautiful, so slim of line, her face so lovely. She sat gracefully, one leg under her, the other outstretched, brown and soft of skin. She gazed down the hill out to the valley, and her eyes were sad.

"Never go back to Hamilton," she murmured. "Missus Silver Jasmine so kind, she smile much. She make dress, she talk and read. Never see her again?"

"Maybe you can go back," comforted Louis. "I must leave the island, though."

She glanced sharply at him, her eyes wide. "Why—leave?"

"All black men must leave, or be killed. White man's justice," he said bitterly. "Some whites were killed. No stay. Go to other islands. Go far away. Hide."

"Ah, I fear," she said. "When red-haired man came, I think trouble gone, all trouble gone. He is good man, like my Mr. Hamilton. But trouble came. Judson came," and she shuddered convulsively.

Abaco was quiet. If Judson remained alive—and Abaco thought it took much killing to get that man!—then Odette would never be safe here on Elysia.

He thought about it, studying the purity of line of

her face and jaw, the soft youth of her chin, the dark shadows under her beautiful large eyes.

"I would take care of you forever," he said finally, boldly.

She turned to glance at him, then lowered her lashes. "Why, care of me?"

"Because I—I feel love for you, Odette. Always, many months. Since I first see you."

She was silent. He thought, it is too soon, too soon after the horror of Bernardo's death, her own rape.

He said, humbly for him, "You are fine girl. You will make good wife. I will take care, I will be kind forever, fight for you, keep other men away. You will go away with me?"

She was thinking about it, her throat moving convulsively. Her small hand moved restlessly over the grass beside her. He gazed at her, then away.

"It is too soon?" he said softly.

She shook her head, dismally. "I feel trouble near. Need strong man," she said, like a child, woefully. "Men want. What can Odette do?"

He bit his lips. He had loved her long, but she had loved Bernardo, and he had been cruelly wrenched from her. It was too soon. He said, finally, with a wrench, "I make promise. Not touch Odette until Odette wishes. Make wife, but not touch. Take care of all the time. Keep bad men away."

He waited breathlessly, to see what she would say. Her dark eyes lifted to his, she shyly searched his hard face, his dark bold pirate's eyes. Then quietly, she put her small hand on his hard tanned hand.

"Odette like you much. You good man. I will be wife," she said.

She had accepted his terms, and he nodded. It would be difficult, but one day she would turn to him. He did not grab the hand and pull her to him as he would wish, but he smiled down at her.

"Now—you eat. We go back to fire, get warm," he said. "You sleep tonight between me and Malkia again. Nobody touch."

Odette leaned toward him, and he felt her cheek press lightly against his hard unshaven cheek. He held his breath, held his arms still against himself. She turned her head, and her soft lips brushed against his chin.

"Thank you—Louis."

They went down the hill, hand in hand. As they moved, they heard another shot, ringing, and another. Clear, in the still evening air. Louis frowned, and halted them on the path. He put the spyglass to his eye, and searched.

The spyglass reached more than a mile, it was clear and sharp. Even in the approaching dusk, Louis could make out the forms in the cane, and he counted, one, two, three, four men in dark garments. One carried a torch, and it flared against the darkness.

He raised the glass to the large white house of Hamilton's plantation. A curtain moved slightly, he saw the rifle poked from the window behind the white curtain. He could make out no faces. The torch moved closer to the house, the rifle barked and a shot echoed again across the hills and bounced back.

He set the glass down against his thigh, and stood scowling in thought. Odette watched him anxiously, then took the glass and put it to her eye. She adjusted it clumsily, he put his arm about her and helped her set it right.

"Oh, no, no!" she breathed. "The slaves attack again! Against Mr. Hamilton, who is good and kind!"

"They must be drunk," said Louis angrily. "I thought they sleep, then come back to hills. Drunken fools!" He was furious with them. Drunken as they were Hamilton could manage them. But Hamilton would not be lenient with the blacks now, after they attacked him and his house!

Odette had tears in her eyes as she returned the spyglass to Louis. "They must not! They must not hurt kind Mr. Hamilton and kind Silver Jasmine," she begged. She caught at his hard bronzed arm. "Louis—you help?"

He hesitated. Drunken slaves might be fools, but they could be dangerous fools. They might turn on him and knife or shoot him.

Odette begged, her dark eyes misty with tears. "Please, Louis. I beg—you be good to Odette, yes? You help them, yes?"

He finally nodded. "I'll go down, see if I can talk to them. Make sense talk. They are damn fools!" he added angrily, half angry at himself for interfering, yet more concerned than he wanted to admit.

Morgan Hamilton had sat down with him, had eaten with him, listened to him with belief, asked him his story. He had stood with Louis and Bernardo at the grave of his uncle, and believed what they told him. He had *believed* the word of a black man.

"Yes, I will go," he said more quietly, and they continued toward the clearing. He was furious to see the fires were still blazing brightly. He strode among them.

"What are you doing? Why are not the fires dying? Do you want to draw Judson up into the hills? Do you wish to signal to him that you are here, to come and get us?" he raged, as he kicked out one fire after another.

Gamba staggered to his feet, holding his head uneasily. "We get cold, Abaco," he said. "I say, more fire!"

"Take children in cave," Louis said curtly to the women. They nodded and obeyed him, drawing the children and their few blankets into the cave. "You men, I talk to you!"

He stood facing them over the last fire, which was dying down. His hard glance dared Gamba to add more wood to the fire. "I hear shooting from Hamilton's plantation. Who goes there? Who missing?"

They looked about in surprise, began counting each other. "Some fool men gone, drunk," said Gamba. "They want to burn down Hamilton house too. Good! All white men's houses burn! We take island! Run plantations, build houses for us! Grow cane, keep money!"

"Fool talk," said Abaco. "When all calm, we must all leave Elysia. White men will come after, chase us all. All must go, men, women, children, leave island. Go to other islands, one family here, another there," and his broad expressive gestures indicated the scattering of them through all the islands. The women came from the cave to listen to him. The men grew silent, their eyes wide and scared.

Leave Elysia for the unknown? How could they do that?

"No, we stay, burn, kill!" said Gamba. "Kill white men. Kill white women. Kill all! Burn, kill!" He beat his chest, bragging, "I, Gamba, lead all! I am chief of all!"

"We cannot kill all the whites. Many whites in St. Michael. Kill all?" asked Abaco, with contempt. "You kill six hundred whites, eight hundred, one thousand? I think maybe not!"

"Not kill," said Odette. "Not kill anymore. Too much killing now! No more kill," her voice pleaded. The women murmured behind her.

Louis nodded at her quietly. She slipped back into the shadows, followed by the hungry knowing look of Gamba. He had a new assurance, and a new bolder arrogance about him. He wanted that woman, he had proved himself a leader, he said. Well, he could not have Odette, Louis promised to himself. If he had to leave Elysia, he would take Odette with him. She was pledged to Abaco now!

He said, "Men shoot at Hamilton plantation house. We will go down, tell them to stop, drag them back. They are drunken fools. Go down, bring back. Maybe Hamilton okay then."

They thought about it, muttering. One man stepped up, a quiet older man, his shoulders stooped. "I will come alongside Abaco," he said.

That moved several others, and they nodded, and came forward. Louis looked at Gamba, who stood scowling. "You come, Gamba," he said. "You chief, you leader." He made it a statement. He would prefer to go without Gamba, but he would not leave him alone near Odette!

About a dozen men followed Louis down the hill. Two rode on each horse, and they had four horses there; others walked, slipping and sliding down the darkened paths. Gamba followed reluctantly, grumbling all the way. Fools, to go stop men from killing whites!

They moved quietly through the fields, and finally left the horses tied to a stunted pine tree, to proceed more softly. Something troubled Abaco. He had looked through the spyglass and seen the dark men moving with assurance through the cane, boldly running through it, one running with a torch.

He finally got hold of the idea that had been in the back of his mind. They had such assurance!

Would drunken blacks walk so?

They grew closer. The firing had ceased. He hoped the blacks would be tired of the battle, and be gone. But as they approached more closely, he could see the little

442

group of men huddled together just out of rifle range of the white house.

A curtain moved upstairs. He glanced up, but could see no face. Hamilton was probably up there, and his rifle could shoot very straight. Louis Abaco hesitated. He did not want to be killed.

He gestured to Gamba and the men. "You wait here. I will crawl forward. Something is wrong," he said, so imperiously that they nodded, and sank down into the field of burned cane. The growing darkness would hide them if they did not move about.

Louis got down on his hands and knees and crawled slowly forward. He wore his dark thick blue pants and shirt, and the red cummerbund held his long machete and his short dirk. He had not brought a rifle, he had no more bullets for it.

He meant to get closer, reassure the blacks that he was Abaco, their friend. Then he would coax them to return to the hills. After that—

He would worry about that later. For now, all his mind and energies must be bent on this task. One thing at a time, and this was urgent.

He crept closer, until he could just make out the forms of the dark men before him. They stood in the cane, he counted them: one, two, three, four. He was about to speak, when one of them spoke.

He spoke in a coarse heavy growl, not like any of the blacks. He said, "Now this time, I want you to run forward, right at the house, swing your arm, and get that torch on the roof. Got me? If you quit and drop it, and run back, by God, I'll shoot you myself!"

Louis stood paralyzed in shock. Then he dropped down flat, shaking. His head lay on his sweating arms. He could not think for a while.

He heard them talking. He heard the slow contemptuous drawl of the Englishman, the distinctive voice so different from the soft drawl of the Cajun speech of the black slaves.

"I say, this is a damn fool thing to do. Why don't we get some sleep and come back in daylight?"

Judson turned on him furiously. "Because they can shoot even straighter in daylight, you damn—" He caught himself, his voice became placating. "I don't mean that. You're smart enough back home in England, shooting foxes, and such like," and the sneer was back in his tone. "But this is the Caribees! You got to figure the men here are different. We got to burn them out tonight!"

Burn them out! Louis lay gasping. He could make out the men now, the form and stance of them. They had black hands and faces, all right, but it was black smeared on. They were white men in blackface, Caleb Judson and two of his overseers, and the sneering cold-blooded Marquess of Tweed who had come to be his guest. The Marquess even carried his rifle over his arm, in the gesture of an Englishman hunting deer!

And they were attacking the house of Mr. Morgan Hamilton! In blackface.

Louis began to crawl backward, until he was far enough away that he could turn around and crawl to where he left the men. He gestured to them, and they moved quietly after him farther back in the fields. He was cold and sweating, all at once.

"What is it?" asked one of the older men, the one who had volunteered first. "What happened?"

Louis said in a low voice, "They are not black slaves, they are not our friends. It is Caleb Judson, and his Englishman guest, and two overseers."

"No, they are blacks," said Gamba, wagging his head.

"They wear black on white faces," said Louis flatly. There was a long silence, as the men struggled to comprehend this mystery. He could just make out their faces, mostly the whites of their eyes as they rolled their eyes and wondered. The silence was unbroken, by bird-song, or even the scratching of any small animal in the cane. Men had frightened away all of nature.

Gamba finally asked, "Why blackface? Why look like black? It is not carnival!"

Louis would have smiled, but he was too intent on the problem. "I think—Judson hates Hamilton," he said slowly. "Wants to burn him out, get woman."

"Let him!" said Gamba. "We go back to hills! Run, hide. Go to islands!" He started to turn.

Abaco, taking his arm, said, "No, we cannot run. You see, if they die, blacks get the trouble. Blacks kill whites. Whites do not kill whites."

"Ahhhh," muttered one man, shaking his head. "Bad, bad!"

"Whites kill whites?" muttered Gamba. "Not our trouble!"

"White men wear blackface. Blacks get trouble," repeated Abaco patiently. He was working out the matter in his mind, and it was getting clearer. "Judson wants Hamilton plantation. Remember, when Mr. Thomas Hamilton die, they blame blacks. But it is not blacks. Judson kill. He wants plantation. Now he tries to kill Mr. Morgan Hamilton. To kill white master, and blame blacks again."

"Ahhhhh!" Now they were understanding, and it worried and angered them, and filled them with fear.

"What can we do?" asked one of them helplessly.

"We help Mr. Hamilton," said Abaco firmly. "We help him. Or else who will believe blacks did not kill Mr. Hamilton? No, he must stay alive!"

That was a strange thought that they must digest. A shot echoed, was followed by another from the house, and they all started violently, looking fearfully toward the plantation house.

"We must go back, help Mr. Morgan Hamilton," said Abaco. He was thinking, he could not go back to Odette and tell her that Silver Jasmine was in danger, and he had not helped. He could never tell her that. And besides, Mr. Hamilton the elder had helped him much, striking off his chains, giving him food. And Mr. Hamilton the younger had been good to him, talked to him, believed him. "We must help Mr. Morgan," he repeated firmly.

"No, no, we go to hills," said Gamba, with more assurance, feeling he had the men with him. "Go to hills, hide. Get boat, escape. Go to more islands!"

"Mr. Hamilton good man, Mr. Judson evil man," said Louis Abaco. "I go help Mr. Hamilton. You do what you wish!"

He began to turn away from them. The men hesitated.

Gamba cried out softly, "But we wish freedom! Go other island, be free men! Hide, run, hide, get away!"

"Then we will never be free men," said Abaco. And he kept on walking. By the sounds of it, they were whispering together. He walked on alone, firmly, through the cane.

If he had to, he would help Mr. Hamilton alone, and die of it. But he could not be a free man anywhere, and live with himself, if he walked away from a man who had befriended him.

And presently, he knew he was being followed, softly, by shuffling feet. Some grumbled under their breaths, but they came. He glanced back, saw it was all of them, all the men, with Gamba standing tall, all six feet four of him following reluctantly. But they were all coming.

29

It was near midnight. Tess shivered in the darkness, her eyes felt heavy and strained with the effort of continuing to search, search in the outside darkness for moving forms of men. She would see a tree, and it seemed to move, and she would lean forward tensely, only to fall back in the chair. It was not a man, just a shadow wavering in the wind.

Would the night never end? Would daylight come, and find them dead? Morgan had said it was the waiting that was the worst. And it was so. The waiting, the dreading, the fear that filled one in the night silences.

This was what separated the good fighters from the poor, she remembered him saying. Glancing across at Morgan's dim form in the other room, she noted how relaxed he seemed, leaning back, his rifle casually across his knees. Yet in an instant he could stand up, get to the

447

window, aim and shoot. Relaxed like a tiger, she thought, a graceful animal of the jungle, ready to tense his muscles and pounce.

Yet he was a man, and he could be gentle and kindly. What was it that made men learn to kill? Evil, she thought, musing in the darkness. The need to protect themselves and their loved ones. Extended, to their country and others.

She blinked. Were her eyes tricking her again? She leaned forward, carefully moved the curtain back two more inches. She stared. Shadows again. Trees?

No. Men. What men could they be? The others, Judson and Lord Tweed and the overseers had stayed at a distance over to the south of the house. This was the west, toward the hills.

She rubbed her eyes, straightened up, stared again for a minute, willing herself to be calm.

"Yes, there are shadows—of men," she muttered. She rose and went to Morgan.

"Morgan, men in the fields—more men!"

He leaned forward at once, flicked back the curtain enough to see, frowning in the distance. "I don't see—where—" he began.

She pointed with her small hand. "There. More to the right—"

He rubbed his eyes as she had, and she knew he was as weary as she was. But his voice was steady and low. "Ah, now—there in the field. But who would it be?"

"They come from the direction of the hills," she whispered. "Are they blacks?"

"I can't tell. They don't carry torches."

The movement continued, there must be about a dozen men out there, Tess thought. Her hand tensed on the pistol. "Shall I tell the others?"

"Not yet. I wonder—I wonder if they could be coming to help us?" he mused.

"Help us? Would they?" It seemed too much to hope for. "Maybe they came to fire the house, and don't know Judson is out there."

Morgan was still for a little time, watching.

Both of them started violently as the silence was broken by a powerful voice.

"Hello, the house! Ahoy there, Morgan Hamilton!"

They saw the forms of the four men nearer to them start violently. They turned to the newcomers, rifles ready.

Morgan yelled, "Is that you, Abaco?"

"Aye, aye, captain! Abaco here! We will help you! What happens there?"

Tess could not help it. She screamed in relief to him. "It is Judson who attacks us! He and Lord Tweed! There are four men! They are wicked, evil!"

A pause, as her voice echoed through the fields. Abaco then called back. "We help, Silver Jasmine! I, Abaco, say it!"

Judson yelled out, evidently infuriated, "You damn bastard! You'll kill us all!"

There was no reply. Morgan was tense at the side of the window. The dark figures moved slowly through the fields, two very tall men, and the others shorter, about a dozen in all.

Morgan suddenly yelled out, "Wait, Abaco! They are armed with rifles and pistols! Wait for the morning!"

The rifles of the four whites were already raised, waiting for the blacks to come closer. Morgan grimaced.

"I'll have to go out there," he muttered, worried.

Vincent ran into the room on stockinged feet, silently. "What is it? What's going on?" he asked.

"Louis Abaco and about a dozen blacks are out there

449

in the cane. They came down from the hills. Abaco says he will help us," said Morgan calmly.

"Do you believe him?" gasped Vincent. "The blacks have burned two houses already, and killed Florencia and—"

"I believe Abaco," said Morgan. "Let me think— wait—are they moving?"

Tess was peering into the darkness intently. She felt so nervous, she felt as though everything moved out there. But when her gaze steadied, she saw all were still.

"They have stopped moving. They are some distance apart," she whispered.

They waited, tensely. Vincent crept back to tell Inez and Señor Quintero of the new development. No one understood what it could mean. The blacks might kill Judson, then turn on the Hamiltons.

"Judson's moving," said Morgan suddenly. "Abaco!" he yelled loudly.

"Yes, Mr. Hamilton!" roared back the powerful voice from the fields.

"Judson is coming toward you! He has a rifle!"

"I see him!" roared the voice.

The whites paused, baffled, furious. More waiting, Morgan watched intently; he was so tense that Tess could see the quiver of his lean body as he bent to the window to watch.

"In the daylight, they will see to kill the blacks," murmured Tess, worried. "And they will have no mercy on them—does Abaco have a rifle?"

"I don't see one. And I cannot ask him." Morgan whispered.

They waited, watched. A half hour crept by. Then the whites muttered together, and began to move.

Morgan yelled at once, "Abaco, they come again! Do you see them and their rifles?"

"I see them, Mr. Hamilton!" roared the powerful voice of Abaco. "They cover their faces with black, but they have black souls, I think!"

The roar of sarcasm seemed to fill the darkened fields. With a yell, Judson ran forward, and the others with him. There was firing in the darkness, the single shots of the rifles roared.

Morgan exploded into action. He shot once from the windows at the racing whites, then flung the empty rifle from him. He picked up one of the sharpened machetes, then raced for the stairs.

"Tess, come with me, I want you to bolt the door after me!" He was running down the stairs, she ran after him on her light slippers.

She wanted to plead, to beg him not to go out there. But his mind was set on it. He was unbolting the door, squeezing through, yanked it shut after him.

Morgan heard her whisper, "God bless—" Then the door shut, he heard the slam of the bolt. Good girl, she had followed orders! He smiled grimly into the darkness, then raced off, machete in hand.

He ran lightly through the back quarters, past the slave huts, and into the fields. He was trying to see, but it didn't take much seeing to find the action. He could hear the grunting, the clash of blades, see the moonlight now on the flashing steel, hear the yells of the wounded.

He found Abaco by his height. He was in a fight with Caleb Judson. Judson had an immense long sword, and tried to keep Abaco at a distance with it. Abaco circled him in silence, using the machete as he would a sword, whirling it before him, his long arms almost making up the distance, the gap between the length of the machete and the length of the long sword.

It was tough, fighting in the darkness. But Morgan was accustomed to that from the Navy. Then, he had sometimes had the blaze of ship's fires, the fires of the shot pots near the cannons. But often they had fought in darkness, panting, on some distant shore, with nothing to light them but a dim moon.

So it was now. And his cat's eyes found their prey. The tall slim Marquess of Tweed stood near him, sword out, finding a mark in one black.

The sword went in, slid out, darkened with blood. The Marquess was grinning, pleased, as the black went down with a cry of stifled pain.

Morgan tapped his back with the tip of the machete. "I am here, Lord Tweed," he said, with deadly politeness.

They were at the side of the small milling crowd. The Marquess whirled like a tiger, and his eyes blazed in the dimness. He was on guard in a moment, and their blades clashed.

Morgan found himself at a disadvantage. His own blade was much shorter—but it was harder and tougher, and well-honed. He went inside the guard once, and slashed open the shirt and coat sleeve, opening it to the arm and drawing blood. The Marquess gasped, fell back a step, and Morgan pressed him instantly.

Morgan was thinking of the time he had first met the Marquess. Of the card game they had played. Of the cruelty in the man's face, of how he would have taken Tess, used her like a rag doll, and discarded her.

He must stay cool, he reminded himself. and tried to think only of the duel before him. It was hard to do so, he got so angry when he thought of how Tess would have been treated. His own gallant, bighearted wife! So valiant, so strong, so much a partner in his life.

This man would still take her, use her, kill her. He drew a deep, steadying breath, and put his thoughts entirely to the duel. The Marquess was circling. catlike. turning him so that his back was to the fight behind him.

Morgan went tense. He must expect no help from the blacks—he could count on nothing. But Judson at his back was not what he wanted.

He forced the Marquess into a new semicircle by forcing the fight, his machete whirled against the sword, slid off, slashed fiercely down in an effort to make the Marquess drop his sword. Lord Tweed cursed in a monotone.

"Damn you, Hamilton! Always—in my way—on this bloody island—curse you—damn you—"

Morgan now had turned the man so his back was to the rest of the battle. Judson was fighting for his life against the tall swift Abaco. The stocky man was grunting, swearing, Abaco was silent, deadly. Judson was slashing wildly—

Morgan pressed the man before him, pressed him back, into the crowd of blacks. Lord Tweed cried out, afraid, as he felt the body of a man behind him. He half turned, fearful—

Morgan was after him in a moment, his machete got inside the guard of the long sword, and he forced the tip to the heart. He slashed the jacket open. Lord Tweed brought up his sword, in one last effort. His hat was gone, and though the blackening on his face hid his expression, Morgan saw the rolling eyes in the blackened face.

He got in another stroke, and hit home, right into the chest and throat. Blood gushed. Lord Tweed flung up his arms, the sword fell from the lifeless hand.

He crumpled to the ground like a broken puppet.

Morgan stood breathing deeply for a moment, he had to catch his breath after that fight. It was then he witnessed the end of the fight between Abaco and Judson.

The tall pirate was moving with coolness and precision, moving closer, then darting out, moving closer and closer, then out and away from the deadly long sword.

Judson's arm was tiring, he seemed unable to get the sword higher.

Then—Abaco moved in, and the machete sliced. Judson's limp arm dropped the sword, his body went down one way, and his head rolled horribly in another direction. Abaco had cut his enemy's head completely off with one stroke of the machete.

Behind Abaco, an overseer moved. He had lost himself in the fighting men, afraid. Morgan was gazing down fascinated, horrified, at the rolling head of Judson that bounced on the ground.

He glanced up in time to see the flash of the overseer's knife. It was at Abaco's back!

"Look out—Abaco!" Morgan cried out, and dashed forward. But beside him another tall figure had turned, and a knife slashed. Tall Gamba swayed, groaned, his knife fell. Abaco had flung about at Morgan's call.

He caught the overseer with the machete, and a second time he slashed fiercely. With both arms, he swung the machete like a precision cutting tool. Half the overseer's head came off, and he crumpled to the ground where he had stood.

Gamba fell also.

Morgan cried out, "Wait—hold—no more! Are there any more here?—let us wait—"

Abaco roared powerfully, "Did we get all them?"

Puffing and silence, then soft voices counting, as the men sorted themselves out. Judson was dead. Lord Tweed was dead, and both overseers. Four blacks were dead, including the tall Gamba, lying face up, eyes opened unseeingly into the darkness.

There were eight blacks left, Abaco, and Morgan. Morgan caught his breath, wiped his hand on his pants. It left a streak of blood. He held out his hand to Abaco.

The man hesitated, then took it, and a strong callused palm struck against Morgan's.

"Thank you, Abaco. I shall never forget what you have done this night," said Morgan fervently.

A white grin slashed the pirate's face. "I will never forget, Mr. Hamilton. Guess I got to be on the run again," he added ruefully.

"No, never. I'll see to that," said Morgan decisively. He raised his voice. "Come to the house, all of you. We'll wash you up, get the wounds taken care of. And you will need food. Come, all of you!"

He led the way back to the house, and called. Tess opened the back door at once, she must have been standing there at the dining room window, he thought, but did not scold her. Her face was white in the candlelight as she lit the candles with unsteady hands.

Vincent rattled down the stairs, eagerly. His eyes opened wide as he saw the blacks following Morgan timidly into the dining room. Inez came down. Quintero was lying on a bed upstairs, exhausted and semiconscious.

Tess brought basins of water, cloth, and ointment. She helped bandage the injured. When she came to Abaco, lounging in one chair, she smiled.

"Mr. Abaco—any injuries?" she asked gently, her great blue eyes studying him.

"Just one, on the arm, missus," he said softly. He showed his arm, she bent to study the wound.

He watched soberly as she washed it carefully, put ointment on it, bound a white bandage around it.

"Is—Odette all right?" she asked him when she had finished. "I have been so worried—is she in the hills?"

Abaco nodded. "Judson raped her. I took with me, into hills. She will be all right."

Her eyes showed her shock. "Judson—took her? Oh, no! No, I had wanted her spared of that horror!"

His hard dark gaze softened a little. "I kill, Odette all right now. She will be my woman," he added simply, his eyes glowing. "She need strong man."

"I am glad for you, and for Odette," said Tess soberly. "Will Odette return to me? What will you do?"

Abaco shrugged. "I think I must run, run, all blacks. Two houses burn, many dead."

"I've been thinking about that," said Morgan. He paused in slicing the cold roast beef, Inez took over from him, to make the sandwiches. "I think no running, Abaco."

"If no running, white men kill," he said simply. "Blacks kill whites. So blacks hang or chased by dogs."

Tess shivered. "No, no, that must not be! You saved us, Mr. Abaco! Morgan, what can we do?"

He put his hand on her slim shoulder. "Don't worry, honey. Nobody is going to kill the blacks. This time, I won't let them. Bernardo has suffered enough for them all," and his mouth moved strangely, as he shook his head as though to shake off that memory. "No, no more killing. Judson is dead. And the five of them will remain there, until I can bring some authority from town and show them. Judson must bear the burden of this evil."

"He did start it, but always the blacks are blamed," said Tess passionately.

"Not this time," said Morgan firmly. He turned to the listening men. "You take food to hills, meat, and fruit. You need water?"

"There is much water in hills," said Abaco.

"All right. Take much food and fruit to hills. Feed the people. Tell them, I speak to white men, swear to God that all was the fault of Judson, as it was. They shall not be punished for this, not while I am alive!"

They listened and believed. Two of the most injured men remained in the slave huts, sleeping, while the others returned to the hills to take food and the story of what had happened.

Morgan went up to sleep, but instead he lay awake. He felt sick with revulsion, he always did after a fight and killing. It seemed cowardly, but after a fight he always felt sick at his stomach. Some of the finest men did. It was something that revolted in them at killing another human being, no matter how evil the person, or how just the cause.

He rose at dawn, washed and shaved, and put on fresh clothes for the first time in two days. Then he went to talk to Quintero. He found the Spaniard awake, slightly feverish, but coherent.

He sat down with him, and told him his plan. "I mean to say that all the killing of the whites was done by Judson and his evil. Morally, that is right," Morgan told him earnestly. "If we tell of the death of Florencia and your two overseers, the whites may turn on our blacks and kill them. It is not right, don't you see? They revolted because of Judson and his deeds."

Quintero shook his head. "They killed—my dear Florencia." His voice quivered. "Someone must pay."

"Gamba has paid," said Morgan quietly. "He paid in blood, helping to save our lives! And other blacks have died, three of them out there in the cane, saving us, Quintero!"

He let that thought soak in, then told him again what he would do. Finally Quintero agreed, and swore on his honor he would never reveal any other facts of the slave rebellion. Inez promised the same, and Vincent and Tess. The truth would remain a secret between them.

"After all, Judson did plenty of evil for which he never paid," said Tess passionately, her blue eyes flashing. "It is only right he should die for it! And be blamed for other deaths! He did cause them, because if he had treated the blacks decently they would not have turned on the Quinteros as well as himself."

They were eating a hasty breakfast about ten o'clock when they heard the sound of carriage wheels. Abaco was coming through the fields at the same time. He reached the back door first.

His dark eyes flashed at Morgan. "Whites come, many men with rifles, Mr. Hamilton," he said.

"A little late, but welcome," said Morgan. "I shall show them what has happened. I have made my promise, and I shall keep it. No running, Abaco. No blame."

Abaco bent his head, but his dark eyes were dubious, and his face clouded with some suspicion, as Morgan went out to meet the carriage. Abaco followed, and Vincent. The girls remained indoors, waiting. They had opened the front doors wide, and the windows had been unbolted and the shutters opened. Fresh breezes blew through the house for the first time in several days, and it smelled good there, with the fragrance of jasmine and plumeria.

Tess glanced out at the carriages, and her eyes widened. "Why—Mrs. Judson has come!" she exclaimed. "I thought she had died at Judson's!"

Tess and Inez went out to greet her. Morgan had strode around the side of the house, to look at the town men who had come armed with rifles, pistols and knives. One held his rifle on Abaco, as the tall pirate followed Morgan. They all were staring at the forms in the cane.

"So you were attacked by the blacks," said one older man, in agitation. He kept glancing nervously at Abaco. "Isn't he one of them?"

"Put the rifle down," ordered Morgan. "Mr. Abaco helped save our lives last night. I want you men to come and see the bodies of the men who attacked us. Not you, Mrs. Judson," he added hastily. Morgan went to help her

458

down from the carriage. "I fear it is a terrible sight, and your husband—is dead."

She did not sway or cling to him. Her head was up, her face pale but composed under the black bonnet. She glanced at Abaco, her eyes flickered a moment.

"Judson is dead?" she asked, and drew a sigh. "Well, I am not surprised. He was brutal to people. They had to turn on him one day."

"Tess, take Mrs. Judson into the house, while we show the bodies," said Morgan. "I don't want the women in this," he said to the older man who seemed to lead them.

Tess went up to Mrs. Judson, greeted her, and escorted her into the house. Tess wore her fresh white muslin, and Inez was gowned in one of Tess's dresses, a pink one that set off her glossy blue black hair and golden face.

Mrs. Judson turned, with composure, to Tess. But her hands were shaking as she drew off her black driving gloves. "Is Mr. Judson—really dead?" she asked.

Tess nodded soberly. "I'm afraid so, Mrs. Judson."

"Afraid?" exclaimed the woman. "I am relieved of a horrible nightmare! I want only to be sure he is dead, before I can begin to live again!" she added passionately.

She was pale. Tess softened to her. "I'll prepare some coffee, Mrs. Judson. Please be calm, sit down. Inez?"

The Spanish girl nodded, and helped Mrs. Judson sympathetically to a sofa. They talked in low tones as Tess went to prepare fresh hot coffee.

Meantime, outside the whites were staring down at the bodies that lay strewn over the cane fields. They shuddered at the sight of the two men whose heads had been severed. "But they are blacks," said one man uneasily.

Morgan bent down, wiped a cloth over the severed head of Judson until his tanned white skin could be seen. "Judson," he said. He showed them the hair, lanky and brown. "He and Lord Tweed and three overseers put black on their faces and hands, and came to attack us yesterday afternoon. It was Tess who guessed who they were. She saw their clothing, the way they walked. I could scarce believe it at first. They must have hoped to kill us, then blame the blacks for it."

"But we'll hang the blacks for starting this," said one man, with fire in his tone. He glared at Abaco uneasily. "I am still not convinced this man wasn't part of it. He's the pirate slave!"

"I am not a slave!" said Abaco, his dark eyes blazing. "I am a free man!"

"He is a free man," Morgan agreed. "And he aided us. Yes, two houses were burned, but the cruelty to the blacks brought that on. Judson had had one of my blacks torn to pieces by dogs," and he went on to tell them patiently all that had happened. These were the men who would take the story back to St. Michael, and he wanted it told his way.

They had to see for themselves how the five men were in blackface, they had to talk and argue and grumble, before they were convinced that the blacks were not to be hanged for it. Abaco stood and listened to it all in silence, his face impassive, his head high in spite of their suspicious looks.

Then Morgan invited them all into the house, for food and drinks. He turned to Abaco. "You will join us," he said.

"Now wait a minute," one of the white men began, flushed. "I ain't eating with no damned black!"

"He is my overseer now," said Morgan firmly, a hint of a smile about his mouth. "You best get used to my method of working! I mean to be here in Elysia all my days, and I will not have mistreatment of my blacks!"

Abaco finally spoke. "I thank you, Mr. Hamilton, but I cannot eat with you. This is not done. I return to hills, and speak to the slaves. Maybe so they come back soon, and work."

Morgan turned to him. "I meant it, Abaco," he said. "I wish you to work with me. We will make some arrangement."

Abaco bent his head in agreement. "That is good. I come back soon, Mr. Hamilton."

He strode on his way, his tall back straight and proud. When he was out of earshot, one of the whites said curiously, "You didn't mean it, that you would eat with him, did you?"

"He is a man," said Morgan, "and he saved our lives. What would you do?"

"Huh—pay him some coins, and tell him you will give him a job. He's a strong man," said the man.

Morgan nodded. "He's a strong man, but most of all, he is a man." But they did not seem to understand him, and sighing, he led the way into the house. He could not fight the whole system; not yet, he thought, dissatisfied.

Tess had prepared a lavish meal for them, with the aid of Inez and Mrs. Judson. The woman recently widowed showed no sign of grief. Rather she was sparkling, happy in a subdued fashion. Some of the men sat at the table; the women waited on them, to eat later, since there was not much room there.

The men decided to return to St. Michael that afternoon, and Quintero would go with them, he thought. He must see a doctor, and rest for a time in his home. Inez went with him, reluctantly, and they gathered up the body of Florencia, in a blanket, to bury her in the churchyard at St. Michael.

Mrs. Judson told them before she left, "I believe I shall settle down in St. Michael. I am not sure yet what I shall do. I may depend on you for aid in my decision, may I not, Mr. Hamilton?"

Morgan said, "Surely. I shall be happy to be of any aid, Mrs. Judson."

He caught a glare from Tess, but she said nothing, merely adding her polite farewells to his. Then they turned to the task of cleaning up the house.

Odette returned the next day, and the blacks began to come back. Tess greeted her warmly, hugged her, cried with her over what had happened. Then they settled down to work again, to cut out new dresses to replace the torn and burned ones, to prepare meals, and sweep the sand out of the house which the wind had blown in. Malkia settled in to helping the injured men recover, and when evening came, to sit and rock in her favorite chair outside the back door on the veranda, pipe in her mouth.

And Morgan counted out what money they had, thought over his plans, and talked to Tess about them. There was much to do, and they must help heal the wounds of the events of years. It would mean selling some of the six-year and five-year rums, managing everything differently and taking a big chance, but they meant to do it.

He meant to free all their slaves, and hope they would come to work for him anyway, for money and their food, clothing and shelter. A different life. Would the blacks accept it? Or would they run off, with no law to chase after them?

30

The following weeks were busy ones, but the tension was gone. The blacks returned to work, to sing at nights, to laugh about their slave huts, to bathe in the ocean waters, to come shyly to the kitchens and beam at Tess and Morgan.

The nightmare was over. Tess heard much singing and chanting one night, and went out with Morgan to witness a voodoo ceremony presided over by Malkia, Odette, and several other men and women. It seemed to be a ceremony for thanking the gods. The next day Odette confirmed that that was what it had been.

"We thank Erzulie, and Damballa, and many other gods, for goodness, for saving life. We ask them to take care of blacks who die, and give them a good hereafter up there." She pointed up to the sky.

"It was like a funeral, Morgan," Tess said later to

her husband. "She wanted the dead ones remembered; the living ones thanked the gods for their safety."

"Yes, like the ceremony of the dead at sea, as we commit them to the waves," said Morgan.

The work in the cane was finished. The molasses had spoiled, and had to be thrown out. Now the summer's work would soon begin, clearing the fields of rubble and burnt stubs, preparing the ground for a new planting in the fall.

But first, they must celebrate with a cane party. Morgan, Tess and Vincent drove into town, taking three husky blacks with them, leaving Abaco to take charge of all three plantations. Mrs. Judson had written, asking them to bring her husband's huge iron safe with them.

But it was too heavy to move, so she wrote to them, giving the combination. Morgan and Vincent opened it, exclaiming over the contents. There were piles of coins and paper money, jewelry, gold, deeds of land. They stacked everything into cloth bags and wooden boxes, and waited uneasily to go into St. Michael with it. They had listed the contents on papers.

They drove into St. Michael, and the small town of about three hundred houses looked immense to them after the cane fields. They drove at once to Quintero's, where the Spaniard had invited them all to stay with him.

He greeted them happily, his pipe waving in his hand. Inez came at once to the hall, to smile and blush at Vincent's hungry look, and the clasp of his hand.

There was much work to do in St. Michael. They remained a week. Morgan and Vincent took the heavy safe contents to Mrs. Judson, had her check over the contents. She, too, was amazed at how much money her husband had had.

"I shall buy a small house here in St. Michael," she said happily. "I never want to live on a plantation again.

However, I must be near enough to keep check on the work." Her beautiful face shadowed. "And I will never return to live in Martinique. My father might sell me to yet another husband! I shall be my own woman!"

Morgan repeated this to Tess, who nodded thoughtfully. "I don't blame her," she said, with a shudder. "Imagine being married to a man like Judson!"

Morgan and Tess were married as he had promised, in a second ceremony in the beautiful cathedral of St. Michael. It was attended by all their friends, and some curious new acquaintances. Morgan put a new ring on Tess's finger, a golden one set with a sapphire, which made her catch her breath whenever she looked at it. It looked much too grand for her small self, she decided. But Morgan said it matched her eyes perfectly.

Vincent said to them that he wished just such a wedding. And Inez blushed, and looked at him with a gentle gaze. Vincent and Quintero had had long conversations. The older man did not wish to return to the hard work of the plantation, and he wanted Vincent to take over the property and manage it for him.

So it was quietly decided that Inez and Vincent would marry that week, and return to Morgan's until their own house could be rebuilt. Meantime, Morgan and Tess had gone to the bank, to speak to the bankers there, and decide what to do about many matters. The bankers had much shrewd advice for them.

"There is a ship in port now, with a fine captain you can trust," they advised. "We suggest you commit your rums to him. He will pay you a fair price for them."

So about a dozen barrels, and a hundred bottles of rum were consigned to the captain. He tested them, pronounced them good, and paid them a fair price, in gold. That money was then put in the bank.

They discussed with the bankers the problems of

freeing the blacks. The bankers were dubious, yet one progressive man said, "It must be done one day. The English government is against slavery. I can see the day when all black men will be freed. You may as well make the first move. We shall stand behind you, should any protests arise. I don't see why they should on Elysia. There are only three plantations here."

A lawyer drew up a form for them to follow. Tess bought a quantity of fine white paper at a shop, some black ink, and fresh pens. She also bought new account ledgers, and Morgan teased her that she took more interest in those purchases than in buying the new dresses and bonnets and slippers that he insisted she needed.

The days were full and happy. Inez came shopping with them, and was of great help in buying lengths of cloth, pants, shoes, dresses, small garments for the slave children, and candies, besides practical items.

The cane party was the time that Thomas Hamilton had always used to distribute new clothes and presents to all his slaves. They bought pounds of good tobacco, new pipes, cups and spoons, new machetes, lengths of cotton and wool and linen.

There were also little sewing baskets for the women, and needles and thread and pins. Tess picked out a beautiful one for Odette, and also a gold bracelet.

Morgan raised his eyebrows at that purchase. Tess said, "Louis Abaco asked me to buy her a gold bracelet: he will marry her with the bracelet, rather than a ring."

"Ahah! So that's the way the wind blows." He grinned.

Tess nodded seriously. "Yes, and it's a good thing. She needs someone strong like Abaco."

They looked about for more overseers. Mrs. Judson had chosen a man, and they talked with him. Quintero and

Vincent would choose someone to aid him on that plantation.

And so the visit stretched to ten days, until Tess said, "We have to go home, the carriages will not hold us all now! We need another carriage to carry all this."

They had come with three carriages, borrowed from Judson's and Quintero's. Morgan bought another one, and two more horses. Mrs. Judson came to them one evening, and asked to return home with them, for a brief visit. "I would like to discuss some more business with Mr. Hamilton," she said sweetly.

Tess gave her a dubious look. She had been sorry for the woman, but if she tried to get her claws into Morgan, she would be in for a fight, Tess resolved fiercely. They had just-been married, a real ceremony, and he was tightly married to Tess!

All St. Michael was buzzing with the rumors that Morgan meant to release his slaves. "Who will work for you?" asked one elderly man bluntly. "You can't hope to get whites to do that tough labor! You're out of your mind!"

"I hope they will work for us, for wages," said Morgan firmly.

"Hope!" he snorted. "Hope, is it? You'd best think twice about freeing them, and buy more whips!"

Tess said to Morgan on the ride home, "Morgan, you will truly release the slaves, won't you? Don't let anybody talk you out of it! I hate to think of people like Odette, and Malkia, being slaves all their lives!"

He put her hand on his sleeve, tucking it into his arm, and smiled down at her, as he clucked to the horse. "Don't fret, Tess, I'll do what is best."

"The best thing is to free them," and she set her chin stubbornly. "I have a feeling Mrs. Judson will try to sweet-talk you into keeping them as slaves!" She suspected the woman's motives in coming along with them.

"Her slaves are her property, that decision is hers," was all Morgan would say. But he seemed quite satisfied about the whole situation.

At home they were greeted with shy delight by the blacks. The house servants came running, the house was polished and swept free of sand, and fresh flowers were set in bowls about all the rooms. Odette came, her hand in Abaco's, fresh color in her cheeks, and a sparkle in her dark eyes.

Everyone helped unload the goods from the carriages. Odette took Mrs. Judson up to her chamber across from Tess's, and Inez and Vincent took the middle bedroom. Señor Quintero took the back bedroom, where Morgan had sat up for nights, watching for the slave attack.

The yard goods and presents were stacked freely about the study and back parlor across from the dining area. The blacks came to peep in and look with big black eyes at the pile of presents.

Their own blacks were there, but not those of Judson's and of Quintero's. Those had returned to their own homes. But Morgan and Tess had quietly bought presents for all of them, for all had been involved in the troubles.

The new overseers would not arrive for another two weeks. Morgan wanted to get matters all settled first.

He told three of the blacks to go over to Judson's, and to Quintero's. "Tell all the slaves to come tomorrow evening for a cane party. Everybody come," he urged. "Party one, two, three days maybe. Plenty food, plenty drink, many presents."

"All blacks come?" asked one of their men dubiously. "All blacks come alike?"

"Yes, all come, alike," said Morgan, nodding firmly. "All were in trouble, all helped, all have party. Cane party, with party queen and king. Much dancing, much food, many presents for all blacks! Tell everybody to come. Forget work!"

They ran off to spread the word, and to dash over to the other two plantations. Morgan led his own people in to dinner, which was a happy occasion.

Antoinette Judson revealed an unexpected sense of humor. Evidently her years under Judson's subjection had subdued her own personality. Now her wit flashed, and kept them laughing, as she told stories of Martinique, rather risque stories of people she knew in society in the Caribbees, incidents her father had told her. She was gay, beautiful, in a violet silk dress, with matching plumes in her dark hair.

Tess and Inez had helped prepare the dinner, and planned it. They ate freely of the slices of roast beef, bowls of golden yellow yams with melted butter, hot biscuits and fresh honey bought from the ship's captain, greens from their gardens, and a huge dessert bowl of mixed fruits. There were pink mangoes, yellow papayas, creamy white little sweet bananas, and thick chunks of ripe coconut, all covered with a delicious coconut liqueur supplied by Señor Quintero. Rums accompanied each course, his six-year rums, and some liqueurs of coconut, lime and berry.

It was late when they finished, and later still before they fell into bed. But Morgan was up early.

He had plans for that day, and he meant to make it a day to remember. He had blacks bring out a sturdy desk from the study, and two chairs. The piles of fresh white paper were brought, and two ink pots and fresh pens. When Tess came down yawning, he had it all set up, and the blacks were beginning to gather in curiosity.

Morgan said nothing yet. He waited until the others were up and dressed, and all having their breakfast before he made the announcement.

"Today is freedom day," he said. "Today, Tess and I are going to make out papers for all our blacks, from Malkia down to the smallest child, giving them their freedom."

Odette stared at him with wide pansy-dark eyes. The other maids gawked. None of the whites seemed surprised, even Mrs. Judson, he thought. Odette wore a golden bracelet on her honey-colored arm.

They went on eating and drinking. Tess was flushed and excited, and subdued all at once. He thought she was worried, about whether the blacks would accept work after that. They were taking a big chance. Would any blacks remain if they were free? They could not run the plantation alone or with white labor. The whites disdained that heavy labor in the fields.

They finished the bowls of fresh fruit, the thick cuts of crisp bacon, the hen's eggs, and more hot biscuits with honey. They drank cups and cups of black coffee, sweetened with their own muscavado sugar, in brown sweet chunks.

Then it was over, and they went out to the veranda. Morgan seated Inez and Antoinette in comfortable chairs, and Vincent stood near to help identify the slaves by name and age. Abaco came around the corner of the house, with Odette by the hand, watching and waiting. The other blacks came, some from the other plantations. The word had spread quickly.

Tess sat down at the desk. She had the form the lawyer had made out. Morgan looked at Malkia.

"I would say to you all," he said, standing at the doorway of the large plantation house, "that my wife and I are most grateful to you for your good work for us. We thank you for being loyal to us when trouble came. There was much trouble, but some of you came from hills, helped us fight. We say, thank you."

He paused. Quintero had come from the house, in his white suit and panama straw hat, and stood listening gravely. Some of his slaves were there, and they looked briefly at him, then politely down at the ground.

"My wife will write out a paper for each one of you," said Morgan slowly, choosing the simple words carefully. "This paper says, this man or woman or child is a free person. We set you free from this day on. This is freedom day. All blacks of the Hamilton plantation are free, and no man may enslave you."

There was a brief murmur of bewilderment, and some whispering. He waited until it ceased, then went on carefully.

"This is strange to you. What does it mean? It means you may go where you wish, work where you will, be idle if you like. It means you do not have to live here if you wish to go."

They frowned and looked at each other. "Go where?" he caught the whisper.

"You may go to St. Michael, or to another island, you may seek work for wages. But I want you to stay here, with me. You will get a paper saying you are free. Also you will live in your hut. I do not beat and whip. I work alongside you. I will give you food, clothes, take care of you. And I will pay to every man and woman who works for me, one shilling English money for every week you work. This money come to you at cane party time, and at Christmas time."

Their faces were blank. Morgan stared at them helplessly. He had said it, didn't they understand?

He glanced at Abaco, saw Odette looking bewildered also. Didn't they understand what freedom was? On impulse he said, "Abaco, you tell them what is freedom, what I wish them to do. Be free, go if they wish. Or stay and work for money. Tell them."

Abaco nodded, and turned to the blacks. None of the whites understood what he said as he spoke rapidly in the Cajun, the brief short abbreviated words of the blacks when they spoke to each other. Morgan caught a word or two, that was all. "Free—paper—work—money—"

The black faces cleared, turned eager. They began to nod, and clap, led by Malkia, pipe in mouth, clapping her old hands. They clapped in rhythm, beaming, and some of the women began to dance on light bare feet on the bare earth.

Abaco nodded at Morgan. "They know now," he said simply.

"Fine. First is Malkia, who is eldest and most respected of women," said Morgan.

Malkia came forward proudly. Tess wrote out the paper, everyone peered forward, craning their necks to watch her scratch on paper and make black marks that meant things.

Morgan took the paper when she finished, and read it aloud as the ink dried. "I, Morgan Hamilton, do swear and attest that one Malkia is a free woman. This day, June 16, 1816." He signed his name with a flourish, dusted sand on the ink to dry it, then handed it to Malkia.

Malkia bowed, took it, beaming with gaping teeth. She went back to the people, showed the paper proudly.

Tess began to write the next paper, and filled in the name and age of the oldest black man. He accepted it after Morgan had signed it.

It took all the morning, until early afternoon, to write out all the papers and sign them, after ascertaining as much of a name and age as each slave knew. Some did not know their ages, but Malkia would say something, with authority, and everyone nodded, satisfied.

He gave papers to all their slaves. The other blacks

had gathered also, and looked wistfully at Morgan, but he shook his head. "You belong Quintero," he said to one. The man looked at Quintero.

"I suppose I'll have to do it also," growled Quintero. "Tomorrow morning, you come here," he said to the man. "I give you paper."

"And I also," said Antoinette Judson's clear musical voice, unexpectedly. "Come the next day, all those from my plantation. Tomorrow Quintero, the next day all Judson. All free. All come."

Morgan looked at her with surprise, she smiled in a twisted manner. "I was going to ask you, Morgan," she said informally. "But the freedom day caught me up." There was a little mist in her eyes.

"You wish to set your slaves free?" he asked slowly. The blacks were quiet, craning to listen. She nodded, and looked at them.

"They have suffered enough. What you offer, I offer. Only, I cannot remain on the plantation, I could not bear to live there again. Will you look after my place for me, Morgan?"

Morgan was aware of the jealous look in Tess's blue eyes, but he could not disregard the appeal. "Gladly, Mrs. Judson," he said. "If that is your wish."

"It is. I shall live in St. Michael, in my little house, and if you will send me enough to live on, I shall be grateful." She added more briskly, "The same arrangement for me. Freedom, then hire all who will remain, for a shilling a week, English money. That is good for all, the men and women alike. When any grow old enough to work, any child may receive the same money."

Morgan turned and announced it in a clear voice. They stared at Mrs. Judson, whispered to each other.

"They don't believe it yet," said Mrs. Judson. "After

all those years—I cannot believe in freedom myself! Not yet. But one day." She went abruptly into the house.

The slaves dispersed slowly, casting backward looks at the veranda. Morgan had told them to return after luncheon, he would give them presents from St. Michael. Everyone was to come, and then cane party would start.

Louis Abaco approached the steps, releasing Odette's hand. She held the precious white paper in it. He said to Morgan, "You will give paper to Abaco?"

Morgan stared. "But Louis, you are not my slave! You are a free man!"

The big mouth twisted in irony. "I know, you know, but some men catch me anyway! I need paper."

Morgan hesitated, "I don't know if it is legal. You are not my slave."

Tess said quickly, "I don't know why we couldn't make out a paper, Morgan! It could say that you attest you know Louis Abaco is a free man!"

Her blue eyes pleaded, he smiled. "All right, Tess. Make it out."

They all watched as Tess wrote quickly. She read it aloud.

"I, Morgan Hamilton, affirm and attest that the former pirate and ex-slave Louis Abaco is known to me to be a free man, and will remain free. Signed this day, June 16, 1816."

Morgan read it over, and signed it with a flourish. He handed it to Abaco, who grinned as he studied the words.

"Now, I am also free!" he said triumphantly, his tall head uplifted, his bronzed face glowing. "I am free!"

That afternoon, they handed out the presents, the lengths of cloth, tobacco, pipes, and all the rest. The slaves came up, received their presents, and retreated, beaming. Morgan called for Judson's slaves, and gave them presents, watched by Antoinette, who protested in a low voice.

"I should have purchased presents for them, I didn't think of it. Really, Morgan—"

"You may repay us if you wish," he said happily. "But presents they will get, the same to all!"

She laughed, and began to help hand out the presents. She smiled especially at one plump woman who came up with her small children, five of them in all.

"Leonie, you will make the children clothes, all of them, yes?" she asked, as she handed cotton cloths to the woman.

The woman nodded, her dark brooding gaze on Antoinette's face. "Where you live, missus?" she asked unexpectedly.

"In St. Michael, Leonie. You will come with me, I pay? You will be a free woman all the time."

Leonie thought a moment. "You get married, missus?"

Antoinette shook her head decidedly.

"Then I come, missus," said Leonie with relief.

The party went on all the afternoon. When all the presents were given out, the fun began, and went on all night and into the next day.

Morgan and the others sat on the veranda in the evening, with bright torches set in the sand about the front of the house. Blacks came up spontaneously, and began dancing and singing, sometimes one at a time, sometimes in a little group.

Odette gave a pretty little dance, formal, rather like a cotillion, except she danced and bowed alone, to clapping by some of the women. She retreated with a shy smile after their applause, to stand beside Louis Abaco, his big hand possessively on her arm, her golden bracelet shining in the firelight.

Others came, and danced in the old ways: some from Africa; some from vaguely remembered balls they had seen; some comic; some romantic as a man danced before a girl and seemed to court her, offering her flowers.

At midnight, the whites retreated to bed. But the blacks danced and sang, ate and drank all the night. They would pause only briefly for sleep, lying down where they were, the children curled up on the skirts of their mothers. Then they would rouse again, and they would get up and jump up and down, and dance and sing again.

It went on all the next day. Morgan wrote out papers with Tess, for the freedom of Quintero's blacks, as Quintero watched with melancholy approval. Quintero signed them all, scrawling his signature with a big flourish of the letters.

On the third day, Judson's slaves were freed. Mrs. Judson sat at the desk beside Tess, watched her make out the papers carefully, then signed her own name to them. Morgan noticed the coolness between the women, the jealous flash of Tess's large blue eyes when Mrs. Judson smiled up at Morgan.

The party went on and on, until the blacks were all weary, satisfied, and ready to go back home.

On the fourth and fifth day, the party slowed, and on the sixth day, most of the blacks from Quintero's and Judson's had returned home, to their own huts.

They would rest, sleep, talk over the days, their freedom. The women would make new clothes for their men and children and for themselves. The men would go fishing, sleep late, rest after the long year of labor.

By July they would be ready to start again, to clean the fields, weed, dig the furrows for the cane. And the year would begin again.

Mrs. Judson thanked them for their hospitality, said she would send a new overseer to Morgan for his orders, and departed for St. Michael, with Señor Quintero to

476

accompany her in her carriage. The house seemed much more quiet when they had departed.

Morgan dared to tease Tess about her. "Did you think she would cling forever, my dear?"

"She would have, if we hadn't gotten married again," said Tess tartly. "I notice she couldn't let go your arm for a while!"

Morgan laughed, caught her up off her small feet, and kissed her soundly. "Tell me you love me," he commanded.

She scowled down at him, kicked out futilely. He shook her a little.

"Come on, Tess, I won't let you down until you do!"

"Oh—I love you," she said, and then smiled, her gamine grin. He set her down, and kissed her soundly again.

"That's my girl!" he mocked. "My wife," he said, more quietly. He held her close for a long moment.

Vincent and Inez were strolling up from the beach. He was carrying a sign and post. "Hey, Morgan, this fell down in the wind last night. I saw it leaning the other day." He held up the sign that read in faded letters, "Last Hope. T. Hamilton."

"We need a new sign, and I wish we could take a new name," said Tess, smoothing back her blond curls. She frowned in thought. "Happiness? Or Hamilton's Place?"

"Or New Hope?" asked Inez. They all thought about it, made suggestions.

Finally Tess came up with one. "What about Joyous Hope?" And they all approved of that.

Morgan cut a new board of smooth white pine, and scraped it clean carefully. Vincent had been cutting a tall fine post of pine. They nailed it together; then Tess got out the thick black ink, and added black pitch to it to make it firmer.

Then in careful beautiful script, she printed the new sign: "Joyous Hope. Morgan Hamilton."

"There," she said, standing back to look at it. "That's better! I am tired of thinking of Last Inn, and Last Hope. This is a new beginning for us all!" Her small face glowed with pleasure.

"Yes, for all of us," echoed Vincent, looking down at the dark-haired girl in the curve of his arm. "Me and my wife, and Morgan and Tess. All of us. A new start, a joyous hope for the future."

"And not long ago, I thought I had no future," Morgan said softly, to Tess. She gazed up at him, blue eyes adoring, and understood, and her hand went to his.

"We all do—a beautiful future for us, if we can but work hard for our dreams," she murmured. She smiled impishly. As Vincent and Inez walked down the path toward the beach, carrying the post and sign to put in place, she caught Morgan's hand and held him back.

"Morgan—I have some news for you," she said.

He held her small hand closely in his, and studied her face. "You mean—you're going to tell me at last— that you are going to have my child?" He said it slowly, and began to grin at her pretended outrage.

"You knew! Why didn't you say!" She began to pummel him, but he only laughed, and caught her to him. His lips met hers in a long kiss.

Vincent and Inez looked back. "Guess we better put the sign up ourselves," he said to his wife. "They get all involved, don't they?"

"They are much in love, as we are," she said, with a blush and a smile for him. "I never thought to be so—so joyous, Vincent."

They went on down to the beach, and took their time at putting up the sign.

OUTSTANDING READING FROM
WARNER BOOKS

IN SEARCH OF HISTORY
by Theodore H. White   (97-146, $5.95)

This is a book about the people who, making history have
changed your life - and about a great correspondent who lis
tened to their stories for forty years. Now he has woven all those
stories into this splendid tale of his own. "IN SEARCH OF HIS
TORY is the most fascinating and most useful personal memoir
of this generation."

—William Safire

THE CULTURE OF NARCISSISM
by Christopher Lasch   (93-264, $2.95)

Have we fallen in love with ourselves? Have we bargained away
our future for self gratification now? With an unsentimental eye
Christopher Lasch examines our society and our values and dis
covers that we are in thrall to a new enchantment self involve-
ment. We live today in THE CULTURE OF NARCISSISM.

THE NEW TYRANNY: How Nuclear Power Enslaves Us
by Robert Jungk   (91-351, $2.50)

From the inner circles of nuclear scientists . . . From the mouths
of embittered plant workers . . . From the records of the inter
national Atomic Authority . . . comes Robert Jungk's inside
information about the dangers of the Nuclear Age. A frightening
indictment of the nuclear power industry. It predicts —convinc
ingly—that the industry will eventually rob us of our freedoms,
if not our lives."

—Benjamin Spock, M.D.

ALEXANDER SOLZHENITSYN
by Steven Allaback   (71-926, $2.50)

In ALEXANDER SOLZHENITSYN Steven Allaback explores the
rich world of Solzhenitsyn's imagination for us the
craftsmanship and vast creative energy of this 20th Century
literary giant. Allaback's interpretations are lucid and lively free
of academic abstraction, and his final assessment of the Rus-
sian's fiction is positive."

—Publishers Weekly

A CAPTIVE OF TIME
by Olga Ivinskaya   (83-968, $2.95)

A CAPTIVE OF TIME is the story behind "Doctor Zhivago" —the
extraordinary romance that inspired it—the passion between the
genius poet and the woman who shared his life and his work and
who went to prison for loving him. It is the story that only Olga
Ivinskaya could write, revealing the man she alone knew.

THE BEST OF BESTSELLERS
FROM WARNER BOOKS

BLOODLINE
by Sidney Sheldon (85-205, $2.75)
The Number One Bestseller by the author of THE OTHER SIDE OF MIDNIGHT and A STRANGER IN THE MIRROR. "Exotic, confident, knowledgeable, mysterious, romantic . . . a story to be quickly and robustly told and pleasurably consumed."
—Los Angeles Times.

PALOVERDE
by Jacqueline Briskin (83-845, $2.95)
"Briskin lets the reader peek into the lives of three generations of a mighty California family. Hear their conversations . . . learn their secrets . . . as they bring in a gusher, prospect for gold, rub shoulders with the elite of Hollywood. Every page is a new adventure, and the reader is caught up in the excitement. Truly a book that's hard to put down . . . and gutsy enough to appeal to men as well as women."
—United Press International.

SCRUPLES
by Judith Krantz (85-641, $2.75)
The most titillating, name-dropping, gossipy, can't-put-it-down #1 bestseller of the decade! The fascinating story of one woman who went after everything she wanted—fame, wealth, power, love—and got it all!